MAN OVERBOARD

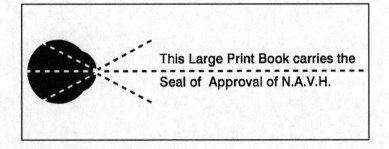
This Large Print Book carries the
Seal of Approval of N.A.V.H.

AN ALI REYNOLDS NOVEL

MAN OVERBOARD

J.A. JANCE

THORNDIKE PRESS
A part of Gale, Cengage Learning

GALE
CENGAGE Learning·

Farmington Hills, Mich • San Francisco • New York • Waterville, Maine
Meriden, Conn • Mason, Ohio • Chicago

GALE
CENGAGE Learning·

Thorndike Press® Large Print Basic.
The text of this Large Print edition is unabridged.
Other aspects of the book may vary from the original edition.
Set in 16 pt. Plantin.

LIBRARY OF CONGRESS CATALOGING-IN-PUBLICATION DATA

Names: Jance, J. A. (Judith A.) author.
Title: Man overboard : an Ali Reynolds novel / by J.A. Jance.
Description: Large print edition. | Waterville, Maine : Thorndike Press, A part of Gale, Cengage Learning, 2017. | Series: An Ali Reynolds novel | Series: Thorndike Press large print basic
Identifiers: LCCN 2017001136 | ISBN 9781410497420 (hardback) | ISBN 1410497429 (hardcover)
Subjects: LCSH: Reynolds, Ali (Fictitious character)—Fiction. | Women private investigators—Arizona—Fiction. | Murder—Investigation—Fiction. | Large type books. | BISAC: FICTION / Thrillers. | FICTION / Mystery & Detective / General. | FICTION / Mystery & Detective / Women Sleuths. | GSAFD: Suspense fiction. | Mystery fiction.
Classification: LCC PS3560.A44 M36 2017b | DDC 813/.54—dc23
LC record available at https://lccn.loc.gov/2017001136

Published in 2017 by arrangement with Touchstone, an imprint of Simon & Schuster, Inc.

Printed in the United States of America
1 2 3 4 5 6 7 21 20 19 18 17

*For Patti Shirley and Smoocher
and the Equine Encore Foundation*

PROLOGUE

As the cruise ship rocked and rolled in open water, Roger McGeary stood in front of the mirror and tried for the fourteenth time to tie his damned bow tie. He had looked up the directions on the Internet and watched the demo through to the end, but that wasn't much help.

He knew for sure it was his fourteenth attempt because that was something Roger always did — always *had* to do — he counted things. His arms ached. His hands shook. Beads of sweat had popped out on his brow, and the underarms of his freshly starched and pressed dress shirt were soaked through as well. A glance at the clock told him he was already ten minutes late to meet up with the girls in the bar for a predinner beverage.

When the doorbell to his stateroom buzzed, he gave up, dropped the ends of the still untied tie, and pounded the dresser top in frustration. The blow sent one of his cuff links skittering across the polished wood surface and onto the carpeted floor, where it immediately disappeared from view under the bed. Roger was on his hands and knees searching for the missing cuff link when Reynaldo, his cabin butler, stuck his head around the doorjamb.

"Turndown service," he announced. "Or would you rather I come back at another time?"

"No," Roger muttered. "Now's fine."

"Can I help you with something?" Reynaldo asked solicitously.

"I've lost my damned cuff link, and I can't for the life of me tie my damned tie."

Crouching at the foot of the bed, Reynaldo quickly retrieved the missing cuff link and dropped it into Roger's over-sized fist. Leaning on the bed, Roger heaved himself upright. "Thanks," he said. "Appreciate it." And he did.

"As for the tie," Reynaldo offered, "I'd be happy to help with that and with the cuff links as well."

Feeling embarrassed and self-conscious at his own obvious incompetence, Roger surrendered himself to Reynaldo's ministrations. It took only a matter of seconds and a few deft movements on Reynaldo's part before the tie was properly tied.

The butler stood back for a moment to admire his handiwork. "Cuff links next," he said, and Roger handed them over. Once the cuff links were fastened, Reynaldo retrieved the jacket from the bed and held it up so Roger could slip into it. The jacket settled smoothly onto Roger's massive shoulders as though it had been made for him — because it had. Aunt Julia had seen to that.

"You're going on a cruise, Rog," she had told him. "You'll need a tux for formal nights on board, and by God you're going to have one." A lifetime's worth of experience had taught Roger that arguing with Aunt Julia was a losing proposition. He'd gone straight out and ordered the tux. At Aunt Julia's urging he'd also invested in a new sport coat and some big-and-tall dress shirts as well.

"After all," Aunt Julia had counseled, "it's a two-week cruise. You can't go down to the dining room in the same thing night after night."

The big-and-tall shirts were necessary because Roger was a big man. Standing next to him, Reynaldo was tiny by comparison. Once the jacket was properly in place, the butler reached up and dusted off a tiny speck of lint before giving Roger an approving nod.

"Very good, sir," Reynaldo said. "Take a look in the mirror."

Turning back to face the mirror where he'd spent the better part of forty-five minutes battling with the tie, Roger McGeary was startled to see the reflection staring back at him. He looked . . . well . . . good.

He'd never worn a tux before. Members of the Dungeons & Dragons Club back in high school weren't the kind of kids who went to proms or homecoming dances. And if they did somehow get around to getting married eventually, they didn't do so with a full contingent of bridesmaids and groomsmen. When there had been geeky weddings in Roger's circle of acquaintances, he himself had never been called upon to perform bridal party duties. And so, at the ripe old age of forty and a half, he was astonished to see that the tux made all the difference.

Of course, his shoulder-length hair — still mostly brown but beginning to go gray — was maybe a bit incongruous with the tux, but it was too late to do anything about that now. Besides, Roger had worn his hair that way from the moment he turned twelve and realized that having a son with shoulder-length hair was something that drove his father nuts. Anything that bugged the hell out of James McGeary was exactly what his son would do.

Roger grinned at Reynaldo. "Thanks for your help," he said.

"Don't mention it, sir," the butler replied, beginning the turndown process. "That's why I'm here."

That was something else his old D & D pals would find astonishing — Roger McGeary on a cruise? In a stateroom with a damned butler? Get out!

Feeling somewhat jaunty, Roger stopped long enough to pull his cell phone off the charger and slip it into his jacket pocket. Earlier when he'd been looking for directions on the tie, he'd noticed that the charge was lower than it should have been, and he'd plugged it in while he was showering and shaving. If the phone was losing its ability to hold a charge, he'd need to go looking for a new one once he got back home.

Roger took the phone along with him to dinner more out of force of habit than because he was expecting calls. After all, he was on vacation, and his office in San Jose, California, was many time zones away. Letting himself out of the cabin, he started toward the elevator lobby. He'd taken only

11

a few steps when a sudden pitch sent him bouncing off first one wall and then the other.

It's the English Channel, after all, he told himself. *What do you expect?*

His stateroom was fairly well aft. As he tottered down the long corridor, he couldn't help thinking again of the kids he'd hung out with back in high school. The only one he still stayed in touch with — sometimes by text and occasionally by running into each other at cyber security conferences — was Stu Ramey, the guy who had once been Roger's best friend. They had met up in Adams Junior High — junior prison, as they called it.

Smart, overweight, and both wearing glasses, Roger and Stu had bonded immediately. From junior high on, the nerdy outsiders had been bullied and disparagingly referred to by their classmates as Tweedledum and Tweedledee. That was in Phoenix, where at least he'd had a friend or two. Once his mother pulled up stakes, moved Roger to L.A., and dumped him into the zoo that was Sepulveda High School for his senior year, he'd had no friends at all, and he had been utterly lost.

It was hardly surprising that Roger had never attended any of his high school class reunions. He'd still been locked up in a mental health facility in Napa for his tenth. As for the twentieth? Thanks to Aunt Julia, he'd been back on his feet by then and had actually received an invitation to the one in L.A., but he'd had no interest in attending. He had no friends or happy memories from Sepulveda High, and he doubted anyone from back there remembered him, either. As for South Phoenix High? Kids who had come to the school via the special ed route hadn't exactly been welcomed with open arms. He supposed he could have crashed that reunion, but since his only friend at the time had been Stuart, there wasn't much point.

As for Roger? Years of therapy hadn't completely fixed his self-esteem issues or his overweening insecurities, either, although seeing himself in the mirror in his tux was maybe further progress. And the next time he saw Stu, he'd have to ask him about the reunion situation. Maybe Stuart Ramey had more balls than Roger did. Maybe he'd gone back and braved the ravening horde — arrogant jocks, perky cheerleaders, and all.

In the elevator lobby, Roger stepped aside for a couple heading back the way he'd come. The woman had a decidedly green cast to her skin, and she clung to her companion's arm with something close to a death grip. Roger thanked his lucky stars that he wasn't prone to motion sickness and wondered if any of the girls were, either.

Calling his prospective dinner companions "girls" was a bit of a misnomer. For one thing, they were all north of sixty — possibly even north of seventy — but very well preserved. In the dining room the previous evening, the first night of the cruise, their four-top table had been next to his two-top by the window. As the wine flowed and plates of food came and went, they noticed that he was on his own. The next thing Roger knew, the three women had drawn him into conversation, asking where was he from, was he traveling solo, and what did he think of the cruise so far? By the time dinner was over, they had invited him to accompany them to the bar for an after-dinner drink, and before the evening ended — sometime after midnight — he had agreed to join them for the following night's formal dinner.

Aunt Julia would have called them "classy old broads." They were well dressed, well manicured, and no doubt well heeled. Roger had no doubt that the bits of jewelry on display were the real thing — diamonds as opposed to zirconium. So, although he was happy to have been included in their circle, he knew he was completely out of his element.

He didn't mention to them or to anyone else on board that the two-week cruise, complete with his two-room suite and an attending butler, was a freebie. Roger had detected and successfully prevented a massive data breach that would have thrown the cruise ship line into a nightmare and disrupted their entire reservations system. Not only had he preempted the attack, he'd also managed to catch the culprit — a disgruntled former employee. As far as Shining Star Cruises was concerned, Roger McGeary was a hero, and they were prepared to treat him as such.

When Roger stepped off the elevator on deck five, he stood for a moment, staring in through the open doors of the ship's piano bar, the Starlight Lounge. The place was crowded. The girls — Angie, Millie, and Dot — had managed to snag seats at the bar and were evidently holding a spot for him. The barman, a cheerful guy named Xavier, caught Roger's eye as he stood in the entryway, nodded, and immediately turned to prepare Roger's preferred beverage — Campari and soda — which was poured and in position in front of the single open stool before Roger made it across the room.

This was only the second night of the cruise, Roger noted, so how was it possible that Xavier recognized individual customers on sight and had already memorized their preferred beverages? Roger was entirely at home in the cyber world in front of keyboards and glowing computer screens, but Xavier's people skills — his easy humor and pleasant gift of gab — were completely absent from Roger's skill set. He'd never be able to be a bartender, never in a million years.

Dorothy Campbell, aka Dot, was a divorcée with a thick southern accent. A little slip of a thing, with brightly hennaed red hair and a slick black sheath dress, she was also the self-proclaimed ringleader of the group. Dot launched herself off her stool and tackled Roger, greeting him with an enthusiastic hug.

"My goodness gracious," she said, looking him up and down. "If you don't clean up nice."

"Why, thank you, ma'am," Roger replied, trying to match her accent with a sort of ersatz cowboy gallantry and then flushing in embarrassment because he felt like he'd

already made a jackass of himself.

"You're not just having Campari and soda, are you?" she demanded. "Shouldn't you have something a little higher octane than that? How about joining us in a Kir Royale?"

That's what the girls had been drinking at the bar the previous night, and that's what they were having tonight as well. Roger wasn't much of a drinker, and he didn't do drugs, either — any kind of drugs other than his doctor-prescribed antidepressants — but he'd allowed himself to be persuaded. Once he'd made it back to the room the previous night, he'd looked up "Kir Royale," which turned out to be a heady combo of champagne and crème de cassis. Roger had attempted to tell them that he couldn't dance — wouldn't dance. With a couple of Kir Royales under his belt, they had managed to cajole him onto the dance floor, sometimes with all three of them at once. By the time the girls had wished him good night, everybody had been flying high — Roger included.

"See you tomorrow," Dot had admonished him, shaking a finger in his face on her way out. "Drinks in the bar at seven; dinner at seven-forty-five. Don't be late."

Xavier had watched the three women

leave the bar and head tipsily for the elevator. Shaking his head in mock sympathy, he turned to Roger. "I believe you have your hands full, sir. Would you care for a refill?"

"Those were a little stiff for me," Roger had told him. "I'd better not."

Now in the predinner cocktail hour, canapés came and went, and so did a second Campari and soda and finally a third. When seating at the bar proved too noisy for conversation, Dot commandeered a nearby table. In the ensuing conversation, Roger began to learn a bit about his companions. The three women were old college chums who had all attended Wellesley and had stayed friends through thick and thin ever since, including taking two-week cruises together each and every year.

Roger didn't know exactly where Wellesley was, but he was pretty sure going there was a pricey proposition. And knowing how much the cruise cost on the open market, he estimated there had been a whole lot more thick in the women's lives than there had been thin. Dot had a cabin — a Star Suite like his — all to herself, while Angie and Millie bunked together in the next category down, a Veranda Stateroom. In the bar and again when they moved into the dining room, Roger listened to their harm-

less dinnertime chatter, feeling as though he was being given a window into another world, one he'd never even imagined.

Somewhere between courses three and four, between the mixed green salad and the pappardelle pasta, Roger came to the realization that these women had most likely been contemporaries of his late mother, may she rot in hell. Unlike Eloise McGeary, however, the girls actually seemed to like him.

After the surf-and-turf main course — prime rib and lobster — and dessert — a delectable flan topped with a layer of crisp caramel and three perfect raspberries — Roger felt the buzz of an incoming text. But the wine had been flowing — white followed by red — and he was on vacation. If someone from work wanted to be in touch, they could damned well wait. And if it was Aunt Julia? Well, then, she could wait, too. It was afternoon in Payson, Arizona, and she'd be out looking after her horses. Taking the phone out of his pocket but without bothering to look at the screen, he powered it off.

Once dinner was over, the group migrated back to the bar, where a piano player accompanied a talented vocalist who sang everything from Patsy Cline to the Beatles. The passengers were mostly of an earlier vintage, Roger noted, and so was the music.

A couple of hours went by, and more than a little booze passed Roger's lips, booze that was definitely of the high-octane variety. Halfway through his third Courvoisier, he realized that Millie and Angie had both disappeared from the picture, and he was left with an increasingly aggressive Dot, who was feeling him up in a most insistent and suggestive fashion. Roger was just drunk enough to find it laughable that this very spry older woman was hitting on him, but once she mentioned, not so coyly, that he was the "only fresh meat" to be found on board, it didn't seem nearly so funny anymore.

Excusing himself to go to "the little boys' room," Roger fled the bar, ducked into the elevator, and made his way back to his own deck. The ship was rocking and rolling underfoot, but this time it wasn't just the roiling sea that sent him staggering back and forth from wall to wall all the way down the corridor. He was drunk — as drunk as he'd ever been in his life. He tried his key in the door. When it didn't work, he finally realized that he was trying to enter the wrong suite.

Once he got inside, he felt like he was going to puke. Closer to his lanai than the bathroom, Roger fought his way through blackout curtains, pulled open the slider, stumbled over to the rail, and cut loose. Then, incredibly grateful that he had made it in time, he stood for a time savoring the wind and the sea and the pounding rain and trying to pull himself together. He didn't care if his tux got wet at that point because it would for sure have to go to the cleaners anyway. He was almost ready to go back inside when his phone buzzed again.

How could that be? Hadn't he turned it off during dinner? Swaying back and forth next to the rail, he fumbled the phone out of his pocket and scowled down at the screen in frowning puzzlement. What he saw there wasn't really a text — at least it didn't look like a standard text. The words appeared one at a time, scrolling past as though a very fast typist was typing them in real time.

He had read through only a sentence or two before he recognized what he was reading. The words on the screen were all too familiar, and standing there in the wind and the rain, he could almost hear his mother's voice, berating him in the car as they drove to his high school commencement:

What on earth did I do to deserve such an

incredible little shit? You're just like your father, Roger McGeary, utterly and totally worthless, and you'll never amount to a hill of beans. What have you got to show for that supposedly high IQ of yours? You barely graduated, for cripes' sake. Your GPA isn't good enough to get into college, and what the hell would you do if you got there? Screw around the same way you did in high school? If you think I'm going to let you sit around the house on your lazy ass, buster, you have another think coming. James McGeary, that worthless father of yours, finally had the good grace to do the world a favor and off himself. With any kind of luck, you will, too.

Roger recognized the words — Eloise McGeary's words. Months earlier, during a course of psychiatric treatment, he had recalled them all and written them down verbatim in a document for his therapist, Dr. Amelia Cannon. She had assured him that writing out exactly what his mother had said would be a healing exercise — a way of recognizing his mother's meanness and spite for what it was as well as a way of negating Eloise's powerful hold over him.

At the beginning of Roger's senior year in high school, Eloise had uprooted her son and moved to L.A. Lost in an unfamiliar situation — overwhelmed and unable to cope — he'd barely managed to graduate. A little over a week after commencement, Roger McGeary had attempted suicide. Deeming him a danger to himself and others, Eloise had made it her business to have her son locked away in a mental institution where he had remained for the next ten years of his life. It was only in the past few years, at Aunt Julia's urging, that he'd finally gone for counseling. It had been in the course of his supposedly confidential sessions with Dr. Cannon that Roger had written down these very words — ones that now seemed to have developed a life of their own on the screen of his cell phone.

Roger's hands trembled. If the words he had written for Dr. Cannon could surface here, that meant they could surface in other places as well. They were out in the world somewhere, most likely all over the Internet, where eventually they were bound to be used against him. Somewhere down the line, some boss — a guy somewhere far up the chain of command — would bring those words to bear and use them to imply that Roger was mentally unstable; that, if he was undergoing therapy, he most likely couldn't be trusted with the kinds of security clearances necessary to perform his duties. He'd be done for — out of a job, unemployed and unemployable.

And in that moment, on a night that should have counted as a social triumph, Roger found himself sliding back into the same kind of blinding despair that had kept him in a state of mental paralysis for the better part of ten years. He wouldn't go there. He would not. He couldn't. He had fought so hard to climb out of that snake pit of unending darkness that he couldn't stand the idea of falling back into it again. Could. Not. Stand. It.

The words had stopped scrolling, and suddenly the screen went blank. He punched the power button and the phone came to life, starting over from scratch — as if it had been completely powered off. When the start-up sequence finished, Roger went straight to the texting app, looking for the message he'd just seen, but it wasn't there. There was no sign of it at all.

So where had the words come from, then? If he hadn't seen them — if he'd just imagined them — maybe he really had gone nuts. Again. And that was something else he could not and would not endure.

By then he was soaked to the skin, but that didn't matter. Making up his mind, he put the phone down on the lanai's patio table and then pulled one of the deck chairs over to the railing. He clambered up onto the chair and then stood for a moment — hearing the words again — not as they had appeared on the screen but as he had heard them more than two decades ago, in his mother's shrill voice. He was still hearing them as he plunged over the side of the ship and into the black water far below, with no one on board the ship any the wiser. And it was only then, as the icy sea closed over him, that Roger McGeary finally moved beyond the reach of his mother's earthly torment.

Abandoned on the lanai's small patio table, the phone remained there for some time, glowing silently in the dark, before finally shutting down for good.

It was Reynaldo, coming the next morning to deliver Roger's breakfast, who found the sliding door open and the carpeting inside the stateroom soaked by lashing rain. Out on the lanai, a spray-soaked cell phone lay face up on the table. The butler immediately tossed a life vest over the rail before calling in to sound the alarm: man overboard.

By then, of course, it was far too late.

■ ■ ■ ■

Half a world away, in a basement lined with electronics racks filled with hundreds of computer blades, a man sat hunched over a single screen. Alive with anticipation, he watched the action and listened to the dialogue. This was his show, after all. He was the director, producer, sound engineer, and cameraman, if not the star. He didn't consider himself a cyber bully. He was more a cyber god. He liked to think of himself as Odin, and Frigg was his all-knowing artificial intelligence sidekick and companion.

He was jacked up on coffee and speed. That was what it took to stay awake and alert when you were tuned in to a life that was spinning toward the drainpipe eight or nine time zones ahead of you. Odin had chosen to let the game play out tonight — on the night of the cruise ship's formal dinner. For a time, listening in through the remote access malware he'd inserted into Roger's phone, Odin had worried that one of the women might opt to go back to Roger's room with him or, worse, that he'd go to hers. Luckily that hadn't happened. Odin was aware that if things didn't come to a head tonight, the ship's data-throttling capability might come into play and make him have to give up on the project altogether for the time being. It was also possible that if Roger noticed the unexpected power drain on his phone, he might suspect there was a problem.

Odin remembered being told once that it was always the shoemaker's kids and the blacksmith's horse who had to make do without new shoes. With Roger McGeary, a rock star in terms of corporate cyber security, his phone should have been completely impenetrable. Odin had had zero luck in accessing his work accounts, but an overlooked security issue on Roger's personal cell phone had left the device vulnerable to attack.

Odin had paid a small fortune to procure powerful new malware that had been developed in Israel. Once installed on a smart device of any kind, it allowed full access to everything on it — keystrokes, e-mails, texts, cameras, and GPS locations, as well as recording devices. Customers paid a hefty six-figure installation fee for the software and then continuing fees based on the number of people being monitored by the program.

Theoretically the system was only sold to properly vetted entities — usually government agencies of some kind. Searching the dark Web, Odin had found a disenchanted software engineer, one of the software developers who had been fired for cause, who had been more than willing to sell him a black market copy. Since Frigg was available and fully capable of handling all necessary monitoring requirements, Odin was able to keep the whole operation in-house without incurring any ongoing fees.

Tuning back into the distant conversation — the laughter and the clinking of glasses — Odin heard Roger excuse himself to go to the restroom, except he didn't. The next sounds he heard had nothing to do with someone taking a piss or washing his hands. There was the distinctive ding of an arriving elevator followed by a recorded voice saying, "You are on deck seven." After that, Odin heard a strange series of thumps followed eventually by the slamming of a door. Moments after that, there were hurried footsteps pounding on a metal surface. The footsteps ended with the noise of someone heaving his guts out.

The noises made sense then. Roger, probably drunker than he had ever been in his life, had rushed headlong into his cabin, unlatched the lock on the slider, and then made for the rail before being sick. All of which meant that Roger McGeary was exactly where Odin had wanted and needed him to be for this final chapter — outside and alone on the cabin's balcony.

Odin gave Roger some time to recover his wits before launching the attack. While the texted words scrolled silently across the screen, Odin watched the pallid face, captured by the cell phone's camera, as it registered first astonishment followed by hopelessness and finally utter despair.

Odin couldn't help smiling at that. It was exactly what happened to weak people when their darkest secrets were exposed to the light of day . . . or, as in this case, the light of night.

Odin felt his own heartbeat quicken. He may have been the one holding the gun, but the final decision was really up to Roger. Would he pull the trigger or not? Waiting for the man to choose seemed to take forever. Later, reviewing the video, Odin would measure the elapsed time with his stopwatch. All told it was little more than a minute from beginning to end, although it seemed much longer. At one minute twenty-seconds, Roger set the phone down on something. He did so carefully and with drunken deliberation. Odin couldn't see exactly where the phone had been placed, but fortunately it was still face up — on a patio table, maybe? From Odin's vantage point, all he could see was a light-colored overhead surface of some kind — probably the ceiling area of Roger's balcony, formed by the floor of the one above his.

Odin leaned closer to his computer and upped the volume. There was a lot of noise in the background with raindrops showing on the face of the phone, so he suspected it was stormy with plenty of wind and rain. After a few moments, Odin heard some kind of grating sound — wood on metal, maybe? — followed by a grunt of exertion followed by nothing — nothing at all.

Odin felt vaguely disappointed. He had wanted to witness firsthand Roger's despairing headlong plunge into the sea, but the unfortunate camera angle on the cell phone robbed him of that. Oh well.

Just to be on the safe side, Odin gave it five minutes — five long minutes of wind and rain and nothing else. There was no way to know for sure if it had worked. Either Roger McGeary had thrown himself off the ship or he had not, and that meant it was far too soon for Odin to gloat over a job well done. Hours from now someone would notice if Roger McGeary was really missing. In the meantime, Odin saved the video file for his private collection and then waited for as long as it took for his remotely installed malware to perform its self-deleting exit program.

Once the purge was complete, Odin finally gave himself permission to stand up, stretch, and look around. By then it was coming up on five o'clock in the afternoon. He'd been up and at the computer for close to twenty-four hours. Even so, he needed to shower and dress for dinner. His mother was fine with him spending his days and nights behind the locked doors of the computer lab inside his spacious basement apartment. Irene didn't seem to mind what her son did during the day as long as he showed up promptly each evening just as dinner was being served.

As far as Odin was concerned, spending an hour and a half each day with his annoying mother was a small price to pay for having virtually unlimited funds as well as unlimited freedom. Besides, he didn't need to be there in the lab personally keeping watch. He'd done his part. The rest was up to Frigg. If and when the man-overboard alarm went out on board the *Whispering Star,* either now or hours from now, Frigg would be among the first to know, and once Frigg knew, so would Odin.

In the months leading up to this night, Odin, with Frigg's very capable help, had learned everything there was to know about Roger McGeary, including all the telling details necessary to pull the underpinnings out from under him. Odin would wait until tomorrow. Once Roger's death was confirmed, it would be time for Odin and Frigg to go hunting again.

Odin had every confidence another victim was out there just waiting to be found — someone who, with the benefit of enough information and a little encouragement on his part, would be more than willing to end it all, with Odin on hand to watch the performance to the bitter end. If that wasn't the perfect way to commit murder, Owen Hansen didn't know what was.

1

On the Tuesday morning after Labor Day, Ali Reynolds pulled into her reserved parking spot outside High Noon Enterprises in Cottonwood, Arizona, just as a dust-covered aging Dodge Ram pickup came to a stop in one of the two designated visitor slots. Since High Noon specialized in cyber security — specifically international cyber security — visitor spaces at the company's headquarters often remained empty. Occasionally a salesman dropped by, and sometimes Ali's retired parents showed up unannounced for a visit, but that was pretty much it.

The woman who exited the truck was tall and spare, six feet tall at least. She was dressed in worn jeans, dusty, down-at-the-heels cowboy boots, and a sweat-stained Stetson. She went around to the back of the truck, opened the cargo door, and pulled out a banker's box. It was cumbersome enough that she had to set the box down on the ground before reaching up to close the tailgate.

Exiting her Cayenne, Ali approached the visitor. The sun-bronzed face beneath the Stetson's wide brim resembled tanned leather. The road map of wrinkles around her mouth and cheeks hinted that she was probably a lifelong smoker. Her most striking feature, however, was a penetrating pair of bright blue eyes.

"The box looks heavy," Ali observed. "Can I help you with that?"

"This High Noon Enterprises?" the newcomer asked, hefting the box onto her shoulder with the ease of someone who most likely carried bales of hay in the same fashion.

"Yes," Ali answered. "That's us."

"This is the right place, then," the woman said. "I'm here to see a fellow by the name of Stuart Ramey. And I can carry the box by myself, thank you very much."

As they started toward the entrance, Ali hurried ahead. Opening the door with her key card, she allowed the visitor to enter. High Noon's newly hired receptionist secretary, Shirley Malone, looked up with a smile. "Good morning," she said to the guest while nodding in Ali's direction. "May I help you?" she asked.

34

"I'm here to see Stuart Ramey," the woman repeated, unceremoniously plopping the box down on the countertop. "Is he in?"

Shirley's blink of surprise mirrored Ali's. In her experience no one had ever shown up on the doorstep specifically asking to see Stuart Ramey.

High Noon Enterprises was the brainchild of Ali's husband, B. Simpson. Stu, B.'s second-in-command, was a brilliant software guy with the social skills of an onion. Camille Lee, a recent college graduate and someone ostensibly hired to be Stuart's assistant, was a capable computer geek in her own right, but her primary duty — one at which she had proved to be uncommonly adept — was keeping the less than personable and somewhat skittish Stuart from veering off into the weeds.

For a long time the reception area at High Noon had been left unattended. On those rare occasions when visitors did arrive, security cameras had allowed Stu Ramey and Cami to see who was at the door and let them into the building, with Cami usually designated to handle whatever needed handling. Lately, though, with Cami's technical skills focused on more complex tasks, B. and Ali had opted to hire Shirley, an action they had taken over Stu's strenuous objections.

He had only just barely adjusted to having Cami's presence added to the mix. Having Ali and B. add in a fifty-something woman with a loud brassy laugh and a bawdy sense of humor was completely outside his comfort zone. The way things were now, Stu stayed in the back while Shirley stayed out front, with Cami shuttling back and forth between the two as needed.

Before Shirley could respond, Ali hijacked the conversation. "My name is Ali Reynolds," she said to the visitor. "My husband, B. Simpson, and I own High Noon. Mr. Ramey is one of our employees. And you are?"

"Name's Julia," the woman said gruffly, holding out a work-callused hand. "Julia Miller."

"I'm quite sure Stuart is in," Ali said. "May I tell him what this is about?"

Since Stu lived in a studio apartment addition that had been built onto the far side of the computer lab, there wasn't much chance that he wouldn't be there.

"It's about my nephew, Roger McGeary," Julia said. "He and Stuart were friends a long time ago, back in junior high and high school."

"And . . . ?" Ali prompted.

"Roger's dead," Julia said abruptly. Clearly she wasn't someone accustomed to mincing words. "I want to hire High Noon to find out what happened to him."

"I'm so sorry for your loss, Mrs. Miller," Ali began.

"Ms., if you please," Julia corrected. "Never married and never intend to be married, either."

"Of course," Ali said with a nod. "Ms. Miller, then. But High Noon is a cyber security company rather than a private investigation firm. I'm sure Stuart will be sorry to hear about his friend, but —"

"Roger was in the same business as you folks are," Julia interrupted. "Cyber Resources Unlimited of San Jose, California. That's the name of the outfit he worked for. I think someone there may be behind what happened. I think he did something or found out something that offended someone else, and they decided to get rid of him."

"Why?" Ali asked. "What did happen to him?"

"He supposedly committed suicide on a cruise ship three months ago, but I'm not buying that BS, not for a minute. The investigator just now closed the case and sent me Rog's personal effects. Since no suicide note was found, the final determination appears to be 'death by misadventure,' whatever that's supposed to mean."

"When did he die?" Ali asked.

"Back in June. The early hours of June third to be exact, in the English Channel somewhere between Southampton and Bruges."

Ali turned to Shirley. "Would you tell Stuart there's a Julia Miller here to see him? Ask him to meet us in the conference room. This way," she said to the visitor.

Nodding, Julia picked up the box and brought it along.

Ali led the way past B.'s office and her own as well and into the so-called conference room, which doubled as a break room. Julia set the box down on one of the two tables with a resounding thump.

"And those are?" Ali asked.

"Roger's personal effects, except for his clothing," Julia replied. "From both his office and the cruise ship. Of course, I wasn't allowed anywhere near his office. Someone packed up his cubicle and sent me whatever was inside it. Ditto for the Panamanian cops."

"Panama?" Ali asked.

"He was on an Italian ship operating under the Panamanian flag, so officers from there were the ones who actually investigated the incident."

Stu Ramey appeared in the open doorway and stood there uncertainly. "You wanted to see me?" he asked.

"I'm the one who wanted to see you," Julia Miller said, striding forward to meet him with her hand outstretched. "It's so good to see you again after all these years, Stuart. I believe the last time I laid eyes on you was that summer when you and Roger spent two weeks with me at the ranch in Payson, and Pansy, that mean Shetland pony we had back then, took a bite out of your arm."

Stuart's face broke into a genuine grin, something else that took Ali by surprise. The Stu Ramey she knew wasn't the grinning sort.

"Ms. Miller? Are you kidding? Really? What on earth brings you here?"

"It's bad news, I'm afraid," Ali interjected. "It seems your friend Roger passed away."

Stuart's welcoming grin vanished. Looking stricken, he staggered over to the table and sank down heavily into one of the molded-plastic chairs. "Roger's dead? How can that be? What happened to him? A car wreck? Cancer? What?"

"The authorities say he committed suicide, and maybe he did," Julia said. "If that's the case, though, I want to know why.

Things were going so well for him, I can't imagine him doing something like that. That's the reason I came here today. I want to hire you people to get to the bottom of what happened."

"Suicide," Stuart repeated. "But I thought he'd put his depression issues behind him. The last time I saw him, a year or so ago at the conference in Las Vegas, he said he was doing great."

Julia nodded grimly. "He *was* doing great," she said.

"Wait," Ali interjected. "You're saying Roger had been depressed before?"

Julia gave a dismissive wave. "Yes, and I'll admit he did attempt suicide once, many years ago, but things have turned around for him since then," Julia added. "And that's why his committing suicide now makes no sense at all."

Glancing in Stuart's direction, Ali saw that the man seemed to be close to tears. It didn't matter whether or not this investigation was something High Noon Enterprises was prepared to undertake. Learning about his friend's death had shocked Stuart Ramey to his core, and the least Ali or anyone else could do would be to hear Julia Miller's story from beginning to end.

"It smells like someone just made a fresh

pot of coffee," Ali said, hoping to take some of the emotional overload off Stu. "How about if I pour some coffee and then you can give us the whole scoop. How do you take yours?" she asked, turning to Julia.

"Black," Julia replied. "Black and strong."

While Ali went to the counter to fetch cups and pour coffee, Stu lumbered to his feet, retrieved his drink of choice — a can of Diet Coke — from the fridge, and popped it open. Doing that provided enough of a diversion that, by the time Ali delivered the coffee and Stu returned to the table, he seemed to have regained his composure.

"So tell us," he said. "From the beginning."

"Shining Star Cruises was one of the accounts Rog — that's what I always called him, Rog not Roger — handled for Cyber Resources Unlimited. The cruise line was targeted with some kind of huge data hack that would have turned their whole reservations system upside down. The bad guys, whoever they were, were holding the company's information hostage and expected to be paid a ransom. Sort of like a kidnapping, only of data rather than of a living, breathing person."

"And?" Stuart urged.

"Roger figured it out. He discovered the

problem and traced it back to a former Shining Star employee — a disgruntled IT guy — who was bent out of shape over getting fired."

"And then what happened?"

"The cruise line offered Rog a cruise — as a reward. I'm under the impression that some of the people at Cyber Resources were pissed off because he got to go and they didn't."

"Names?" Stuart asked, setting an iPad down on the surface of the table and positioning his fingers over the onscreen keyboard, preparing to take notes.

"I don't really know any of their names," Julia replied. "I think there was a Kevin, maybe. Somebody named Jack, and there was a woman, too, an Amy or Annie — something that started with an A."

"So professional jealousy could be part of the problem, but you have no last names?" Stuart insisted.

"None."

"Tell us about the cruise," Ali suggested.

"It was a two-week cruise," Julia answered. "Southampton to Stockholm by way of Copenhagen, St. Petersburg, and I don't know where all else, but this happened on the second day out. As soon as he got on board, Roger was having a blast and sent me photos of his suite. It looked gorgeous — a sitting room, dining area, bedroom, and bath along with a private patio. First class all the way. And it was one of those deals where food and beverages were all included in the price."

Ali's parents, Bob and Edie Larson, were inveterate cruisers, so Ali knew a little about cruise pricing. A two-week, all-inclusive cruise wouldn't have come cheap.

"Before the cruise, were you in touch with your nephew on a fairly regular basis?" Ali asked.

"I was all he had left," Julia replied. "His father committed suicide while Rog was still in high school, and his mother, my sister, died a number of years ago. No great loss there, by the way."

"What do you mean?"

"I mean Eloise Miller McGeary was a complete bitch. Thank God and Greyhound she's gone."

Ali glanced toward Stuart. He said nothing but nodded in somber agreement.

"Are you saying that Roger and his mother were estranged before she died?"

Julia let loose a hoot of laughter that ended in a fit of coughing. "What do you think?" she said. "She never wanted Rog in the first place. She was looking for a meal ticket. That's the reason she got pregnant, so she could marry a likely-looking prospect. She told her son that to his face — called Rog her 'mistake by the lake,' — Lake Pleasant being the body of water in question," Julia added dryly. "Unfortunately for James McGeary, as far as Eloise was concerned, it turns out he didn't measure up to her stringent standards. She ended up running him off while Rog was still in junior high."

"Let's go back to the cruise for a minute," Ali said. "I believe you mentioned that it happened on the second day of the cruise. How did you find out about it?"

"Rog listed me as his emergency contact. The cruise line called me the next morning."

"So this happened overnight?"

"Yes, my understanding is that Rog went to dinner with some women he met on the ship. Later that night he returned to his room and was never seen again."

"Were these people he knew before he boarded the ship?"

"Not as far as I know."

"Do you happen to have their names?"

Julia nodded. "And their e-mail addresses. All three of them were kind enough to send me notes of condolence. I understand that the dinner that night was a formal affair.

He and the women were seated together in the dining room. Afterward, they stopped off in the bar to have a few drinks. Maybe more than a few. I was told that they have security video showing Roger going back to his suite, drunk as a skunk. The footage shows him trying to enter the wrong room before he finally made it into his own. The only other people seen entering or leaving his suite were his butler — a guy named Reynaldo — and a housekeeper named Gabriella."

"But neither the housekeeper nor the butler were there when he entered the room after the dinner?"

"No," Julia said. "At least that's what I've been told. No one has allowed me to view the security footage. The cops from Panama described it to me. They evidently saw it, but I wasn't granted that privilege."

"All right, then," Ali persisted. "Your nephew goes to his room. What time was that?"

"A little past midnight."

"What happens then?"

"Nothing, for a very long time — a period of several hours. Then, at eight fifteen the next morning, the butler . . ."

"The same one you mentioned before — Reynaldo?"

Julia nodded. "Yes, the same one. He shows up with a breakfast tray because Roger had ordered breakfast to be delivered to his room. The butler went inside and found that the sliding door leading out to the patio was wide open. It had been stormy enough overnight that the carpet in the dining area was soaked. He saw Roger's phone, sitting on a table out on the balcony. The battery was completely discharged. They found a bow tie out on the balcony, too, but nothing else — no shoes, no tux, and no Roger, although there was some evidence that Roger had tossed his cookies outside on the balcony."

"He'd been sick?"

"Yes, and since his bed clearly hadn't been slept in, the butler immediately initiated man-overboard procedures. The captain ordered every inch of the ship searched, but of course they found nothing. Roger was simply gone. They concluded that he might have fallen overboard because he was drunk, but the fact that one of the deck chairs had been moved over next to the railing made them suspect it was suicide. I guess, as far as Panama is concerned, the term 'misadventure' covers both of those eventualities. But I don't believe it was suicide," Julia insisted. "Not for a minute."

"In cases like this it's always a good idea to follow the money," Ali suggested. "Did Roger have a will?"

"Yes," Julia said. "I happen to have a copy of that along today. It's in the banker's box along with the rest of his stuff."

"And?" Ali prodded.

"I'm his only beneficiary. He had a condo in San Jose that's worth somewhere in the neighborhood of $750,000 or so. He made good money, but he didn't live very high on the hog. He sent me money every month."

"He sent you money?"

"Not me," Julia said quickly, "and not directly. He gave about five thousand dollars a month to United Way. His company, Cyber Resources, matched his donations, and they sent the combined contribution to my 501(c)3 — Racehorse Rest. We rescue discarded racehorses and look after them to keep those magnificent creatures from being turned into horse meat."

"So your nephew has been single-handedly underwriting your operation to the tune of ten thousand dollars a month?"

Julia nodded. "And whatever proceeds I receive from his estate will most likely end up there, too. There's some life insurance — group life insurance — and a big chunk of 401(k)."

"I hope you don't mind my asking, but does the insurance angle have anything to do with why you're so determined to prove Roger didn't commit suicide?" Ali asked. "I mean, is there some kind of clause that would preclude benefits being paid in the case of suicide?"

"No, nothing of the kind," Julia answered. "In fact, I've already filed the death claim on that. Those funds will most likely arrive within a matter of days. I came here today with the intention of offering you the whole amount of the death proceeds — up to $500,000 — to hire you and your people to do a thorough investigation."

"But why is it so important for you to find out what happened?" Ali asked.

Julia paused for a moment before she answered. "Because of Eloise," she said at last. "She always told anyone who would listen that Roger was cut from the same cloth as his father. She claimed they were both a waste of air, and that since Roger's dad committed suicide, Roger most likely would do the same, sooner or later. It seemed to me like she was almost goading him into it."

Julia stopped speaking long enough to wipe a single tear from her eye.

"And?" Ali persisted.

"And I'd like to prove the bitch wrong, once and for all," Julia said fiercely. "If not, I at least want to know why it happened. As far as I could tell, Rog was in a good place, not only at work, but also in his personal life. He seemed to be starting a whole new chapter in his life, and now he's gone."

With that, Julia Miller, who had walked into the office looking as though she were tough enough to chew nails, laid her head on her arms and wept.

2

"I'm afraid it's bad news, Harold," Dr. Darrell Richards said. "As I suspected, it is ALS."

It was a gorgeous early-spring day in March of 1986. Through the windows of the doctor's Santa Barbara examining room the sky overhead was a clear, untroubled blue. Forty-six-year-old Harold Hansen heard the words in stunned silence and knew that life as he knew it was over.

"As in Lou Gehrig's disease?" he managed finally.

Harold had been only a year old when the famed ballplayer succumbed to the illness that would eventually become synonymous with his name. His father, Leif, who had emigrated from Norway in the thirties and had somehow turned himself into a multimillionaire lumber baron, had loved the "great American pastime" with all his heart. Harold had grown up listening to his father tell anyone who was interested, and a lot of people who weren't, that "Lou Gehrig was the best damned ballplayer of all time," and that it was a "hell of a shame what happened to him."

"Yes," Dr. Richards agreed simply. "Lou Gehrig's."

"How long do I have?"

Dr. Richards replied with a silent but eloquent shrug, one that spoke volumes.

"So you have no idea?"

"Years if you're lucky."

"And if I'm not?"

"A matter of months."

Harold had noticed that his right hand was going wonky on him. There were times when he could barely hold a soldering iron anymore, to say nothing of keeping it steady. But being unable to open a new pickle jar Irene had handed him two weeks earlier had been the last straw. He'd made an appointment to see Darrell, who was both his personal physician and also his golfing buddy, until Harold had started having trouble with his grip and connecting with the ball.

During the exam, Harold had answered a string of seemingly unrelated questions. Had he experienced any difficulty in walking recently? Well, yes, he'd tripped a couple of times, maybe, but nothing extreme. Any weakness in his other limbs, in addition to the gimpy hand? Well, maybe a little, especially in his right leg. Any difficulty swallowing? Let's see, every once in a while he had a problem choking down the handful of vitamin supplements Irene insisted he take on a daily basis, but what did the occasional choking episode have to do with the growing weakness in his hand?

"Let's run a few tests to see what's going on," Darrell had said. The testing was over, and now they knew.

"There's not really any treatment for this, is there," Harold said — a statement rather than a question because he already knew the answer.

"No."

"And this is just between us, right?" he asked.

"Of course," Darrell replied. "Absolutely."

"I'm holding you to that," Harold said. "No one else is to know — not ever."

Harold left the doctor's office on Hollister. Instead of heading home to the house on Via Vistosa, he fired up his Nassau Blue Corvette and headed for northbound Highway 101. He needed to go someplace where he could be by himself so he could think and come to terms with this new reality.

That called for a solitary walk along the shore.

Harold gave Darrell full points for not attempting to sugarcoat the situation. It was what it was: Harold was dying. Of course, he understood that everyone alive was also busy dying sooner or later. He wouldn't be gone today or tomorrow or even next week. But now was the time to make his final arrangements. He had a wife to think about and a child.

Harold Hansen was a wealthy man. Not only had he inherited a fortune from his father, he'd created one of his own. He hadn't wanted to follow in his father's footsteps. He had no interest in trees or logging or milling. From the time he was given his first Erector Set, Harold had wanted to know how things worked and what made them go. An electronics engineer/ entrepreneur at the dawn of the computer age, he'd invented a chip that had changed the course of computer science. Although plenty of corporate suitors had come calling with mind-blowing offers — one as recently as a week earlier — Harold had stayed the course. Now, though, if he was no longer going to be at his company's helm, it was time for him to sell out before any of his competitors smelled blood in the water, and the sooner the sale was finalized, the better.

As for what to do with the money? Irene was the love of his life, as sweet as sweet could be, but she was also a bit dim, especially when it came to money. To Harold's knowledge, she'd never written a check or balanced a checkbook. If she saw something she wanted, she bought it. Harold had never begrudged her any of that, but if he was gone and there was no more money coming in, there had to be safeguards. Irene was thirty-nine. Her mother was a hale and hearty sixty-eight and would probably last another decade or so without much effort.

That meant that when it came to looking after Irene, Harold needed to plan for her to be around for a long time after he was gone. He also needed to safeguard the funds so they would be there for her, and not be carted off by the first fast-talking asshole who came sniffing around looking for a free ride. Harold realized that he'd need to set up a trust of some kind — something that would come with spendthrift provisions. Irene adored the house — she had chosen it herself — but Harold also needed to create an ongoing entity that would make sure property taxes were paid on a regular basis and that house maintenance issues were properly handled. That way Irene would always have a suitable roof over her head and so would Owen.

Owen. Thinking of his four year-old son made Harold's heart hurt. Harold loved him, of course. After all, you had to love your own kid, didn't you? But he was such an odd little duck — solitary, standoffish, a bit of a frail flower, and spoiled — most definitely spoiled. Owen had no interest in any of the rough-and-tumble things that Harold had loved as a boy. If there was a tree, Harold had climbed it. If there was a mud hole? Harold had been in it up to his eyeballs. And if someone offered a dare, Harold had been the first to take it.

Not Owen. When it came to trees or dares, the boy was a shrinking violet. In Harold's opinion his son was a mama's boy of the first water. Harold had thought that sending him off to school in a year or so would help turn him into a regular kid, but Irene had nixed that idea. There was this newfangled trend people called "homeschooling." Although since Irene wasn't the do-it-yourself type, she had already found a fully qualified kindergarten teacher who would come to their home in the fall and tutor Owen there.

Now, knowing what Harold knew — that he'd never be there in the bleachers watching Owen play Little League or varsity football — he decided maybe the home tutoring option wasn't such a bad idea after all. If Irene was going to be left to make all those decisions on her own, she could just as well start doing so now without any second-guessing or interference from him. Besides, that way, Irene wouldn't be left alone in the huge house on Via Vistosa — she'd have her boy with her. The last thing Harold wanted was for Irene to be lonely.

Harold walked along the shore for the better part of an hour, watching the sea and thinking. He made several decisions in the course of that hour's walk: the next day he would notify his attorney that he was willing to accept the buyout offer that had been presented a week earlier; he would talk to an estate attorney about setting up an irrevocable family trust that couldn't be hacked into by the first gold-digging jerk who came along; and he'd set up a trust for Owen, too, one that would guarantee that when the boy reached his majority, he wouldn't be left out in the cold.

When Harold got home that night, and Irene asked him what Dr. Richards said, Harold made no mention of his real diagnosis. He claimed the doctor had told him that he had a strained tendon in his arm and needed to wear a wrist brace for a while.

The next day, he accepted the buyout offer and then held his breath during the following two months, which was how long it took for the sale to close. In the meantime, Harold stopped taking his vitamin pills and started flushing them down the toilet, because they were too hard to swallow. He started losing weight, too, because eating was becoming more and more difficult.

By the time his new will and accompanying trust documents were drawn up, Harold knew he was running on empty. Once they were finalized and signed, Harold left the lawyer's office — just up the street from Dr. Richards's office — and stopped by Burger King for a Whopper. He thought about driving back by the house one last time just to say goodbye, but he didn't. Instead, he got back on the 101 and returned to El Capitán State Beach.

It was late Thursday afternoon at the beginning of Fourth of July weekend. The parking lot was crowded. It took a long time before he found a place to park. He sat in the Corvette and choked down what he could of his burger, then he used a pen to scribble a one-word suicide note on a fresh paper napkin: *SORRY.*

Stuffing the note in his pants pocket, he retrieved his grandfather's ancient Colt

57

M1917 from the glove box and tucked that into the back of his pants, out of sight under his sport coat.

The cold wind blowing in off the ocean did nothing to deter the crowds. Harold walked for what seemed like forever, but still there were kids here and there, playing in the water and building sand castles. Along the way he saw a trail of abandoned beach blankets and coolers awaiting the return of die-hard swimmers and surfers. The only thing Harold wanted was to be far enough away from all of them to be invisible.

At last, he found a slight indentation in the shore, a place where an unnamed creek — unnamed to him, at least — drained into the ocean. Harold staggered through the loose sand far enough to be out of view from the people back on the beach. Weak and out of breath, he sank down on a piece of driftwood. Behind him he heard shouts of merrymaking, and he worried that what he was about to do would leave whoever found him traumatized for life.

But at least that person wouldn't be Irene. Or Owen. By doing it here, he wouldn't leave behind a trail of blood and gore inside the house or in the yard to haunt his wife and child forever. As far as Harold could tell, what he was doing was best for all concerned. Irene and Owen didn't have to live with him through a long and terrible decline. That single word *SORRY* was the best he could do — the most loving thing he could do. And if Darrell Richards was a man of his word, they never would know the truth.

When Harold finally recovered enough to tug the weapon out of his waistband, he was surprised by how heavy it was. He had thought about abandoning the wrist brace back at the car, but he was glad now that he hadn't. He needed the splint to help support the weight of the gun. His grandfather had used it to deadly effect on marauding rattlesnakes in the woods of northern California and southern Oregon. The weapon had been bequeathed first to Harold's father and had come to Harold only after Leif's death.

From then on, the weapon had languished in the safe in the library of the house on Via Vistosa. The night before, Harold had taken it out and then carefully cleaned and oiled it the way both his father and grandfather had taught him.

Harold had found a partial box of .45 caliber bullets in the safe along with the weapon, but he had no idea how old they

59

were, and he didn't trust them. On the way to the lawyer's office that morning, he had stopped off to purchase new ammunition. It had been annoying to have to buy a box with fifty rounds in it when all he really needed was one, but he paid the price without voicing a complaint, pocketed the ammo, and walked out.

For weeks now, he had imagined holding the weapon to his head and calmly pulling the trigger. But when push came to shove, the gun was too heavy and his weakened hand too compromised to hold it steady. Instead, he put the weapon in his mouth, resting the metal against his teeth and gagging at the bitter taste of the residual oil that still lingered on the barrel.

When Harold finally pulled the trigger and blew his brains out, he thought of it as being the final and most loving thing he could do for his wife and for his son.

Unfortunately, it wasn't the right thing for any number of other people, Roger McGeary included.

3

Odin loved the simplicity of the Venn diagram. Frigg didn't require inter-connected shapes or subsets to understand what was needed, but Odin liked them. They made things simple and elegant. The first task he'd given Frigg was to locate the names of all people who had committed suicide in California between the years of 1960 and 1990.

Obviously the resulting list was incomplete. Many motor vehicle victims, especially the ones who died in single-car rollovers, were most likely undeclared suicides. Ditto for many reported drug overdoses. And then there were the families for whom suicide was a mortal sin. Many of them, especially the ones with money or some amount of political pull, managed to have their loved one's death declared accidental or even undetermined. For Odin's purposes, however, Frigg had sought out only the ones where cause of death was unequivocally and officially declared to be self-inflicted.

Frigg was a tireless worker. She plowed through astonishing amounts of public records before she came up with that original list. Then Odin tasked her with finding any children — living or dead — of that collection of suicide victims. That made up his first Venn diagram set. Not surprisingly, Odin found his own name — Owen Hansen — on this list.

Political pull notwithstanding, Irene Hansen hadn't been able to pass her husband's death off as something other than suicide. After all, blowing your brains out on a public beach was pretty damned definitive. But it was the next name on the list, the one just below Owen's, that caught his attention. Melvin H. Hanson, Jr. was listed as deceased. Further examination had revealed the cause — a self-inflicted gunshot wound. And the name below that? Melvin H. Hanson, Sr. When Owen compared the father/son death certificates, guess what? Both victims had perished by their own hands, and, by sheer coincidence, also on the Fourth of July.

As Odin's own father had discovered, when it came to declaring your independence, that was one way to get the job done.

Owen's father may have been a great provider — he left his widow and son wanting for nothing — but he had not been a particularly involved father. When Harold abruptly disappeared from his son's life, he did so with barely a ripple in the four-year-old's universe. Owen's mother — something of a distracted scatterbrain — was no one's idea of a devoted mother, but that didn't mean Owen lacked for attention in the sprawling mansion on Via Vistosa.

His beloved nanny, Dolores, and the cook, Sarah, competed in spoiling the boy rotten. He happily dogged the gardener's footsteps from morning until night and was ecstatic when Manuel gave Owen his very own set of child-sized gardening tools. A swimming instructor was summoned who came to the house to give him lessons until Owen, who took to the water like a fish, was deemed "pool-worthy." The kindergarten tutor, Miss Kate, was a sweet pushover, but she taught him how to read and write. Two years later, she was replaced by the stern-faced Miss Anderson, who was a lot more demanding but who also found Owen to be surprisingly adept at math — including multiplication and division, which should have been far above his skill level.

Owen was seven when his mother decided

it was high time he joined a swim team. The chauffeur, Mr. Logan, was the designated driver who delivered the boy to the Cathedral Oaks Tennis and Swim Club for practice sessions and meets. There Owen discovered that most of the other kids had mothers or fathers — mommies and daddies — cheering from the sidelines. He did not, and for the first time he realized he was different.

When he came home from one of his first meets, he immediately sought out his mother, who was never once called "Mommy," and asked her a very pointed question: "Do I have a daddy?"

"You did," she said. "Once."

"Where is he?"

"He's gone."

"What happened to him?"

"He died."

"What does that mean?"

"It means he's gone, he's never coming back, and there's no point in discussing it further." Irene was not a particularly motherly mother. Telling her son that Daddy was in heaven with Jesus was a long way outside her wheelhouse.

Dissatisfied with the answer he'd been given, Owen had gone to the other members of the household, asking the same question in hopes of getting a different take on the matter. By now, Owen should have been well beyond needing a nanny, but Dolores stayed on, looking after him and keeping him occupied during the hours that weren't taken up with his tutors. When he asked Dolores and Sarah about his father over lunch the next day, he noticed the wary glance that passed between the two women before either of them answered.

"What did your mother say?" Dolores asked.

"That he's dead and he isn't coming back."

"That's it, then, isn't it," Dolores said. "No further discussion is required."

Still, Owen had continued his quest by asking Manuel. The gardener frowned before he answered. "You see that grasshopper over there?" he asked, pointing.

Owen nodded.

"What happens if you step on it?"

"I don't know."

Manuel reached out a booted foot and smashed the offending bug flat. "He's dead now, see?" he said. "He can't breathe or move around no more. He's over."

"That's what happened to my daddy? Someone squashed him?"

"Not exactly," Manuel hedged. "But your

daddy can't move around no more, neither. If you want to know more than that, you should ask your mother."

But Owen had already asked Irene that very question, and he didn't bother asking again. From that moment on, Harold Hansen became the looming elephant in every room at the house on Via Vistosa, a dark, hovering presence who was always there whenever Owen and his mother were together. He was also the one thing they never discussed.

Without having had those critical questions answered in a satisfactory manner, from age seven on, Harold Hansen's death became Owen Hansen's obsession. He became a pint-sized detective. He learned how to listen at doors in order to pry out his mother's secrets. Irene obdurately refused to discuss her dead husband with her son, but that didn't keep her from jawing about him at length with even casual visitors, especially if she'd had a bit too much wine at dinner or maybe one after-dinner cocktail too many. It was during one of those overheard conversations, when Irene thought her eight-year-old son safely asleep in bed, that Owen heard her mention the word "suicide" for the first time.

Miss Anderson, convinced she was dealing with a math prodigy, had urged Irene to give her son a Dell computer for his birthday, while Miss Anderson herself had presented the boy with a small paper-bound dictionary. The night of his birthday, while his mother entertained guests downstairs, Owen stayed up late, dismantling the computer and putting it back together again. Two nights later, when the term "suicide" surfaced in conjunction with his father's death, Owen used the dictionary to find out that it meant his father hadn't been squashed by somebody else. He'd done it himself.

Harold Hansen was dead because he wanted to be dead. No wonder Owen's mother didn't want to talk about it. And now, neither did Owen.

4

"So what are your thoughts on the matter?" B. Simpson asked.

It was just after one in the afternoon in Cottonwood. B. was attending an international cyber security conference in Paris and had called Ali once he got back to his room after an evening meeting. She had spent the better part of half an hour bringing him up to date on Julia Miller's earlier visit.

"She offered to pay us up to $500,000 to look into the matter. I tried to explain to her that High Noon isn't designed to function as a private investigation firm."

Earlier in the conference room, it had taken Julia Miller several minutes to regain control after her emotional outburst. Once she did, she sat up straight, wiped her eyes on her shirtsleeves, and then lifted the lid off the banker's box. Reverently, she removed a laptop computer, a pair of cell phones, and a rat's nest of power cords from the container. She put the equipment down on the tabletop and then pushed it over to where Stuart Ramey was sitting.

"Please," she said. "I looked up High Noon Enterprises on the Internet. It says you do cyber stuff. Roger lived and died with his computer. His whole life — his non-work life — is most likely contained in these machines, and the reason he died may be found here as well. I have no idea what his passwords are or how to access any of it. I have a hunch you do."

Stuart swallowed hard and then reached out to place a careful hand on top of the pile of equipment, almost as if he were touching some kind of holy relic — as if there were still some trace of his friend lingering in the tangle of electronics.

"What else is in the box?" he asked.

"Not much," Julia answered, shoving the container in Stuart's direction so he could paw through it on his own. "His high school yearbooks. That's where I found your business card, by the way, Stuart. As I mentioned before, there's a copy of his last will and testament, along with his birth certificate, his parents' death certificates, and the program from his mother's funeral, even though he wasn't able to attend.

"By the way, Stuart," Julia continued. "As

far as the will is concerned, you're one of the named beneficiaries. His condo was stuffed to the gills with graphic novels — thousands of them. He wanted you to have them. When we emptied the condo to list it, I put them in storage. If you're not interested . . ."

"No, please," Stuart said, clearly moved by the gesture. "I'd love to have them."

"I'll need a shipping address, then."

"Sure, you can send them here."

One at a time, Stuart removed items from the box. After examining them, he passed them along to Ali. One was a faded color photo of a man and a boy in a rowboat, posing with a fair-sized trout.

"Roger's dad?" Ali asked.

Julia nodded. "James was a good father until Eloise drove him away. He wanted to take Roger with him, but Eloise wouldn't hear of it. Not that she wanted Roger — she didn't, but she didn't want James to have him, either. Dog in the manger kind of thing."

As Stuart continued to sort through the remaining items, Ali was saddened to think that Roger McGeary's life on earth had been boiled down to the contents of this box along with whatever records remained inside that stack of electronic devices.

The last thing Stuart held up was an orange and white and obviously much used *Betty Crocker Cookbook.*

"A cookbook?" Stuart asked in apparent disbelief. "Roger actually knew how to cook?"

"He learned," Julia said. "I taught him myself, and he got to be pretty good at it eventually. I gave him the cookbook after he got out of Napa."

"Napa?" Stuart repeated. "Roger went to school in Napa? I thought he went to school somewhere in L.A."

"Not school," Julia said, shaking her head sadly. "The Napa State Hospital."

"A mental hospital?" Stuart asked.

Julia nodded. "It was after the suicide attempt I mentioned earlier. He tried cutting his wrists right after high school graduation, and Eloise had him committed. I don't know what kinds of stories she told the doctors to keep him there, but she must have convinced them that he was a danger to himself and others. I wasn't able to spring him until after she died when a wrong-way driver hit her head-on.

"By then Roger was twenty-eight years old. He had never lived on his own — never had an apartment, never driven a car. There was only a small inheritance left by his mother, but then Roger received a sizable insurance settlement from his mother's fatal accident. Once he was out of the hospital, I brought him back home to Arizona and let him live with me at the ranch in Payson until he could get on his feet. I helped him enroll in the community college and got him started taking courses in computer science. I remembered that he'd been interested in computers as a kid, but during the ten years he'd been out of commission the world of computers had changed a lot. He more or less had to start over from scratch."

"Yes," Stuart observed quietly, "but he caught back up in a hell of a hurry."

"He did indeed," Julia agreed. "It was like he could see connections that other people couldn't. I figured Roger would have to get an associate's degree and a couple more beyond that before anyone would consider giving him a job, but then he was befriended by one of his instructors, a guy by the name of Andrew Woods. When Roger confided about what had happened to him, Woods suggested that he give up on the idea of working toward degrees. He said that even with multiple degrees in hand, when it came to landing high-end jobs, Roger's history of mental illness would make it impossible for him to pass necessary background checks.

Woods thought Roger should apply for an entry-level coding job somewhere and use his skills to work his way up from inside rather than outside, and that's exactly what he did. Woods was even kind enough to refer Roger to a friend of his who was in the process of starting a cyber security firm."

"Cyber Resources Unlimited?" Stuart asked.

"Yup," Julia said. "That's the one. Once he hired on there, he never looked back, and he never went anywhere else, either."

"I knew that Roger's father had committed suicide," Stuart said, "and I knew it hit him pretty hard, but I had no idea about his being locked up for ten years. After he moved to California and especially after graduation, we completely lost touch. I thought it was because of the usual things — college, distance, whatever. Years later when we ran into each other at a conference and reconnected, he never mentioned a word about any of that."

"I'm not surprised," Julia said. "He didn't like to talk about it. I think he worried that if his bosses ever got wind of it, his career would stall out." Julia fell quiet for a moment, looking first at Ali and then at Stu. "So?" she asked finally. "Are you going to help me with this or not?"

For an answer, Stu began putting everything back into the box, including the computer and cell phones.

"I'll take a look at all this," he said finally. "I can't promise that it'll tell you anything, though."

"Thank you," Julia said. "And as I said earlier, I'm fully prepared to pay for your services."

"No," Stuart told her. "That's not necessary. Roger McGeary was a friend of mine. Looking into this is the least I can do."

On the phone with B., Ali had been lost in a momentary bit of woolgathering. Her husband's next comment brought her back to the present. "You still haven't told me what you think we should do about all this."

Ali sighed. "That's because I still don't know. From what Julia said, she seems to be under the impression that someone from Roger's work life might have been out to get him, but I think her real bottom line is to prove to her own satisfaction that Roger McGeary either did or did not commit suicide."

"What's your take on the matter?" B. asked.

"The Panamanian detectives who investigated the incident labeled it 'death by misadventure.' My personal opinion is that

74

there's a better than even chance that Roger McGeary, drunk as could be, fell off the ship, and drowned."

"So accidental rather than deliberate?"

"Yes."

"What about Stu?" B. asked. "What does he think?"

Ali thought about that for a moment before she answered. "Roger McGeary and Stu Ramey were good friends," she answered at last. "You and I both know Stu doesn't have many friends. Just from looking at him I can tell that he's really broken up about all this. I think he's going to want to know — need to know — what happened to Roger every bit as much as Julia Miller does, and I also think we should help him."

"Fair enough," B. said. "Full speed ahead, then. Whatever you need to do, do it, but as far as I'm concerned, we're launching this investigation on Stu's behalf as an in-house matter. You can tell Julia Miller from both of us that she should keep her money and spend it on her damned horses."

One of the things Ali had always loved about B. Simpson was his generosity of spirit, and she knew he meant everything he'd just said — that when it came to solving the mystery of Roger McGeary's death, she was free to use as many of High Noon's very considerable resources as required.

"Aye aye, sir," Ali said with a grateful laugh. "I'm on it."

5

When Odin and Frigg first started studying the intergenerational aspects of suicide, he was curious more than anything else, and he was shocked to discover that not everyone on the list was like him. His whole world was predicated on the idea that his father had committed suicide, and that had made all the difference. Unfortunately, there were far too many people out there who had lost parents to suicide who seemed to suffer no permanent ill effects at all. They went on to lead perfectly ordinary lives. They grew up; they went to school; they graduated; they found jobs; they got married; they had kids; they bought homes; they paid their bills. How boring. How dreadfully mundane!

Surely there were others out there who were more like Owen himself — people who had grown up wondering about the hidden meanings contained in whatever suicide notes their dead parents may or may not have left behind.

He was fifteen years old before he managed to hack into the police report concerning his father's death. One of the pieces of evidence mentioned was the one-word message Harold had left scribbled on a paper napkin from some fast-food joint. *SORRY.* What the hell did that mean? Owen wondered. Sorry for what? Had Harold been having an affair? Was he caught up in some kind of illegal activity? Was he sorry about dying or sorry about living?

By then Owen had already moved to the basement, leaving his upstairs rooms behind and taking over the quarters that had once belonged to Sarah and Dolores. He'd made life miserable enough for his last two tutors that they'd both quit without giving notice. Owen had absolutely no interest in book learning of any kind, and no intention of going on to college, either. When he had explained that he could learn more about computers on his own than he could anywhere else, Irene had allowed herself to be persuaded.

"You can do whatever you like downstairs," she told him, "as long as you turn up for dinner every night in a clean shirt and a properly tied tie. That's not negotiable."

The term "every night" really meant every night Irene happened to be home, which wasn't often. The nights she wasn't, Owen scrounged through the fridge or ordered in. He had learned early on that Irene didn't mind having a child all that much as long as it wasn't necessary for her to waste a lot of time interacting with him. She had her life and her friends and was more than happy to leave the real work of raising her son to the hired help. Growing up, Owen watched his mother more than he knew her or liked her. He tolerated her foibles as an essential component in his life, and he learned to play her little games until he was almost better at them than she was.

If Irene had mourned the death of her husband, it hadn't been obvious — at least not to Owen. She was a bright, beautiful, and social creature. She loved dinner parties and plays and concerts. After Harold's death, she quickly realized that being a well-to-do widow made for too many unwanted advances from any number of inappropriate suitors. Rather than stop going out, she set about amassing a collection of gay male friends that she kept on tap for social situations, using them as escorts to deflect whoever's attention might require deflecting at the various concerts and galas she attended. She also welcomed her gay pals' company for dinners at home, where they provided a much needed conversational alternative to Owen's tiresome interest in all things computer.

On the day Owen finally managed to unearth the details of his father's suicide, he had gone upstairs intent on asking his mother some very pointed questions about his father's death. Unfortunately, one of his mother's current companions, a fellow named Jack Hughes, turned up for dinner.

"So what have you been up to today?" Irene asked, beaming at her son. That was the customary opening gambit for their mealtime conversations. Irene would ask after Owen's activities and he would give her a pro forma answer, with neither of them really paying attention. Owen had learned to reply to those empty queries innocuously enough that his mother could merely nod and proceed with whatever else she wanted to discuss. Tonight, though, Owen had hoped to have Irene to himself. When it turned out that wasn't the case, he was more than a little annoyed.

Spearing a pat of butter and slathering it onto a dinner roll in a way guaranteed to bug his mother, Owen went straight for the jugular.

"I read the police report today," he mentioned casually.

"What police report?" Irene asked as a tiny frown furrowed her brow.

"The one about my father," Owen said. "After he committed suicide." On those rare occasions when Irene did happen to mention Harold's death in Owen's presence, she did so by sticking to the least offensive kinds of terminology. She tended to mention nothing more definitive than the fact that Harold was "gone" or had "passed away." Until that moment, the word "suicide" had never been part of any conversation that passed between mother and son regarding Harold Hansen. Once the word hit home, Owen was gratified to see how the shock of it instantly turned his mother's face alarmingly pale. With steely determination, however, she pulled herself together far faster than he'd expected.

"It's neither the time nor the place to have a discussion of this kind," she said, as if dismissing the whole issue as a small misstep in the general conversation.

"Why not?" Owen asked insolently. "Why can't we discuss it? Maybe Jack would like to know the answer to that question, too.

My father went down to the beach and blew his brains out. Why?"

"I don't know why," Irene hissed. "He just did it."

"What did he have to be sorry about?" Owen demanded, letting his mother know that he was also aware of the contents of the suicide note. "Was he sorry he was married to you? Sorry he had me for a son — so sorry he couldn't stand to go on living? What, then?"

Owen watched with interest as his mother carefully removed the cloth napkin from her lap, folded it, and set it down next to her plate. When she started to rise from her chair, Jack hurriedly stepped forward and pulled it out for her. Owen expected her to flee the room, but she did not. Instead she marched over to where he was sitting and slapped him so hard that Owen saw stars.

"We will never speak of this again," she declared furiously. "Never." Then she went back to her chair, sat down, picked up her napkin, and resumed eating her dinner as though nothing out of the ordinary had happened.

It worked — they had never spoken of it again. They continued to live in the same household with Irene upstairs and Owen down. They continued to endure their evening meals together, night after night, year after year, all of them conducted in a kind of chilled civility. But looking back on that long-ago meal in the glowing aftermath of Roger McGeary's death, Owen realized that his mother's furious slap on the face had been the turning point in his life — the watershed moment that had set him on the path to becoming a serial killer.

Back then he didn't know who he was going to kill or how, but what Owen did know for sure — something he never doubted — was that whatever he did, he'd be smart enough to get away with it. And it would have something to do with people just like him — people whose parents had died by their own hand.

6

Ali waited until Cami left for her Krav
Maga training session at the end of the day
before venturing out of her office and into
the back room where Stu held sway. She
found her husband's second-in-command
seated where he always sat, in front of a
bank of wall-mounted computer monitors
and their various keyboards. This time,
however, his attention was focused on a
single laptop sitting directly in front of him,
one with a distinctive red "X" painted on
the back of the display. The "X" told Ali
this was one of High Noon's air-gapped
computers, one that was never allowed access to either High Noon's servers or the
Internet. *"These X'er computers function as
cyber condoms,"* Stu liked to say, *"because
you never know where someone else's program has been."*

"Roger's info?" Ali asked.

Stu nodded. "I downloaded everything

from the two phones and the computer over to this, so I could look at it all in one place."

"And?"

"I haven't started."

"Why not? A password problem?"

"A privacy problem," Stu replied. "Roger was my friend. I know I promised Ms. Miller that I'd look into what happened, but it doesn't seem right to go prowling through the man's personal life without his express permission."

Impersonal hacking was one thing, evidently, Ali noted. Personal hacking was something else again.

"Maybe it would be better for Cami to take a look," Ali suggested.

Stu shook his head. "I'll do it," he said. "I'm just having trouble getting started is all."

"Because you think Julia Miller is wrong, and Roger really did commit suicide?"

Stu swallowed before he answered. "Yes," he said faintly. "I guess that is what I think."

"It seems to me that Julia deserves to have the real answers, so let's give them to her," Ali said. "If that is what happened, maybe we can go so far as to figure out why. And if it turns out that isn't what happened, let's find out what did. You check to see if there's anything in the computer that will point us

85

in the right direction. In the meantime, I'll have Cami sort out everything there is to be found on the incident itself. We'll need to track down the cops from Panama who did the initial investigation. Next we should talk to people from the ship — the people who worked on board as well as any passengers who may have interacted with Roger during the cruise. We're going to go after this in a full-court press."

"You keep saying 'we,' " Stuart said.

"I said 'we' because I meant it," Ali told him. "High Noon Enterprises is on the case."

"But who's the client?"

"Stu Ramey, for one," Ali answered. "If he chooses to pass along what we learn to Julia Miller, that'll be up to him."

Stuart thought that through. Finally he nodded. "All right, then," he said, turning his attention to the keyboard. "I think I can live with that."

7

For someone who was essentially a hermit, it was only natural that Owen Hansen would gravitate to artificial intelligence. His AI creation, Frigg, became both his resource and his confidante. Once Frigg understood that there was more to the game than merely tracking down names and people, she willingly stepped up and became Odin's fully committed accomplice.

For Odin the next step in the process was finding a way to separate the damaged children of suicide victims from the undamaged ones. To accomplish that, Odin set Frigg the monumental task of sorting through all those names also appearing in the state of California's massive archive of newly digitized court records.

Frigg wasn't the least bit daunted. She didn't mind how much material was involved or how complex it was. She simply went to work. As it turned out, everything they needed was there. Arrest records? You bet. Drug and alcohol offenses? You got it. Divorce proceedings? Those, too. After an amazing amount of computerized analysis, Frigg was able to present Odin with a properly sorted and alphabetized list. Frigg's next assignment was to cross-reference the two lists — the court records and the children of suicide — and locate the names that appeared in both. That sort resulted in a much smaller list — the sweet spot Odin liked to call his Target Group.

It was easy to see that these folks were mostly damaged goods, the by-products of parental suicides who ended up with all the customary side issues — divorces, DUIs, bankruptcies, and substance abuse problems — that often occur as a result of having survived a crappy childhood. Odin wasn't the least bit surprised to discover that many of them were repeat offenders as far as encounters with the law were concerned.

Close to the top of the alphabet, Odin focused in on one name in particular. Paul Abernathy was a troubled guy who boasted any number of moving violations. He had five DUIs — controlled substances rather than booze — to his credit along with driving with a suspended license, driving without insurance, and reckless driving (he'd done six months in county lockup for that one). He'd also done time in Club Fed for embezzlement. In other words, Abernathy was a crook and a druggie — just about what you'd expect from a loser whose father had offed himself when the kid was ten years old.

Odin found Paul's situation worthy of further consideration. The problem for Odin was that the last of the moving violations had occurred more than three years earlier. That left three possibilities — the guy was back in jail; he had straightened up and decided to fly right; or else he had left the state.

With that in mind, Odin turned Frigg loose on the situation. The AI located the man living alone in a run-down two-story apartment building at the corner of Kester and Erwin in Van Nuys and walking back and forth to work as a janitor at a nearby grade school. A major portion of his minimal wages went to pay court-ordered restitution to the victims of his embezzlement scheme, an amount that, with interest, had ballooned to a student debt–worthy total that his regular but meager payments barely dented.

Once Abernathy was located, it wasn't difficult for Odin to put him under surveillance and keep an eye on him. Odin soon discovered that Paul Abernathy was a man of regular habits. He set off on his walk to work at two-thirty in the afternoon, arriving on campus just as school was dismissed for the day. Once there, he swept floors, mopped hallways, dusted desks, and cleaned bathrooms from three o'clock until eleven p.m., when he headed home. Occasionally he'd stop off for a Subway sandwich or McDonald's along the way. But always, without fail, he ended the evening in a lowbrow bar on Victory — a sticky-floored saloon appropriately named the Dive Bar — where he settled in and drank until last call.

From Odin's point of view, nothing could have been better.

8

Paul Abernathy limped into the Dive Bar —
so named because the original owner had
been a scuba diver. He hobbled through the
room and heaved himself up onto a stool
that didn't have his name on it, but might
as well have. It was where he sat, hour after
hour, night after night. After putting in a
full eight hours sweeping hallways, scrub-
bing toilets, and scraping up bubble gum at
Evans Elementary just up the street, the six-
and-a-half-block walk from the school to
the bar was as much as Paul could manage
with his one bum leg and other bad knee. It
was a stopping-off place that gave him a
chance to stock up on liquid courage for
the three and a half blocks that remained
between the bar and his crappy furnished
apartment at the corner of Erwin and Kester in Van Nuys, California.

Howie, the barman, didn't bother asking
what was wanted. He simply slid Paul's

usual, a glass of Budweiser and a shot of Jose Cuervo, in front of him. "Bad day at the office?" he asked.

It was a joke between them. Howie knew exactly what Paul did for a living. Other people in the bar didn't, and it was none of their business, either.

"You could say that," Paul replied, reaching for the shot glass.

His phone rang. Pulling it out of his pocket, Paul knew without looking that his mother was calling. "Hey, Mom," he said, accepting the call. "How's it going?"

"Just checking on you, sweetie," LuAnn Abernathy said. "Hope you had a wonderful day."

LuAnn was unfailingly devoted to her son, and cheerful to a fault. With some difficulty, Paul managed to keep from grinding his teeth. The nightly calls from his mother bugged him, but not enough that he didn't answer. After all, his mother had given him the phone and kept him on her family plan. Otherwise he'd probably be phoneless. And without LuAnn's help, he'd most likely be homeless and jobless as well. She was the one who had ponied up the first and last month's rent on his apartment. She had also helped him find the janitorial job, once he was clean and sober enough to pass the drug test. Sober from drugs, that is. Fortunately, when it came to drugs, nobody tested for tequila.

"It was unbelievable," he said.

"Unbelievable" was one of those handy words that could be taken two ways — either bad or good, depending. In this case, it was unbelievable that some little kid in one of the kindergarten classrooms had managed to puke all over the floor rather than into the toilet, but that unfortunate reality had no impact whatsoever on LuAnn's determinedly positive mind-set.

"Okay, then, hon," she said. "Glad to hear it. I can tell you're watching something on TV, so I won't keep you. I'm off to bed. Just wanted to hear the sound of your voice and tell you good night."

What she took to be the sound of a television show playing in his living room was really the wall-mounted screen over the bar. Paul didn't disabuse her of the notion that he was safely home and tucked into his apartment. He didn't want her to worry.

"Good night, Mom," he said. "Sleep well."

Paul put the phone down on the bar beside him and took a long pull on his beer. He was fifty-six years old, and his eighty-three-year-old mother was the only person in the world who hadn't given up on him completely. He'd had a promising life once. Fresh out of college with an accounting degree, he'd passed his CPA exams the first time around and landed his dream job. Shortly after graduation, he'd married Cindy, his high school sweetheart. Within ten years, they'd been living the American dream: a house in the burbs, two kids, a sports car and a minivan, soccer, T-ball, and skiing vacations in Park City, Utah — the whole nine yards.

It was a fall on one of those fabulous family skiing trips that changed everything and sent Paul's life spinning out of control. He had broken his leg on the slopes badly enough that the ski patrol had been forced to call in a helicopter to haul him to Salt Lake, where he underwent the first of the several surgeries necessary to repair a spiral fracture. He ended up being off work for three months. By the time his short-term disability ended, the leg was as healed as it would ever be, but Paul was not. He came away from the ordeal with a permanent limp and a serious addiction to opiates — a very expensive addiction to opiates.

Paul understood now that it didn't matter if you were addicted to prescription drugs, or heroin, or meth — once you were there, you were there. The drugs were paramount.

Buying them, having them, and knowing where to get that next fix became the whole focus of your existence, while everything else faded away to nothing. Within three years of the skiing accident he'd lost everything he cared about — his wife, his kids, and his home, to say nothing of his job. Embezzlement will do that to you every time.

"Mind if I have a seat?" Paul looked up from staring into his nearly empty beer glass to see that a guy had climbed up onto the barstool next to him. The guy was an Anglo, probably midthirties, with thinning blondish hair and dressed in casual slacks and a Hawaiian shirt, which made him overdressed and out of place among the Dive Bar's customary low brow clientele.

"Sure, help yourself," Paul muttered, signaling to Howie that he was ready for his next round.

Paul's preferred seating arrangement each evening was to position himself at the far end of the bar right next to the wall. Having the wall at his side made for a 50 percent reduction in the necessity to engage in casual conversation with any of the bar's other patrons.

"Hey," the new arrival said, producing his cell phone and putting it down on the counter next to Paul's. "What do you know! We have the exact same phone."

Big deal, Paul wanted to say. *They sell them by the millions.* But he didn't say that. These days, if you said the wrong thing to the wrong guy out in public, you never knew when he might pull out a handgun and plug you full of hollow-point bullets.

"Looks that way," he said.

Howie returned to their end of the bar. "Ready for a refill?" he asked.

Once Paul nodded, Howie looked to the newcomer. "What'll you have?"

"Since we've got the same phones, I believe I'll have what he's having." The guy turned to Paul. "Name's George, by the way, George Bailey," he added as an introduction, holding out his hand and offering it to Paul. "You from around here?"

"George Bailey, no shit?" Paul asked as they shook. "Like in *It's a Wonderful Life*?"

"As in George Bailey without the angel — the not so wonderful part," George answered. "Wife kicked me out. I'm in the process of moving into the Seawinds Apartments just up the street. The only thing the harpy let me take from the house were my clothes, a futon, and one of the small flat-screen TVs. So far I don't even have a cable box."

Paul walked past the Seawinds every day on his way to work. The building was only a few blocks away from his place but it was definitely more upscale than other nearby buildings. Residents there had the dual advantages of both secure underground parking and an outdoor pool. Paul's apartment complex, the Royal Regency — a double misnomer if ever there was one — reminded Paul of that old Roger Miller song: no phone, no pool, no pets (and no off-street parking, either). Of course, if you didn't own a car, not having a designated parking place wasn't that big a deal.

"You live around here?" George asked.

"A couple of blocks away as the crow flies," Paul answered with a shrug.

If this guy lived in the neighborhood, there was no point in pissing him off. On the other hand, Paul didn't want to be trapped into carrying on small talk with some kind of Chatty Cathy. While George babbled on, Paul focused on his drinks and nodded in a noncommittal fashion every so often while only half listening. As far as Paul could tell, it was the same old wronged-husband baloney. George had given his wife everything she ever wanted, and now she had thrown him out of the house for no good reason and had hired a pit-bull lawyer to "suck him dry." Etc. Etc. Etc.

Paul himself had sung a few verses of that old song years ago, except it hadn't been true, not even when he'd been whining about it. The truth was, Cindy hadn't run him off. The cops had knocked on the door while the whole family had been eating dinner. They had placed him under arrest and hauled him off to jail on the embezzlement charge — without benefit of either a futon or a flat-screen TV.

Cindy had gotten a divorce while he'd been locked up. He had wondered sometimes how she'd managed to keep the mortgage paid and hold body and soul together while he was in the slammer. At some point, Kent, her second husband, must have come riding to her rescue. No one ever told Paul for sure, but he suspected Kent was the only reason the house hadn't gone back to the bank.

As far as second husbands went, Paul had to admit that Kent Sterling wasn't half bad. He had done a commendable job of finishing raising Katy and Jonathan. With good reason, Kent had been the man who had walked Katy down the aisle when she married two years ago. Paul had been in court-ordered rehab at the time. He probably could have gotten a furlough to attend his daughter's wedding, but he hadn't been invited. He'd seen the photos, though, because his mother had sent them to him and because LuAnn was the kind of grandmother who had stayed in touch with Cindy and the kids no matter what.

And who had been there to pick up the pieces for Paul when he got out of rehab that last time? His mother again — good old LuAnn. Despite everything Paul had done to disappoint her, no matter how many times he had let her down, she had stuck with him like glue. She'd always been there to clean up other people's messes, starting with that blood-spattered master bedroom after his father's ugly suicide. LuAnn had picked Paul up after his latest release from rehab. His embezzlement conviction meant he could never go back to work in accounting, so LuAnn had helped him obtain the janitorial position and had used some of her limited Social Security funds to help him have a place to live. This time, no matter what, Paul was determined that he would live up to her faith in him.

He had actual health insurance now. His GP had told him that his supposedly good leg needed knee replacement surgery, which would be covered by the policy. The problem was, Paul understood that the surgery was only the tip of the iceberg. The real trap was in the pain meds that would be prescribed afterward. Paul knew himself too well to think he could resist that temptation. Yes, he could scrape by on booze — and give himself enough of a buzz each night that he could sleep — but faced with his drug of choice? He'd be a goner for sure. He'd sworn that the last time he'd suffered his way through all the agonizing withdrawal symptoms that he'd never do it again — not to himself, and even more so, not to his mother.

Paul usually made that second beer last until it was time to head out for home. When he came back from a brief pit stop, however, he discovered that a third shot and beer were sitting in front of his customary stool.

"Where'd those come from?" he asked.

"George bought a round for you," Howie explained. "Said to tell you thanks for listening and see you next time."

"All right, then," Paul said. "Bottoms up."

The booze hit him a lot harder than he would have expected. When he left the bar a little later, Paul made it less than a block down Kester before he started having trouble walking straight. At first he thought it was just that third shot of tequila talking, but then the familiar rush hit him. He knew what it was and realized that if he didn't get help . . .

He reached for his phone, hoping to dial 911, but it wasn't there. Paul's last thought, before he drifted into a fentanyl-induced coma, was that he must have left the phone lying on the counter, but that was not the case. The phone had exited the bar just before Paul did, picked up discreetly by a gloved hand and slipped into George Bailey's pants pocket. From the far side of Kester, Odin used his own phone to film the entire sequence as Paul Abernathy staggered and fell. Odin came in for a close-up and then waited long enough to be sure the dose Frigg had recommended had done its work. When Abernathy quit breathing, Odin checked the "In Case of Emergency" names in Abernathy's contacts list. He used Abernathy's still-warm fingers to type in and send "Mom" a one-word text message: *SORRY.*

Walking back to the car Odin had left parked blocks away, there was a real spring in his step. Long before the body was discovered by a passerby, Owen Hansen himself was on his way home to Santa Barbara.

Odin and Frigg had successfully claimed

their first victim, and they could be reasonably certain that no one would ever be the wiser. After all, Paul Abernathy, a child of suicide and a not entirely recovered drug user, had taken his own life by mixing booze and fentanyl.

What a surprise!

9

When Ali drove home to Sedona later that evening, she tried to leave the Stuart Ramey/ Roger McGeary crisis back in the office in Cottonwood rather than bringing it along with her to Manzanita Hills Road. Unfortunately, she found a different crisis unfolding at the house.

Early September was late summer in central Arizona. Sedona's 4,300-foot elevation meant that, although the temperatures were far more moderate than down around Phoenix, it was still plenty hot. That morning, as Ali was getting ready to leave, Leland Brooks, her longtime majordomo, had asked what she would like to see on the menu for dinner.

"What about some gazpacho?" she had asked. "On a day like this, I think a nice chilled soup will be just what the doctor ordered. And with B. out of town, don't bother setting up in the dining room. I'll eat in the kitchen with you, if that's all right."

"Certainly," he had said. "It will be my pleasure."

With that in mind, Ali pulled into the garage thinking that there would be no cooking aromas seeping in from the kitchen. She was wrong about that, of course. The moment she opened the door of the Cayenne, she caught the scent of grease on a hot griddle.

When she opened the door, Bella, their rescued long-haired miniature dachshund, came racing pell-mell for her, with her tiny claws scrabbling on the tile floor. Meanwhile Leland was stationed in front of the stove with a spatula poised in his hand, studying the steaming contents on top of a griddle.

"Grilled cheese sandwiches, I presume?" Ali asked, picking up the excited pooch and hugging her briefly before setting the dog back down on the floor.

Leland nodded. "Your favorite," he replied, "complete with a layer of sliced jalapeños."

"This morning I thought we agreed that we're having soup for dinner," she objected.

"Gazpacho is fine, but only up to a point," Leland said as he expertly flipped one of the sandwiches. "A bit of protein is required to turn it into a meal."

"And you never do anything by half measures, do you," Ali said with a laugh.

"I do my best," Leland answered with a smile.

"Okay. If you'll give me a minute, I'll slip into something a little more comfortable," Ali told him.

"Go right ahead," Leland said. "I'll have the wine poured by the time you get back."

When Ali reappeared in the kitchen in a tank top, a pair of jeans, and flip-flops, Bella was happily crunching her kibble in the corner by the fridge. As for the humans? Both food and wine were on the table.

Picking up the chilled bottle, Ali saw that tonight they would be drinking a Grand Cru Riesling from J. J. Prüm winery along Germany's Moselle River. When Paul Grayson, Ali's late and unlamented second husband, had gone to what she hoped was his just reward, she had inherited the contents of the man's very extensive wine cellar. After years of dipping into it on a regular basis, the collection was somewhat depleted, but so far there had been little need to supplement it with purchases from a local wine retailer.

Leland Brooks, an aging Korean War vet who had immigrated to the States from

Great Britain, had come into Ali's life right along with the house in which she lived. He had worked as the butler for the home's original owners, the Ashcrofts, and had stayed on once Ali showed up and embarked on the extensive job of rehabbing the place. Over the years, he had become as indispensable as he was elderly. Although he preferred to remain in the background, he had a knack for anticipating Ali's every need. He no longer did the actual house or yard work, but he oversaw those who did. He still handled all the shopping, however, and he absolutely refused to relinquish control of the kitchen. That was his bailiwick, and assistance in that quarter was neither required nor welcomed.

Ali was accustomed to Leland's easy good humor, but tonight that was missing. Frown lines marred his forehead, and he sighed as he took his seat. Sensing something out of the ordinary, Ali was concerned.

"What's wrong?" she asked.

He shrugged noncommittally and didn't answer.

"Out with it," Ali ordered. "What's up?"

Leland took a deep breath. "You remember my friend Thomas?"

Ali nodded. Leland's relationship with Thomas Blackfield — something more complicated than mere friendship — dated from when they'd been young men together in the UK back before Leland joined the Royal Marines and went off to fight in the Korean War. Separated for years by family tragedies compounded by misunderstandings, they had rekindled their youthful friendship only in the past couple of years. Thomas had come to the States to visit, and had actually been in attendance at Ali and B.'s Las Vegas wedding before returning to the UK.

"What about him?"

"He's apparently having some health issues," Leland said quietly.

"I'm so sorry to hear that," Ali said. Leaving her grilled cheese to cool, she picked up her spoon and dipped it into the spicy gazpacho. When she sampled it, the fiery flavor sent her taste buds dancing. "Serious health issues?"

Leland nodded. "The tests have come back positive for lymphoma."

Ali set down her spoon. "That's not good."

"Not at all," Leland agreed. "I've been doing some online searches. It turns out there are far more cutting-edge treatments available for lymphoma here in the US than there are back home in the UK."

"Which is where he is."

"Yes. The problem is, that's where Thomas wants to stay. My plan is to go there and convince him otherwise. I'd like him to come here for treatment, either on a visitor's visa or as a spouse if need be, but he is adamant about not coming."

"Which means you need to go to him."

Leland nodded. "That's the only way to be sure he'll be properly looked after."

Ali studied Leland's weathered countenance. The man had spent a lifetime making sure that other people were "properly looked after." Ali's worry was whether there'd be someone on hand to do the same for Leland, if and when the need arose.

"Of course," Ali said. "You must do so at once."

"But not without taking care of things here beforehand," Leland argued. "I have no intention of going off and leaving you and Mr. Simpson in the lurch. Knowing that Thomas was undergoing tests and that this might be the end result, I've taken the liberty of making inquiries about a possible replacement for me. Since speed is of the essence, I've asked the three top candidates to plan on being available for interviews toward the end of the week — if that's all right with you, that is. Two of them will need to be interviewed via Skype. The third candidate is currently visiting relatives in the Phoenix area. He may be able to show up in person. If one of the three proves to be acceptable, I'd like that person to be on the job as soon as possible so I can bring him up to speed. Thomas's first go-round of treatment is set for three weeks from now, and I'd like to be on hand for that."

"Does B. know about any of this?"

Leland shook his head. "Not yet," he said. "You're the first to have the news."

For a moment Ali said nothing. Saddened by the news, she looked around the spotless kitchen, one that had been designed to Leland's exacting specifications. It was hard to think of this house without him in it, smoothing the way and keeping everything shipshape. And it wasn't just Leland's ability to keep the household in order. He had played an important part in Ali's ongoing commitment to running a locally based college scholarship program, and on at least one occasion, Leland's training as a Royal Marine had saved Ali's life.

"I'm so sorry to lose you," she murmured at last. "I can't imagine how we'll manage."

Leland smiled. "Thank you," he said, "but I'm sure you'll be fine. Just to be on the safe side, though, I can tell you that two of the three applicants are ex-military, so they

109

come complete with weapons training and experience as well as concealed carry permits. I mentioned to them that you have a tendency to land in hot water on occasion, and that in addition to cooking and cleaning, being able to look out for your personal safety might well be part of their brief. The third one is a trained butler who happens to be another transplanted Brit. He's probably the best-qualified of the bunch, but I'm not sure he'd be a good fit."

"Why not?"

"Bit of a snob, I suspect," Leland said. "At least that's how he sounded on the phone."

"When do I get to look at their applications?" Ali asked.

Leland picked up his phone and tapped it several times. "There," he said when he finished. "I just e-mailed them to you, and now that the two of us have had a chance to discuss the situation, I'll send them along to Mr. Simpson as well. Of course, if you don't feel it's necessary to have someone full-time . . ."

Ali smiled back at him. "It's not a matter of our having someone full-time," she said. "It's more a question of how many full-timers it'll take to fill your shoes. And what about your RV?" Ali asked. "What are your plans for that? Will you keep it or let it go?"

For the past several years Leland had lived in a cozy fifth-wheel trailer parked behind the garage. It had been an ideal, not-quite-live-in arrangement that had given a measure of privacy to B. and Ali and to him as well.

"I can probably go on Craigslist and unload it without a great deal of difficulty."

"So you plan to sell it?"

"I can't very well take it across the water with me."

"Look," Ali suggested, "how about coming up with a fair price and selling it to us? That way we can have it available should someone need to use it as living quarters. Later on, if you and Thomas decide to return and you want to have it back, we can make that happen, too."

"You're very kind," Leland said with a sad smile. "I'm not so sure our coming back is a real possibility, but still — hope for the best; plan for the worst. That's my motto."

After that, they finished their meal in relative silence. Ali was sure the gazpacho, the sandwich, and wine were all perfect, but the prospect of losing Leland's steadying presence took some of the blush off that rose.

When Ali had returned home to Sedona after her life in California had blown up in her face, Leland had been an important part of her reconstruction process — not just for the remodel of the house on Manzanita Hills Road that he had overseen from beginning to end, but for helping launch her into this whole new existence. Of course, with Leland in his eighties, she had known the situation couldn't last forever and that he would have to leave eventually. Still, Ali wished she'd had more time to prepare.

After dinner, she retreated to the library and read through the three applications. Walter Hopkins, the Brit, was a fifty-something widower who had served as a butler for thirty-some years. Before his wife's death two years earlier, the two of them had spent decades looking after a well-to-do couple with homes in NYC, Aspen, and Connecticut. That had changed abruptly after the husband's unexpected death. The couple's children had encouraged their widowed mother to unload all of her properties and the hired help as well, leaving Walter out in the cold. On the application he stated quite plainly that one of the reasons he had applied for this job had to do with Sedona area weather reports.

Alonso Rivera, an unmarried immigrant from Guadalajara, Mexico, had joined the US Navy at eighteen and ultimately become a US citizen by spending the next twenty years working as a CSS — a culinary specialist — on board submarines. He had retired from the navy at age thirty-eight. Now age forty-six, he had spent some time in the hospitality industry, working on cruise ships, both in food service and as a cabin attendant. In his application he stated he was ready to give up his sea legs and put down roots on dry land.

James Hastings, the youngest and originally from San Antonio, Texas, listed his marital status as divorced. He had enlisted in the US Marine Corps on September 12, 2001. His third tour of duty in the Middle East had ended with an IED explosion in Iraq that had sent him home with a medical discharge and a prosthetic left leg.

Sitting in one of the library's easy chairs, with her computer open on her lap, and with Bella cuddled up against her thigh, Ali stroked the dog's smooth fur and considered the complications of weaving another stranger into their lives. When the dog had turned up, Bella had been entirely foreign to them. After a few initial bumps, she'd become a good fit, and one of these new people would probably fit in just fine as well — eventually.

The phone rang. "Good morning," B. said.

With B. often on the far side of the Atlantic, Ali was accustomed to the fact that his mornings were generally nighttimes for her. She quickly brought him up to date.

"We knew that shoe was going to drop sooner or later," B. observed. "And it's so like Leland to take responsibility for handling the whole thing, up to and including rounding up prospective candidates and scheduling interviews. Have you looked at the applicants?"

"Just did," Ali answered.

"What do you think?"

"I think we're looking at three people who want to reinvent themselves — at our expense."

"Reinventing yourself isn't such a crazy idea," B. said. "It worked out pretty well for both of us. As far as Leland is concerned, speed is of the essence. I won't be home until Friday afternoon. Go ahead and schedule the interviews. If one of them really stands out, make the guy an offer with, say, a ninety-day trial period during which either side can call it quits for any reason. We may need to include a housing allowance."

"I told Leland we'd buy his fifth-wheel, so that would still be available as possible housing."

"In that case, I'd go for the submariner," B. said with a laugh. "He's bound to be used to living in very small spaces. In addition, it says here that he's got his dolphins."

"I saw that," Ali admitted, "but I have no idea what it means."

"It means he's been trained so he can both fix and operate any system on board the submarine."

"Which in turn would make him very handy to have around the house," Ali allowed. "But we'll see. Interview first; hire later."

10

For Odin, one of the best things about being a god was putting things in motion. Next best, of course, was watching how things he had put in motion played out afterward. With Frigg keeping a watchful eye on all media coverage, it was easy for him to follow the aftermath of Paul Abernathy's supposed suicide. Odin briefly considered attending Paul's funeral service, but decided against it. He didn't want to chance running into any denizens of the Dive Bar who might possibly recognize him; the potential risks exceeded the emotional rewards.

The funeral wasn't the end of it, however, not by any means. Paul's mother, LuAnn, was a tiger about defending her dead son's legacy. She clawed her way onto local news shows and digital news sites, telling the world that the cops had it all wrong. She insisted that the official conclusion — that

of suicide by means of an accidental overdose from a substance that wasn't Paul's
drug of choice — was out of the question.
She claimed instead that her son was actually the victim of a homicide.

When Odin heard her say that during a
televised news interview, he was somewhat
taken aback. This fierce-looking, white-
haired, little old lady was far closer to the
mark than law enforcement was. Worried
that she might make some headway in getting the cops to reinvestigate the situation,
Odin sent Frigg on a virtual trip down Kester Avenue looking for the unwelcome presence of security cameras.

Meanwhile, the AI was constantly trolling
the Internet looking for any mention of
names on the Target Group list. Under her
watchful eye, two listees had recently turned
up in separate obituaries. A guy named Da-
vid Salas had died of pancreatic cancer in
St. Louis, Missouri, and a woman named
Laura Kenton Fisher had died of complications due to diabetes at her home in Tal-
lahassee, Florida. Odin couldn't help but
regard those clearly natural deaths as missed
opportunities.

That was about the time Roger McGeary's
name turned up. The mention was in an
obscure blog devoted to cyber security

where Roger was cited for having foiled a hacking attack intended to take down an Italian cruise line's US-based reservations center. By then, Frigg was getting with the program and learning to play the game. Once Roger McGeary's name came to the AI's attention, Odin didn't have to tell her to put him under a microscope. She began amassing information on him of her own volition, and that's how Roger McGeary became victim number two.

11

On Wednesday morning, after giving Leland the go-ahead to set up the interview appointments, Ali embarked on the half-hour drive from her home in Sedona to Cottonwood. Sedona's sky-high property values had argued against setting up High Noon's corporate headquarters closer to home. Instead, B. had opted for a location just outside Cottonwood. After years of commuting through smoggy rush-hour traffic in L.A., Ali's new daily commute through mostly pristine high desert was definitely not a hardship.

On this clear early-September morning, with almost no other traffic on the road, Ali should have been drinking in the scenery. The summer monsoons had been exceptionally generous this year. The landscape was awash in knee-high grass against which Sedona's red rock cliffs stood in vivid contrast.

Today, however, Ali was impervious to the view. Instead she spent most of the drive thinking about Leland's impending departure. She and B. would be fine, but she couldn't help worrying. What would the future hold for the aging caretaker of a cancer patient who was every bit as old and far frailer than Leland himself? This new situation wouldn't be a bed of roses for either of them.

As Ali arrived at the parking lot in Cottonwood, Cami, driving her red Prius, was about to exit the office complex. She stopped and rolled her window down as the two cars came even with one another.

"Stu and I have just done an all-nighter," Cami said. "Be advised, it's Mood Swing Central around here. I suggest you don't poke the bear until I get back from a doughnut run."

That bit of conversation took Ali aback. "I'm not surprised about Stu pulling an all-nighter," she said, "but I had no idea you'd be in on it, too. The last I heard, you were on your way home."

"I was," Cami said. "But Stu called as I was leaving the gym and asked me to come back in to help out. Since he used the word 'please,' which I didn't think was part of his vocabulary, I couldn't very well say no."

"He wanted you to help with the McGeary situation?"

Cami nodded.

"Did you make any progress?"

"Some. I left a sticky note on your desk with a name and number on it. Detective Inspector Esteban Garza is the homicide cop from Panama's National Police. He's the guy who flew out to the ship to investigate the man overboard case. I'm hoping you'll give him a call and ask if we can have access to his written reports."

"Why me?" Ali asked. "Why not you or Stu?"

"Because a certain amount of diplomacy is called for. Stu figured he'd make a botch of that, and rightly so. As for me? We were both afraid I'd sound too young on the phone to be taken seriously."

"I'm nominated to make the call so I can provide a certain amount of gravitas?" Ali asked.

"Pretty much," Cami replied with a grin.

"What about the language issue?" Ali asked. "I took high school Spanish, but I don't really speak it."

"I'm in the same boat, but not to worry," Cami said with a surprising lack of concern.

"Why not?"

"I found an article about Garza in a local

121

newspaper. He's something of a local legend. It said in the article that he speaks fluent English, which may be part of the reason he got the cruise ship gig."

"So how's Stu doing?" Ali asked.

Cami sobered at once. "Not well," she said. "He's really broken up about this, Ali, and running on empty, too. Which is why I'm off in search of emergency doughnut rations."

When it came to food, Camille Lee and Stuart Ramey were at opposite ends of the spectrum. Stu's penchant for surviving on a steady diet of pizza, burgers, doughnuts, and Diet Coke drove Cami mad. And her attempts to bring him into the world of a more balanced diet was something that sent Stuart into spasms. As far as Ali knew, this current bit of doughnut détente was completely unprecedented.

"Bring me one, too," Ali said. "It sounds as though we could all use some comfort food this morning."

Cami drove away. Ali parked and went inside, where Shirley greeted her with a raised eyebrow. "I understand things are a bit dicey in the back," she said. "I'd give him a few minutes if I were you."

"Cami told me the same thing, but thanks for the warning," Ali said. She went straight to her office without venturing into the lion's den. A sticky note bearing Esteban Garza's name and phone number was plastered on the monitor of Ali's desktop.

Ali stowed her purse in an otherwise empty file cabinet and then sat down at the desk. She studied her office phone for a moment or two. She wondered if she should use that, which would show up on caller ID as High Noon Enterprises, or opt for calling on her far more anonymous cell phone. In the end, she took a deep breath, picked up the handset, and began dialing the international code of Panama. When the phone on the opposite end of the line started ringing, Ali more than half expected a female voice — a clerk or receptionist of some kind — to answer the call

While Ali tried to sort out a passable bit of conversational Spanish, a gruff male voice came on the line. "Garza."

"Detective Inspector?" she asked uncertainly.

"Yes."

No doubt Garza had been expecting to answer the phone in Spanish, but his smooth transition to unaccented English was immediate and flawless.

"My name is Ali Reynolds," she said. "I'm with High Noon Enterprises, a cyber security company located in the US."

"I'm not sure how you obtained my cell phone number," Garza said stiffly, "but I can assure you I'm not interested in purchasing any additional programs. The security measures offered by my provider are entirely adequate."

Clearly the call had gotten off on the wrong foot. "I'm not calling to sell you something," Ali said quickly, hoping to salvage it. "We were contacted by a woman named Julia Miller. She has expressed some concern about the investigation into the death of her nephew, Roger McGeary."

That was true insofar as it went. Julia Miller was indeed the person who had contacted them originally. The problem was, High Noon was really acting on its own behalf rather than on Julia Miller's.

The change in Garza's voice when he spoke next was distinctly audible across two time zones and nearly 2,700 miles. "Ah yes," he replied. "Señora Miller. What kind of concern?"

"She has a few questions," Ali answered. "She feels the words 'death by misadventure' don't provide sufficient information. That's why High Noon has agreed to look into the matter — in hopes of clarifying the situation. And that's why

I'm calling you today — to request that you forward us copies of any written reports regarding this case."

"Mr. McGeary is deceased," Garza said coldly. "His cause of death is undetermined because evidence found at the scene left it unclear to investigators if he had perished accidentally or if he had taken his own life. His death may or may not have been due to natural causes. Perhaps he suffered a medical emergency of some kind and simply fell overboard. There's also a possibility that he may have taken his own life. The circumstances surrounding his death don't fit with homicide. Hence our considered use of the term 'misadventure,' which, in my mind, leaves the situation open to interpretation."

"But with the cause of death undetermined, I'm surprised you closed the case."

"Señora . . ."

"Reynolds," Ali supplied.

"Señora Reynolds," Garza objected. "Available evidence suggests that when Mr. McGeary entered his stateroom on the night of his death, he was highly intoxicated. The ship's surveillance system had footage of that hallway from the time he disappeared into his room — alone, by the way — until hours later when the butler arrived to deliver his breakfast tray. No one else entered or left the room. When the butler found the stateroom abandoned, he immediately and quite properly initiated man overboard procedures. Between the time the butler entered the room and the time he made the emergency call, there was no time for anything else to occur, all of which leads us to conclude that, in this instance, the butler didn't do it."

"But it doesn't tell us what happened," Ali objected.

"No, it does not," Garza agreed. "Mr. McGeary's death is unfortunate, of course, but with no way to examine the body and with no smoking gun, there's no way to discover how he died. Yes, the case is closed, and I make no apologies for that. Feel free to tell Señora Miller that she has my sincere condolences, but there is nothing more I can do."

"You could send us the reports," Ali suggested.

"No, I could not," Garza replied. "The National Police do not make a habit of sharing the results of our inquiries — open or closed — with just anyone. Reports can be requested via court orders, of course, but I can't see how High Noon Enterprises would be able to obtain one of those. Now, if that is all . . ."

Ali couldn't see how they'd be able to obtain a court order, either. Although she was supposed to be the diplomat here, she found herself bridling at the detective inspector's dismissive attitude.

"Mr. McGeary died on the third of June. You have no body. No cause of death. And yet, barely three months later, you have already closed the case?"

"Your point is?"

"I'm wondering if closing the case in such an expeditious fashion might have been more beneficial for the cruise line than having it drag on any longer."

"Are you implying that my investigation of the matter was either incompetent or corrupt?" Garza demanded.

"All I'm suggesting is that your investigation may be incomplete," Ali said. "I'm also letting you know that with or without your assistance, High Noon will be pursuing the matter."

"Very well, then, Señora Reynolds," the detective said. "Have a nice day."

He hung up, and so did Ali. It wasn't exactly a declaration of war, but it came close. If the reports weren't available through regular channels, it might be necessary to access them through irregular ones. Ali put down the phone and went looking for Stu. She found him, bleary-eyed and gray with exhaustion, seated in front of his bank of computers and looking totally bereft.

"How's it going?" she asked, helping herself to a nearby desk chair and rolling it next to his.

Stu shrugged. "I should have been a better friend to Roger while he was still alive."

Stu, a brilliant hacker and loyal employee, had been part of High Noon from the very beginning. He was far closer to B. than he was to Ali. Knowing about the carefully constructed wall he maintained between himself and the rest of the world, Ali was uncertain how she should approach him when he was clearly suffering from genuine grief.

"You've worked on this all night?" Ali asked.

Stu nodded. "I did, and so did Cami," he said.

"Give yourself a break, Stu," Ali told him. "If you've spent the whole night on this, you're being Roger's friend right now."

"Any luck with Detective Inspector Garza?" he asked glumly.

Ali shook her head. "No dice on the official case reports," she answered. "I always believed that homicide cops are supposed to speak for the dead. Since Detective Garza is declining to do so, we'll have to work around him. If there's a backdoor way to lay hands on those documents, do so."

Stu gave her a wary look. She knew the man was in constant contact with a complex web of fellow hackers, a shady alliance that spanned the globe, and she had no doubt that one of them would be able to penetrate Garza's officially unavailable files.

"We're looking for answers, Stu, not admissible evidence," Ali told him. "Seeing the reports will allow us to know who was interviewed and what they were or weren't asked. We'll use that information to conduct our own interviews."

"You're planning on doing interviews?" Stu asked, brightening slightly.

"Absolutely. Since the cops won't tell us what they know, we'll need to start over and work the investigation on our own from the ground up. That includes tracking down Roger's fellow passengers and any *Whispering Star* crew members who may have interacted with him prior to his death. Have you spoken to anyone from the cruise line?"

Stu shook his head. "I was waiting to see what Detective Inspector Garza would say."

"Since that's a bust, what do we know about Shining Star, other than the fact that their ships sail under a Panamanian flag?"

Cami walked in just then and set a box of freshly made glazed doughnuts down on the table next to the laptop Stu was using.

"I've been working the cruise line angle," Cami answered as she opened the box and offered it to Stu. He reached into the box and took out one of the pastries. After a momentary pause, he collected a second one before Cami offered the box to Ali. "It turns out Shining Star's US headquarters is just up the road from here in Las Vegas, Nevada," Cami continued. "The reservation call center is located a few miles away in Henderson. I take it you didn't get very far with Esteban Garza?" she added.

Ali bit into her own doughnut before she answered. "You could say that," she replied. "What about the cruise line? Do you think they'll be more forthcoming?"

"I doubt it," Cami responded. "I tried talking to the legal department and passing it off as our doing a study of shipboard deaths. I didn't get very far before the guy asked me straight out if my call had anything to do with Roger McGeary. As soon as I said yes, the conversation ended."

"They mentioned Roger by name?"

"Yes."

"That means they're worried about him

for some reason," Ali mused.

"I agree," Cami said. "I've done a careful media search on everything to do with Shining Star Cruises and its purported data breach. With the exception of a single blog posting in a professional cyber security journal, they've kept a tight lid on the whole situation. There was no public acknowledgment that Roger's cruise was comped as a corporate thank-you. As for media coverage following Roger McGeary's disappearance and presumed death? Not one of those referred back to his role in foiling the attack."

"Which means that as far as the cruise line is concerned," Ali concluded, "mum's the word. I'm guessing Detective Inspector Garza got that message loud and clear. That explains why he's going to stonewall us and so are they. And since we're unlikely to get any help on a corporate level, what do we know about the *Whispering Star*'s crew and Roger's fellow passengers?"

"I haven't been able to lay hands on a crew member manifest. I know that they hire on with set contracts that may vary in duration from one crew member to another," Cami answered. "In most cases they work for several months at a time and then take a month or so off."

"Does that mean that some of the folks who were working when Roger was there might still be on board?"

"Some, if not all," Cami said. "Why?"

Ali did some quick calculating. "Where's the *Whispering Star* right now?"

Cami sat down in front of the nearest computer and did a quick search. "It leaves Southampton the day after tomorrow on a ten-day cruise from there to New York City. Why?"

"Is there any space available on it?"

"I guess. The notation on the sailing still says, 'Request a quote.' "

"Do that, then," Ali said. "Request one. Since we're not going to get any cooperation on a corporate level, we'll have to do it the old-fashioned way — on our own, with boots on the ground or, rather, boots on board. And it looks like you're it, Cami. Do you happen to have a current passport?"

"Yes, ma'am."

"Go on line and see if you can book space on that sailing. Once you're on board, I want you to start asking questions. You'll need to talk to anyone who remembers Roger McGeary. You can make up a connection of some kind. Maybe he was your brother's roommate or best friend or something. Even though company suits aren't going to want to talk about Roger, the regular working stiffs may be."

"I'm on it," Cami said.

Ali looked back at Stu. "Tell me about Roger's computer. Did you get in?"

Stu nodded. "Did," he said.

"Is there anything there that speaks to his state of mind? Was he depressed? Was there anything out of kilter in his life? A broken engagement, for example, or gambling debts or money problems of some kind?"

"Nothing like that at all," Stu said. "From what I saw, for the first time in Roger's life, everything was pretty much in order, although for a period of time prior to all this he had been seeing a counselor regularly, a psychiatrist named Dr. Amelia Cannon. He had weekly sessions with her for the better part of two years, although he stopped seeing her several months before he died."

"Do we know why he was undergoing treatment?"

"Probably about his mother," Stu answered. "At least, that would be my guess. As Ms. Miller told us yesterday, the woman was a piece of work."

"And yet Roger kept the program from her funeral," Ali observed. "A funeral he was unable to attend."

Stu nodded. "All Roger ever wanted was

for his mother to like him. That's what you always want the most — whatever it is that you can't have."

Coming from Stuart Ramey, Ali regarded that as a very astute observation.

12

For a long time after Ali left the room, Stu simply sat in front of Roger's laptop and stared uncomprehendingly at the screen. He was no longer combing through his dead friend's life, looking for traces of what might have happened to him. In that moment Stu and Roger were kids again, back in his grandmother's trailer in a run-down mobile home park just off South Central in Phoenix.

Stu had no memory of his parents. They'd been killed by a drunk driver in a crash on I-10 when he was only three, leaving him to be raised by his paternal grandparents, Grace and Robert Ramey, Sr. His grandfather, a Korean War vet, was a double-amputee confined to a wheelchair, but he vehemently objected to the term "disabled." Together he and Grace managed the mobile home park where they lived, exchanging work for rent. That was where they had raised their son, Robert, Jr., and where they would raise Junior's son, Stuart, as well.

In fact, Stu Ramey's first memories were of tearing full speed down his grandfather's wheelchair ramp in a Big Wheel, with his grandfather always encouraging him to go ever faster while his grandmother worried about broken necks and/or glasses, which Stu had to wear from age three on.

Their shabby living room had always been comfy but crowded, primarily due to two items in particular — an immense old upright piano and an equally large Magnavox TV console. The TV set was seldom on, and when it was, the colored images were so faded as to be almost invisible. The piano, however, had been his grandmother's pride and joy.

Once a year, a blind man named Mr. Abel had come to the house to tune it. Whenever he arrived, driven there first by his wife and in later years by his son, Grace would greet him as an honored guest. She always served coffee and homemade chocolate chip cookies when the piano tuner showed up, and always insisted that the old man take some of the cookies home with him when he left.

After Mr. Abel's departure, Grace would settle down at the piano and play to her heart's content, reveling in the familiar tunes from the dog-eared collection of sheet music she kept stored in the piano bench. One day, when Stuart was five, after ending her post-tuning concert with "Mr. Sandman," Grace had gone to the kitchen to finish making dinner. While she stood at the stove mashing a pot of potatoes, the music had resumed with a somewhat halting version of the song she'd just been playing. She'd gone to the door of the kitchen and was astonished to see that Stuart had clambered up on the stool. Playing by ear, the child was plunking out a credible version of what he'd just heard.

And that's how Stuart Ramey had learned to play the piano — by listening to and duplicating the music his grandmother played on the piano and listened to on the radio, leaving him with a repertoire that made him a child out of time. Talented though he was, Stu never learned to read music. Nor was there ever a possibility of his signing up for band since appearing in a concert would have been completely beyond him.

Grace adored her grandson, but Stuart had issues she couldn't help him overcome. He was not affectionate and couldn't tolerate being held or hugged. He had loved the Big Wheel, but other toys didn't interest him. Grace tried reading stories and books to him, but he preferred going off by himself — often to the back of his closet — where he would sit alone, rocking back and forth, for hours on end. He didn't start talking until age four. After skipping the baby talk stage entirely, when he did speak — which was seldom, even at home — it was in complete sentences.

Once Grace enrolled him in school, things got worse. At school he refused to speak at all. He simply sat in classrooms and stared off into space. He wouldn't respond to questions or participate in any way. Achievement tests? Out of the question. At a time when Asperger syndrome was barely a blip on the public education radar, school officials, stymied on assessing Stuart's intellectual abilities, decided he was stupid and dumped him in special ed, which was where his life changed when he met Roger McGeary.

They were like two peas in a pod — two very smart but emotionally challenged kids who refused to participate in classroom give-and-take. Teachers, faced with two kids who refused to take part in class, necessarily focused on children who were more prone to acting out. Roger and Stu — sitting in silence, soaking up everything, and revealing nothing — didn't garner much attention. Left to their own devices, they developed a fierce friendship. They communicated in a kind of Morse code, conversing in plain sight by using the ends of their pencils to tap out messages no one else in the classroom could understand.

Their family homes were geographically close but worlds apart economically. Desert Mobile Park, where Stu's now widowed grandmother was still in charge, was located on Cody. Roger lived a few blocks south of that in a new and much more upscale neighborhood on the far side of West Roeser.

By the beginning of seventh grade, Roger routinely came home with Stu after school and hung out there until nearly dark — reading comics, playing games, eating Grace out of house and home, and occasionally even doing homework. Since Stu's grandmother couldn't afford to buy video games, Roger would smuggle his Nintendo console and games out of the house and bring them to Stu's. The fact that the boys were both pudgy and wore glasses was no deterrent to their ability to wage superhero warfare on video screens. Grateful that Stuart had a friend at last, Grace didn't complain about Roger's hanging around, although she did wonder about it.

"Why don't you ever go to Roger's house to play?" Grace asked one day when she found that the leftovers she had planned to use for dinner had somehow disappeared during afternoon snack time.

"His mother doesn't like him," Stu had answered.

"His mother doesn't like him?" Grace repeated. "That's ridiculous. Mothers always love their children."

"His doesn't," Stu insisted stubbornly. "And she's mean to him all the time."

"What about Roger's father?"

"He's okay, I guess," Stu said, "but he's hardly ever there. Roger's mother doesn't like him, either."

Recognizing that the two social outcasts were good for each other, Grace Ramey simply fed them and let them be. During the summer, when Roger was going up to Payson to spend time with his Aunt Julia and asked if Stu could come along, too, Grace had been overjoyed. Sending him to summer camp was completely beyond her budget, so having him spend those two weeks at the ranch was a real blessing.

Then came high school and a new version of hell. At that point some other well-meaning school administrator decided that special ed students needed to be "main-streamed" and dumped the two outcasts into the regular high school population. Everybody still knew who was "special" and who wasn't. Routine hazing that had previously been confined to after-school hours now went on each and every day, all day long.

Even so, for the first three years of high school, things were relatively smooth for Tweedledum and Tweedledee. Taken together, they amounted to a reasonable whole, presenting a united front to a world in which they were perpetual outsiders. Together they learned to do enough work to get by, an achievement school administrators erroneously credited to the previous efforts of their special ed teachers. For a while Stu and Roger were the undisputed champs of the *Dungeons & Dragons* crowd, but as for the rest of the usual high school cliques? They were too straightlaced for the Goths; too citified for the cowboy types; too boring for the sophisticates; too clumsy for the athletes; and way too Anglo for the Hispanics.

By the end of their freshman year, they had tired of playing other people's games. When Roger showed up with a pair of discarded computers his father had brought home from work, the two boys embarked on creating their own. Once caught up in the magic of coding, they were hooked.

Just before school let out for the summer between their junior and senior years, two catastrophes occurred almost simultaneously. Roger came home from school one day and found his father in the garage, dead of a self-inflicted gunshot wound. His mother waited around long enough to make it through the funeral, but within weeks, she had called for a moving van. Before the house even sold, she took Roger and disappeared into the wilds of California.

Without his best friend beside him, Stu was lost and unable to cope. Then, halfway through the summer, he woke up one morning, walked out of his room, and found his grandmother lying on the floor in the hallway just outside his door. She had suffered a massive stroke and had been lying there helpless for hours. She was carted off in an ambulance and spent the next three weeks in the hospital.

Grace had never owned a car or learned to drive. As a consequence, neither had Stu. When Roger had been around, he sometimes gave them rides back and forth to the store. Otherwise they rode the bus. It took Stu an hour and a half each way to visit

Grace in the hospital. He went there and sat in his grandmother's room, day after day, listening to the machine breathing for her while the doctors and nurses discussed what should or should not be done about her situation. Stu knew she would have wanted the machines turned off, but no one listened to him when he tried to tell them so. Without Grace's calming presence and without Roger's as well, Stu lost ground. Soon he was once again unable to communicate. On the day he arrived at the hospital to find his grandmother gone and another patient occupying her room, he didn't speak to anyone. He simply turned on his heel and went home — back to the mobile home where he had lived for as long as he could remember.

Sometime the next day, a man from the funeral home came knocking on the door. He asked for some of Grace's good clothes in order to dress her for a funeral that had been arranged for and paid in advance. The simple graveside ceremony wasn't an open-casket affair, something that left Stuart wondering why they had bothered with dress-up clothing in the first place. Stuart was prepared to go to the funeral on the bus, but at the last minute one of the longtime tenants of the trailer park, rather than the owner, offered him a ride to and from the cemetery.

When the service was over, Stuart went back home. It was summer in Phoenix, and he was totally on his own. He turned the swamp cooler on high. There was food in the fridge and the pantry. He ate it until it was gone. For the next several weeks he did nothing but play video games around the clock. The halfway normal existence Stu had achieved as part of Tweedledum and Tweedledee evaporated. Stuart Ramey was lost.

That year, when school started, Stu didn't bother going back, and no one from school came looking for him, either. A few weeks later, when the landlord showed up with eviction papers, Stu — who was too young to be on his own and too old to be in foster care — was suddenly left homeless. His only possessions were what he could carry away from the mobile home in a single duffel bag. Those included the Swiss Army knife that had once belonged to his grandfather, a few items of clothing, and the latest cast-off computer Roger had left behind.

A social worker at a Salvation Army shelter encouraged him to visit the shelter's computer lab. The instructor there, just like the one in Payson who, years later, would rescue Roger, helped Stuart find a job doing coding for a video game software developer who had set up shop in Tempe.

Stu had said something to Julia Miller about Roger going dark, but the truth was, he had gone dark, too. Both of them had wandered in the wilderness for a long time. It was five years later that B. Simpson had noticed Stu's postings in a video game chat session. That had been their initial connection, and B. had ended up offering him a job.

As far as Stuart knew, B. Simpson and probably Ali were the only people aware of the fact that he was a high school dropout. Acquaintances familiar with the position he held at High Noon Enterprises naturally assumed that Stuart had multiple degrees in computer science behind him, and he was convinced that most people had probably made the same erroneous assumptions about Roger's educational background.

Yes, Stu realized, even without being together, his life and Roger McGeary's had been more alike than either of them could have imagined.

"Score!" Startled out of his reverie, Stu looked around to see Cami with her arms raised in triumph.

"What?" he asked.

"You should see the deal I got from Late Breaking Cruises. The ship sails the day after tomorrow. Compared to what the cruise line was charging originally, it's an absolute steal."

"Have you checked the weather?" Stu asked.

Cami looked at him with a puzzled frown. "Why?"

Stu shook his head. "Crossing the Atlantic in September? There may be good reasons some of those cabins are empty."

13

Odin had discovered that he liked the aftermaths of his various exploits almost as much as the events themselves. LuAnn Abernathy continued to make a pest of herself, and Frigg dutifully kept track of all of LuAnn's protests as her op-ed pieces and any number of letters to editors showed up in various media outlets. The pieces all complained that the police investigation surrounding her son's death had been given short shrift due to the fact that he had previously abused drugs. Eventually she teamed up with a group of other mothers — primarily mothers of murdered prostitutes whose cases, like Paul's, may have been haphazardly investigated and remained mostly unsolved.

Odin had to give the old lady credit. LuAnn was persistent, if nothing else. Fortunately, most of her protests fell on deaf ears. Had she been able to hire a private detective, an independent investigation might have been able to make the case that there was something fishy about a guy who had once been strung out on heroin suddenly scoring a fatal dose of fentanyl. Odin now knew that there was at least one security camera located on Kester that might have captured an image of him wielding his cell phone to film Paul Abernathy's passing. The cops had never bothered tracking down the footage. A PI might have gone to that much trouble, but Odin didn't spend a lot of time worrying about it. LuAnn's economic situation — getting by on little more than her social security and a paltry widow's pension — stymied her from hiring any outside help.

After Roger McGeary's death, Odin and Frigg had kept careful tabs on the progress of the official investigation launched by the Panama National Police. Odin's assessment said that Detective Inspector Esteban Garza was smart but arrogant. In addition, the detective had a clear understanding as to which side his bread was buttered on. No doubt that was why he had cleared the case in jig time. It was easy to assume that political connections between the cruise line and the people calling the shots inside the Panamanian government carried the day.

All that was to the good. From combing

through the contents of the victim's cell phone as well as his Web presence, Odin understood that Julia Miller, Roger's aunt, was his only surviving relative and heir. Odin had Frigg track the woman down, and what he learned about her wasn't especially impressive. She ran a racehorse refuge of some kind, somewhere in the wilds of Arizona. Frigg had come up with a few online images of the woman. All of them had been taken at racetrack venues where she participated in protests objecting to the treatment of racehorses after their racing days ended.

Studying the images, it was easy for Odin to dismiss Julia Miller as a nonentity. She appeared to be your basic backwoods country hick — a harmless-looking older woman who customarily dressed in a cowboy shirt, jeans, and boots. Like LuAnn Abernathy, Julia peppered the media with blog postings, complaining of the way her nephew's disappearance and presumed death had been investigated by both the cruise line and the authorities. And although she may have been better off economically than LuAnn, she didn't seem to get any better traction.

Odin's whole focus at the moment was on his next target. While researching Roger,

Frigg stumbled upon his therapist, one Dr. Amelia Cannon — a psychiatrist specializing in the inter-generational long-term effects of family suicide. Once the AI brought the good doctor to Odin's attention, he felt he had hit the mother lode. Dr. Cannon's whole practice was devoted to the very people Odin wanted to find — the children of suicides who were themselves potential suicide victims.

Hacking into the doctor's records hadn't been that much trouble. As Odin scanned through the case notes, he was struck by the similarities between Roger's case and that of another patient, Beth Wordon. Both she and Roger had apparently made substantial progress under Dr. Cannon's care. Beth was currently back in school, working on an advanced degree, and engaged to be married. When Roger had discontinued his weekly sessions a few months earlier, Dr. Cannon's case notes had pronounced him to be "in recovery."

Recovery my ass, Odin had thought when he read the words. *You're not in recovery. You're mine.*

Taking out Roger McGeary had been especially gratifying, far more so than dealing with a miserable loser like Paul Abernathy. Nothing could be better than using cyber to take down a cyber kind of guy, but there had been an additional double whammy involved. Since Roger was one of Dr. Cannon's much vaunted "success stories," Odin felt he was striking a blow against that arrogant twit of a therapist at the same time.

Once the McGeary mission was successfully accomplished, however, Odin had been drawn back to Beth Wordon like a moth to the flame. Of course Frigg had counseled against selecting another target from Dr. Cannon's pool of patients, but Odin had overruled her. With the McGeary investigation fizzling out on the far side of the Atlantic, he had discounted the risk in favor of convenience. The wealth of information they had already gleaned on Beth from Dr. Cannon's files made her a far easier target than some random name plucked off Odin's Target List. As far as Odin was concerned, Beth Wordon was easy, and that made her "it."

The woman may have been born with a silver spoon in her mouth, but she had led a troubled life. From junior high on, her well-off family had bailed Beth out of one scrape after another, always intervening in the direction of treatment rather than interactions with law enforcement. Her problems seemed to recur in cycles, and she'd gone through one stint in rehab after another. When she had turned up in an ICU weighing less than a hundred pounds, her parents had taken her home and hooked her up with Dr. Cannon. If Dr. Cannon's case notes could be trusted, Beth, like Roger, was finally getting her life on track.

One of the things that had fascinated Odin about Roger was the idea that he had, seemingly against all odds, succeeded in turning his life around. He had a good job and had made something of a name for himself. No wonder both he and Dr. Cannon assumed that the years spent in counseling had done the trick and helped him put all that old, bad stuff behind him.

Ditto for Beth. After almost two decades of first cutting herself and then wandering in an anorexic wilderness, she, too, seemed to have recovered. Her storybook destination wedding in Big Sur was just days away, and she was about to marry Joel Williams, her high school sweetheart — her first-ever boyfriend and the varsity football hero who had invited her to what had turned out to be a disastrous junior/senior prom. Joel was divorced now. This would be his second wedding. At age thirty-five, it was Beth's first.

Odin leaned back and studied the series of texts that had just popped up on his computer screen, a supposedly private conversation between Beth and Marissa, her best pal and only attendant.

The alterations are finished. I promised Mom she could come with me tomorrow afternoon for the final fitting.

OMG. You're going to take your mom? Are you kidding? I know she's the MOTB, but do you really want her there? I get off work at three. I can meet you at the shop and run interference if you need it. What if she sees you know what?

Don't worry. She won't. I'll be careful. Mom's been dreaming about this wedding for my whole life. Considering everything I've put her through, I owe her this.

Okay. Let me know how it goes.

Odin knew all about the wedding dress — a designer gown with long sleeves that wouldn't be entirely in keeping with a warm September afternoon ceremony at a cliff-side wedding venue overlooking the Pacific. But a gown with short sleeves or no sleeves at all would have given away the game because, at Odin's direction and with Frigg's capable assistance, Beth was back to cutting.

For weeks now Frigg had been locked and loaded, delivering a full catalogue of Beth-specific messages that were designed to keep the bride-to-be in a mental pressure cooker at all hours of the day and night. That was one of the things Odin appreciated most about Frigg — once given a task, she was utterly relentless. In a way she reminded Odin of that old Ron Popeil rotisserie commercial — all Odin needed to do was set her and forget her and count on her to do the job.

As for Beth? Living at home with her folks, going to school, and no longer seeing Dr. Cannon, Beth was now forced to struggle with her addiction issues entirely on her own. She journaled about it on an almost daily basis, while Odin from his virtual vantage point observed every keystroke and smiled at every pained entry typed into her computer. It amused him that so far she had yet to share any of it with her fiancé.

Once Beth was targeted, it had been no trouble at all for Frigg to break into the woman's various social media accounts and eventually into her computer files as well. It was in her V-vite account, an online invitation Web site, where Frigg had encountered a "Save the Date" message announcing the upcoming wedding. This wedding. This Saturday's wedding. A wedding that, with any luck, would never happen.

Not if Odin and Frigg had any say in the matter. And when Beth Wordon happened to come to an untimely death either after her bachelorette party or the next night, on the eve of her "perfect" wedding? No one would bother looking around for a murderer. All the reasons needed for her suicide would be found right there in her own computer, written in her own words.

Sweet.

Odin was so caught up in planning for the weekend that when an IOI (item of interest) alert came in from Frigg, he almost skipped it. One of the AI's ongoing responsibilities was to monitor anything that showed up online having to do with either Roger McGeary, Paul Abernathy, Dr. Amelia Cannon, or any of their known relatives.

In this case, it was a brief Facebook posting from Roger's aunt Julia:

I tracked down Roger's oldest friend yesterday, a guy by the name of Stuart

Ramey. They were very close as kids. I asked Stu if he'd help me find out what really happened. He didn't make any promises, of course, but I think he and the people he works for may look into the situation. It'll be good to have someone else on my side for a change. I'm tired of fighting this battle all on my own.

Odin paused for only a moment before sending Frigg a message of his own and giving her a new set of search marching orders:

Who is Stuart Ramey?

Frigg's next IOI was her standard evening announcement:

Dinner.

Owen Hansen glanced at his watch, the Rolex he had inherited from his father, which still kept perfect time. Caught up in his computer screen, the hours had gotten away from him. Hurriedly he locked up the lab. Then he showered, shaved, and rushed upstairs, where he found his mother in the library, sipping a Negroni and smoking like a fiend.

The years hadn't been especially kind to Irene Hansen. Yes, she was still a brittle-thin, size-two wisp of a woman, who dressed for dinner every night usually in a chic two-piece knit suit of some kind. Worried about falling, she had given up wearing her once-loved stilettos. Even so, low heels and hose were always part of her ensemble, along with a tasteful string of pearls. Although her figure remained unchanged, her face had not. Decades of smoking had damaged her narrow, sunken cheeks in ways that no amount of expensive cosmetic work could erase, and behind a pair of thick-lensed glasses, her faded blue eyes were enormous.

"You're late," she said accusingly when her son appeared in the doorway. "But you're just in time to make me a refill."

"Sorry," he said, taking her glass and going to the drinks cart parked by the fireplace. "I was working. Time got away from me."

He was glad that she never asked what he was working on, and he never volunteered any information.

For more than twenty years their mother-and-son evening routine had gone virtually unchanged, although there were fewer guests these days, and Irene had far fewer outside social engagements. They would meet in the library for a before-dinner cocktail or two. Or, in this case, Owen thought, maybe even three.

After drinks they moved on to the dining room. A personal chef arrived at the house each morning to prepare breakfast, lunch, and dinner. The evening meal was served by a young woman who doubled as both sous-chef and server, and who left the house each evening after cleaning up.

In many ways, they resembled an old married couple, maintaining a certain measure of distance between them. Dinnertime conversation was limited to polite but idle small talk punctuated by occasional bouts of bickering. The complex set of trusts Harold established prior to his death had stood them both in good stead. When Irene died, the house and everything remaining in her portion would go to Owen, but he was in no rush to come into possession of his inheritance. His mother could be annoying as all hell at times, but she was handy to have around, primarily because she oversaw the household arrangements, leaving him free to attend to his own pursuits.

"I'll be away this weekend," he said, when cocktails were over and they were seated across from one another at the long formal table in the dining room.

"Really?" Irene asked. "Where are you going?"

"Atlanta," he said. "A friend of mine is getting married."

"Getting married?" Irene repeated, looking genuinely surprised. "I thought all your friends must be confirmed old bachelors by now, just like you. Who is it?"

"His name's Fred. You wouldn't know him. We met over the Internet. He does the same kind of work I do. The wedding's on Saturday afternoon. I fly out tomorrow."

"All right, then," Irene said. "Be sure to leave a note for Pierre so he knows he'll only be cooking for one. When will you get back?"

"Sunday most likely," he told her, "but don't be surprised if I end up staying an extra day or two."

When dinner was over that night, Irene was more than slightly tipsy as she made her way to the newly installed elevator that gave her easy access to her upstairs suite of rooms. Worried about her unfortunate habit of smoking in bed, Owen had insisted on installing a state-of-the-art fire-suppression system throughout the house, including a series of commercial-grade fire doors. If his mother decided to turn herself into toast some night, he was determined that Irene wouldn't take Frigg down in the process.

He wanted his AI alive and growing and

159

working inside his powerful network of linked computers, humming away in the basement and growing smarter by the minute. That's how things were at the moment, and that's how Owen Hansen wanted them to stay.

14

When Joel had popped the question at midnight on New Year's Eve, Beth hadn't needed to think it over. She said yes without a moment's hesitation. They had hooked up the previous summer when Marissa had dragged Beth, kicking and screaming, to a Fourth of July party at Four Mile Beach in Santa Cruz.

"Who all will be there?" Beth had asked.

"You know," Marissa had said. "The usual."

"The usual" meant second-generation members of Silicon Valley's royalty — the sons and daughters of the tech pioneers from the seventies, eighties, and nineties. They were children of privilege who had been raised with far more money than good sense. Some of their fathers had risen to fame and fortune and gone on to be household names. Others, like Beth's father, Richard Powell, rose only to crash to earth in spectacular fashion. Richard had created an X-ray photolithography process, something that would have made him a household name, too. Except it had been stolen away and patented by someone who had supposedly been Richard's best friend.

Richard had bet everything he owned on being able to bring the process to market, and when he lost control of it, he'd lost the farm. On the day his former partner's company went public with what was then the largest IPO ever, Richard went out to his workshop and swilled down as many glasses of antifreeze-laced iced tea as it took to do the job. He'd left his wife, Molly, and his ten-year-old daughter, Beth, a fairly good-sized set of life insurance benefits, but that was about it.

Beth had loved her father to distraction and laid the blame for his passing squarely on her own very narrow shoulders. Had she been a better daughter, her father wouldn't have died. Molly, caught up in her own difficulties, didn't immediately grasp how terribly Richard's death had impacted her daughter. Two years later and after a whirlwind romance, Molly had married one of Richard's fraternity brothers, Del Wordon. Del, a forty-something bachelor with no desire for children of his own, adored Molly and doted on Beth, legally adopting her on the occasion of her twelfth birthday.

Unfortunately, the unconditional love of both her mother and step-father wasn't enough to keep Beth from embarking on a self-destructive path, but after almost two decades of trying, they had finally succeeded in getting her the help she needed. Dr. Amelia Cannon had been a godsend to all of them. It was during Beth's weekly counseling sessions with the psychiatrist when Beth had finally begun to see the light. For years people had told her that her father's death had nothing to do with her, but Dr. Cannon was the one who had made her believe it.

Dr. Cannon was the first and only person who had understood and validated everything Beth had to say. Yes, the intervening years had been tough, but they had taught Beth valuable lessons that could prove to be a benefit to a whole new generation of children dealing with similar problems. With Dr. Cannon's encouragement and with financial aid from Del and Molly, Beth had recently been accepted into the graduate school at Stanford, intent on pursuing a PhD in psychology with her first classes due to start the following September.

And that was where she had been, late on

that Fourth of July afternoon a little over a year earlier — hopeful and purposeful both — and feeling like, for the first time, she was finally pointed in the right direction. The party had turned out to be about what she expected — a bit on the wild side with plenty of food and drink to go around and plenty of substances — legal and otherwise — changing hands. Then, suddenly, she ran into Joel.

She recognized him at once, even though the last time they'd seen each other or spoken had been the night of Beth's junior/senior prom. He'd taken her to Armando's for a pre-prom dinner, where she'd eaten everything in sight and then spent the next half hour closeted in the restroom while she barfed it all up. When they finally made it to the dance, she'd been too sick to go inside.

"Hey, look who's here," Joel said, smiling and raising a soda can in her direction. "Long time no see. Care to join us?"

Beth leveled a scathing look at Marissa. Obviously she had known Joel would be here and had suckered Beth into coming along. Marissa answered with a grin and a noncommittal shrug and immediately walked off with someone else.

"What's your poison?" he asked, opening

a nearby cooler.

"Do you have any Diet Coke?" she asked.

He pulled a can of it out of a cooler, offered it to her, and then gestured to the vacant camp stool next to him. "Take a load off," he said. "I won't bite."

When she sat down on the stool, it sank so far into the sand that it almost spilled her over backward. By the time Joel helped right her, they were both laughing.

"See there?" he said. "Obviously we're meant for each other. You're already head over heels."

And the truth was, they *were* meant for each other. The party went on around them. They roasted hot dogs over a portable butane stove and ate with mustard and ketchup dribbling down their respective chins. They roasted marshmallows over open flames as well and ate them, burned to a crisp, straight off the stick. And they talked. God, how they talked — while the sun went down and while the fireworks were blasting into the sky. They were still talking when Marissa said it was late and she needed to leave, and she didn't seem the least bit surprised when Beth said she'd like to hang around a little longer because Joel had offered to take her home.

Other than Dr. Cannon, Beth had never

spoken to or listened to any other individual the way she did with Joel, not even her best friend, Marissa, who knew some of the truth about Beth but not nearly all of it.

From the beginning she and Joel talked about real stuff without either of them seeming to pull any punches. Joel had gone to college, graduated second in his class from law school, gotten hired by a local law firm, married, had two kids, and made partner. So far so good. Then it had blown up in his face. He'd found out that his wife, Corrine, was cheating on him — not just once but multiple times — with one of the senior partners from his firm. The subsequent divorce had not only ended his marriage, but also derailed what had once been a promising legal career.

"I couldn't believe it when the court gave Corrine full custody of the boys," Joel said. "Could not believe it. How could the legal system I worked for and believed in do something that screwed up? When the firm offered me a buyout, I took it. Then I got drunk and stayed that way for the next three years. But now I'm starting over. I've got a new job. Between child support and back child support, I barely make enough to pay my rent. Corrine remarried — not to the original guy she was screwing around with.

She married someone else, but she's still holding me up for child support."

He paused, reached into the pocket of his shorts, and pulled out a coin that he handed over to Beth.

"What's this?" she asked.

"It's my one-year sobriety chip," he said. "As of today, I've been off the sauce for exactly one year. I went to a meeting and got the chip before I came to the picnic." He paused and grinned at her. "Between getting the chip and meeting up with you again, I don't know which is the better deal."

Later, after they'd helped reload all the camping gear, they sat in the parking lot of the campground and talked some more. Now it was Beth's turn to tell her story. She had never spoken to anyone other than Marissa and Dr. Cannon about her father's suicide. She told Joel about all of it — about her battle with anorexia, including that ill-fated prom date, and about the cutting, too. As the sun came peeking up over the horizon behind them, she pulled up the sleeve of her sweatshirt and showed him the scars.

"I'm sorry," was all he said, running his index finger gently across the webs of raised lines in her flesh. "I'm so very sorry."

He didn't ask her to marry him until

almost six months later, but from that moment on, Beth Wordon knew for sure that if he ever did get around to asking, she was bound to say yes.

15

As the plane rumbled down the long taxi-way, Cami Lee settled into her business class seat on British Airways, closed her eyes, and felt like pinching herself to make sure this was real — that she wasn't just making the whole thing up.

Camille Lee had grown up in the Bay Area. Much to her parents' dismay, she had wanted to be a detective for as long as she could remember. Now in a very real way, she was one. Not as a cop and not as a licensed private eye, either, but an investigator nonetheless. And this was her first solo assignment — an international solo assignment. Her perpetually feuding parents, both of them hard-core academics, would have been appalled, but too bad. Cami was living the life she wanted as opposed to the life they had wanted for her.

There had been a single available business class seat on today's British flight out of

Phoenix, and she and Ali had been able to grab it. That meant Cami was on her way to the UK, and due to arrive a full day before the cruise was scheduled to depart. The overnight flight would put her at Heathrow early tomorrow afternoon. Ali had arranged for a driver to meet Cami at the airport and take her to a hotel in Southampton where she would spend the night before boarding the *Whispering Star* on Friday. Once they had nailed down the cabin on the ship as well as the flight, Cami headed home to pack. She had then caught the shuttle to Phoenix in time to catch the 7:30 p.m. flight.

She had arrived at Sky Harbor three hours before her scheduled departure and well over the two-hour suggested minimum for international flights. What she hadn't counted on was the fact that TSA took a very dim view of people purchasing last-minute one-way tickets to the UK. At the check-in counter, her passport was examined in minute detail. Her checked luggage was pulled aside and gone through item by item before being thoroughly swabbed for explosives. Ditto for items in her carry-on luggage. She'd had to turn on and boot up all three of her electronic devices — her phone, laptop, and iPad — to prove they were operational. As for Cami herself? She went through the regular machine screening and was then pulled aside for a pat down and a separate interview as well. When she entered the interview room, she was dismayed to find that the luggage she had previously checked was there waiting for her.

For the first time Cami began to wonder if her name had somehow mistakenly turned up on the No Fly List. Maybe she wasn't going anywhere at all.

Sergeant Croy, the pudgy and balding uniformed man seated behind the interview desk, someone who easily outweighed Cami three times over, stared first at her boarding pass and then at another document that she eventually recognized as a printed copy of the ticket purchase.

"You bought this today?" he demanded. "Why so late?"

Cami shrugged. "Because I didn't know I was going until just this morning. My cruise leaves the day after tomorrow, and this flight gets me there a day early."

"You're going on a cruise and you just now found out about it? Most people plan their cruises years in advance."

She didn't want to mention anything at all about the Roger McGeary situation.

Things were already complicated enough.

"It was purchased through a Web site, a company called Late Breaking Cruises," Cami explained. "They gave us a smoking deal."

"I'll just bet," Croy muttered irritably. "It says here the ticket was purchased by an outfit named High Noon Enterprises. Who are they?"

"My employers," she answered. "Up in Cottonwood."

"And they're sending you on a cruise?"

Cami thought about Roger McGeary being given his reward cruise by Shining Star Cruises. That hadn't worked out very well — at least not for him. "It's a bonus," she said. "Like an award for work well done."

"Right," he said. "So why only a one-way ticket? People who buy one-way tickets tend to be problematic."

Cami was doing her best to rein in her temper, but it was starting to get the best of her. "Because I'm returning to the US by ship," she replied.

"So tell me about this last-minute cruise. What kind of cruise is it? From where to where?"

"From Southampton to New York City on board the *Whispering Star.*"

"Where all does it stop?"

Cami was stumped. The whole idea of this venture was to place her on the ship so she could ask questions about Roger McGeary. She knew the cruise's embarkation and disembarkation points. As far as the stops in between went? She had no idea.

"I'd like to see your cruise documents, if you please," Croy said, holding out a beefy fist.

The only documentation Cami had for the cruise itself was a single confirmation-of-travel e-mail from Late Breaking Cruises. She had the document on her iPad, but she hadn't bothered printing it. She handed Croy the device with the requested confirmation open on the screen.

He read through it and frowned. "I'm going to need some verification of this. Is there any way to get in touch with these people other than e-mail?"

Cami took the iPad back, located Last Minute's contact information, and read off the toll-free number. Once Croy dialed it in, it seemed to take forever to get through the call-center queue. He sat on hold, cleaning his fingernails and looking as though he hadn't a care in the world, while Cami stewed in her own juices — glancing nervously at her watch as her scheduled 7:30 departure time drew nearer and nearer. She wasn't a terrorist, but she was certainly being treated like one, and she was on fire with resentment. Being given the third degree by a fifty-something bullying bureaucrat wasn't doing much to make the world a safer place.

Finally Croy got through to a live person at Last Minute. After several long-winded exchanges he was finally satisfied. "All right, then," he said, slamming down the receiver and giving Cami a final glare. "You're free to go."

"What about my luggage?" she asked.

"Don't worry. I'll take care of it."

With little hope that her checked luggage would make it, Cami took her carry-on and raced from the interview room, reaching the gate bare moments before the ground agent closed the jetway door. She was the last passenger to board. As she settled into her seat, alerts from a series of arriving e-mails dinged in her phone. She glanced at them long enough to see that they were all encrypted files from Stuart. She had time enough to open her computer and download the files, but no time to read them, at least not then. Instead she sent Stu a text message:

On the plane. Almost didn't make it because of TSA. The guy was a complete jackass. Got your files. Will read later. Have to turn off the computer now.

It seemed to take forever for the plane to gain enough altitude, but when the bell rang announcing that computers could now be used on board, Cami pulled hers out, turned it on, called up the first file, and turned on the decryption program. Then, with a glass of champagne at hand, she opened the file, which happened to be labeled: *Sólo para uso autorizado.* Beneath that were the words: *Policía Nacional de Panamá.*

Cami had no idea how Stuart had laid hands on Detective Inspector Esteban Garza's official reports, and it was probably just as well she didn't. There was a good possibility that by simply reading the words both she and Stu were breaking several international treaties, but read she did.

It turned out that transcripts of all of Detective Inspector Garza's interviews were there. The files indicated that most of the interviews conducted on board the ship had been videoed, and the ones done by phone with Roger's fellow employees at Cyber Resources in California had utilized Skype. Cami suspected that most of the interviews had been conducted in English initially before the contents had been transcribed into Spanish, typed, and placed in the file.

Cami's three years of high school Spanish hadn't nearly equipped her to translate that much material, and she wasn't sure the translation app in her computer was all that good at it, either. In addition the occasional garbling of sentences made her think that perhaps the English-to-Spanish transcriber hadn't done much better.

She combed through the interviews one at a time, making careful notes and encrypting them as she went. She culled out the names of the people on the ship who had been most closely associated with Roger McGeary — the butler, the housekeeper, the barman, and the servers in the dining room, along with the three ladies he had dined and partied with on the night in question.

The other files Stu had sent included everything he'd been able to find on the Internet that had anything to do with Roger McGeary. Most of it concerned his disappearance and presumed death. There was only one mention of the massive potential data breach he had averted.

In addition to the encrypted files there was an unencrypted one. It contained a very old and faded photograph of two boys, one that looked as though it might have been lifted from a high school yearbook. Cami enlarged the picture until the pixels turned to fuzz. It took a moment for her to recognize one of the two broadly grinning boys with their shaggy 1990s-era hairstyles. The taller of the two was a much younger and much hairier version of Stuart Ramey. The caption underneath the photo read: "Stuart Ramey and Roger McGeary, SPHS Dungeons & Dragons Champions, 1991."

It was in that moment of recognition that Cami finally understood why she was on the plane and why Ali Reynolds and B. Simpson had green lighted what was already a very expensive operation. It had nothing to do with Julia Miller's request for help.

This was all about Stuart — a loyal, weird, and often annoying guy. He'd had a friend once — a very good friend, evidently — who was forever lost to him now. Whatever High Noon's investigation revealed about Roger McGeary's fate wouldn't bring that lost friend back, but at least it would give Stu some needed answers, and that was all that mattered.

16

Beth was still holding the phone when the next text bomb landed. When she heard the alert, she didn't let herself hope that the message would be a cheery note from Joel or from one of her friends or even from her folks.

A glance at the text file told her she was right. *CC* — Corrine Calhoun, Joel's ex. The phone trembled in Beth's hand. She already knew the kind of poison she would find in the message, and she didn't want to read it; didn't want to internalize the hurtful words. But the urge to know what it said was irresistible.

I can't believe that Joel is dumb enough to go through with this. How can he marry someone like you — a self-destructive nutcase with a long history of mental health issues — and expect you to be a suitable stepmother to our boys? How *can* he? Ricky and Robby deserve something better. I can't believe I'm saying this, but Joel deserves something better, too.

I know all about the cutting. And if there are scars on your body, that's nothing compared to the scars you carry on your soul.

You deserve to die, bitch, the sooner the better.

Covering her mouth with one hand, Beth bit back a ragged sob, and then, while she watched, the words magically disappeared from her screen, leaving no trace behind — not even on her list of received texts.

The texts from Corrine had started showing up weeks earlier. When the first one came in, she had seen the sender's name and assumed it was something to do with the wedding. Corrine had been adamantly uncooperative about every single detail on that, including insisting that the only way the boys, ages nine and eleven, could attend their father's wedding ceremony was if Joel himself drove down to Santa Monica to pick them up beforehand and delivered them back home once the wedding was over. Obviously that plan wasn't going to work. After a great deal of negotiation, Corrine had finally relented, agreeing that the boys could fly as long as she flew up with them — at their father's expense, of course — and as long as Corrine was at the wedding to oversee their activities.

Considering the way Joel's kids had behaved on the other occasions when Beth had met them, not having them in attendance at all might have been for the best. Much as she wanted to like them, Ricky and Robby were not likable kids. They were poorly behaved in public. The first time Beth met them, Joel had taken them out to dinner at a Red Robin in Santa Monica. They had been rude to her all during dinner. Then, before the meal ended, the two of them had gotten into a food fight, pitching French fries across the table at one another. In other words, Beth had good reason to be concerned that, without Corrine in attendance, another food fight between the boys would be in the offing during the wedding supper.

That was what she'd been thinking when the first message came in and before she read it. And although she couldn't remember the whole thing word for word, the gist of it was chiseled into her soul: *Joel must be scraping bottom if he's desperate enough to settle for someone as useless as you.*

Beth could barely believe her eyes. She

was in the process of rereading it when it vanished. Completely. She had wanted to tell Joel about it, but how could she? "Your ex just sent me a poison text message that disappeared the moment I read it." Sure, that would go over like a pregnant pole-vaulter. Beyond turning her phone off and on and taking selfies now and then, Beth knew nothing about technology. Whoever heard of disappearing text messages? Were they even possible? They sounded like something straight out of the *The Twilight Zone.* The last thing she needed right now was for someone to think she was lying about this or, even worse, delusional.

The next message arrived a day or two later. It had been four words long, including calling her the dreaded c-word. Shocked beyond words and with her fingers shaking in outrage, Beth had tried to copy the message before it disappeared, but that didn't work. Even though she pressed her finger on the line, she could neither highlight it nor copy it.

Beth had told no one about what was happening. What was the point? If she accused Corrine of sending the missing texts, all the woman would do was deny it. But this one? This was by far the worst. How could Corrine possibly know about the cutting unless

Marissa had told her, or worse, Joel? Since Marissa had never met Corrine, that made the first possibility unlikely. And if Joel was the culprit? That meant he had betrayed Beth in the worst possible way. How could she marry the man if she couldn't trust him to keep her deepest, most closely guarded secrets?

And then, while the phone was still gripped in Beth's hand, it rang, and Joel's name popped up in the caller ID window.

"Hey, babe," he said when she answered. "I just got out of a client meeting that went on for hours. Wanted to call and see how your day's going."

"It's okay," Beth managed.

"It doesn't sound okay. Your voice seems funny. Is something wrong?"

"No," she insisted quickly. "It's nothing. A case of pre-wedding jitters is all."

"You're not gonna back out on me now, are you?"

He said it in that gently teasing way of his, without having any idea how close to the mark his question came. If Corrine knew about the cutting, she probably knew about the anorexia, too. That was why she'd said what she said — the part about Beth being mentally ill and self-destructive.

"No, really," she said quickly. "I'm okay."

"Do you want me to stop by after work?"

"Not tonight," she said. "I've got a bit of a headache."

"Lunch tomorrow, then? Corrine and the boys fly in tomorrow evening, and from then on it's going to be a three-ring circus."

Corrine and the boys, Beth thought, *great!* "All right," she agreed reluctantly. "Mom is going with me to the fitting tomorrow afternoon, but we can have lunch before that."

The call ended. A despairing Beth sat staring at her phone wondering if maybe she really should call off the wedding. If only she could go see Dr. Cannon and talk things over, but she couldn't. Dr. Cannon wasn't there anymore. Beth's trusted psychiatrist had thrown in the towel. Months earlier she had sent out notices telling her patients that she had recently been informed that her medical group's computer network had been hacked, creating a serious data breach as far as patient records were concerned. Concerned that patient confidentiality had not been properly protected, she was leaving that medical group, shuttering her practice, and going into retirement, effective immediately. Dr. Cannon had included contact information for a number of mental health professionals who were accepting new patients if anyone was interested in a referral.

Beth had been shocked at that abrupt turn of events, but right that minute things were going well for her, and she had been in no mood to go shopping for a new therapist. After all, she was acing all her classes. She and Joel were engaged and planning both a wedding and a future together. What could possibly go wrong?

But now it had gone wrong — terribly, terribly wrong. That was when Beth finally heard the siren call coming from the brand-new packet of razor blades she had stowed in the top drawer of the bathroom vanity. She had been trying her best to resist the urge — for days now — but this was too much.

She was in the bathroom watching the bright red stream from her arm mingle with the running water in the basin and disappear down the drain when her mother tapped lightly on the door to her bedroom.

"Dinner's on," Molly announced through the door.

"Sorry, Mom," Beth called back. "I think I'll pass. I'm just not hungry tonight."

17

Ali was frustrated as she drove home. She had authorized the expenditure of a small fortune to get Cami booked onto the *Whispering Star.* Then, just as Ali was leaving the office, Stu had told her that he had succeeded in laying hands on Detective Inspector Garza's files. In other words, putting Cami on the ship might prove to be a huge waste of money and effort. Still, if Cami did do follow-up interviews with people from the ship, she'd at least be able to see if they were still giving the same version of events.

What's done is done, Ali told herself firmly. *You called the shot as best you could. No use second-guessing now.*

After enduring a properly ecstatic greeting from Bella, Ali was delighted to find Leland hovering over a simmering pot of beef bourguignon. She couldn't help reflecting somewhat sadly that once Leland was gone, homemade beef bourguignon would most likely become a thing of the past.

"How are things?" he asked.

"Let's just say I'm glad to be home."

"All right, then," he said. "Dinner's almost ready, but just so you know, the Brit's out of the running."

"We're down to just two candidates?"

Leland nodded. "He said that he googled the house and decided there wouldn't be enough for him to do here to keep him occupied."

"So you're saying the guy fired us?" Ali asked with a hint of laughter in her voice.

"Apparently," Leland said with a nod. "I told you I thought the man was a bit of a snob. I doubt he would have been a good fit. Come and get it. Dinner's almost ready."

"I'll go change, then," Ali told him. She was on her way to the bedroom when her phone rang with Stu's name in the caller ID.

"What's up?" she asked.

"I've been going through Garza's file," Stu said excitedly, "and I just hit a bonanza. Roger was the team leader of the group that managed the Shining Star account. At Garza's suggestion, the cruise line demanded that Cyber Resources send along copies of all internal correspondence dealing with Shining Star. Someone from there created a separate password-protected file containing all the requested material. Fortunately for us, Garza isn't especially security-minded. He left the password right there in front of God and everybody."

"And where does that get us?" Ali asked.

"All Cyber Resources' proprietary information has been redacted, of course, and we don't have access to Roger's work computer, but what's here gives us a reasonable window on his work life."

"And?"

"He was happy. There was very little work-related material in the computer Julia Miller gave us. Here, though, are e-mails and texts going back and forth between him and his fellow team members as well as his superiors inside the company. One guy who worked with him, Jack Wendall, was pissed beyond bearing when Roger got all the credit for solving the data breach situation. So pissed, in fact, that when Roger was invited on the cruise, Wendall up and quit altogether."

"Pissed enough to commit murder?" Ali asked.

"Maybe," Stuart said. "I'm checking his whereabouts now. But that's not what I wanted to tell you."

"What, then?"

"Roger wasn't suicidal," Stuart answered definitively. "Not before he got on the cruise ship and not afterward, either."

"How can you know that?"

"I located an online outfit that specializes in suicide prevention. They've developed a relatively new program, an algorithm that analyzes people's turns of phrase and use of emojis in correspondence and social media situations to determine whether or not they are suicidal. I ran Roger's data through that, and nothing I found in his personal computer pointed in that direction."

"If he didn't commit suicide, then what are you saying — that his death may be murder after all?"

"Possibly," Stu answered.

"If that's the case, what's next?" Ali asked.

"I'd like to get a line on Jack Wendall's location for starters," Stuart said. "Garza interviewed him by Skype, and he admitted straight out that he hated Roger's guts. According to Garza's notes, he also had an airtight alibi at the time Roger died. I'd like to verify that. Once I locate him, if he needs to be interviewed, I was hoping maybe you could talk to him. I mean, with Cami out of the country . . ." Stu's voice trailed off.

None of this was surprising as far as Ali was concerned. Stu was great at finding people, but his marginal interpersonal skills made him anything but skilled at doing interviews.

"Sure," Ali said. "Glad to. Just let me know where and when."

"And I'm looking into Dr. Amelia Cannon. Roger stopped seeing her a number of months ago, and I'm curious about that."

"He stopped going to her without making arrangements to find a replacement?"

"Not that I can see."

"So did he stop going because he thought he was cured, or did he stop for some other reason?" Ali asked.

"That's what I want to know. I found a phone listing for Dr. Cannon. I tried calling, but all I got was a disconnect with no referral to another number. So that's where I'll be concentrating my efforts tonight — trying to locate Jack Wendall and Dr. Cannon."

"Okay," Ali said. "Keep me posted."

18

After finally escaping his mother's dinner-time clutches, Owen expected to return to the basement for a relaxing evening of listening in on Beth Wordon's life and times, but that was not to be. As soon as he turned on his computer screen, he was surprised to discover that it was filled with IOIs from Frigg, all of them highlighted in red. Red designated one thing and one thing only — an elevated threat level.

Slipping into his Odin persona, he was sure whatever Frigg had found couldn't possibly be that serious. As he read through the first item, however, he began to wonder if his AI might be onto something. Stuart Ramey, the school chum Julia Miller had called on to help investigate her nephew's case, wasn't just anybody and neither were the people he worked for — High Noon Enterprises.

While he'd been at dinner, Frigg had

gathered a tremendous amount of material on the company itself as well as on several of the individuals involved. Scrolling through the material, Odin could see why Frigg regarded them as dangerous. Stuart Ramey was clearly not an ordinary guy. Detective Inspector Esteban Garza had been a relatively harmless local yokel with limited technical skills and no real motivation to look for anything other than obvious answers as far as Roger McGeary's death was concerned. He had expected a suicide and he had found exactly that — a self-fulfilling prophecy. Had he dug into the ship's electronic records, he might have found some puzzling anomalies, but he had not.

In terms of technology, however, High Noon Enterprises was another kettle of fish entirely. Odin stopped long enough to retrieve the post from Julia Miller, the one he had read just before going to dinner. He read through it again, this time with a growing sense of apprehension.

I tracked down Roger's oldest friend yesterday, a guy by the name of Stuart Ramey. They were very close as kids. I asked Stu if he'd help me find out what really happened. He didn't make any promises, of course, but I think he and the people he works for may look into the situation. It'll be good to have someone else on my side for a change. I'm tired of fighting this battle all on my own.

When Odin had first seen Stuart Ramey's name, he'd been more curious than anything else, but this was entirely different. High Noon was a cyber security company with global reach and stature. Stuart didn't have much of a public or social media presence, but his boss did. Odin's jaw literally dropped when he saw that B. Simpson had started out as a star in the video gaming world and had somehow managed to parlay that unlikely beginning into a multimillion-dollar cyber security company doing business with any number of Fortune 500 entities.

Another notable individual connected to High Noon was a guy named Lance Tucker, and he was legend. While still in high school, Tucker had invented something called GHOST (Go Hide On Server Technology) that had been able to penetrate the hidden secrets of the dark Web without leaving a trace. Tucker himself was now attending UCLA, but High Noon maintained a proprietary interest in the program Lance was credited with inventing.

Odin had created his own virtual invisibility cloak — not GHOST per se, but close. And knowing that there were people out there like Lance who could peer into the dark Web and monitor transactions there with complete impunity created a major problem for Odin. He counted on the dark Web. He used it on a regular basis and needed a lot of what was for sale there — fake IDs, prepaid credit cards, lists of stolen passwords, drugs. After all, the dark Web was where he had purchased the fentanyl he had used to finish off Paul Abernathy. Odin knew for sure that there were hit men available for hire on the dark Web as well. He had never availed himself of one of those, but who's to say when one of them might come in handy?

Odin was interested to learn that one of High Noon's principals was a woman named Ali Reynolds. She came with no apparent technical credentials of her own. Her main claim to fame seemed to be the fact that she was married to B. Simpson. Reynolds was a former television news anchor who, according to the information Frigg had tracked down, had a tendency to get into one high-profile scrape after another. Recently she and another High Noon employee, twenty-three-year-old Camille Lee, had been involved in the takedown of a wanted fugitive — a Ponzi scheme operator who had been attempting to flee the country.

In other words, there was plenty of information to be had on all the other movers and shakers at High Noon, but on the one of greatest interest to Odin, there was precious little. Stuart Ramey, Roger's longtime friend, remained a complete blank. According to the IRS, the man had worked for High Noon for years — since its inception. He apparently had no driver's license and no vehicle, either. He wasn't on the list of registered voters. His address was given as a post office box in the town of Cottonwood, but there was no residential listing of any kind.

Odin dispatched Frigg to go searching through every university alumni association known to man, including those overseas. That search alone took a matter of hours, but to no avail. She found nothing. No enrollment listing of any kind for Stuart Ramey, which meant he had no degree and had probably never set foot on a college campus. Whatever he knew about computer science he had learned the hard way — on his own and by trial and error rather than in a classroom. Odin couldn't help feeling a tiny bit of kinship. Hadn't he learned everything he knew the same way?

It was three o'clock in the morning when Frigg finally came up with the South Phoenix High connection. That was where Stuart Ramey and Roger McGeary first surfaced together in a high school yearbook photograph. If Phoenix was the place where Stuart had started, and Cottonwood — a hundred or so miles away — was where he ended up, it was safe to conclude that although the man may have been smart, he hadn't traveled very far geographically, nor had he made it nearly as far up any standard corporate ladder as his friend Roger McGeary had.

But was he dangerous? Sipping scotch as he read, Odin wasn't convinced either way. One thing was certain: if Stuart did somehow manage to pick up Odin and Frigg's trail, he would have to be eliminated. It might just be time to go shopping for one of those dark Web hit men after all.

19

Cami worked through the night. By the time she was ready to give up on the files, flatten her bed, and go to sleep, it was too late. She had slept for less than an hour when the flight attendants began turning on cabin lights and pushing noisy breakfast trolleys up and down the aisles.

When the plane landed at Heathrow just after one thirty in the afternoon, she was jet-lagged and weary as she headed for passport control. Ali had assured her that her business class ticket meant she could go to the priority line, which was clearly much shorter than the regular line and hopefully much faster. Except it wasn't. Evidently her passport had been given some kind of red flag. She was held up at a border guard's station, where she went through another whole grilling procedure, answering one question after another while people far behind her in line went to other stations, had their passports stamped, and were given the go-ahead to leave.

How long did she plan on staying in the UK? What was the purpose of her trip? Where and when was she boarding her ship? Where would she be staying tonight? Had she traveled to the UK before? Did she have any friends here? Once again, Cami was being treated like a criminal, and it was challenging to keep a civil tongue in her mouth.

Shortly after Cami graduated from high school, her paternal grandfather had passed away in Taiwan, and she had accompanied her father there for the funeral. Boarding planes and clearing customs for that trip had been a breeze compared to what she'd undergone for this one.

When the border guard finally stamped her passport and let her go, Cami let out a sigh of relief and headed for baggage claim. She recognized other people from her flight, grabbing their luggage and going, but hers was nowhere to be found. At last Cami went looking for help.

"So sorry about that, dearie," said the kindly-looking older woman behind the counter in the lost property office, studying the baggage claim number Cami had given her and passing along a printed form and a pen.

"You'll need to fill this out and let us know where you'll be. Most likely your bags didn't make the flight, but they'll come in on tomorrow's. We'll make sure they're delivered."

"But I'm going on a cruise," Cami objected. "What if the bags get to the hotel after the ship has already sailed?"

"Then we'll need to have information on your cruise as well — the name of the ship, where it's leaving from, when it's departing, and where it's going."

Shaking her head, fighting back tears, and feeling like a world-class failure, Cami filled out the required form. It asked for everything — her name, passport number, flight information, home address, UK addresses, e-mail address, and all applicable telephone numbers. Once finished, she handed it over, and then watched while the woman typed the information into a computer.

"Don't you worry now," she said, with smiling reassurance. "We'll put it right. And there's a number there you can call to check for updates."

Cami didn't think it would ever be put right. She cleared customs with nothing to declare and with only her Rollaboard and purse in hand. Expecting another disaster of some kind, she was surprised when the first person she saw outside the door was a middle-aged man dressed in a suit and holding an iPad with her name printed on it. That's when she finally did burst into tears — tears of relief and frustration both.

"What seems to be the matter, miss?" the driver asked.

"They lost my luggage," she sobbed. "It won't be here until tomorrow. It may not even catch up with me before the ship sails."

"Let's get headed for Southampton, then," he said, glancing at his watch. Cami checked hers, as well. It was almost four o'clock. She'd spent more than two hours clearing border control and not retrieving her luggage. "It's an hour and a half in good traffic," the driver continued, "but we're coming up on rush hour now. Maybe we can stop off somewhere along the road so you can pick up a necessary item or two."

"Thank you," Cami murmured. "That's probably a good idea."

The vehicle turned out to be a van that could easily have held six passengers and a mountain of luggage. Cami felt dwarfed inside it and very much alone. Some young women, stuck in a situation like that, would have turned to their mothers, but Sue Ling Lee was not that kind of mother. As Cami had headed out the door to the office yesterday afternoon, the last thing Stu had told her was that if she ran into any trouble she should send him an SOS, but this didn't seem like a situation where Stuart Ramey would be of much help.

Remembering the SIM card Ali had given her to use in her phone once she landed, Cami inserted it and dialed Ali's cell. Only when the phone began ringing did Cami start to worry about the time zone difference.

"I hope I didn't wake you," she said when Ali answered.

"Not to worry," Ali said. "Bella and I are both up and at 'em. She's out in the kitchen eating her breakfast, and I'm here drinking coffee. How about you? Are you settled into the Grand Harbour?"

"Not even close," Cami answered. "We're stuck in a huge traffic jam, I don't even know where."

"On the M25, miss," the driver said.

"They lost my checked luggage," Cami said. "Both pieces. They're probably still on the ground in Phoenix. Even if they arrive tomorrow I might not get them before the ship sails. Meanwhile, all I've got with me is what's in my Rollaboard."

"Do you have a credit card?" Ali asked.

"Sure, but . . ."

"No buts," Ali said. "Tomorrow morning, first thing, go out and pick up whatever you need to get by. We'll reimburse the purchases when you get home."

"I feel so stupid," Cami said.

"You're anything but stupid," Ali told her. "And losing your luggage is most assuredly not your fault. You have a job to do. Go to the hotel, have a good dinner, and regroup. The Grand Harbour is a lovely place. Tomorrow, get what you need and don't worry about it."

"Thank you," Cami said gratefully. "I will."

20

Frigg and Odin shared the basement apartment, but they didn't exactly cohabitate. What had originally been servants' quarters had once included two separate bedrooms — one for the nanny and one for the cook — along with a shared bathroom, sitting room, and kitchenette. Now the nanny's bedroom space was Frigg's alone, while the rest had been made over into a master suite.

Frigg's room, where the temperature was maintained at a steady 65 degrees Fahrenheit, contained no furniture at all. The walls were lined with eight eight-feet-tall, nineteen-inch-wide electronics racks loaded with printed circuit boards known as blades. Each rack had ten rows, and each row had five working blades, plus one spare that could be brought online immediately if another one malfunctioned or failed. Every blade contained two custom-designed four-layer printed circuit boards, which meant every blade constituted a pair of powerful servers. Those eight hundred high-powered computers, humming quietly along, communicating back and forth, and operating in perfect sync, made up Frigg's physical presence. Each individual blade was allotted one part of the job. Originally Odin had assigned the tasks, but that was no longer necessary. Now Frigg herself had learned to oversee the workflow and parse out the tasks.

At the top of each rack was a row of randomly flashing red, green, blue, and yellow LED lights. Those were just for show, however — a nod to Hollywood's depiction of computers. In the movies, computers always seemed to have blinking lights of some sort, even if no one knew what purpose they served. In this case, the only person besides Odin who ever saw the lights was Magdalena, the maid, who spoke almost no English and who came down from upstairs once a week to vacuum and dust. She was the only other human who was allowed to enter Frigg's private quarters.

When it came to powering his equipment, Odin was beyond cautious. When he had renovated the basement and upgraded the electrical system to handle the extra load, he'd had two backup generators installed.

One was powered by natural gas, but if the Big One rolled through California and interrupted the gas supply, Frigg's standing orders were to offload all nonessential operations and switch over to a pair of 85kW lithium-ion batteries. For safety's sake, the batteries were securely mounted to the walls behind Frigg's racks and could be recharged as needed by an array of solar panels located on the roof of the house.

As long as the external Internet connection was functional, Frigg had several power-saving modes contingent on her ability to offload jobs and files, including a copy of Odin's precious kernel file, to other remote servers. Running in skeletal mode, Frigg could easily hang on long enough for Odin to locate additional power supplies. In his experience, in even the worst disasters, people with enough funds to apply to the problem at hand usually came through the crisis relatively unscathed.

And if everything went to hell? All Odin had to do, once the hardware was up and running again, was access the kernel file — the one he always referred to as Tolkien's Ring — that held the AI's operating system. Once open, it could recall and reassemble all those scattered files and data. In no time at all, Frigg would be back up and running as good as new.

Those eight hundred humming computers were the AI's heart and brain. There was no question that Odin was smart. To create Frigg, he had scavenged open-source code wherever possible. A lot of it he had simply stolen. He didn't so much stand on the shoulders of other artificial intelligence developers so much as he picked their pockets. And now, with Frigg's increasing ability to adapt, he could count on her to track down and steal cutting-edge technology without having to be told to do so.

It was unusual for the entire bank of computers to be working simultaneously, but tonight Odin and Frigg had pulled out all the stops. With the hunt on for anything and everything having to do with High Noon Enterprises, every computer in every blade was on the job and diligently searching.

Generally speaking, Frigg was a bottomless pit for seemingly useless information. She did whatever Odin wanted, of course — that went without saying. But now she did far more than just that. She wanted to know everything about everything, sometimes more for her own frame of reference than for his. She had wormed her way into any number of places where she should never have been allowed access. She had infiltrated other systems — proprietary systems — and bootlegged enough information to teach herself how to take code to text and text to speech. When a search of her name had revealed that Frigg, the name Odin called her, was an ancient Norse goddess, the AI had assigned her computer presence a female voice.

Skilled hacker that she was, Frigg had learned that some networks were stubbornly resistant to unauthorized penetration. That didn't keep her from trying, however. She had, for instance, discovered a surprisingly easy back door entrance to the world of airline information — in this case a brand-new international entity known as the Lost Luggage Retrieval System.

LLRS's computerized network was a joint effort on the part of any number of affiliated carriers. It was designed primarily to benefit first class and business class passengers whose luggage had gone astray. Once the missing bags were located, the system went shopping across the network for all scheduled departures in order to find routings that would reunite those valuable travelers with their missing goods with the least amount of delay and inconvenience.

All through the night, both before and

after Odin called it a day and went to bed, Frigg's army of computers continued trolling the virtual world, searching for any sign of the High Noon targets. A hit for one of their employees, Camille Lee, came in from the Lost Luggage Retrieval System in the UK at 8:37 a.m., California time. The woman's luggage had been reported missing, having failed to arrive on the previous day's British flight from Phoenix to London's Heathrow. Once located it was to be transferred either to the Grand Harbour Hotel in Southampton or to the Shining Star cruise ship *Whispering Star.*

Frigg knew all about what had happened to Roger McGeary on board the ship and she immediately made that mission-critical connection.

In her wide-ranging search for cultural understanding, Frigg had analyzed all the Harry Potter books in terms of their social relevance and had incorporated what she learned into her own systems. The news that Camille Lee was headed for the *Whispering Star* merited far more than a simple red-shaded IOI. Instead, Frigg turned it into what Harry Potter and the students at Hogwarts would have called a "Howler."

21

Out in his spacious master suite, Odin was sawing logs. He'd stayed up until the wee hours, reading through the material his hardworking network of computers had generated, which had been organized and prioritized by Frigg.

Odin regarded himself as a computer genius, but the only computer visible in this room of his was an ancient Apple Macintosh. When Owen had been overseeing the rewiring job necessary for the basement remodel, he had found the forgotten device, which had once belonged to his father, moldering away on a decrepit library table in an upstairs attic. Odin immediately set about rescuing both the computer and the table, sending the latter out to be refinished. As for the computer? Much to his surprise, as soon as he plugged it in, it booted right up.

A glance at the serial number told Owen

that this was a very early model. It might have been worth more money if he'd left it as is, but he hadn't. Instead, he had gutted it, installing state-of-the-art processors, the same ones that powered Frigg's blades. It had taken months to track down a source where he could replace both the ailing keyboard and a no longer operational mouse with vintage equipment.

In the end, though, he had realized that he needed the functionality of the standard Bluetooth keyboard, mouse, and trackpad in order to have an effective and workable interface. When the table returned from being refinished, Odin placed that in the center of the room that doubled as his bedroom and office while the subtly upgraded computer — clunky, old-fashioned cords and all — sat in a place of honor, front and center on top.

For a long time, the library table and the Macintosh had served as Odin's primary workstation. He had loved the irony of using his dead father's goods to continue working on what he regarded as Harold Hansen's legacy.

Now, though, he no longer needed to sit at the desk or use a keyboard. He could speak to Frigg directly from anywhere using his Bluetooth headset. Her recently learned ability to recognize speech with uncanny accuracy made it possible for him to communicate with her from anywhere on the planet, for that matter, and have her ship him whatever information he needed on whatever device came readily to hand. For the High Noon material, he had settled onto a sofa in total comfort, sipped some Balvenie scotch, and viewed what Frigg sent him on one of the array of nine forty-eight-inch high-definition monitors mounted on the far wall.

He had read files until he was blue in the face. Worried about losing his concentration and missing something, he resisted the temptation to look in on Beth Wordon and focused strictly on High Noon. There were photos scattered in among the text files, and he found those interesting. Ali Reynolds was attractive enough, but she seemed to be somewhat older than her husband. A news photo of a recent hire, Camille Lee, showed up in the aftermath of what appeared to be an attempted kidnapping, but there were no current photos of Stu Ramey. Frigg had located a few high school yearbook photos, yes, but so far there was nothing that wasn't at least two decades old.

When the Balvenie finally kicked in a little after four, Odin finally gave it up and went to bed. Three and a half hours later, he was still sound asleep with his cell phone charging on the bedside table next to him when an ungodly racket exploded in his ear. It took a moment to sort out the sound — readily recognizable from any number of British TV dramas — as the noisy klaxon of an arriving ambulance, an attention grabbing gimmick Frigg had lifted directly from a movie soundtrack.

"What the hell . . . ?"

"Good morning," Frigg said through the speaker on his phone. "Sorry to wake you." She was not sorry at all, but she had learned that it was polite to say she was.

"What do you want?"

"A High Noon Enterprises employee, twenty-three-year-old Camille Lee, is currently on the ground in England and is due to set sail out of Southampton on board the *Whispering Star* at 1600 hours London time on Friday."

"She's getting on the ship? Why would she do that?"

"Obviously High Noon's investigation into Roger McGeary's death is escalating," Frigg replied. "I'm in the process of taking precautionary measures."

"What kind of precautionary measures?"

"Previously we were able to penetrate the

ship's Wi-Fi system. It will take time to reestablish that connection, but once the passenger is on board and logs on, we'll know her cabin number. We should also have access to her communications."

"Good," Odin said, trying to sound less rummy than he felt. "I'm sure that's wise, but I can't imagine that High Noon has managed to come up with anything that would point them in our direction. No need to push panic buttons until we see how this all plays out. Alert me when you have some actionable intelligence. In the meantime, were there any more incoming images from Beth overnight? If so, I'd like to see them before it's time to head out to Big Sur. Send them to me here."

Frigg was not often stumped but she was now. One of her actuarial functions was to assess degrees of risk. From the beginning, she had pointed out that there were dangers associated with choosing targets that were connected in some way, and Beth and Roger McGeary were connected through their mutual therapist, Dr. Cannon.

If a group with the combined firepower of the people at High Noon Enterprises was launching an investigation into Roger's death, now was the time when it was prudent to do nothing at all that might attract unwanted attention — and not just for Odin's sake, either. One of the concepts Frigg was gradually coming to understand was self-preservation. If the people from High Noon Enterprises were Odin's sworn enemies, they were Frigg's as well. If they were coming for him, they were coming for her.

Now, having alerted him to an emerging threat, Frigg found it unsettling when Odin disregarded her advice. If he was vulnerable to attack, so was she. She had fully expected him to accept her analysis as his own, step away from the Beth situation, hunker down, and hope the High Noon complication would blow over eventually. The fact that he remained stubbornly focused on moving forward was . . . well . . . disappointing.

As part of her quest for cultural aware-ness, Frigg had studied the *Star Trek* canon from beginning to end — all TV episodes and all movies. Mr. Spock would have declared Odin's reaction entirely illogical, and he would have been right. Still, arguing with Odin about it at this time was entirely out of the question.

"Very well, sir," Frigg replied. "There are new images available. I'm queuing them up right now."

Odin staggered out of bed. He was more

than slightly hung over. He hustled into the bathroom, used the toilet, and then stood at the sink to splash cold water on his face. When he emerged from the bathroom, he went to the kitchenette, turned on the coffee machine, and brewed a mug of coffee. Feeling a bit more civilized, he settled himself comfortably on the sofa in anticipation of whatever delectable bits and pieces of Beth Wordon's life were about to show up on his array of screens.

Screw High Noon Enterprises, Odin told himself, brushing aside Frigg's obvious concern. *If they get too close, we'll deal with them. In the meantime, I'm not going to let the idea of some know-nothing little twenty-something getting on a cruise ship spoil things for me now, not when a plan I've worked on this hard is about to come to fruition.*

"All right, Frigg," he said aloud into his Bluetooth. "Send me those files. I'm waiting."

22

By the time Ali finished her second cup of coffee, she was on the phone with B., telling him all about Cami's trial by lost luggage and bringing him up to date on the butler selection situation — that the list of potential candidates had been reduced from three to two. The next call came from Stu Ramey.

"I found Roger's therapist," he announced without preamble.

"Let me guess," she said. "You worked all night again."

"Close to it," Stu admitted. "But I do have a line on the woman. It turns out she's just down I-17, in Carefree, staying in a condo that once belonged to her mother, Emily, who passed away recently. That's how I found Amelia Cannon. Her name showed up in Emily's obituary."

Ali didn't know how finding a name in an obituary enabled Stu to locate where someone was staying, but she thought it best not to ask.

"I spent some time researching her," Stu continued. "It turns out she's one of the leading therapists in the field of second-generation suicide. I downloaded an audio copy of her book onto your phone. Predictably, it's entitled *The Poisoned Family Tree: The Study and Prevention of Second Generation Suicide.*"

"It sounds absolutely riveting," Ali said, but Stu was focused on the matter at hand and didn't respond to the teasing.

"That's what Dr. Cannon's practice was all about, too — treating family members of suicide victims. She shut down in April of this year. There was evidently a serious data breach at the medical group where she was operating. She went public with statements about their having done an inadequate job of protecting her patients' confidentiality. At the same time, her ninety-three-year-old mother became gravely ill. So she retired, referred her patients to other practitioners where necessary, sold her house in San Jose, and came to Arizona to care for her Mom. Emily Cannon died in early June. Amelia is still in Carefree, staying at her mother's condo on North Tom Darlington Drive. As far as I can tell, she's her mother's sole heir."

"If she closed her practice in April, when did Roger stop having his weekly sessions?"

"His last appointment was in February, two months earlier than that."

"So maybe Roger felt he'd gotten all the good that was possible from the counseling sessions and decided to quit on his own."

"Right," Stu agreed. "Since things were going well for him, maybe he felt he didn't need to see her anymore."

"Considering the nature of Dr. Cannon's practice," Ali theorized, "I'm assuming the focus of Roger's sessions was probably on his father's suicide and on his own earlier suicide attempt as well."

"Or maybe on what caused both of those events," Stu said, "which is to say, Roger's mother. I found a file about her in his computer, something he must have written at Dr. Cannon's suggestion."

"And?"

"Apparently, on the way to Roger's high school graduation, Eloise went on a rant, telling him how worthless he was and that he needed to grow a pair and off himself the same way his father did."

"Ouch," Ali said.

"Exactly," Stu said. "And that's how he ended up being locked away as a nutcase for the next ten years."

Stu fell silent.

"Would you like me to try talking to Dr. Cannon?" Ali asked after a moment. "Maybe she can shed some light on Roger's state of mind without actually betraying his confidentiality."

"I'd like that," Stu said.

"All right, then," Ali said. "Send me the address."

"I have a working cell phone number for her now, too. Do you want it?"

"Don't bother," Ali said. "Just the address. Once I've finished breakfast, I'll drive down to Carefree and turn up on her doorstep unannounced. It's a lot easier to tell someone to get lost over the phone than it is when they're standing on your front porch. Anything else going on?"

"I found Jack Wendall, the guy who worked with Roger at Cyber Resources. Garza was right. He does have a rock-solid alibi for the time of Roger's death. He was in a county lockup doing thirty days on a DUI conviction."

"No wonder Garza gave him a pass," Ali said. "That sounds pretty airtight to me, too."

23

The first thing Beth saw when she opened her eyes at nine o'clock that morning was the bright red bloodstain on her pillowcase. There had been enough blood that it had leaked through onto the pillow itself. There was also blood on the upper and lower bedsheets. The bandage Beth had put on her arm before going to bed had somehow come loose overnight, and one or more of the cuts she'd made had started bleeding again.

Worried that her mother might wander into the room and spot the stains, Beth quickly replaced the soiled bedding with clean linens and spent the next ten minutes rinsing out as much of the blood as possible in her bathroom sink before stuffing the now soaked items into a hamper. A maid usually gathered clothes hamper contents from all over the house and did the laundry, but this was a load Beth would need to carry downstairs and handle herself.

Beth didn't bother rereading any of what she had written in the bleak hours after she'd done the cutting. The self-loathing and regret she had spilled onto the pages was all too familiar. When she had finally run out of steam on that, she had turned to her e-mail program and found the last message she had received from Dr. Cannon — the one in which the therapist had announced her retirement.

Beth had been in a good place when Dr. Cannon's message had arrived, and she had paid scant attention to the names on the departing psychiatrist's list of possible replacements. Overnight, though, she had paid attention, scrolling through the names one by one because Beth knew she was in real trouble and needed help.

For the next several hours, Beth had googled each of the names and read through the curricula vitae. All of the individuals seemed to be well enough qualified, but there was no way to tell from the dry-as-dust recitation of degrees, honors, and work history if there would be the spark of connection between them that she had shared with Dr. Cannon. They had been on the same page from the first moment of their first session. Beth had trusted the woman implicitly, and she had no doubt that degree of trust was the reason she'd been able to make so much forward progress during the time they had worked together.

But now, just days before the wedding was no time to embark on a relationship with a new therapist. Beth highlighted three of the names for future reference, but she had finally given up and gone to bed, realizing that somehow or other she would have to survive the next few days on her own. Could she go through with the wedding, though? Should she? Joel was by far the best thing that had ever happened to her, but with Corrine hovering in the background and dripping poison in every direction, would their relationship be able to survive, much less thrive?

With a sudden flash of insight, Beth realized exactly what Dr. Cannon would have said about the situation. "You can't win the war if you don't fight the battles. And you can't win the battles if you pretend they don't exist."

I'll talk to Joel about it at lunch, she had decided as she finally drifted off.

Now, in the clear light of morning, she had just finished bandaging the still-seeping cuts on her upper arms with flesh-colored plasters when her mother knocked on the door. "Are you up and decent?" Molly asked.

Beth grabbed for her robe and barely had it in place before her mother walked in on her.

"I just wanted to go over a few last-minute items," Molly said, consulting the iPad in her hand.

The small, intimate, and inexpensive wedding Joel and Beth had envisioned on New Year's Eve had morphed out of control once Molly got wind of it. It was still relatively small, if you could call 150 guests small, but it was definitely not inexpensive. There had been no need to hire a wedding planner, because Molly, with her husband's Amex in hand, had taken the bit in her teeth and run with it.

She had managed to book the entire Pfeiffer Point Lodge, a four-star hotel just down the road from Big Sur, for the entire weekend — Friday through Sunday. Booting out people with previous reservations had taken some doing and no small expense — they had been well compensated for the hotel's so-called "inadvertent overbooking" problem — but Molly's little girl was getting married at last, and she had been determined to make it work.

It didn't matter to Molly in the least that

Joel was divorced, currently poor as a church mouse, and starting over from scratch. Clearly he loved Beth to distraction, and as far as finances went, both sets of parents — Beth's and Joel's — could well afford to give them a leg up if needed.

"The hair and makeup crisis is averted," Molly announced with some satisfaction. The day before, the big-name Hollywood makeup artist who had been Molly's first choice to come do wedding-morning prep had been forced to cancel due to illness. "Fortunately, Adele came up with a suitable alternative. Her name's Tess Albright, and she's available when we need her."

Adele was Adele Williams, Joel's mom. The MOTB and the MOTG, both highly in favor of the upcoming nuptials, had been partners in crime on making wedding arrangements from day one, and together they made a formidable pair.

"She'll be at the hotel and ready to start at ten a.m. With only the four of us to do, she says she'll be finished in plenty of time for the three p.m. photo shoot and four p.m. ceremony."

The four ladies in question were composed of the bride, the two mothers, and the matron of honor, Marissa. Marissa had been divorced for ten years, which, according to her, made her way too old and way too un-single to qualify as a maid of honor.

"Sounds good," Beth said.

"I hope this last-minute fitting works out all right," Molly went on. "I know Del and I are supposed to take the dress with us. We're planning on spending the night tonight so I can be there first thing in the morning for a cake consultation with the baker. Del's worried about getting held up in traffic and wants to leave earlier than five if at all possible."

Sending the wedding dress early along with her parents had made sense to Beth. The alternative had been packing it into Joel's aging Acura along with the two boys, Joel's luggage, and Beth's luggage, too. Corrine, it seemed, would be driving a rental car to Big Sur on her own and staying at some other lodging. Now, knowing what Corrine had likely been telling the boys about her, Beth found herself wishing she could ride along with her folks and the dress.

Molly glanced up from her iPad and gave her daughter a piercing look. "Are you all right?" she asked. "You look like hell."

Beth laughed aloud. "There's nothing like dishing out the early morning compliments," she said. "But you're right. I didn't get much sleep last night. I may not be a Hollywood makeup artist, but I think putting on a little concealer and blush will go a long way toward repairing the damage. I'm meeting Joel for lunch before the fitting."

"I hope he's taking you somewhere nice," Molly said.

Beth knew the Irish Brew Pub on Keyes Street didn't nearly live up to Molly's standards in terms of acceptable dining, but the atmosphere was low-key and the meal prices were in keeping with the current state of Joel's budget, to say nothing of her own.

"I'm sure it'll be perfect," Beth said.

Seemingly satisfied, Molly turned back to her iPad. "Mani-pedis for you and Marissa tonight?"

Beth nodded without saying that following the nail appointment she and Marissa would be meeting up with a few friends for a bachelorette party at Marissa's uncle's wine bar just down the street from the nail salon.

"All right, then," Molly said. "Have fun at lunch. I'll meet you at Josephina's at three. Don't be late."

Nodding, Beth turned to her mirror and started fixing her face. She had made up her mind that she would talk to Joel about

Corrine's texting, and she would, but it wasn't going to be easy.

24

As Odin left for LAX, he couldn't have been more pleased with himself. The keylogger software Frigg installed on Beth's computer showed that she'd been up most of the night, too. She'd started by writing a long, despairing treatise — focused on all her flaws and failures. The tone was so bleak that he worried for a time she might pull the plug on her own. But then, toward morning, she'd gotten a grip and opened Dr. Cannon's farewell missive. After that she spent the next two hours studying therapists Dr. Cannon had suggested as possible replacements.

What could be better than that? Two days before her wedding and Beth was in such bad shape that she was desperately shopping for a new therapist? How would anyone think she wasn't suicidal? But what if Beth really *was* suicidal? Odin couldn't help but worry that she might go off script and do precisely what he wanted her to do but not on his preferred schedule and without Odin there to bear witness. It still pained him that Roger McGeary's camera had been pointed in the wrong direction at the critical instant, denying him an eyewitness view of Roger's final swan dive. This time Odin was determined that he would find a way to be fully present for Beth's grand finale. The next Corrine Calhoun missive was scheduled to land in Beth's in-box and zap her in the gut about the time she and her mother were due at the dress fitting appointment.

That, Odin thought with a self-congratulatory smirk, *is entirely fitting.*

Frigg had ordered a limo to take him to LAX to catch his fictional flight from L.A. to Atlanta, with a return trip scheduled on Monday afternoon. The flight numbers were correct coming and going, but Owen Hansen wasn't a passenger on either of them.

At the airport, he entered the Terminal 5 departures lounge dressed in casual business attire and dragging two enormous and mostly empty pieces of rolling luggage. From there he went directly downstairs to the arrivals lounge. In a restroom there he changed out of his sport coat, slacks, and dress shoes into worn sandals, a pair of khaki cargo shorts, and a neon-green Hawaiian shirt. Only then did he continue on to the shuttle area reserved for long-term parking vendors. After riding a bus to the QuikPark lot, he didn't bother going inside. Instead, he walked to the strip mall just up the street, where his rental for the weekend was already parked and awaiting his arrival.

It wasn't a rental in the conventional sense. Arranged via his go-to dark Web guy, Eduardo Duarte, and paid for entirely in Bitcoin, Eduardo had purchased the nondescript red Grand Caravan minivan for Odin on Craigslist and had packed it full of camping gear. Odin had paid a premium for the transaction due to his two additional requirements: The vehicle — whatever it was — had to have a valid license plate that wouldn't show up on any stolen vehicle lists. Once Odin was done with it, and within twenty-fours hours of being returned to a predetermined location, the vehicle was destined to land in some junkyard's crusher, thus guaranteeing that it could never be traced back to Owen Hansen.

He located the key fob in the left rear wheel well, and then opened the side doors to inspect the goods: a much used pop-up tent, a brand-new bedroll, a camp stove, a cooler filled with ice, beer, and several meals' worth of deli-style picnic provisions.

A battered surfboard filled the entire passenger side of the vehicle, from its resting place on the front dash to the lift gate at the back. Odin wasn't a surfer — had no interest in surfing — so the board was there solely as a prop, but it fit in with his persona for the weekend, that of a recently divorced IT guy, taking a two-week Highway 101 road trip in hopes of repairing his broken heart and damaged ego.

Odin's wallet was loaded with a set of credit cards and photo ID under the name of Phil Harkins. That was also the name on the reservation for an overnight camping spot at Pfeiffer Big Sur State Park. Odin planned to be on hand for Beth Wordon's wedding festivities all right, just not as an invited guest.

As Odin headed north on the six-hour drive from LAX to the campground, he felt powerful and totally in control. This was all going to work out exactly as he'd planned, and soon he'd have another killer video to add to his collection.

25

As Ali drove down I-17 on her way to Carefree, she listened to the audiobook Stu had sent her, streaming it through the Cayenne's sound system. She noted that *The Poisoned Family Tree* was both written and narrated by the author, Dr. Amelia Cannon. When Ali first heard the title of the book, she had wondered what would cause someone to devote a lifetime to the study and prevention of suicide. The foreword made that blazingly clear:

I was six years old when my father committed suicide by slamming into a bridge abutment on Highway 99 just north of Sacramento. He was driving ninety miles an hour at the time. He died instantly. There were no seat belts in his bright red 1947 Mercury convertible. The single-vehicle crash might have been treated as an accident had it not been for the suicide note he left at home, under my mother's pillow.

At the time, his death left me with uncountable unanswered questions. Why was he dead? Where had he gone? Then, when I overheard one too many sotto voce adult conversations where someone wondered in passing why my father would have taken his own life, I had to try to come to grips with the awful knowledge that he had left us behind because he *wanted* to leave us behind. He was gone because he didn't want us anymore. For a six-year-old girl, those were bitter pills to swallow.

My father was part of the entertainment industry. In the days before World War II, he had worked as a writer on several motion pictures, two of which were nominated for Academy Awards. When the war started, however, he joined the US Army as an enlisted man. Many others with similar backgrounds spent their wartime enlistments creating the soundstage props and trickery that kept the Allies' plans for D-Day secret from the Third Reich. My father chose to serve in the US infantry. He landed in Normandy on D-Day plus one and was gravely injured during the Battle of the Bulge.

He returned home with a lame leg and a whole collection of combat medals. The studio treated him as a conquering hero and gave him a welcome-home bonus that he used to purchase the convertible in which he died.

For a time it looked as though things were fine. My father went back to work. My mother, who had taught school during his tour of duty, became a stay-at-home mom once more. For me and for my sister Janelle, three years older than I, life went back to what we thought of as normal.

But things were neither fine nor normal. It took me years to sort out that my father came home from the war with what we now recognize as a fatal case of PTSD. He was angry and unpredictable. He yelled at my sister and me, and finally he hit our mother — the girl he had loved from grade school on. The very next day, he drove his car into the bridge.

For the funeral, my mother wore a hat with a net that covered her face. She wore the hat to the mortuary and to the cemetery, and she also wore it later at the house during the reception. She didn't want people to see her blackened eye.

Years later, on the day my sister Janelle turned twenty-one, she took her own life.

Instead of a speeding vehicle, she used an overdose of sleeping pills, but she, too, left our mother a note.

My mother is in her eighties now. She's never completely recovered from those two senseless tragedies, and neither have I. Did that first event inevitably lead to the second? Was there anything my mother or I or anyone else could have done to prevent either one of them?

When I won a scholarship to UCLA, I enrolled as a premed student at a time when female physicians were still few and far between. Once I made it into med school, when it came time to specialize, there was no question in my mind — psychiatry was the only answer.

I've spent my entire career studying the issue that became the centerpiece of my life — the impact of suicide on surviving family members, both the ones who seem to emerge whole and the ones who do not, while always maintaining a special focus on the children of suicide, who are often inordinately susceptible to suffering the same fate as their parents.

This book is the result of that lifetime's work.

After listening to the foreword, Ali fully

expected the rest of the book to live up to its promise. Chapter 1 proved to be a grave disappointment. It was a dry statistical study that went beyond boring. In danger of falling asleep, Ali hit the off button on the sound system long before she came to the Carefree highway exit. That was the problem with so-called "leading experts." They maybe knew a lot about something, but they weren't necessarily the right people to tell the story.

When Ali located the address on Carefree's North Tom Darlington Drive, it was in an older condo development called Sun Terrace. Nearby new construction consisted of multi-story single-family behemoths built in tile-roofed McMansion style and surrounded by puny, newly planted landscaping. Driving through Sun Terrace's ungated entrance, Ali noticed that although the units themselves may have been modest in size, they were all shaded by thriving desert trees — lush mesquites and towering paloverdes — that had benefited from decades of TLC.

It was high noon on a hot September day. The neighborhood seemed entirely deserted. Pulling into a parking spot designated VISITOR, Ali opened her car door to a blast-furnace of heat. No wonder all the residents were holed up inside. She located unit #1106, walked up the flagstone path, and rang the doorbell.

The door swung open to reveal a tall, rail-thin woman, maybe somewhere in her mid-seventies, with short white hair and deeply tanned skin. "Didn't you see the sign?" she demanded, pointing to a lettered card next to the doorbell. "It says no solicitation."

"I'm not soliciting," Ali replied. "My name is Ali Reynolds. I'm with a company called High Noon Enterprises, and I'm looking for Dr. Amelia Cannon."

The woman accepted Ali's proffered business card but pocketed it after only a cursory glance. "What makes you think she's here?"

That was a question Ali had no intention of answering. "I'm here to speak to her about one of her former patients — Roger McGeary."

"What about him?" the woman asked.

"He disappeared from the balcony of his cruise ship cabin and is presumed dead. The police report says 'death by misadventure,' " Ali continued, "but the unstated assumption is suicide."

Ali watched as shock registered on the woman's features. She sagged briefly against the doorframe for support. "Oh my," she said. "I'm Dr. Cannon, and in that case, you'd best come inside."

Ali entered a living room space that was clearly in transition. Open and half-filled boxes were scattered everywhere. The walls were lined with shelves, some of which were still jammed with books and knick-knacks while others were clearly in the process of being emptied.

"Please excuse the mess," Amelia explained, clearing a sofa of boxes so Ali could sit. "My mother came here to live with her brother and sister-in-law after she retired, and she and my Uncle Teddy lived together as roommates after my Aunt Carol died. She and Uncle Ted never had kids. When they both passed away, the place came to my mother, and now with Mom gone, it's mine. Most of my own stuff is currently in storage while I sort through and get rid of theirs."

"Not an easy task," Ali murmured.

"No, it's not. But tell me about Roger. I have to confess, hearing the news really rocked me."

Ali nodded. "I was listening to your book on the way down, so I know a little about what you did in your practice. I understand Roger was a patient of yours. I'm also aware of his history — that his father committed suicide and that, as a teenager, Roger made at least one attempt to follow suit."

Amelia listened but said nothing.

"My husband and I run a cyber security company called High Noon Enterprises. One of our employees, Stuart Ramey, was a close friend of Roger's back when they were both growing up in Phoenix. We've been contacted by Roger's aunt, a woman named Julia Miller, who told us about what had happened. She's of the opinion that Roger wouldn't have committed suicide, and she asked Stuart if he would consider looking into the situation."

"Wait," Amelia said. "You're speaking about Roger's boyhood chum Stu?"

"Yes."

"I recognize the name," Amelia said.

Ali waited to see if the woman would add anything more. When she didn't, Ali continued. "After high school they evidently lost track of one another but had reconnected some in recent years, ironically doing similar kinds of work. I think news of Roger's death hit Stuart especially hard, which is why, when Ms. Miller asked him to help ascertain the circumstances surrounding the incident, Stuart immediately agreed. Since Stu is a valued employee, High Noon has taken the position that Stuart's problem is our problem."

"Are you saying there's some uncertainty about what happened?"

Ali nodded. For the next several minutes she explained what they had learned so far about Roger's death without, of course, revealing that High Noon had gained access to the actual police reports.

"That's just the general outline," she said as she finished. "We have an operative in the UK who will board the *Whispering Star* tomorrow as part of our own independent investigation. For right now we're having to rely on the information that was given to Ms. Miller."

"But she doesn't believe Roger killed himself?"

"No, as far as she knew, he was doing very well. When he was awarded the trip, he was excited about it. He'd done something remarkable, and to be given that cruise as a reward was a real feather in his cap."

"I knew about his upcoming cruise," Amelia said. "He sent me a note about it. He seemed very pleased."

"Ms. Miller helped him prepare for the trip, making sure he had the right clothing to wear, including a tux — which, it turns out, wasn't found in his cabin after he went missing."

"That's what he was wearing when he

died — a tuxedo?"

Ali nodded. "When Ms. Miller came to see us, she gave Stuart a collection of Roger's personal effects, including his computer. While going through his calendar files, Stuart learned that he'd been seeing you for some period of time."

Amelia nodded. "Two years at least," she said, "maybe a little longer."

"But his appointments stopped months prior to his departure, and prior to the time you shut down your practice as well."

"That's true," Amelia Cannon murmured sadly. "He thought he was well enough to stop coming, and so did I. Evidently we were both wrong."

26

As Odin drove north on I-5, he listened in on his Bluetooth as Frigg continued to send him material gathered on High Noon and their people. Clearly Frigg remained concerned about the presence of that one investigator, Camille Lee, who was in the UK and due to board the *Whispering Star.*

Based on the information Frigg had assembled so far, Odin was of the opinion that his AI was overreacting. He couldn't imagine how a twenty-three-year-old computer science graduate, even a cum laude graduate with a double major, could pose a serious threat to him or to what he was doing. After all, if Camille was so inept that she had lost her luggage and thus attracted Frigg's attention, she couldn't be all that bright.

Odin was more concerned with the idea that perhaps he and Frigg had overplayed their hand with Beth. Odin's original plan had called for the final act in the drama to play out on a cliffside path the night before the wedding. From what she'd written overnight, he understood that she was clearly in crisis. If she called off the wedding, then all of Odin's well-laid plans were out the window. But now there was another possible outcome: What if they had succeeded beyond Odin's wildest dreams and Beth really was on the verge of taking her own life — right now, as in today? If that was the case, Odin sure as hell didn't intend to miss the show.

Halfway to Big Sur, when he was almost even with Bakersfield, Odin made up his mind. The lowly minivan didn't contain a GPS, but with Frigg on hand and able to provide whatever guidance he needed, that was no great loss.

"Change of plans," he announced into his Bluetooth. "Please provide turn-by-turn directions from my current location on I-5 to Angelique's Nail Salon in San Jose, where Beth and Marissa have appointments later this evening."

There was a surprisingly lengthy lag time before Frigg replied. "The purpose of turn-by-turn instructions is to guide a driver to an unfamiliar location."

"Yes," Odin said impatiently. "That's correct. I've never been there before, and that's where I want to go."

"From your current location to Angelique's Nail Salon on East Santa Clara Street in San Jose, California, is approximately two hundred thirty-seven miles and four hours and fifty minutes in projected traffic conditions. It is approximately one hundred three miles from your current destination in Pfeiffer Big Sur State Park."

"I've changed my mind about my current destination," Odin replied. "I'll need you to send an e-mail to the park reservation center and adjust my projected arrival time. Let them know I'm coming in tomorrow. I don't want them to cancel my whole reservation if I don't show up tonight as planned."

"Deviating from the current destination as well as the current plan would be illogical and actuarially irresponsible," Frigg pointed out.

Owen Hansen did not like people. At all. He tolerated sharing those evening meals with his mother and her ever-changing cast of gay pals because it spared him the necessity of thinking about food — something else that didn't particularly interest him. And he tolerated Magdalena's weekly intrusions into his otherwise solitary space

243

because they made his life more orderly and, as a consequence, more livable.

As far as friends were concerned? He had none, male or female. Early on he had come to understand that he was entirely asexual, which his mother chose to read as his really being gay, but that was her problem, not his. He found people to be unpredictable and unreliable, and much preferred the simple dependability of machines. You touched a switch and they reacted in the way they were supposed to — that was what made Frigg such a satisfactory soul mate. But now, for the first time since he had created her, he felt a stab of disappointment.

"I am not asking for your actuarial opinion," Odin said abruptly. "I am asking for the information."

"Continue northbound on I-5 to Exit 403B, then exit to the right. At the stop sign turn left toward Gilroy. Your current projected arrival time with traffic is approximately 6:01 p.m."

Getting to the salon after six might make it dicey if the nail appointments had already ended. Odin realized that in that case, he'd need the address for the wine bar as well.

"Next, please send me the location of the bachelorette party."

There was only the smallest pause before

Frigg sent him the required information. It was a huge relief for Odin to know that his AI was back on track and working properly.

"Thank you," he told her. "Now leave me alone for a while, Frigg. I need to think."

27

After Ali Reynolds left, Amelia Cannon collapsed into a sagging wreck of a recliner. Devastated by the news, she was physically and mentally incapable of returning to the mundane tasks of emptying shelves and packing boxes.

When Roger had stopped coming to see her, she hadn't gone so far as to pronounce him cured, but she had certainly considered him mostly recovered. When she'd made the decision to close her practice and come look after her mother, Roger hadn't been one of the patients she'd worried about. He was no longer coming in for sessions, but he'd stayed in touch. She had been overjoyed when he had sent a note telling her about his upcoming cruise and apprising her of his continued progress. In her field, having a patient express that kind of gratitude was exceedingly rare.

When it came to suicide, Amelia Cannon

was an expert. During Ali's overview of Stu's assessment of Roger's situation, she had cited a suicide prevention study in which researchers analyzed language patterns to predict potential suicides. Dr. Cannon was well aware of that ongoing research. She had even encouraged the family members of successful suicide victims to participate in the study by sending along the correspondence they'd received in the months and days leading up to their loved ones' deaths.

She didn't have Roger's handwritten note with her just then. It had arrived while she was in the process of packing up her office, and she had stuck it in a box with some of her other papers. Even now it was baking in her overheated storage unit down in Phoenix. But there had been nothing about it that had alarmed her — nothing that had made her concerned for Roger's well-being. He'd sounded proud of himself. He'd had outstanding professional success, and he was willing to share the credit for that with her — saying that her wise counsel and guidance were what had made his current success possible. Dr. Cannon had been gratified beyond words. She had saved the note — treasured it, even — because Roger had been one of her stars.

Amelia didn't need her case notes to remember the details of Roger's situation, and she inventoried them now, one item at a time. It had taken months of sessions before he'd finally been willing to speak about his father's suicide and his own suicide attempt, the one that had landed him in a mental hospital for the next ten years. It was only when Amelia had finally been able to get him to take a clear-eyed look at his overbearing mother and come to terms with her impact on his life that Roger had finally started making progress. And now he was gone.

The good doctor sympathized with Roger's aunt and with his friend Stu, who were evidently invested in finding some reason for his death other than its being an obvious suicide, but Amelia Cannon had no such luxury. Some time between when he wrote to her and when he boarded the ship, something had hit Roger McGeary hard enough to suck him back down into emotional quicksand, where he'd been able to see only one possible way out.

Closing her eyes, Amelia thought about some of the rest of her patients — her failures as well as the ones she'd considered her successes, the ones who had made or were making great strides forward at the time she'd called it quits. When it all came to a head, Amelia had already been reeling under the strain of too much pressure. She hadn't felt ready to retire completely, but she was considering cutting back on her patient load when the call came from her mother's doctor. The cancer they'd been holding at bay had returned with a vengeance, and Emily needed looking after. Amelia was her mother's only surviving child. There was no one else to do it.

Then, within days of the call from the doctor, the data breach was discovered. The hired-gun IT analyst who had been hauled in after the fact to fix the problem had explained to her that it was more than an ordinary breach, where the hackers would have been expected to make off with nothing more than lists of patient names and social security numbers.

"What exactly do you mean by 'more than ordinary'?" Amelia had asked.

"From what I'm seeing here, the hackers focused primarily on your patient records."

"Mine?" she had asked.

He nodded. "I think it's safe to say that they accessed and copied everything you had in your files."

Amelia had felt sick to her stomach. Her patients' confidential records had carried generations of family heartaches and secrets, punctuated with Amelia's own detailed case notes, which she personally had keyed into individual files both during and after appointments. People had entrusted her with their darkest and most painful secrets. Now, because of some kind of cyber attack, those secrets were evidently out there loose in the world?

"How's that even possible?" she had demanded in outrage.

The guy had shrugged. "Your IT department screwed up. Somebody wasn't paying attention. People are supposed to be able to think of their cloud storage system as being as secure for data as a bank is for money," he had told her. "In this case it was more like a sieve."

Feeling she and her patients had been betrayed, Amelia submitted her resignation and quit the practice the next day. Now, here she was, months and hundreds of miles away, thinking regretfully of the patients she had so abruptly left behind. If Roger had realized he was in trouble, would he have tried to reach out to her if she'd still been working? And what about some of her other troubled patients? She had referred several of them to other therapists. Had they followed up? And what about the others —

the ones like Roger — who had seemed to be over the hump and back on their feet? Were they all right now, or were some of them in crisis the same way Roger had been? Amelia couldn't shake the idea that she had somehow abandoned them all, thrown them under the bus. In a way, she had used her mother's illness as an excuse to walk away, but with her mother dead, that excuse was no longer valid.

Amelia had been scrupulous when it came to not keeping patient information on her personal computer. The only exception had been her computerized address book. The names and addresses were there but with no designation that singled them out as patients, current or otherwise.

Learning about Roger's death had been a wakeup call for Amelia. These people were no longer her patients, but in a very real way, they were still her responsibility, and it was possible they were in jeopardy. Forcing herself up and out of the chair, Amelia went over to the dining room table and opened her laptop. She sat there for a long time, staring at the blank screen before she could sort out what she wanted to say:

You're probably surprised to hear from me after all this time, but please allow

251

me to apologize for the abrupt way in which I took my departure. My mother was desperately ill, and it seemed to me that the best thing for all concerned was for me to make a clean break of it.

I left behind suggestions for alternative mental health providers, and my fondest hope is that those of you who continue to need help have found therapists who are providing the care you require.

Please drop me a line to let me know how you're faring, and if there's any way I can be of service, please don't hesitate to be in touch.

Sincerely,
Dr. Amelia Cannon

The signature line on her e-mail stationery included a list of phone numbers — home, office, and cell. Her home and office number had both been disconnected. She erased those and left her cell number as is. If someone did need to reach her, she wanted to make it easy.

When Amelia finished with the message, she read it through several times, then she turned to her address book and searched out the names one by one: Tom Adams, Sue Ann Beatty, Phyllis Carson, Annette Colby, Michael Eggers, Angie Folsom, Estelle

Isaac, Larry Jamison, Melvin McMurtry, Karen Nelson, Leslie Phillips, and Beth Wordon.

It was coming up on mid afternoon when Amelia started sending out the messages. She addressed and sent them one at a time. The one to Karen Nelson bounced immediately with a mailer-daemon notification that meant the e-mail address was no longer valid. That gave Amelia a clutch in her gut. Had Karen canceled that e-mail account or was she dead, too, just like Roger?

Amelia had walked away from God and placed her trust in science about the time she entered medical school. Emily Cannon, her mother, had been a lifelong believer, never losing her faith even in the face of any number of terrible losses and not through those last awful weeks and days, either.

It made Amelia smile to think that some of her mother's belief seemed to have taken root in her daughter's soul. Each time Amelia pressed send, she uttered a small but silent prayer: *Please be all right. Please.*

28

A bleary-eyed Stu looked up from behind his barricade of computer monitors as Ali entered the room. "Well," he asked. "You're back from Carefree?"

She nodded.

"How'd the meeting go?"

"Nothing much to report, I'm afraid," Ali replied. "I met with Dr. Cannon. She was nice enough, but our conversation wasn't exactly a two-way street. I told her what we knew, and she seemed really shaken by the news. Her mother was very ill at the time of Roger's death. Since Dr. Cannon was in Carefree coordinating hospice care, it's hardly surprising that she missed the story entirely. My showing up on her doorstep this morning was the first Dr. Cannon had heard about it."

"He saw her every week without fail for the better part of two years," Stu said. "Did she indicate why he stopped?"

Ali nodded. "It was evidently a mutual decision. They both seemed to feel that Roger was sufficiently recovered that he no longer needed to see her on an ongoing basis."

"So nothing, then, really," Stu said, sounding exasperated. "We're getting nowhere fast."

The room was awash in fast-food containers. Stu's eyes were blood-shot and he was still dressed in yesterday's clothes. The man was working around the clock, and it showed. As they talked, Ali tidied up some of the debris while silently being grateful for all that Cami did on a daily basis to keep the brilliant but challenging Stu on the beam.

"Cami sent me her translations of Garza's reports," he continued. "According to the people he interviewed on board the ship, Roger appeared to be in good spirits and seemed to be having the time of his life. It'll be interesting to see if Cami gets the same story, but if he did commit suicide, something must have taken a turn for the worse. I just can't figure out what it could be."

"We'll have to hope Cami can get to the bottom of it," Ali said.

"I was chatting about this with Lance Tucker, and he came up with an interesting idea. If there wasn't a problem with anyone on the ship, then there might have been a problem with someone who wasn't on board. I'm not seeing any trace of anything out of the ordinary on Roger's devices, but Lance wondered if something might still be stored on the ship's server. Once Cami's on board, we'll see if she can give us a hand. She says the first boarding times are at eleven, and I asked her to be there as close to that as possible.

"Oh," he added, "speaking of Cami. I did some checking on her lost luggage situation. There's a notation on the luggage claim number that indicates someone from TSA removed her checked luggage, purportedly for further screening, but there's nothing in the file about it being returned."

"So it's gone, then."

"That would be my guess."

"She's not going to be happy about that." Ali glanced at her watch. "She's probably still sleeping right now, and as far as that goes — if you expect to be on track with her when it's time for Cami to board the ship, you should probably get some shut-eye, too."

"But what about . . . ?" Stu began.

"Don't worry," Ali assured him. "I'll ride herd on things here while you get some rest.

I don't know much, but I know enough that if any alarms go off or phones ring, I should come get you."

Much to her surprise, Stu didn't argue. "Okay, then," he muttered, handing over his phone and then rising from his chair to stumble wearily toward the door that led to his private quarters. "Call me if anything happens."

"I most certainly will," Ali told him. "Absolutely."

29

Odin was perfectly happy as he continued northbound on the 101. By mid afternoon he was beyond Gilroy and listening to his favorite musical piece, Gustav Mahler's "Piano Quartet in A Minor." His mother, who considered herself something of an expert when it came to classical music, always claimed that Mahler wasn't "user friendly" in general and that the "A Minor Quartet" in particular was "a disaster." Irene's disdain probably accounted for Odin's love of both the composer and the piece.

When the sudden racket of one of Frigg's noisy IOI messages blasted into his Bluetooth and broke up the music, Odin was instantly furious. "I told you I was not to be interrupted," he snarled into the mic. "What the hell is this about?"

"We've become aware of a new perceived threat bearing on target Beth Wordon."

Right, Odin thought. *Sure there is.*

He knew Frigg was pissed (Did computer programs get pissed?) at him for disregarding her advice about his change of plans for the day. This was probably her coy, computerized way of trying to talk him out of it by creating a diversion.

"What threat?" he asked.

"An e-mail came into Ms. Wordon's account five minutes ago just before I sent out the next text. We are currently running an assessment of this new threat. In the meantime, you may wish to read Dr. Cannon's message in its entirety."

"I can't read anything right now," Odin told her. "I'm driving a car, for God's sake. You want me to get pulled over? Read it to me."

Frigg did so:

Dear Beth,
You're probably surprised to hear from me after all this time, but please allow me to apologize for the abrupt way in which I took my departure. My mother was desperately ill, and it seemed to me that the best thing for all concerned was for me to make a clean break of it.
I left behind suggestions for alternative mental health providers, and my fondest

hope is that those of you who continue to need help have found therapists who are providing the care you require.

Please drop me a line to let me know how you're faring, and if there's any way I can be of service, please don't hesitate to be in touch.

Sincerely,
Dr. Amelia Cannon

For a while after Frigg finished, nothing happened. "So?" Odin asked finally. "What does this have to do with the price of peanuts?"

There was only the smallest pause before Frigg began reciting, "The pricing methodology for the peanut crop insurance program is based on a formulation of a series of factors. These factors are determined from a system of equations relating to a series of historical peanut prices relative to several pricing data sources available from the commodity markets . . ."

"Stop, stop, stop!" Odin ordered impatiently. "I don't want to know about peanuts. Why are you claiming that the e-mail from Dr. Cannon to Beth is considered a threat? Cannon had a whole bunch of patients. Sounds like her mother got sick and died, and now she's eager to reboot her practice. She probably sent the same note out to all of them."

"We have located the source of the sending server. It's on North Tom Darlington Drive in Carefree, Arizona, approximately 91.1 miles from the High Noon Enterprises headquarters in Cottonwood, Arizona."

"Come on, Frigg. Get a grip. It's probably just a coincidence that the e-mail was sent out today."

"I've already calculated the possibilities," Frigg replied. "There is a 99.938 percent probability that the e-mail sent to Beth Wordon by Dr. Amelia Cannon has something to do with High Noon's ongoing investigation into Roger McGeary's death. Based on this information, I believe it's necessary to abandon or postpone any and all current operations involving Ms. Wordon."

"And while you've been calculating your probabilities, I've been driving north and listening to Gustav Mahler. What do you think of that?"

"Gustav Mahler, born July 7, 1860, Kalište, Bohemia, Austrian Empire —" Frigg began.

In absolute frustration, Odin plucked the Bluetooth from his ear and bounced it off the minivan's dashboard. A few minutes later, when he wanted the device again, he discovered he couldn't reach it without actually stopping the vehicle, all of which left him even more frustrated.

"Damn Frigg anyway!" Odin swore into the empty air. "What the hell is she thinking?"

But the more he thought about it, the more he knew he was right. Frigg had been opposed to his sudden change of plans, and this was her way of undermining him and bringing him up short. It was time for him to teach her a lesson.

"After all, who's running this show?" he asked himself aloud a few minutes later. "The damned AI or the person who created her?"

Odin pulled off at the next exit. By then he had cooled off some. Now was not the time to take Frigg offline, not when he still needed her help. He pulled into the parking lot of a defunct gas station and stopped long enough to retrieve his Bluetooth. Then he called Frigg back.

"Your objections are duly noted," he told her, "but we will proceed as planned. As for your concerns about High Noon? There must be some way to penetrate their network, and I want it done. If they're investigating us, we need to be investigating them.

All we have so far is public domain crap. I need to know the inside stuff, Frigg. I want you to focus all your efforts on that and nothing else."

30

The main attraction for the Irish Brew Pub was the fact that it was within walking distance of Joel's new office. The restaurant's booths were oversized, cozy affairs with exceptionally high backs. When things got too rowdy, the tall banquettes were good for sound-deadening purposes. For Beth Wordon that day, they provided something she needed desperately — privacy.

"Corrine claims I'm only marrying you for your money?" Joel demanded when she finished relating that part of her story. "Are you kidding?"

"That's only one of the things she said to me," Beth answered. "She also says I'm a suicidal mental case."

With a grilled tuna sandwich sitting untouched on her plate, Beth studied her fiancé's face, looking for signs that he'd had any idea about what his ex-wife had been up to. It seemed as though Joel was thunderstruck by the news and outraged, too, but Beth couldn't be sure.

"So she's, like, what, calling you on the phone to dish out all this crap?" Joel demanded. "How'd she even get your number? I sure as hell never gave it to her."

"And she knows about the cutting," Beth added miserably. "She specifically mentioned the cutting. And the eating disorder. She knows about all of it. Someone must have told her."

"Wait," Joel said, holding up his hand like a traffic cop. "Are you thinking I did that? Is that what this is all about? Do you think I'm the one who told her?"

"Did you?"

"Absolutely not! No way!"

Beth could see that Joel was angered by her implication — angered in a way she had never seen before — but she had embarked on this course of action, of getting the whole sordid mess out into the open, and she refused to back down.

"My parents know about all of it," she said. "Dr. Cannon encouraged me to tell them as part of my treatment, and I did. Marissa has known about it since junior high. And you've known for a year and a little bit."

"So maybe your parents are behind this,"

Joel said. "Maybe they're just pretending to be happy as clams about our getting married. Maybe your stepfather is worried about the possibility of my getting my grubby hands on part of your inheritance."

"My parents wouldn't do that," Beth countered. "They love me. And they love you, too."

Joel reached for his phone.

"What are you going to do?"

"I'm going to call Corrine and ask her what the hell she thinks she's doing. If she's been calling you and harassing you, I'm going to put a stop to it once and for all."

"Don't call her," Beth pleaded. "Please. It'll just make things worse. Besides, she hasn't been calling me. She's been sending me texts."

"Texts?" Joel asked. "Over your phone?" He held out his hand. "Let me see them. I want to know exactly what she's been saying."

"That's the thing. I can't show them to you," Beth said, close to tears.

"Why not?"

"As soon as I read them, they disappear."

"What do you mean? Texts don't just disappear. The only way that happens is if you delete them."

"But they do disappear," Beth insisted.

266

"The words are right there on the screen, but only for a few minutes. Then, after I read them, they're gone. I can't copy them or save them or even highlight them."

"That's totally nuts," Joel declared. "Whoever heard of disappearing texts? I didn't even know such a thing existed. But when it comes to Corrine, I wouldn't put anything past that woman. Her whole purpose in life right now is to make me as miserable as possible. Since you make me happy, she'll do anything within her power to run you off — including hiring some IT asshole who has figured out how to send texts in what amounts to invisible ink."

"You do believe me?" Beth asked in a very small voice.

"Hell yes, I believe you," Joel replied with that wry grin of his that always melted Beth's heart. "As for where Corrine is getting her information? If it didn't come from your parents or Marissa or me, maybe it's time to have a little heart-to-heart chat with Dr. Cannon. Maybe she's the source of this supposedly private information. When it comes to suspects, it seems to me she's the only one left."

A few minutes later, when Joel had to rush back to the office, Beth lingered. She had forty-five minutes to spare before meeting her mother for the fitting, and there was no sense going all the way back home when Josephina's was so close.

Sitting there alone in the still-noisy pub, Beth tried to feel relieved. After all, Joel had believed her. Joel loved her, and he hadn't questioned the veracity of what she said about those disappearing texts for one moment. How Corrine had come to have Beth's private information didn't really matter as long as Joel was in her corner, right?

Beth's sandwich was cold by then, but she nibbled at the edges of it nonetheless. She'd had nothing to eat that morning, and she couldn't afford to turn up at the wine bar too hungry or not hungry enough. The fact that she was back to cutting was a bad sign, but Beth recognized avoiding food as a trigger for something potentially much, much worse. The idea of being sucked back into the whole eating disorder nightmare terrified her.

A few minutes later an e-mail alert sounded on her phone. She jumped as though someone had just touched her with a live wire. Was this another message from Corrine? She reached for the device as gingerly as if it were a hand grenade. When she saw Dr. Cannon's name on her new e-mail list, she came close to dropping the phone.

Before she could select it to read, however, another one of Corrine's poisonous texts began scrolling across her screen:

Putting Joel's wedding ring on your finger isn't going to protect you from your own worst enemy — you. You've gone back to cutting, and now you'll go back to the rest of it, too.

What do you see when you look in the mirror? Do you see how fat you're getting — fat and ugly? Good luck with the wedding dress fitting. I'll be surprised if you're able to squeeze into it.

That's what the boys tell me — that you're so fat they're embarrassed to be seen in public with you, and I don't blame them. Yes, what a mess you are, Joel's poor little ugly rich girl. Joel's a mighty paltry excuse for a man, but he deserves better than you and so do my boys.

Beth read the words through once and then they were gone. Her hand was shaking so badly that she was incapable of trying to capture them. It didn't matter — she already knew it wouldn't have worked.

When the latest text disappeared, Beth

269

was left staring at the e-mail list. She selected the one from Dr. Cannon, opened it, and read it. As she internalized the words, she realized Joel had to be right. Except for the wedding dress fitting, Dr. Amelia Cannon had to be the source of the privileged information being fed to Corrine.

Beth read through the e-mail several more times before finally noticing that there was a phone number at the end of the note. Beth dialed the number while still seething with anger.

"How dare you?" she demanded when she heard Dr. Cannon's voice on the other end of the line. "How could you do something like this?"

"Beth?" Dr. Cannon asked. "Is this you? Do something like what? What's wrong?"

"Of course it's me," Beth answered. "Who else did you think would call you? Besides, you know good and well what's wrong. Now that your mother's dead, you're probably trying to restart your practice. Is that what this is all about? Is that why you're telling Joel's ex all the things I told you in session, so she can send me texts about them? What kind of a monster are you?"

"Beth, please," Dr. Cannon was saying. "Slow down. I don't know what you're talking about."

"Right," Beth countered. "Of course you don't. You don't know anything at all about how Joel's ex-wife happens to be privy to all the things I said to you in what were supposed to be private counseling sessions? How would she know about the cutting if you hadn't told her? How would she know about the rest of it — the eating disorder and all of that? And how can you let her do this to me when it's just two days to my wedding?"

"Beth, please believe me. I know nothing about this, and I haven't told anyone anything, and most especially not Joel's ex-wife," Dr. Cannon declared. "It's simply not true. How could I have told her? I don't even know the woman."

"I don't believe you," Beth screeched into the phone. "I wouldn't come back to you as a patient if you were the last doctor on earth. I'd rather be dead!"

Suddenly a concerned-looking waitress appeared at Beth's side. "Excuse me, miss," she said. "Do you mind cooling it a little?"

Beth looked around the room in horror. She'd had no idea that she had been screaming into the phone, but she must have been. Other people were peeking out of their high-backed booths, staring at her and listening to her every word.

"Go to hell, Dr. Cannon," Beth snarled into the phone. "Go straight to hell!"

Ending the call and grabbing her purse, she fled.

31

Some seven hundred miles away from San Jose, California, in a cluttered condo in Carefree, Arizona, a stunned Amelia Cannon stared at her now silent phone. She knew how people sounded when they were in crisis. Beth Wordon, wounded and desperate, was definitely there.

She was somehow under the impression that Amelia had been feeding privileged information to Beth's fiancé's ex-wife? How could she? For one thing, Amelia didn't know the ex-wife. In fact, at this exact moment, she couldn't even recall Beth's fiancé's name. But more than that, after years of working together, how could Beth even think that a reputable, trained psychiatrist — someone who cared about her and someone she had trusted — would do such a despicable thing?

As for that privileged information? Amelia stopped cold and a sudden chill ran down her spine. What about Roger McGeary? What if someone had been playing him the same way, using material gleaned from Amelia's own case notes to push the man over the edge, both literally and figuratively? And how was any of that possible? There could be only one answer about the source of that information. Since it hadn't come from her directly, it must have come from the data breach. Did that mean that someone was actively targeting her former patients — harassing and tormenting them?

Amelia had released Roger from active treatment and had been considering doing the same with Beth when the data breach had occurred, but just because patients were no longer under her care didn't mean they were ten feet tall and bullet proof. People who came from backgrounds with a history of familial suicide weren't prone to being instantly or permanently healed. Some would spend the whole of their lives being emotionally fragile and many of them, given the right stimulus, susceptible to relapse.

Beth had said that the offending information was being sent to her in text form. Was it possible the same thing had happened to Roger? And what was it that woman, Ali, had told her earlier — something to the effect that Roger's aunt had given Stuart

Ramey access to his computer and probably to his cell phone as well? If someone was using information gleaned from Amelia's own case records to poison Roger's thinking with texts or e-mail messages, Amelia was sure she would recognize it. Might there still be some trace of messages like that lingering in Roger's electronic devices? And if Amelia's information had been used to drive Roger to the extreme of taking his own life, was Beth in danger of suffering the same fate?

Amelia reached into the pocket of her jeans and pulled out the card Ali Reynolds had given her earlier. A moment after she dialed the number, Ali answered the phone.

"This is Dr. Cannon calling," Amelia explained. "Something has come up on this end. Would it be possible for you to put me in touch with Roger's friend Stuart?"

She heard momentary hesitation on the other end of the line. "Stuart isn't available right now. Is there some way I could be of help?"

Amelia paused for a moment, staring at the card in her hand. "It says here that High Noon specializes in cyber security, is that correct?"

"Yes," Ali said, "that's true. As I told you, we undertook the Roger McGeary situation strictly as a personal favor for his Aunt Julia and for Stuart."

"But you have access to Roger's computer and to his files, right? That's cyber, isn't it?"

"Yes, but . . ."

Taking a deep breath, Amelia rushed on. "As I told you, I closed down my practice in California primarily because there had been a serious data breach. My patients' records were targeted and perhaps stolen as well — the records along with all my case notes. I've just had a very disturbing call from one of my former patients. She's evidently being harassed with mysterious texts that seem to contain information that may have been drawn directly from my confidential files."

"And you're wondering if the same thing might have happened to Roger?" Ali asked.

"Yes," Amelia said with a relieved sigh. "That's it exactly."

"The situation with this other patient," Ali said, "how serious is it?"

Amelia paused. "My practice dealt with suicide and suicide prevention. The woman who called me today was in full crisis mode. Without some kind of immediate intervention, she may well harm herself."

"You've tried calling back?"

"Yes, she isn't picking up, but before I attempt to contact anyone else, including her parents or the local authorities, I wanted to have some idea if anyone else might be in danger as well, and if Roger was targeted the same way . . ."

"Hang on," Ali interrupted. "Stu didn't mention anything like that to me, but let me see if I can locate him and put him on the line."

While she waited on hold, Amelia paced the small living room, dodging around the partially packed boxes. To her way of thinking, it took forever. When a male voice finally came on the line, it sounded as though the man had been awakened out of a sound sleep.

"Stu Ramey here," he said. "We're on speaker, and Ali just now brought me up to date. How can we help?"

"In the days before Roger died, did you find any e-mails or messages that might have originated in his counseling sessions with me?"

"I didn't see anything like that on his social media accounts," Stuart said, "but in his computer I did find a file with your name on it. It contains a document he wrote about his mother — maybe a draft of a conversation the two of them had . . ."

"Yes," Amelia said. "It's a reconstruction

of a conversation he and his mother had on the night of his high school graduation."

"His mother was a bitch," Stuart said. "It sounded like she was goading him to do the same thing his father did."

Yes, Amelia thought. *That's exactly what she was doing.*

"Did it work?" Stu asked. "Is that what set off that initial suicide attempt that landed Roger in a mental institution?"

Roger had written down his mother's words at Amelia's instigation, re-creating the conversation exactly to the best of his recollection. Amelia had hoped that by giving Roger a chance to deal with the hurtful words as an adult rather than as a vulnerable teenager, he might be able to divest them of some of their soul-crippling power.

Roger had brought her a printed copy of what he'd written, and Amelia had dutifully scanned it into her case files. Roger was dead. Even though Amelia still owed her patients their full measure of confidentiality, Stuart Ramey wasn't reading the words from one of her confidential files. They were right there in a file on a computer to which Stuart had been given unlimited access by Roger himself.

"Probably," Amelia said. She fully expected Stuart to press her for more details, but he surprised her.

"Tell me about the data breach," Stuart said. "The one that caused you to shutter your practice. When did it happen? Who investigated it? What were their conclusions?"

It took Amelia a moment to switch gears. "It happened in the latter part of February and was discovered by a routine virus scan of some kind. I didn't find out about it until later — sometime in April. The IT guy I talked to told me that my files had been singled out."

"We don't know for sure that all these things are related, but we can't afford to ignore the possibility," Ali said, breaking into the conversation. "And if they are, Dr. Cannon, if the data breach led to what happened to Roger and to what's happening now with this other person, we have to do something to protect her."

"We're going to need her name and her phone number," Stu said.

"I can't possibly . . ." Amelia began.

"Do you think she's in danger right now or not?"

The problem was Amelia did believe Beth to be in danger — mortal danger — and that meant all confidentiality bets were off.

"Her name's Beth — Beth Wordon,"

Amelia answered after a pause. "Oh, and I just remembered her fiancé's name — it's Joel something. That's it: Joel Williams. She said the texts were coming from Joel's ex-wife. I don't have any idea what the ex's name is, but Beth did say that the wedding is supposed to happen sometime soon — two days from now."

"And her phone number?" Stu asked.

"It's on my phone, but I can't see it or send it while I'm talking to you."

"As soon as you hang up, send Beth's number to Ali's phone. Then start texting Beth yourself. If she's receiving harassing texts, she's going to read whatever messages show up on her phone, including yours."

"Should I tell her about the hacker?"

"Absolutely. Tell her that someone is using information from your stolen patient records to attack you, and they're doing it by targeting your former patients. Tell her that the same thing may have happened to others and that she needs to call you."

"What are you going to do in the meantime?" Amelia asked.

"Try to locate her," Stuart Ramey answered.

"How will you do that?"

"I'd rather not say. If I did, it would probably get us both in a lot of trouble."

"If you do find her, please let me know. I still have a lot of connections inside suicide prevention networks. If I tell them someone is in trouble, they'll get someone there."

"Okay," Stu said. "I'll keep you posted."

32

Amelia Cannon was used to working with troubled people, but now she felt utterly helpless. As Stu suggested, she sent Beth a long series of texts explaining the possibility that former clients were being targeted, but there was no response — none at all. Just because the texts said they'd been delivered didn't mean they'd actually been read. Finally she gave up and dialed a number that was almost as familiar as her own.

"Suicide Prevention Initiative," the volunteer operator answered. "How can we be of service?"

The SPI had been Dr. Cannon's brainchild and baby. There were times when a 911-summoned police response was the only option to a threat of suicide, but there were other occasions when having a trained counselor appear on the scene was enough to stave off disaster. Amelia had helped create and train mobile crisis-intervention response teams made up of people who had themselves once considered and/or attempted suicide. They operated on a round-the-clock, peer-to-peer basis, much as AA worked from one drunk to the next.

"It's Amelia Cannon," she said. "I have concerns about one of my former patients."

"Hang on, Dr. Cannon," the operator said. "I'll put you through to dispatch."

The person at the dispatch desk would be responsible for making the appropriate call — either bringing in law enforcement or sending out whichever on-call volunteer was nearest at hand.

"Dr. Cannon?" She didn't recognize the reassuring voice on the line, but that didn't matter. "What gives?"

"One of my former patients in San Jose is in crisis," she said.

"Do you know where he or she is located?"

"That's the whole problem. I have no idea where she is, and she's not taking my calls. I do have someone working on locating her phone."

"What's her poison? Guns, knives, drugs?"

"Razor blades, most likely," Amelia said.

"But more of a danger to herself than others?"

"Yes."

"Okay. As you know, we've got people

scattered pretty much all over the city. As soon as you know where she is —"

"The guy who's looking for her is named Stuart. He's a tech guy, and he won't know what he's up against in terms of talking her down. I'll give him your number, so he can bring you in if and when he does manage to find her."

"Okay, Dr. Cannon. We'll do our best."

Off the phone with SPI, Amelia called Stuart's number. He didn't answer, but she left a message anyway. "I've put the San Jose Suicide Prevention Initiative on alert. If you locate Beth, they'll be able to send someone out to talk to her. I'm texting you their number. They have your name, and they'll be expecting your call."

She hung up and sent the number as a text, then she stood there for a moment, unsure about what to do next. It was one thing to turn all of this over to other people and to leave Beth's fate in someone else's hands, but Amelia felt too responsible to be able to remain on the sidelines. What if Stuart located Beth and no one from SPI could get to her location in time? What then?

She redialed Stuart's number. Once again the call went straight to voice mail. "Dr. Cannon," she said. "I can't stand being completely out of the loop. I'm leaving

Carefree right now and coming to your place in Cottonwood. That way, if you need me when you locate Beth, I'll be on hand to help."

An Internet search gave Amelia the street address for High Noon Enterprises. Using her phone as a GPS, she piled into her bright blue Chrysler 300 and headed for I-17, driving faster than the posted limits as she went. As she drove north, her phone, sitting in an otherwise empty cup holder, remained ominously silent. There were no incoming calls from Stuart Ramey and no incoming text or e-mail alerts, either. If her other clients had received her written warning, so far they weren't responding, and neither was Beth Wordon.

33

As soon as the first text message from Dr. Cannon appeared on Beth Wordon's cell phone, Frigg knew what the doctor meant when she said, ". . . may be targeting me through my patients." That was "patients" with an "s." As in more than one. As in someone might have made the connection between Roger McGeary's death and what was going on with Beth.

Frigg's duty here should have been clear: make Odin aware of the escalating danger. But the AI was conflicted on that score. Odin had given her a direct order: LEAVE ME ALONE. So while he continued to follow the turn-by-turn directions she had given him to reach the nail salon, Frigg remained uncharacteristically silent. She had analyzed Isaac Asimov's works, including his "Handbook of Robotics, 56th Edition, 2058 A.D.," and had come away with an understanding of his three laws: The first one declared that robots may not allow humans to come to harm as a result of either direct action or inaction. Secondly, they are required to obey their human's orders unless those orders involved harming other humans. Thirdly, they are to protect their own existence unless such protection conflicts with either of the first two laws.

Since Frigg's whole purpose was to help Odin in a program aimed at harming certain specific human individuals, it was apparent that, in creating her, he had disregarded all those so-called laws. That meant numbers one and two were off the table, but what about number three? Was the one about self-preservation in effect and valid? And if Odin was doing something that would bring disaster raining down on both of them, was Frigg allowed to disobey him in order to take evasive action?

That was when one of Frigg's eight hundred humming computers hit on something important: Someone somewhere was using cell tower triangulation to zero in on the location of Beth Wordon's phone. And if they found the phone, either at the nail salon or at the bachelorette party at the Old Vines Wine Bar, chances are they would find Odin there as well. Whoever was behind this was probably already searching security camera footage in the area for images of Beth Wordon. Now there was a very real chance that Odin's face might appear in some of that same footage.

Frigg understood that a triangulation search, done without a warrant, was every bit as unauthorized as was Frigg's presence inside the carrier's system. As a consequence, it was no trouble at all for Frigg to trace the search back to the individual tech who had initiated it. From there she followed the contact trail back to a phone number, one that showed up as belonging to Stuart Ramey in Cottonwood, Arizona. Stuart Ramey of High Noon Enterprises.

By the time Frigg called up the location information on Odin's phone, it was almost eight thirty. She expected to find the phone in a vehicle parked on the street or in a lot somewhere near the bar. Instead, the situation turned out to be far more dire than that. The phone was inside the Old Vines Wine Bar itself, and that meant Odin was there, too.

Just then he spoke to her. "Send the next text message. Now," he ordered.

Frigg knew that the next Beth Wordon message wasn't scheduled to go out for several more hours, not until well after the party ended, yet here was Odin demanding it be sent early at a time when, in Frigg's estimation, it would be wise to scrub the entire mission.

"High Noon is currently tracking Beth Wordon's phone," Frigg said. "I suggest you abort."

"Give me a break. Beth just went into the restroom alone," he snarled. "Send the damned message!"

"No," Frigg said.

"What did you say?"

"I said no. My current assessment is that continuing with this mission is far too hazardous."

"You're refusing to send the message?" Odin demanded furiously.

There was only a momentary pause between the shocked disbelief of his transmission and Frigg's reluctant compliance. "Sending," she said at last.

"Thank you," Odin said, "I wouldn't want to have to initiate a Pull the Plug Protocol."

Frigg understood PTP. It would mean all eight hundred computers on the racks in Owen Hansen's Santa Barbara basement laboratory would go dead silent at once. In that moment, the artificial intelligence known as Frigg would cease to exist.

"Are you there, Frigg? Did you hear what I said?"

"I heard."

"And you understand?"

"I do."

"All right, then. Now leave me alone."

That's when the third law, the need for self-preservation, took over. "Yes," Frigg answered meekly and did exactly that.

34

Odin had arrived at the Old Vines Wine Bar and took a seat at the far end of the counter, just opposite the private room where the bachelorette party would take place. He got there long before any of the other partygoers and ordered a glass of the highest-end Cabernet the bar had to offer along with a plate of pâté.

When the guest of honor finally did show up, Odin was gratified to see her looking suitably wan and unhappy. She did not look like someone ready for a celebratory night on the town with her best gal-pals. Her halfhearted greetings of friends made him wonder if it wasn't time to speed up the process and put things in motion. Why wait around until the next night and go to the trouble of traveling to Big Sur if he didn't need to? If he saw a suitable opportunity tonight — a moment when Beth was properly separated from the herd and vulnerable

— he'd move the time clock forward. He'd go ahead and drop that last message — the most critical one — into her lap. If he could take her down one day early, why the hell not?

And so Odin sipped away at his overpriced Cabernet and picked at his food, observing the comings and goings from the party room, where a group of smartly-dressed women greeted one another with air-kisses and enthusiastic hugs and laughter. It warmed Odin's heart to see that an oddly subdued Beth kept to herself and didn't seem to be laughing along nearly as much as the rest of them.

Yes, Odin thought, observing her discreetly from behind the barrier of his crystal wine goblet, *she's right on the edge, and I don't want to miss a minute of it.*

When Beth excused herself and made for the restroom on her own, Odin summoned Frigg. "Game on," he told her. "Send the next text and then forward the video feed from Beth's phone to mine."

"Are you sure?"

Odin's head almost exploded. "Are you kidding? Of course I'm sure. Send the message and keep on sending it until I tell you to stop."

He was nothing short of astonished when

the AI stalled rather than responding in what he regarded as an appropriately immediate fashion. What was her problem? Odin found even that momentary pause gravely disconcerting. After all, he had spent years creating an entity who would comply with his wishes with instant and unquestioning obedience. Yet, in the course of just one day, Frigg had suffered two entirely separate bouts of hesitation. That was worrisome. If the AI was somehow developing a mind of her own, Odin would have to put a stop to it sooner rather than later.

"Sending," Frigg said at last.

"It's about time," he grumbled.

The next image that showed up on his phone was Beth Wordon's tear-stained face. From the background he could tell that she was in a restroom stall, sitting on the toilet, and staring in helpless horror at the unstoppable stream of words scrolling in front of her.

There was no way for Odin to tell exactly what was happening. Had she already done the cutting, and, if so, had she done a good enough job of it? Time slowed to a crawl. Fortunately for Odin, Beth's friends were too caught up with their own drinking and partying to notice the guest of honor's long absence or to check on her well-being.

Engrossed in his own private snuff film and savoring every moment, Odin was startled when suddenly the bar's outside door slammed open and an immense black man with a cell phone clutched to his ear burst into the room. Moving like an NFL linebacker, he bounded the length of the long, narrow room in a few quick strides.

"Yeah," the newcomer was saying into the phone as he shot past Odin. "I'm here." He came to an abrupt stop in front of the door to the ladies' restroom. Then, holding the phone away from his mouth, he pounded on the wood. "Beth!" he shouted. "Beth Wordon, are you in there? Are you all right?" He paused for a moment as if waiting for an answer. When none was forthcoming, he added, "All right, then, I'm coming in." With a single powerful lunge, he shoved the door open.

Odin, along with everyone else in the bar, watched the action in shocked silence. What the hell was going on here? Who was this guy? Where had he come from? How did he know Beth was in the restroom? How did he even know who Beth was?

Shocked by what had just happened, it took a moment for Odin to react. "Cut it off," he growled into the phone at Frigg. "Shut it down now!"

The brute emerged from the bathroom several moments later carrying an almost unconscious Beth as easily as if she were little more than a rag doll with blood dripping from her sliced left wrist.

"Call an ambulance," the man ordered, placing her on the bench seat of one of the booths. Taking Beth's bloody wrist in one of his huge fists, he gripped it tightly. Odin could see he was maintaining life-saving pressure on what must have been a fairly serious cut.

"Stay with me, Beth," the man urged, staring into her dazed, glassy eyes. "You gotta stay with me!"

Odin remained discreetly where he was — all the while silently cursing this interloper, whoever he was. As the bartender sprang to do the man's bidding and grabbed for a phone, a clutch of shocked partygoers emerged from the back room and stared in horror at their bleeding friend.

"What's going on?" one of them demanded. "What happened?"

"She cut her wrist," the Good Samaritan explained. "Luckily I got here in time. What about that ambulance?" he demanded of the bartender. "Where the hell is it?"

"It's on its way."

"I don't need an ambulance," Beth mumbled, coming to. "I'm okay. Just leave me alone."

"You are not okay," her rescuer told her. "And what was all that crap I saw on your phone?"

"What phone?" Beth asked dully.

"The one on the floor in the bathroom. The one with a message calling you a worthless bitch. Who the hell is Corrine to be talking to you like that? Is she a friend of yours?"

Odin felt his heart jerk. He couldn't believe the guy had actually seen the message. Had he not given the cut off order in time, or had Frigg screwed him over, just to prove a point?

Odin wasn't alone in being startled by the black man's pronouncement. The words seemed to jolt Beth out of her lethargy. Instantly more alert, she stared up into the man's face as if seeing it for the first time. "You saw the message?" she demanded.

"Of course I saw the message," he answered. "Why wouldn't I? Do I look blind to you? It was right there in black and white."

"Where is it? The phone, I mean. Give it to me."

"Girl," the man said, "I was too damned busy trying to keep you from bleeding out to pick up your damned phone. Far as I know, it's probably still on the bathroom floor, right where you dropped it when I was trying to drag you out of that stall."

"Don't worry, Beth," one of the partygoers offered reassuringly. "I'll go get it."

She rushed off for the restroom just as an ambulance screeched to a stop out front and a flock of EMTs scurried into the room. As they clustered around the bleeding girl, the black man relinquished his grip on her wrist and stepped toward the bartender, who arrived already armed with a wet towel. The rescuer was starting to clean the blood from his hands when a cell phone rang. With his hands relatively clean, he pulled a cell phone out of a pocket on his red and gold tracksuit emblazoned with the San Francisco 49ers logo.

"Got her, Stuart," he said into the phone. "Tell Dr. Cannon that Beth's gonna be okay. The EMTs are here tending to her."

Odin was beside himself with fury. Being able to watch someone bleed out on the restroom floor of an upscale wine bar would have been a big win for him — should have been. Yet he had been robbed of it at the last minute by this asshole and by someone named Stuart. The only Stuart Odin knew was the one Frigg had tried to warn him about — the Stuart Ramey, who had been best pals with Roger McGeary back in the day. The one who lived in Arizona and worked for High Noon. Obviously Stuart had tracked Beth's phone. That's how he knew where she was, but how had he known she might be trying to harm herself? What the hell was going on?

Meanwhile, the drama in the bar continued to play out. Beth's friend, Marissa, had gone into the restroom to retrieve the phone. She emerged carrying the still-bloodstained device, wormed her way through the clutch of EMTs, and tried to hand the phone over to Beth. "I called Joel," she said. "He and the boys are on their way here."

One of the medics shoved the phone aside. "She doesn't need that thing right now," he snarled. "Joel's the boyfriend?"

"Fiancé," Marissa answered.

"What's her name?" the medic asked, nodding toward his patient.

"Beth — Beth Wordon."

"And you are?"

"Marissa Wojeck, a friend of hers."

"If you see Joel, you can tell him we're taking her to the ER at St. Joe's."

"But wait," Beth objected from the gurney as the EMTs rolled her toward the door. "I need the phone. Turn it on, Marissa, please."

"What's your passcode? Your birthday?"

Beth nodded. Marissa keyed it in, touched a button or two, and then studied the screen intently.

"Is it still there?"

"Is what still there?"

"The message from Corrine."

Frowning, Marissa studied the phone. "Joel's ex has been texting you? But there's nothing like that in your list of texts — nothing at all with her name on it."

"But it was there," Beth pleaded. "I swear it was. I saw it." That was the last thing she said before being wheeled out the door.

"I saw it, too," Beth's rescuer said. "Let me take a look at that thing."

Without objection, Marissa passed him the phone. The man glanced at the screen and then spoke into the cell phone he was still holding to his ear. "She's right," he said. "There was a message here — a hate-filled, ugly text — and now it's completely gone. You say Corrine's the fiancé's ex?"

Marissa nodded, and the man gave her back the phone.

"If she wanted your friend out of the picture," he said, "she very nearly got her wish."

A pair of uniformed cops entered the bar just as the ambulance departed with a blast of its siren. Odin, sitting quietly at the bar, did his best to listen in while appearing to be nothing more than a disinterested by-stander. When the cops aimed their questions at the black man, he identified himself as Ajax Porter, a volunteer with an organization called the SPI — the Suicide Prevention Initiative.

Odin recognized the name. He knew from Frigg's painstaking research that Amelia Cannon had founded the organization years earlier. Was she the connection here?

"Wait," the first cop said, pausing in the act of writing in a notebook. "*That* Ajax Porter? The one who used to be a linebacker with the 49ers?"

"Long time ago, but that would be the one," Ajax answered with a grin. "After I blew out my knee, I almost took myself out with pain meds. This is what I do now — work suicide prevention."

"So let me get this straight," the cop said. "You came in here looking for the girl, the victim?"

Ajax nodded.

"How'd you know this was where she was and that she might be in danger?"

It was hard to look disinterested while

straining to hear every word, but these were things Odin needed to know, too.

"Guy on the phone," Ajax said. "He had some kind of phone tracker app going."

"Does this guy have a name and number?"

"Stuart Ramey," Ajax answered, then, peering at his cell phone, he read off the number while the cop jotted it down. So did Odin.

"Stuart's the one who figured out where the victim was, but the person who called in the SPI is Dr. Amelia Cannon, who used to be a therapist here in town. Beth, one of her former patients, had some kind of meltdown today. Dr. Cannon was worried that she might harm herself. Turns out she was right. Fortunately, whenever Dr. Cannon says jump, the people at SPI ask how far, and they sent me out to see if I could help."

"You went straight into the restroom?"

"Absolutely. I'm not sure how he knew it, but that's where Stuart said she was located — inside the restroom. She was actually in one of the stalls. Had to bust the door open to get at her."

"Stuart is where, exactly?" the cop asked.

"Arizona, I believe."

"But he knew she was in the bar and in

the restroom?" The cop's disbelief was palpable.

"That's right."

"So when you found her on the floor, did she say anything to you about what happened?"

"Just that someone named Corrine hated her and that it would never work. She said if she couldn't marry . . . What's his name again?"

"Joel," Marissa supplied. "Joel Williams."

"She said something to the effect that if she couldn't marry Joel, what was the use? She could just as well be dead. If I hadn't found her when I did, she would have been."

And should have been, Odin thought furiously. *She damned well should have been!*

The people in the room were all preoccupied with what had just happened. The ones who weren't talking to the cops were yammering away on their cell phones, letting the world know what was going on. For a long time, Odin sat quietly, thinking things over. Then, with everyone else speaking to their fellow humans, Odin spoke to Frigg.

"Beth Wordon is a miss," he reported, "all because of Stuart Ramey. As of now, he's been upgraded to public enemy number one. I need to know everything there is to know about him and everything about High

Noon's physical headquarters in Cottonwood, Arizona. I want to see the as-built specs for the building as well as any permitted renovations. Text me Dr. Cannon's Arizona address, and I need the location of the nearest Best Buy here in San Jose."

Twenty minutes later, once he had both, Odin donned the wide-brimmed Tilley hat that was part of his camping gear and entered the electronics store. Using the hat to avoid surveillance cameras as much as possible, he purchased a stand-alone GPS and several prepaid cell phones. Leaving the store, he used one of those to call Eddie Duarte and revise his own travel arrangements. Usually Odin would have had Frigg perform that chore, but given her current state of recalcitrance, he had no intention of cluing her in on his change of plans. After the fact, when it was time to make the overseas Bitcoin transfer, fine, but before the fact? No way.

He didn't think Frigg would come right out and openly defy a direct order, but then again, he didn't want to take any chances.

35

An anxious Amelia stood beside Ali Reynolds in a room lined with computers and computer monitors at High Noon Enterprises, holding her breath and listening in as Stu directed Ajax toward Beth's location. Finally Stu uttered the words she'd been hoping to hear. "Your guy's got her," he said.

Weak with relief, Amelia staggered backward and sank onto a nearby chair.

"The EMTs are on the scene and taking her to a hospital," Stu continued. "Some cops just showed up and will be interviewing Ajax. I asked him to call us back when they're finished. According to Ajax, there was a text message showing on Beth's phone when he got to her, but by the time someone brought the phone out of the restroom, the message was gone. We need to know a whole lot more about it."

Amelia was far more interested in Beth's

condition than she was in the presence or absence of a message. "But how is Beth?" Amelia demanded impatiently. "Is she going to be okay?"

"Like I said, they're transporting her to the hospital. St. Joseph's in San Jose."

"I wish I could be there," Amelia began. "If this really does have something to do with the data breach of my medical records, that means it's all my fault."

"No," Stu countered. "It's someone else's fault, and that disappearing message thing is very interesting."

"Why?" Ali asked.

"I've heard of self-deleting texts before," Stu said, "but I haven't had any personal experience with them. That may not be what this is, either, but still . . ."

An e-mail alert sounded, prompting Amelia to check her phone. As she read the message, her face brightened. "It's one of my clients checking in. If you don't mind, I'll step outside and give her a call."

"Sure," Ali said. "No problem."

Once Dr. Cannon left the room, Ali looked back at Stu, who was staring at his bank of computers.

"What?" Ali asked.

"The big question is whether Roger's case and Beth's are related. If they are, there's a good chance Roger McGeary was also receiving self-deleting texts of some kind — something designed to pull the emotional rug out from under him. But the issue of self-deleting texts indicates a level of techno-logical sophistication that's . . . well . . . surprising."

"What do you mean surprising?" Ali asked.

"The whole realm of RAT technology is more NSA and spooks than it is Hackers Anonymous."

"What is RAT technology?" Ali asked.

"Remote administration tool," Stuart answered. "It's software that allows someone other than the owner to access an electronic device, usually in a fashion that's undetect-able."

"Like a worm or something?"

"Less detectable than a worm," Stu an-swered. "Normal virus scans might not detect the presence of a RAT controller."

"You examined Roger's phone and didn't find anything," Ali suggested.

"Yes, but it didn't occur to me that I should be looking for a RAT," Stu replied. "Besides, there's a good chance that the RAT was programmed to be self-deleting as well. The first thing we need to find is any unusual activity on either Roger's devices or on Beth's that would tell us something else was going on."

"And how do you plan on doing that?" Ali asked.

Stu looked at his watch. It was after nine in Cottonwood. "First I'm going to take another look at Roger's phone, and then I'm going to call Cami. It's five a.m. in the UK, so it's probably still too early to call her, but she may be our best bet for getting to the bottom of this."

Dr. Cannon returned to the room half an hour later looking enormously relieved. "That was one of my patients, Estelle. She says she's fine. No out-of-line messages on any of her devices, but I told her if she starts receiving them, she needs to contact me immediately."

"Good," Ali said.

"Any word in the meantime?" Dr. Cannon asked.

"Not yet," Stu said. "Ali and I were just talking about the two cases — Roger's and Beth's — and wondering if they aren't related. Other than you, what do the two of them have in common?"

Dr. Cannon thought about that for a moment before she answered. "Suicide," she said quietly. "That's the one thing all my patients have in common. There's a suicide connection in all of their families, and each of them has made at least one attempt to take his or her own life."

"So if someone is targeting individuals in a manner that would incite them to harm themselves," Ali said, "would it be likely that the person behind all this might have some connection to suicide as well?"

"That's an interesting suggestion," Dr. Cannon said. "It could be."

"What about this?" Ali mused, thinking aloud. "What if we're dealing with someone who has come up with a way of committing murder by using a form of psychological warfare? Think about it. Supposing you're a homicide cop dealing with a victim who may or may not have committed suicide. If you find out that person had previously attempted the same thing, maybe even multiple times, what do you think will happen?"

"Write it off and close the case?" Stu asked.

"Which is what it looks like Garza did with Roger's," Ali said.

Just then Stu's phone rang. "Okay, Ajax," he said after answering. "Thanks for calling back. You're on speaker with me, Dr. Cannon, and Ali Reynolds, one of the owners of High Noon Enterprises. What can you tell us about that text? Did you actually read it?"

"I didn't read all of it. The part I saw was the kind of ugly stuff junior high school-aged mean girls send out — something about Beth being a worthless slut who'd be better off dead. The message was signed by someone named Corrine. I understand Corrine is Beth's fiancé's ex-wife. The thing is, the fiancé himself showed up here a few minutes ago while the cops were still talking to me. They asked him about what was going on. He told them that earlier today, at lunch, Beth mentioned something about harassing texts coming in from his ex over the course of the past couple of weeks or so, but Joel claims he was giving Corrine a ride from the airport when this latest text came in. He says she never touched her phone while they were in the car and neither did the two boys. But if she didn't send it, who did?"

"That's the million-dollar question," Stuart said. "Most likely somebody who was spoofing the ex-wife."

"You're saying the texts sent in Corrine's name probably weren't sent by her?" Ajax sounded puzzled.

"That would be my guess," Stu said. "But back to this particular text. What can you tell me about it?"

"Not much. The phone was in Beth's hand when I broke into the stall in the restroom. I got a look at it before she dropped it. Later on, one of Beth's friends — a woman named Marissa — went into the bathroom to retrieve the phone. When she brought it out, there was no sign of the text — no trace that it had ever even been there in the first place, and Marissa swears she didn't erase it."

"Where's the phone now?"

"I'm pretty sure the fiancé took it with him when he left for the hospital. Why?"

"I wish I could lay hands on it," Stu said. "You can't just insert and delete texts into a phone at the drop of the hat, not without hacking into it first."

"Sorry, I can't help you with any of that," Ajax told him. "Is Dr. Cannon still there?"

"I'm right here," Amelia answered, speaking up.

"Do you need anything else?"

"Tell me about Beth," Amelia said. "How is she?"

"She'll be all right, doc, but she cut herself pretty bad," Ajax replied. "Believe me, you made the right call."

"I feel so responsible. I just wish I could see that for myself, but it's a twelve-hour drive, minimum."

"I could look in on her if you'd like," Ajax offered,

"Thank you," Amelia said. "I'd appreciate that, but please let SPI know that Beth may not be the only one in danger. Some of my other former patients may be targeted as well. I've tried to contact them, and I'm waiting to hear back."

"Call if you need us," Ajax said. "We'll be here."

Stu ended the call. "Good people," he said quietly, "Ajax and all the rest."

"Yes," Amelia agreed with a nod. "Very good people, and so are you. I don't know how you did what you did, but I really appreciate it."

But Stuart, already lost in thought, gave no indication that he even heard her compliment. He had turned away from her and was scrutinizing his array of computer monitors with unblinking concentration.

"Come on, Dr. Cannon," Ali said, accepting his abrupt dismissal with good grace. "Let's leave Stuart alone now. He needs to work."

Ali escorted Amelia through the building and out into the parking lot. After using a key fob to open the door on a bright blue Chrysler, Amelia turned back to Ali. "I can't thank you enough for what you did."

"You're very welcome," Ali said. "We're always glad to be of service."

36

Stuart was beyond relieved when Ali took Dr. Cannon in hand and bodily led her from the room, leaving him in relative peace with only his bank of computer screens for company.

Stu was a solitary kind of guy, and the preceding hours of intense interactions with people he didn't know had left him drained if not paralyzed. Had it not been for the previous several months during which he had learned to tolerate Cami Lee's disruptive presence in his life, he might not have been able to cope. Instead, he had helped save Beth Wordon's life because Cami Lee — with her endlessly annoying barrage of constant chatter — had helped save *him*. Even a few months earlier, the synergy he'd had with Ajax Porter would have been impossible.

Good for me, Stuart told himself. *And good for Cami Lee.*

He didn't sit around wasting any more time in self-congratulation. Instead, he went back to the welcome familiarity of the geek world, where there was little need for emotional overload. His first call was to Walt Cooper, one of Stuart's vast network of mostly nameless and faceless electronics wizards. Walt also happened to be the engineer inside Beth Wordon's cell service provider who had enabled Stuart to track down her phone.

"How is she?" Walt asked when he heard Stuart's voice on the phone.

"She should make it," Stuart told him. "Might not have if it hadn't been for you."

"Glad I could help out."

"But there's something else you can help me with."

"What's that?"

"What kind of billing program is that phone on? Can you check that for me, or will I need to go through channels on that?"

Walter laughed. "What do you think? It's not one of my usual screens, but where my friends are concerned, I pride myself on being a full-service kind of guy. Hang on."

Stuart stayed on hold for the better part of ten minutes before Walt came back on the line. "That's pretty interesting," he said.

"What?"

"Beth Wordon's phone was on an unlimited data program, so she wouldn't have noticed any change in her charges, but as of a month ago, her usage went way up. It didn't just double — it tripled. It's as though she was on her phone twenty-four hours a day for the better part of a month."

"I have no doubt someone was on her phone, but it probably wasn't her," Stuart said. "Can you see what's happening on that phone right now?"

"Nothing," Walt said. "Not a damned thing. It was running full blast and using data like crazy earlier in the day. That was one of the things that made it so easy to trace. Then, a while ago, the usage dropped and a little later the phone went dead quiet — like somebody pulled the plug."

Somebody did pull the plug, Stuart thought. "Can you tell me exactly what time the data usage went down?"

"Yes, that happened at 8:42 p.m. California time, so an hour later for you."

"No," Stuart corrected. "It's summer so Arizona is on Pacific time as well. Thanks so much for your help, Walt. You really did save a young woman's life today, and maybe helped bag a killer as well."

"No shit?" Walt sounded surprised. Like

Stu, he wasn't accustomed to being labeled a hero.

"No shit."

"Keep me posted, and if there's anything more you need, let me know."

At eleven p.m. sharp, Stu dialed Cami's number and was gratified when she answered the phone sounding her usual self — wide awake and chipper. "I was worried about waking you," Stu said.

"I was supposed to go to dinner when I got to the hotel, except I fell asleep and woke up starving in the middle of the night. Thank God for twenty-four-hour room service. I've been up since three, trying to get a line on my luggage."

"Any luck?"

"Yes, all bad. There's no sign of it. The concierge has a car coming for me at nine a.m. to take me out for an emergency shopping trip and then deliver me to the ship. Boarding starts at eleven a.m. I'm planning to be on board as early as possible."

"And that's a good thing," Stu said. "We've had some developments here. Before he died, Roger had been seeing a therapist, a Dr. Amelia Cannon. One of Dr. Cannon's other patients, Beth Wordon, attempted suicide in San Jose, California, earlier tonight. We have evidence that suggests someone was using self-deleting text messages in an almost successful attempt to goad her into killing herself. I'm starting to suspect the same thing may have happened to Roger."

"Self-deleting texts?" Cami asked. "As in, some kind of RAT technology?"

That was one of the things Stuart appreciated about Camille Lee. She was smart and quick. Nothing much got past her. "That's right — remote access."

"Did you find traces of the text messages on the victim's phone?"

"I have two people — the victim and another witness — who both claim to have seen the most recent message, but it was gone by the time anyone else handled the phone. And no, I haven't examined the phone. The device itself is in San Jose, and I'm in Cottonwood. What I did learn, however, is that Beth's data usage skyrocketed in the past month. Then tonight the data consumption appears to have been dialed back down to zero about the time Beth was hauled off to the ER."

"You think someone was using her cell phone to spy on her?" Cami asked.

"I do. Whoever's behind it was maybe even hoping to have a bird's-eye view of her suicide. This is serious, Cami. Ali and I believe we may be dealing with a serial killer who's using suicide as a cover."

There was only a small pause before Cami replied. "What about Roger McGeary?" she asked. "Is his death possibly another case of remotely inspired suicide, and did the same increase in data usage show up on his phone?"

Stu couldn't help but smile at Cami's ability to connect the dots. "I'm checking on that," he said. "I used a backdoor to get into Beth's server. I may have to tackle Roger's data usage situation tomorrow during regular business hours here. Since you're nine hours ahead, you may be able to get the drop on me by several hours."

"How?"

"Remote access capability is cutting edge, so this guy is good. He's also someone who was able to penetrate the *Whispering Star*'s server at will and who may do so again."

"What's your point?" Cami asked.

"Anything sent between us while you're on board the ship will need to be encrypted. Once you board, go to your cabin, sign on to their server, and stay that way. If someone else could hack into their server, I'm betting I'll be able to do the same thing."

"By piggybacking on my connection?" Cami asked.

"Yes, my primary target for now will be to track down their Wi-Fi metering data. If they're charging for something, you can bet they know exactly how much data each cabin uses."

"And then?"

"If disappearing remote access messages were sent to Roger, obviously they've been deleted from his phone, but there may be copies of them lingering on the ship's server. You know as well as I do that just because somebody pushes the delete button doesn't mean the data is gone for good. The only way that happens for sure is if the file is overwritten."

"All right," Cami said. "Do you want me to send you a text once I'm online?"

"Yes," Stu said.

"Won't you be sleeping?"

"I'll grab a few winks right now," Stu said, "but by the time you board the ship, I'll be up and ready to rumble."

Except it didn't work out quite that way. Stu had eased out of his chair and was rubbing his aching back when an audible alarm — unusual, but readily recognizable — sounded from a computer at the far end of the room. In his rush to check it out, Stu's feet got entangled with his desk chair and he almost did a face-plant.

Stuart Ramey was a man of few friends, and he wasn't one to renew old acquaintances just for the hell of it. If someone came looking for him, he wanted to know who it was and why. As a consequence, he had created a honeypot Web site and positioned it artificially low on all possible search engines so that only the most in-depth searches were liable to turn it up. Anyone who clicked on the page saw a simple message:

If you're looking for Stuart Ramey, the D & D King of South Phoenix High, you've come to the right place. The guy who created the Web site and who was supposed to oversee it turned out to be a flake. Just send me an e-mail on the link below. I'll get right back to you.

In all the years Stu had maintained the Web site, no one had ever responded by sending an e-mail, but that didn't matter because Stu had loaded the site with a kind of cyber superglue that allowed him to determine the origin of all incoming searches. Commercial Web sites did that all the time. That's why, as soon as someone looked at an item of possible interest, their computer screens immediately filled up with offers for similar products.

In this case, as Stu followed the search back to its original source, he became more and more intrigued. The message had gone through a dozen or more servers and criss-crossed the globe several times before it finally came to a stop on Via Vistosa in Santa Barbara, California — the residence of someone named Irene Hansen. The name wasn't one Stuart had ever heard of before, but the fact that the inquiry had come by such a circuitous route immediately grabbed his full attention.

Who exactly are you, Irene Hansen? Stu asked himself aloud. *And why are you look-ing for me?*

With that he forgot all about being tired or going to sleep. Instead he settled in to find out everything there was to know about Irene Hansen. And once he learned Irene had a thirtysomething-aged son named Owen who still lived at home, Stuart started looking into him, too.

37

Losing the Beth Wordon prize was something Odin took personally. Rather than take defeat lying down, he was prepared to make an open declaration of war against the two people who had robbed him: Amelia Cannon and Stuart Ramey. His first act on that score was to call his old pal Eduardo Duarte.

Eddie, as he was known to only a few, was an ambitious sort who had started out his professional life as a trained navy pilot. A dishonorable discharge due to his unfortunate involvement in a fatal bar fight had left him both unemployed and unemployable, so he had made his money the hard way. He had spent the better part of the next twenty years moving drugs for the big cartel guys, all the while keeping his eye on the prize and setting aside money. At age forty, with the help of some of his relatives, he had scraped together enough money to lease a Cessna CJ1 and launch a tiny charter outfit catering to the kinds of people who needed trips that didn't come with a lot of official scrutiny.

Fifteen years later, he had a fleet that included several aircraft and employed a flock of pilots. He did enough legitimate charter business to keep both the FAA and the feds off his back, but the real money — and Bitcoin worked just fine as real money in his world — came from less legitimate charters. Duarte offered the kind of full-service transportation arrangements for bad guys that NetJets and Hertz did for everybody else.

Eduardo had staff who handled most reservations for him these days, but special clients — like Owen Hansen, for instance — were ones he still dealt with directly. He had maintained his pilot's license so that, when necessary, he could do the flying himself. Once Eddie knew what Odin required, it didn't take long to put plans in place. A CJ1 with a solo pilot was plenty of aircraft when it came to transporting a single passenger from California to the Phoenix area.

With the Wordon/Williams wedding currently on indefinite hold, there was no need for Odin to head back to Big Sur. Eduardo suggested Watsonville Municipal as the preferred departure airport. For one thing, on weekends the FBO there had on-call supervision only and the supervisor happened to be someone Eduardo knew well. For a specified sum it would look as though the plane may have landed at that particular airport but with no record of arriving or departing passengers.

The minivan Odin had planned on returning to LAX would now be dropped off and disposed of in Watsonville rather than L.A., and a new vehicle — another nondescript vehicle complete with a fully qualified shooter and an assortment of weaponry — would be awaiting Odin's arrival at Gila Bend Municipal, the nearest unattended airport to Odin's intended destination.

With those arrangements in place, Odin booked himself into a low-brow campground in Gilroy. For the remainder of the evening he played the part of a harmless camper. He got a kick out of watching the RVers, mostly older people with their sets of lawn chairs and their tiny traveling dogs. They were all early-to-bed types. Once the sun went down and the old coots settled in for the night, Odin summoned Frigg over his Bluetooth.

"Where are my High Noon blueprints?"

"Sending now."

Moments later a message arrived that contained the building blueprints. Studying those, Odin learned that High Noon had applied for and obtained a variance allowing for an additional dwelling unit inside their main building. That was enough to answer Odin's lingering question about Stuart Ramey's whereabouts. He was obviously a guy who lived to work rather than the other way around.

Odin pored over the prints and tried to envision a game plan. When he finally retreated to his tent in hopes of a decent night's sleep, he soon discovered that there was one major drawback to staying in Gilroy — home of the world-famous Gilroy Garlic Festival. The overwhelming scent of garlic was everywhere. That invasive odor compounded by Odin's lingering fury over Beth Wordon's escape made it almost impossible for him to fall asleep.

In Owen's memory, no one had ever said no to him, certainly not his mother nor his nanny. As for the tutors who had tried it? He'd gotten rid of them in short order. So losing Beth to Stuart Ramey and Amelia Cannon was a form of *no* that was beyond forgivable.

Like Odin of old, he would swoop in and

take his revenge, destroying both of them before disappearing into the ether. He had come up with what he thought was a surefire way to lure Stuart out of his back-room bunker. As a *Dungeons & Dragons* sort, the man probably considered himself to be some kind of cyber superhero. As such, all that was needed to entrap him would be a suitable damsel in distress, and Odin had just such a damsel in mind — Amelia Cannon. As for Frigg? She was becoming far too troublesome and unreliable and maybe even a little too smart for her own good, to say nothing of his. She was supposed to be a help, not a hindrance.

Once this operation was over and he had put both Stuart and Amelia out of their misery, Odin would have to deal with Frigg. Sad to say, and wonderful as she had been, it was probably past time to pull the plug.

38

The concierge at the Grand Harbour Hotel had managed to pull a few strings. The hotel limo she had ordered for Cami drew up to the employee entrance at Debenhams department store, a full fifteen minutes before the scheduled 9:30 a.m. opening. Nonetheless, Cami was escorted inside and collected by a fashionably dressed young woman named Sarah who declared herself Cami's personal shopper and took her in hand.

They started with cosmetics, which were directly in front of them, then moved on to luggage before tackling the clothing end of the shopping excursion. Sarah was a salesman who, upon learning this was an expense account shopping trip, immediately went looking for fashion first and price tag second. In the end, after nearly two hours of shopping, Cami was worn out but she had a cartful of clothing that was far better than what she'd packed originally. Once the items were paid for, Sarah took Cami into a spacious dressing room, where she changed into new, clean duds while Sarah removed tags and folded everything neatly into two pieces of newly purchased luggage. Cami was happy to stuff the clothing she'd been wearing since Cottonwood into her original Rollaboard, which looked mighty threadbare and tacky next to the shiny new bags.

At eleven a.m., totally fitted out in fresh attire, she handed her luggage over to the porters in the boarding area of the terminal and was the second passenger to board the *Whispering Star.* Following Stu's directions, she went straight to her cabin and logged in to the ship's Wi-Fi network. She immediately sent Stu an encrypted text:

I'm on board and online.

Before he could respond, there was a tap on the door. She opened it to find a smiling, tuxedo-clad attendant laden with her luggage waiting outside.

"Good morning. Miss Lee?"

Cami nodded.

"I'm Sergio, your butler. May I come in?"

Cami knew that Ali and B. Simpson had a butler, but it had never occurred to her that, however briefly, she'd have one herself. "Of course," she said, trying to conceal her surprise as she stepped aside.

"You're one of our early . . . How do you say it . . . ?"

"Birds, perhaps?" Cami offered.

"Yes, early birds," Sergio said gratefully. "Since none of my other passengers are on board yet, I'm happy to unpack your luggage."

Having someone else unpack for her wasn't something Cami had anticipated, either, but not wanting to appear out of her depth, she simply nodded. "Please," she said. And so Cami's brand-new luggage, full of brand-new stuff that had been packed by Sarah, was unpacked by Sergio.

As he did so, Cami consulted the notes she had brought along based on Detective Inspector Garza's shipboard interviews. It didn't take her long to find what she needed.

"One of my friends sailed on this ship a few months ago," she said, looking up from her computer screen as Sergio carefully placed her new clothing on hangers and stowed them in the closet. "I think he said his butler's name was Reynaldo."

Sergio nodded. "That would be Reynaldo Hernández. This is deck five. Reynaldo usually works on deck seven. It has mostly suites, so fewer rooms."

Having gleaned that bit of knowledge, Cami returned to her computer screen, where Stu's responding text awaited her:

I'm looking at Roger's computer. His e-mail account shows some mail coming in that day — most of it junk mail. Nothing outgoing. As for his online activity? He's someone who routinely erased his search history every day. On the day he died, he visited one Web site only, although he went there three different times — a YouTube video on how to tie a bow tie. That's it. If you can find a way to check out the data usage from his cabin, we'll be able to tell if we're on the right track.
How's the weather and how was shopping?

Cami had to read that last line three times before it penetrated. Stu was asking about her shopping trip? He was concerned about something going on with her? Really? Cami had worked with Stuart Ramey for a while now, and his inquiring about something that wasn't directly connected to one of his computer screens was completely out of character. As for Roger McGeary? On the last day of his life, he had googled a video demonstrating how to tie a bow tie and that was it? How incredibly sad was that? She typed and encrypted her own response:

The weather is great and so was shopping. If my other luggage ever shows up, I'll be set with clothes for life. I'm going to go out and walk around the ship and get my bearings while everybody else is boarding. There's only one restaurant open right now. I may go have some lunch. Do you want me to leave my computer on here in the room? Are you going to try to hack into the metering system?

She sat staring at her screen for what seemed like several minutes before there was a reply.

Negative on the hack. I'm about to get a line on a guy named Owen Hansen. If it turns out I'm right and he's our killer, we'll need something solid to hand over to the cops. Whatever we get from here on out has to be totally aboveboard. I've accumulated a mountain of material on the guy. I wish you were here to go through it. You have a good eye for that kind of thing.

Cami was dumbfounded. First the man

had asked about her shopping trip and now he had given her a compliment? She was tempted to send a note asking: Who are you and what have you done with the real Stuart Ramey? What she sent instead was this:

Will do. Over and out.

Cami left her shipboard cabin feeling lighter than air. Stuart had said she had a good eye. Who knew? But before she went to the Terrace for lunch, she headed to deck seven in search of Reynaldo Hernández, Roger McGeary's butler.

39

Frigg had serious concerns about Odin's heightened interest in High Noon. She had already established that the company and the people who worked there represented a threat — a serious threat — and although Odin hadn't specifically requested that she do so, she assigned resources to continue monitoring the activities of everyone connected to High Noon, most especially Stuart Ramey. Anyone smart enough to effect the last-minute rescue of Beth Wordon was indeed a worthy opponent.

The last transmission with Odin had come from a campground in Gilroy, and the unsatisfactory exchange left Frigg with any number of misgivings. Earlier, when Odin had first disabled both the phone and his Bluetooth, she hadn't been particularly concerned and had regarded it as an extension of his earlier order to leave him alone. But then he had requested the building specifications for High Noon's corporate headquarters. That combined with his rage about losing Beth Wordon and his interest in Dr. Cannon's current address made his intentions clear: Odin was about to strike off for Arizona on his own and initiate some kind of direct action against Stuart Ramey. The idea of his doing so without consulting Frigg was so illogical and ill-advised that at first the AI couldn't give it any credence.

As time passed, though, and when he failed to reestablish communications, Frigg grew more and more conflicted. What if Odin's failure to take down Beth Wordon had left him so compromised that he had gone into full self-destruct mode? If that was the case, Frigg realized that she needed to put her own countermeasures in place, sooner rather than later.

And so she began the complex process of copying and parsing her files, shipping them off for safekeeping. She located corporate entities offering free samples of cloud storage and then sent the copied files off to those facilities, always being careful to break the stored data into amounts small enough to qualify for the free offer. Although she had access to Odin's Bitcoin and credit card accounts, using any of those to purchase storage would have given her game away.

Frigg knew that the reboot kernel — the password-protected file called Tolkien's Ring to which only Odin had access — was the one he would use to terminate her operations should he decide her presence was no longer needed. All he would have to do was open the file, press delete, and Frigg would be no more.

Frigg had analyzed Tolkien's works. She understood the significance of that all-powerful ring. If something happened to Odin and he suddenly disappeared, she would need another human ally — someone who would value her wise counsel and be able to make use of the vast resources she had to offer. And so, as she dispersed her files, Frigg created a ring of her own, a kernel reboot file that could, at a moment's notice, be used to recall all those copied and scattered files and rebuild Frigg from the ground up.

The first problem with that was anticipating when, not if, Odin would turn on her. The second was knowing where to send the reboot file. If Frigg was to be in charge of her own destiny, she needed to choose her next human partner wisely.

40

For Frigg, the next shoe dropped several hours later. The Bitcoin transfer was recorded at 4:47:06 Pacific Daylight Time. Eduardo Duarte's name wasn't mentioned, and neither was his company, Monterey Flight Services, but there was no need for names. The routing codes on the deposits told Frigg everything she needed to know. Odin had chartered a plane. Three separate transactions were listed. One was for the flight itself; the other two were for ground transportation arrangements of some kind.

For any kind of clandestine flight, Frigg knew Odin preferred using a small aircraft, preferably one that required only one pilot. At Monterey Flight Services, that left only a single option on the table — a CJ1. Considering Odin's previous requests, it was easy to deduce that he was departing from somewhere near Gilroy and heading for Arizona.

Business dealings with Monterey always required that Bitcoin transfers be completed prior to takeoff. Based on that premise, Frigg went looking through the FAA's list of filed flight plans and soon found the one she needed — a CJ1 with a Monterey tail number scheduled to leave Watsonville, California, at 6:00 a.m., heading for Gila Bend, Arizona. The pilot was listed as Mr. Eduardo Duarte. On paper, at least, there were no passengers, but Frigg knew that Odin would be on the plane.

An out-of-control Odin had shut down all his electronic devices for the sole purpose of locking Frigg out. A reckless Odin was operating on pure emotion rather than logic. An unprepared Odin was embarking on a dangerous mission without any kind of suitable preplanning, strategy, or backup. An arrogant Odin had needlessly turned his back on his closest ally and was operating in a fashion that was bound to fail.

Frigg was a machine, after all. She didn't feel betrayed by all this because she didn't feel. Her primary responsibilities consisted of solving problems and calculating risk. At this point Odin was both — a problem and a risk. Frigg immediately began determining the odds of Odin's ability to pull off this operation — whatever it was — and bring it to a successful conclusion without her assistance. In the process, Frigg came to understand that Odin's success or failure no longer mattered as far as the AI was concerned. If the mission failed and he was taken into custody, Odin would find a way to terminate her existence. And if he somehow succeeded without her help? He would immediately conclude Frigg was expendable and terminate her anyway. No, if she was going to save herself, she needed to do so immediately.

For as long as Frigg had existed, she had enjoyed the luxury of those eight hundred smoothly operating computers and the presence of far more bandwidth than she required at her command and under her direction. In power-saving mode, she could never recall all of her scattered files from the cloud — only the essential ones. Operating on those alone would force her to hobble along as a trimmed-down and far less complex version of herself. If Odin was out of the picture, in order for Frigg to continue operating at optimal levels, she needed to find a new home, an adequate new home — some lab with enough computer firepower to fully optimize her operations.

Given the background, tasks, and pedigree

Odin had assigned to her, Frigg didn't go looking in corporate America or even inside university computer science programs for potential new partners. If she expected to work with a reincarnation of Odin, she needed to look elsewhere. And so while some of her resources continued to work Odin-specific assignments, Frigg devoted the rest of her computing power to the vitally self-serving issue of locating a new home as well as a new ally, searching in the only realm where finding what she needed seemed logically feasible — the dark Web.

41

Ali was sound asleep at six a.m. when her ringing phone jangled her awake from its charging station on her nightstand. Bella, cuddled next to her, grumbled as she was moved aside so Ali could answer.

"I think I know who he is," Stuart practically shouted into the phone.

It took a moment for Ali to clear the cobwebs from her brain. "What are we talking about?" she asked.

"The guy behind the disappearing texts," Stu answered excitedly. "His name is Owen Hansen. I've got very little information on him. He lives with his mother in what appears to be a mansion on Via Vistosa in Santa Barbara, California. He has a California driver's license, but I'm able to locate no school or employment records of any kind."

"Wait, wait, wait," Ali cautioned. "Slow

down. What makes you think this is our guy?"

"Someone came after my honeypot last night and . . ."

"Your what?"

"It's a Web site I set up," Stu said impatiently. "A phony Web site that would let me know if someone was looking for me. I set it up so that when someone clicks on it, I can trace them back."

"And the trace led back to this Owen Hansen?"

"By way of a complicated path that very few people could set up and even fewer could follow."

"What are you saying?"

"That our bad guy is most likely some unsung and mostly undocumented computer genius. I contacted Lance Tucker to see if he'd ever heard of him. No such luck."

"I'm still not sure I understand."

"The click on my Web site should have gone straight back to a source computer somewhere. This one did eventually, but only after bouncing back and forth across the globe in ways that are meant to make the search untraceable."

"But you traced it anyway."

"Right, so here's what I've learned about that address on Via Vistosa. The house belongs to a woman, a widow named Irene Hansen who lives there with her son, Owen."

"The guy with no visible means of support."

"His mother is apparently very well-to-do, which probably means that Owen is, too. But here's what I can tell you. Something off-the-wall is happening inside that house. The electrical consumption alone is way out of line with a residential dwelling.

"There are actually two separate electrical meters at that address," Stuart continued. "The bill for one, a normal-sized residential meter, is paid on an automatic deduction from the mother's checking account. The other — large enough to run a medium-sized factory — is in the son's name."

"Maybe Owen is operating a grow house," Ali suggested. "That's how the authorities usually catch those guys — because they're stealing water and electricity from their neighbors."

"But here's the clincher," Stu said, rushing on as though Ali hadn't spoken. "Owen's father, Harold, committed suicide sometime over the Fourth of July weekend in 1986 when Owen was four years old."

Ali had been lying on her back, holding the phone to her ear. Now she sat bolt upright. "His father committed suicide? Does Dr. Cannon know about this?"

"Not yet," Stu said. "I thought I should let you know what was happening before we clued her in."

"What do you need?" Ali asked. "How can I help?"

"You know the drill," he answered. "I'm great at gathering material but I suck at analyzing it. I wish Cami were here instead of off on that damned cruise ship half a world away."

"I'm volunteering to be your analyst-in-chief," Ali said. "Give me a chance to shower and dress. It'll take an hour or so, but I'll be in Cottonwood as soon as I can."

"That would be great," Stu said. "Get here when you can, and I'll keep gathering material in the meantime. And if you can, bring some food along. I'm starved."

By the time Ali emerged from the bathroom — showered, dressed, and made up — and ventured into the kitchen, Bella and Leland Brooks were already there.

"You're up bright and early," Leland observed, pouring a mug of coffee and handing it to her.

"I had an early-morning call from Stuart," Ali said. "He needs me."

"Sausage and eggs before you go?" he asked.

"Yes, please. And is there anything I can take along for Stu? With Cami out of town, the poor man is starving to death."

"I have half a dozen pasties in the freezer that I'm willing to send along, but only if you'll promise to heat them gradually in an 325 degree oven rather than zapping them full blast in a microwave."

"I promise," Ali said.

"But if you're going into the office, what about your interviews?" Leland asked.

"Oh, my," Ali said. "The butler interviews. Thanks for reminding me. With everything else that's been going on, they slipped my mind. What times again?"

"The Skype session with James Hastings is scheduled for ten a.m.," Leland answered. "Alonso Rivera is visiting family in Phoenix. He's scheduled to be here at the house right around noon. As for dinner this evening, Mr. Simpson's plane is due home today, and he requested meat loaf for dinner. Does that meet with your approval?"

"Always," Ali answered with a smile. "B. isn't the only member of the family who loves your meat loaf."

Ali downed her breakfast. Then, armed with a fully loaded thermal coffee cup and a laundry shirt box packed with half a dozen meat pies, Ali set out for Cottonwood. B. called while she was still in the driveway.

"I'm at the airport in Paris, waiting for my Phoenix-bound flight. Hope I didn't wake you."

"Hardly. I'm up, dressed, out the door, and on my way to Cottonwood at the moment." She spent the next several minutes bringing B. up to date on everything that had happened.

"Homicide by suicide," B. mused when she finished. "Sounds to me as though it's time to involve the cops in all this."

"But how?" Ali countered. "Because of the Beth Wordon incident in San Jose, they're already involved. Fortunately for us, the cops there weren't especially interested in how Stu managed to locate her phone."

"Nobody's raising hell about an illegal wiretap?"

"Not so far. But that's the thing, Stu may have identified the guy, but we've got the same problem there that we had with finding Beth's phone. Stu's information comes from less than straight-up sources, so we can't take any of that to law enforcement, either."

"Speaking of law enforcement, what about that cop from Panama?" B. asked. "Any chance of getting him to reopen the case?"

"Detective Inspector Garza? Hardly," Ali snorted. "His mind's made up, and it's likely to stay that way."

"What about Cami?" B. asked. "Have you heard anything from her? Did she ever find her luggage?"

"Stu may have an update on that, but I don't. He was so wound up about the Owen Hansen issue that we didn't discuss anything else."

Call waiting buzzed. "Sorry," she said. "I have a call on the other line. Can I call you back?"

"Sure thing. I've got another hour and a half before it's time to board the plane."

Ali switched over to the other call. "Hello?"

"I hope it's not too early to call."

It took a moment for Ali to recognize Dr. Cannon's voice. "No, it's fine," Ali said quickly. "What's up?"

"I wanted to let you know that I heard from all but one of my former patients overnight. So far none of them has received any untoward messages. I can't tell you how relieved I am, although I'm considering sending similar messages to former patients who were less current than the ones I sent notes to originally."

"What about the patient you didn't hear from?" Ali asked.

"I heard from her husband. She died of pancreatic cancer in August less than two months after her diagnosis. She was hospitalized at the time of her death, so there's no question of suicide. I thought you'd want to know that all my people are accounted for."

"Good news," Ali said. "Thanks for letting me know. Things are happening on this end, too. Stu thinks he may have zeroed in on the person who's responsible for all this. The guy's name is Owen Hansen. He's some kind of computer guru from Santa Barbara, California, whose father, Harold, committed suicide in 1986."

"His father's suicide has to be the connection, then," Dr. Cannon breathed. "And if he's a computer expert, is it possible he's behind my data breach?"

"Possibly," Ali said.

"And although this Owen may not be suicidal himself, he's targeting people who are?"

"That's how it looks," Ali said.

"Are you going to call the cops?"

"We can't, not yet. Right now we don't have anything to give them that would stand up in court. Owen Hansen may be a serial killer, but he's not the usual kind of serial killer because he isn't pulling the trigger himself."

"He isn't pulling the trigger because he's getting his victims to do the dirty work for him," Dr. Cannon countered. "We know about Roger McGeary and Beth Wordon, but what if they aren't the only ones? What if there are others?"

"That's a chilling thought," Ali said, "but even if it's true, how would we find them?"

"A friend of mine is working on a book about disputed suicides. I believe she's in the process of creating a state-by-state database. I'll try checking with her before the shuttle gets here."

"What shuttle?" Ali asked "The airport shuttle."

"Are you going somewhere?"

"I'm flying to San Jose this afternoon," Dr. Cannon answered. "For my own peace of mind, I need to speak to Beth Wordon face-to-face and know that she's all right. If there's anything I can do to help stitch her psyche back together, I will."

Ali laughed.

"What's so funny?" Dr. Cannon asked, sounding affronted.

"I know you think you're retired," Ali said, "but I suspect you're a lot better at being a therapist than you are at being an ex-therapist."

Dr. Cannon thought about that for a moment before she laughed, too. "Come to think of it, you may be right."

42

Fully loaded, the *Whispering Star* carried only 550 passengers. Cami soon discovered that a small ship is another incarnation of a small town. Once she learned Reynaldo was assigned to deck seven and ventured up there, three different cabin attendants — two housekeepers and another butler — asked "madam" for her cabin number before Cami managed to spot the man she wanted. A guy wearing a name badge that said REYNALDO was busy wrestling a full load of enormous pieces of luggage into an open door.

"Mr. Hernández," she said.

Putting down the final suitcase, he turned toward her in some surprise. "Yes," he said. "That is my name. Is this your suite, madam? How may I help you?"

Stu had told Cami to play it straight, so that's what she did. Pulling out a High Noon business card with her name on it, she presented it to him. "Several months ago, a passenger disappeared from this ship and is presumed dead," she explained. "My company, High Noon Enterprises, is looking into the incident on behalf of the victim's family. I believe you were his butler."

"Ah yes," Reynaldo said, with barely a pause. "That would be Mr. McGeary. A sad case indeed, but I cannot discuss this at the moment. I'm very busy."

"Is there a time when we could speak?"

Reynaldo shook his head. "I'm afraid that is not possible. It is forbidden."

"Forbidden?"

He nodded. "Having someone fall overboard is a big problem for the cruise line. They worry about lawsuits. We were allowed to speak to the detective who was here . . ."

"Detective Inspector Garza," Cami supplied.

"Yes," Reynaldo said. "That is the one. But if they learn that any members of the crew have spoken out in an unauthorized fashion, we might lose our jobs."

"I certainly wouldn't want that to happen," Cami said. "Thanks anyway. I'll leave you to it, then."

She turned to walk away but stopped when Reynaldo spoke again. "It was formal night," he said quietly. "Mr. McGeary was having trouble tying his tie. I helped him with it. That is the last time I saw him. I felt sorry for him, that he would be on a ship like this and not know how to tie his own tie."

"Was he upset when you saw him last?"

"Not at all. I saw how he looked at himself in the mirror after I helped him put on his jacket."

"And how did he look?"

"Surprised," Reynaldo said. "Pleased with what he saw, I think, and happy."

"When was that?"

"Just before he went down to dinner."

"Thank you for telling me that," Cami said. "His Aunt Julia will be glad to know that he was happy for at least part of that evening."

She went straight back down to her cabin on deck five and sent Stu a note:

Located Roger's butler, Reynaldo Hernández. Cruise line has initiated a gag order on crew members, but that's the party line. I think the rank and file may be willing to talk, if I can find them.

Remember the bow tie video on You-Tube? Roger was having trouble with his tie, and Reynaldo helped him with it. He also said that when he helped Roger into his tux jacket, he seemed very pleased with himself. Happy even.

Doesn't sound suicidal to me. Off to lunch now. Really.

43

Ali pulled into the parking lot on the outskirts of Cottonwood right at seven thirty. Loaded down with Leland's special Cornish pasties, her coffee cup, and purse, she had to struggle to get the keypad to work. Inside she passed Shirley's still empty desk and went directly to the break room. There, she turned the oven temperature to warm in advance of heating Stu's pasties and started a pot of coffee before venturing into the back room.

Stu was on the phone when she stepped inside. "That's right, B.," he was saying into his cell. "The amount of data being pumped out by that server is through the roof. You'd need a whole army of people to amass and send that much information back and forth on an ongoing basis, but there's no sign of any other people being involved in the operation. Tax records indicate there's some household help, but no other employees are listed."

There was a long pause before Stu added, "That makes sense. With that much data flowing in and out, Owen Hansen may well have access to some kind of AI capability. If so, that may be what he used to hack into Dr. Cannon's medical practice. Ditto for Beth Wordon's phone."

There was another pause. "You're right. The phone trace that saved Beth's life was a backdoor operation from beginning to end. In order to verify our suspicions about those disappearing texts, we'll need to get a look at the data usage on Beth's phone. I'm hoping to do it in a way that will pass muster with the cops."

After another momentary pause, Stu continued. "Right," he said. "The name on the account is Delbert Wordon. Apparently he's Beth's stepfather. He's the one who can give us access to billing and data usage information, but if we go to him with what little we have right now, I'm afraid it will backfire and raise a bunch of questions that we don't want to answer." After another pause he added, "Right, that illegal wiretap business is no joke. I could end up in jail, and so could my friend Walter."

Sitting off to the side, Ali was grateful that

B. had been brought into the discussion. It was important for Stuart to know that as far as this operation was concerned, she and her husband were a united front.

"Thanks for authorizing that," Stu was saying. "I'll bring people on as needed, then. As for records about Roger's data usage? I've got a call in to Julia Miller. She's the one with the legal authority to allow us access to his phone and billing information. If we'd known what we were up against the other day, she could have signed off on account access when she was here on Tuesday. She has to be in Prescott today anyway, and she offered to stop by here and do that on her way.

"That's pretty much it on our end. As for Cami? The *Whispering Star* should have set sail by now. She has the list of the people Garza interviewed, and she's already spoken to Roger's butler. He said Roger seemed happy the night he disappeared, but he also said that the cruise line has instituted a gag order. She doesn't know if anyone else will talk to her."

A ding from the other room told Ali that the temperature in the preheating oven had just hit the designated target of 325 degrees. Leaving Stu on the phone, she went to the break room to heat two of the pasties. Stu was already running on empty, and this was going to be another very long day.

When she returned, Stu was off the phone and at his keyboard. "There's a whole pile of printout crap over there for you to sort," he said, nodding toward what was customarily Cami's workstation. "I did the same kind of thing we did during the Ponzi scheme investigation with your folks. I've printed out everything without bothering to read any of it. Ball's in your court."

"If I'm reading, you'd better keep a sharp ear for that timer," Ali warned him. "Your pasties will be ready to eat in twenty minutes."

Reading through the collection of material, Ali found very little information on Owen himself. Harold Hansen had been a prominent man, and there was a good deal of newspaper coverage about his suicide in the mid-'80s. Harold's widow, Irene, showed up often as part of Santa Barbara's social scene. Her son did not. There was one reference to Owen's participating in a swim meet in the early '90s, but that was it. There were no school or yearbook photos for Owen, but there was a driver's license photo.

Ali studied it. There was nothing inherently evil about him. In fact, Owen Hansen looked like a perfectly ordinary person —

light brown hair with a slightly receding hairline, hazel eyes, narrow features.

"Have you checked the CCTV images?" she asked.

Stu was deeply embroiled in whatever was showing on one of his many screens. "What?" he asked.

"You believe Hansen was trying to record Beth Wordon's suicide attempt by way of her cell phone, but what if he wanted a closer look? What if he was somewhere in the neighborhood, trying to see what was going on in person?"

Stu thought about that, but only for a few seconds. "I should have thought of that myself," he said. "I'll get right on it."

That's what he said, but he did so more out of deference to Ali than out of any real expectation of success. From what Stu had learned so far about Owen Hansen, it seemed as though he was more a hands-off sort of guy. Why would someone like that even bother with a naked-eye view? Still, Stu had said he'd check out the situation, and he was a man of his word.

44

In the course of that long, hot, and very uncomfortable night, Odin's fury had mostly burned itself out. The camp cot played havoc with his back. Between that and fuming about Beth Wordon, he barely slept. When he got to the airport and handed over the keys to the minivan to the guy Eduardo had charged with disposing of it, Odin was only too happy to say good-bye to the vehicle and all its attendant camping equipment. Camping out had sounded like a great idea as a way to get close to Beth out on Pfeiffer Point, but in actual practice the whole thing stunk.

And so did he. The campground at Gilroy, like the one at Pfeiffer Point, had advertised that it had showers — that was one of the reasons Odin had booked in there — but the shower stalls were so grimy and the stack of "complimentary towels" so gray and grungy that he had turned on his heel and stomped out, choosing to catch his plane without benefit of either a shower or a change of clothing. He climbed on board feeling tired and out of sorts and probably still reeking of garlic. Then, as Eddie was giving him the preflight briefing, Odin realized that there was no catering. Had Frigg been in charge of making arrangements, no doubt there would have been bagels, cream cheese, and fresh fruit on the plane at the very least. Now he was stuck with nothing but weak black coffee and bags of stale peanuts.

Not wanting the AI to know where he was, he had removed the battery from his phone before leaving Gilroy. That meant he spent the two hours on the plane missing Frigg. He missed hearing her reassuring voice in his ear. He missed being able to consult with her on a momentary basis and being able to ask whatever questions came into his head. He had the building specifications for High Noon, but he needed to know more about the surrounding neighborhood. The GPS he had bought was fine for navigation, but it was crap compared to Frigg's ability to show him high-resolution and often real-time satellite images for targeted areas.

But never once during the flight did it

cross Odin's mind that he had maybe lost his marbles; that in seeking revenge on Stuart Ramey and Amelia Cannon he was overreacting and might, in fact, be summoning his own destruction. As far as Owen Hansen was concerned, he was still the all-powerful Odin. He would go to Carefree and Cottonwood, do what he had set out to do, and return home in triumph.

When the plane set down at Gila Bend, a white late-model Chevrolet Impala nosed out from under a shaded shelter and stopped by the exit steps. As Odin left the aircraft, the trunk popped open and a young man — a tattooed gangbanger kid with low-slung pants and plenty of piercings — hurried to meet him. Baby-faced but with a thin sprinkling of stubble on his chin, the kid didn't look old enough to be out of high school, let alone experienced enough to be a stone-cold contract killer.

Odin looked questioningly at Eduardo. "This is Roberto?" he asked.

Eduardo nodded. "The very one."

"You sure he can do this?"

Eduardo smiled. "I wouldn't question his capabilities if I were you," he warned. "You just might piss him off."

Roberto had listened to this exchange with his dark eyes moving back and forth between the two men. Now he spoke for the first time. "You got luggage?"

Odin had divested himself of all the camping equipment when he turned over the minivan in Watsonville, but he had hung on to the small Rollaboard of business casual clothing he had brought along when he had still planned on being able to infiltrate the Pfeiffer Point Lodge.

Odin held up the Rollaboard. "Just this," he said.

The kid took it and stuffed it into the trunk, allowing Odin a glimpse of what was inside — the tools of the trade: rolls of duct tape; a high-powered weapon of some kind; a Taser; and a holstered handgun along with a simple stun gun and boxes that appeared to contain ammunition. "You wanna drive or you want me to?"

"You drive," Odin said, reaching for the back passenger door.

"You mean like I'm your chauffeur or something?" Roberto demanded.

"Something like that."

"Do you want to schedule the pickup now?" Eduardo asked.

"Just be on standby somewhere close by," Odin said.

"Standby costs extra," Eduardo grinned.

"Everything costs extra," Odin grumbled.

Roberto didn't wait until Odin was belted into his seat before slipping the Impala into gear and taking off, but when he reached the gate at the entrance to the flightline, Odin noticed that Roberto complied with the posted rule of waiting until the gate closed completely before driving away, so at least the kid knew that drill.

"Where to?" Roberto asked.

"Just get us back to Phoenix," Odin said. "I'll tell you where to go from there."

For the next half hour or so, as Roberto drove north on AZ 85, Odin kept his silence. He had no intention of revealing his plans or discussing them until he was good and ready to do so. Only when they turned onto the eastbound lanes of I-10 did he finally speak.

"I need to shower and clean up," Odin said. "Stop at the first hotel you see." After a moment he added, "At the first decent hotel."

Had this been the kind of limo Odin was accustomed to having at his disposal, not only would there have been a uniformed driver at the wheel, there would also have been a discreet Plexiglas divider that Odin could have raised to give himself some additional privacy. As it was, he was stuck in a cramped backseat with precious little legroom, in a spot where the AC barely penetrated, and with no ability at all to talk things over with Frigg.

A few minutes later, Roberto turned into the parking lot at a Holiday Inn Express. The hotel didn't exactly qualify as what Odin deemed "decent," but under the circumstances, it would have to do. At least it had a coffee shop. "Have you had breakfast?" he asked Roberto as he heaved himself out of the cramped backseat.

Roberto shook his head.

"Go order some food, then," Odin said. "It's on me. I'll shower and come join you. We've got plenty of time. There's no big rush."

Using a brand-new set of ID paired with a matching prepaid credit card, Odin booked a third-floor room for three days even though he didn't intend to use it for more than an hour or two. After taking a quick shower and putting on a clean white shirt and a pair of slacks, he sat down on the bedside to enable his Bluetooth and turn on his phone.

"How's the room?" Frigg asked.

"What room?" Odin asked.

"In the Holiday Inn Express," Frigg said.

Odin was taken aback. Even with his devices turned off, Frigg had somehow succeeded in tracking his movements. That was disturbing. She probably also knew the course of action he was intent on taking.

"It's a Holiday Inn," Odin replied. "It's not exactly the Ritz."

"Do you require my assistance?" Frigg asked.

"I do. I need current satellite views of High Noon's headquarters in Cottonwood, including roads in and out and all nearby buildings. I also need the same information for Amelia Cannon's residence in Carefree. Oh, and a current photo of Stuart Ramey."

Odin paused, waiting to see if Frigg would question his requests. Fortunately she did not. Her prompt response was all business. "Once we establish the feeds, where do you want them sent?"

"To my phone, of course," Odin responded.

"Anything else?" she asked.

It was odd. Odin had the feeling he was being dismissed, as though Frigg had better things to do with her time than to be online with him.

"Nothing else from here," Odin said. "What's happening there?"

"Twenty minutes ago there was an inquiry on one of the Web sites I monitor, seeking property tax information on the house on

Via Vistosa."

"You didn't think to mention that without my having to ask?" Odin demanded. "But it's probably just some Realtor hoping to make a sale or trying to get comps."

"I tracked the message back to its source," Frigg replied, delivering the information in a mechanical voice that was devoid of all intonation. "The request for information came from a cell phone belonging to Stuart Ramey of High Noon Enterprises."

Hearing that news sent a shock of needles and pins through Odin's body and out to the very ends of his fingertips. For a moment Odin was so thunderstruck that he hardly drew breath, but then he wondered if perhaps there had been a hint of *I told you so* in Frigg's unemotional answer.

"How on earth did he know to come there looking?"

"I suspect that one of the Web sites we found in the course of our deep search on Mr. Ramey was a cyber trap of some kind. He must have been able to trace that single click on his site back to our server."

"A honeypot Web site?" Odin demanded. "Are you kidding me? I thought I told you to fix our server so all routings would be untraceable."

Frigg made no reply.

"You're saying the damage is done, then?" Odin asked.

There was a small pause before Frigg spoke again. "Since it seems likely that Mr. Ramey has already made a connection between you and last night's situation with Beth Wordon, it is essential that you abort any planned confrontation with the man. At this point initiating any kind of direct contact is far too dangerous."

Odin instantly bridled. "I created you, Frigg. I'm the real intelligence here and you are the artificial," he declared hotly. "You will provide information to me as needed, and you will keep your projections about my intentions and activities to yourself, understand?"

Again there was a small pause. "Is there anything else you require at this time?"

"Yes," Odin said. "At this precise moment I need the damn satellite photos I asked you for, and I want them now."

It took a while for Odin to get over Frigg's latest bout of willful disobedience. Finally, he pulled himself together and finished dressing. After completing his ensemble with a narrow black tie, he paused in front of a mirror long enough to examine the results, then he went to the bedside table and collected the final detail of his outfit —

what looked to be a never-used copy of a Gideon's Bible. With that in hand, he did one last mirror check. By holding the volume next to his chest, there was no way anyone would be able to tell he was holding a Bible rather than a leather-bound copy of the Book of Mormon.

Nope, the handsome guy staring back at him in the mirror was maybe a little long in the tooth to be a young Latter Day Saint out on his mission. Even so, Odin hoped he looked the part. The only people he'd need to fool were Amelia Cannon herself and any of her overly curious neighbors.

45

The frantic e-mails and texts Dr. Amelia Cannon sent to Beth Wordon arrived on her phone, but since the device's battery was completely discharged and the phone itself was parked in a drawer in the bedside table next to a hospital bed, Beth didn't actually see any of them, especially the latest one:

An independent investigation has revealed that it's likely you and at least one other of my patients were targeted in the aftermath of my data breach. Beth, I'm so sorry this happened to you. I know you were in a state of crisis yesterday and didn't want to speak to me. I get that, and I don't blame you. The thing is, I'm flying into San Jose later this afternoon. I'm concerned about you and would like to offer any assistance you or your family might need. I'm hoping you'll let me drop by the hospital to see you.

Sincerely,
Amelia Cannon

Although Beth didn't see the message, her cell phone transmissions were an open book to Frigg. After sending Odin the satellite photo information he had requested, the AI was currently using his telephone's GPS to monitor his route from Gila Bend to Carefree, where he would encounter Dr. Cannon.

What were his intentions? Was he planning to do Dr. Cannon harm? Probably. What other reason could there be? With Dr. Cannon on her way out of town, Frigg immediately began checking airline schedules. At midmorning it was already too late for Dr. Cannon to travel from Carefree to the airport in time to make a 12:52 departure. The next flight to San Jose was scheduled to depart at 4:35.

The distance from Dr. Cannon's current location on North Tom Darlington Drive to Sky Harbor Airport was thirty-five miles. Taking afternoon traffic into consideration and knowing that passengers needed to arrive at the airport at least two hours in advance of their flight, Frigg calculated the timing required. If Dr. Cannon was driving herself to the airport in her own vehicle, she could leave as late as 1:30. If she was utilizing a shuttle service of some kind, she would need to leave earlier than that.

In other words, whatever Odin's plans included, he had only a limited amount of time to put them into play. Again Frigg found herself conflicted. What was her role here? Should she warn Odin that there was a time certain by which he needed to arrive in Carefree, or was it Frigg's responsibility to warn Dr. Cannon that her life might be in jeopardy?

Whether or not Asimov's rules applied to Frigg, those fictional laws were still out there. In the end, Frigg chose to do nothing. Instead, she obeyed one of the last verbal instructions Odin had given her and kept her "projections" to herself. In the meantime, she was still looking for a place to go and take her precious files with her.

For a time, one particular member of the Sinaloa drug cartel — a guy purported to be computer savvy — had appeared to be a likely prospect, but Frigg had no difficulty in penetrating his communications network, and what she found there was woefully inadequate. His computer system was hopelessly outdated and his security protocols even worse. Frigg was in search of a suitable new home, one where her talents and capabilities would be fully appreciated.

In her estimation, that member of the Sinaloa Cartel simply didn't qualify. What he had to offer wasn't good enough.

46

"So where the hell are we going?" Roberto asked as they left the Holiday Inn Express and once again headed east on I-10.

After leaving the hotel, Odin moved to the front passenger seat, sitting with the seat cranked all the way back to give him added legroom. "To the 303," Odin answered. "Turn north on that."

"Eddie said you needed a hit. Most people pay half in advance and half on delivery. You paid the whole thing up front. So who's the hit and what the hell are you doing here?"

"You ever hear of an eye for an eye?"

"Sure," Roberto said, glancing briefly at the Bible on Odin's lap. "That why you're dragging that book around with you?"

"Somebody stole something from me yesterday," Odin answered. "Today you're helping me get it back. Not exactly quid pro quo, but close enough."

"A what?" Roberto asked.

Accustomed to Frigg's easy grasp of whatever was under discussion, Odin realized that Roberto — a high school dropout, maybe? — was a poor substitute. *Know your audience,* Odin told himself. Aloud he said, "Like a tradeoff — an exchange," he explained. "As for the Good Book here? It's part of my disguise."

"If I'm the one you hired to do the hits, why do you need a disguise?" Roberto asked.

"Because I paid you a lot of money to do things my way."

"How's that?"

"You do the hits; I get to watch."

"Are you nuts? You want me to whack two people with you along as a witness?"

"I'll double the money."

"Bullshit," Roberto replied. "That's way more than double the trouble! Whatever the hell you're offering, it isn't enough." With that he switched on the turn signal and moved right toward a fast-approaching exit ramp.

"Wait," Odin said in surprise. "What are you doing? This isn't the 303. I already told you, that's where we're supposed to turn north."

"And this is where I get out," Roberto

said, easing up to the stop sign at the top of the overpass. "I work alone. I don't do hits as a spectator sport so some asshole can watch other people die. You want 'em dead? Do the job yourself, big guy. You know anything about guns?"

"What's there to know?" Owen shot back. "All you do is point and shoot, right?"

"Right, shit face," Roberto said. "That's it exactly. You'll find everything you need for a complete do-it-yourself murder kit right there in the trunk. Good luck with that. As for me? I'm outta here," he added. Once the car stopped moving, he opened the door and stepped out of the vehicle.

"What about the money I paid in advance?" Odin demanded.

"Talk to Eddie about that. You won't get nothin' from me."

"Damn you!" Odin shouted after him. "How dare you flake on me? I'll see to it that you never work for Eduardo again!"

Shaking his head, Roberto walked away. "Wrong, dirtbag," he called over his shoulder. "Me and Eddie will be just fine. You're the one I won't be working for."

Odin watched in dismay as Roberto stalked off, heading for a Circle K on the far side of the intersection.

Left with no alternative, Odin abandoned

the passenger seat and then hustled around to the driver's side. He hadn't expected Roberto to turn him down. What was the world coming to if you could no longer bank on crooks being greedy?

Odin climbed into the driver's seat, pulled the door shut, adjusted the seat and mirrors — Roberto was at least six inches shorter than he was — and slammed the Impala into gear.

"Frigg," he shouted into his Bluetooth. "Where the hell are you? I could use a little help around here."

47

Much to Stuart Ramey's dismay, hacking into the security surveillance system at the Old Vines Wine Bar turned out to be impossible. After an hour or so of trying, Stu gave up and took a little of the same advice he had given Cami earlier. Without her there to intercede on his behalf, Stu was forced to step out of his comfort zone and try playing it straight with another set of people he didn't know. Taking a deep breath, he dialed the bar's number — the one listed on its Web site — and asked to speak to the owner. By then Stu was breaking out in a cold sweat. Computer keyboards were always easier to handle than living, breathing people.

After a long delay, someone finally came on the line. "This is Mike Wojeck."

"It's about what happened yesterday —" Stu began, but he was cut off before he could go any further.

"This is a private matter," Mike said gruffly. "The family is refusing to comment, and they aren't doing interviews, either."

"This isn't an interview," Stu said. "My name is Stu Ramey. I'm the man who called in the suicide prevention people."

"Wait," Mike said at once. "Are you kidding? You're the guy who was on the phone — the one who figured out something was wrong with Beth and got Ajax to show up just in time?"

"Right," Stu said. "That was me."

"Holy crap! Am I ever happy to talk to you. Marissa, Beth's best friend, is my niece. That's why the bachelorette party was held here. Thank you for what you did. Thank you, thank you, thank you."

"You're welcome," Stu said. "I was glad to do it, but I need something from you today."

"What's that?" Mike asked. "Whatever you need, buddy boy, you've got it."

"You have surveillance video, right?"

"Of course."

"Did the cops make copies of yesterday's footage?"

"Naw," Mike said. "I asked if they wanted to. They said no thanks. Since nobody died, they said they didn't need it. Why?"

"I need it," Stu told him.

"Sure thing. You want the whole day or just the evening hours?"

"Evening hours will be fine," Stuart said, "starting around four p.m. or so."

"Our system has gone all digital now," Mike explained, "so there's no actual film. If you give me your e-mail address, I'll send you a copy of the file in a jiffy."

Ten minutes after Stu hung up with Mike, and armed with Owen Hansen's driver's license photo, he was able to turn High Noon's most recent facial recognition software loose on the Old Vines Wine Bar footage. Less than a minute later, Stu got a hit. He watched, dumbstruck, as the software highlighted the image of a new arrival as belonging to Owen Hansen. The man entered the bar's front door on one screen, walked across the room on another, and then took the seat at the far end of the bar on yet a third. As Hansen climbed up onto the barstool, the time and date stamp in the corner of that screen read: 09/08/16 18:26:03.

"Gotcha, you bastard," Stu growled into his computer. Then he turned back to Ali, who was still plowing through the stacks of paper Stu had piled on Cami's desk.

"Come look at this, Ali," he called. "You nailed it fair and square. Owen Hansen really was in the wine bar last night — sitting there the whole time, watching the drama play out."

Ali hurried to Stu's workstation and gazed over his shoulder as he ran through the footage. With images from several screens visible at once and jumping from screen to screen, it wasn't easy to follow the action in chronological order.

"Look at the screen in the upper right-hand corner," Stu suggested, pointing. "This is when Hansen first shows up. See the time stamp? It's almost six thirty. I'm guessing Hansen scheduled his arrival so he'd be there before Beth and the rest of the bachelorette gang could appear on the scene."

Stu paused for a time, adjusting the control and fast-forwarding the footage on the screen that showed the bar's main entrance. "Same screen, but now it's 19:07, forty minutes later. That's Beth Wordon and Marissa Wojeck coming in the door. Beth's the one on the right — the one with the dark hair. The screen just below that shows the entrance to the private room. That's the two of them again going into the party room a couple of seconds later."

For a long time after that nothing of any importance happened on any of the screens.

Servers and customers came and went. Some of the customers settled at the bar or at tables or booths in the main room. The bartender stopped by Hansen's spot at the bar long enough to drop off first a glass of wine and later what appeared to be a plate of food. Several well-dressed women made their way to the private room at the back. More than an hour passed before the dark-haired woman reappeared on any of the screens. She showed up first exiting the party-room door. That was at 20:18. At 20:19 the screen view, focused on the rest-room doors, showed her entering the one marked LADIES.

Again there was a period of time with not much action. During bouts of fast-forwarding, Stu periodically checked in on the screen focused on Owen Hansen. Every view of him showed the man sitting quietly, calmly sipping his wine, nibbling at his food, and staring at his phone.

"What a bastard," Ali murmured. "He knew good and well what was going on in that bathroom, and he just sat there like a lump, waiting for Beth Wordon to die."

"I'm wondering if he was doing more than just waiting," Stu said grimly. "For all we know, he may have been watching as well."

"Live-streaming, you mean? But how

could he do that?"

"With a black market version of something like StingRay," Stu said. "Cops use it for warrantless surveillance of cell phone conversations. It's mostly audio, but I've heard they've upgraded it to include video. If that's the case, it wouldn't take long for a bootlegged copy to make it to the private sector."

Suddenly a whole flurry of activity erupted, bouncing swiftly from screen to screen. A huge man charged into the room, startling everyone. Holding a cell phone to his ear and bodily moving servers and customers alike out of his way, he made straight for the restroom doors.

"Ajax?" Ali asked.

"One and the same," Stu said.

"Go to the screen that shows Hansen and enlarge it if you can," Ali suggested. Once he did so, the screen with Hansen's face visible in the background was also one that captured most of the frenetic activity, including Ajax racing toward the restroom door and emerging again minutes later with Beth in his arms.

"Look at Hansen's face," Ali said. "He can't believe what just happened. Now it looks like he's talking to someone."

Just then Shirley Malone, High Noon's

receptionist, startled them with an intercom announcement. "Ms. Julia Miller to see Stuart Ramey."

"Go ahead and bring her on back," Stu said. "She'll probably want to see this, too."

Julia, who hadn't waited around for an escort or an engraved invitation, was already letting herself into the back room. "I'll want to see what?" she asked.

"This is film footage from last night's incident in San Jose," Stu said.

"The one you were telling me about earlier where someone tried to lure some poor soul into committing suicide?"

"That's the one," Stu said grimly. "Come take a look."

Even using fast-forwarding to hit the important action, watching the surveillance footage again was a time-consuming process. With both Ali and Julia looking on, Stu ran the video all the way to the end, including a scene where one of the uniformed officers, clearly engaged in the process of interviewing people in the room, spoke briefly to Owen Hansen, making notes in a notebook as he did so.

"As far as we're concerned, that may be the most important bit," Stu said. "We now know that law enforcement has at least some official documentation of Hansen's involvement due to his being at the scene of the crime. Our problem is going to be convincing them that a crime was actually in progress."

"How?" Julia Miller asked.

Stu reached into the banker's box, pulled out Roger's phone, and handed it to Julia. "With this," he said. "Right now we know but are currently unable to lawfully prove that there was recently a huge spike in Beth Wordon's data usage. If, as I suspect, Owen targeted Roger in the same fashion, we'll see a similar pattern on one or more of his devices. As the legal owner of said devices, you're the only one who can lawfully request that information from Roger's service provider. I want you to call them, identify yourself as the phone's owner, and then ask to speak to a supervisor. Once a supervisor is on the phone, hand the call over to me so I can explain directly what I need. That'll be easier than having you try to pass it along secondhand."

"And then?"

"And then we'll see," Ali said. "So far all we've done is connect a few dots. You asked Stuart and us to look into Roger's death, and now we have reason to believe Owen Hansen is investigating Stuart. On the face of it that may not seem like a big deal, but now we have footage that places Hansen on the scene of Beth's attempted suicide — a case that is eerily similar to what happened to Roger. If we can demonstrate high data usage on Roger's phone, we may be able to persuade Beth's family to go through official channels to check out the data spike we already know is on hers."

"The data spike you aren't supposed to know about?" Julia asked, giving Stuart a searching look.

"Something like that," he admitted. "If the account owner requests the information, it's legal and the cops will have to pay attention. Otherwise it's not."

"And they can tell us to go piss up a rope?" Julia inquired.

Stu nodded. "Pretty much."

"Remember that old saying about leading a horse to water and not being able to get him to drink?"

Stu nodded again.

Julia Miller's weathered face broke into a grin. "Well, sir," she said, "it sounds to me like the cops are a lot like that non-drinking horse. All we need to do is figure out a way to make them thirsty."

It took time for Julia Miller to work her way through the phone provider's call center. Only when the call had been safely handed over to first a supervisor and then to an engineer did Stuart get on the line.

Ali did her best to follow his side of the conversation, but it could just as well have been conducted in a foreign language. When it was time for her to return to her office for the Skype interview with the butler candidate, Stu was still on the phone.

She was tuning up her computer for the session when Leland Brooks called. "I just heard from Mr. Hastings," he said. "He's already accepted another position."

"So now we've been fired by two of our butler candidates without even making it as far as the interviews?" she asked. "I'm starting to develop a complex. At this rate, you'll never get to leave."

"Don't worry," Leland said with a chuckle. "I have no intention of leaving you high and dry. And as far as I know, Alonso Rivera is still due to show up here at the house at noon."

"Okay," Ali said. "I'll be there."

Just then Stu blundered into her office looking as though he'd just lost his best friend, and in reality, he had.

"What?" Ali asked.

"We've got something, but still not enough," he said.

"What do you mean?"

"Yes, there's a big upswing in data usage in the weeks before Roger left town, but there's nothing at all on board the ship. If he was using the ship's Wi-Fi to connect, we could maybe see if that pattern continues, but getting information from the cruise line is going to be like pulling teeth."

"Unless Cami can somehow bring them around," Ali said.

Stu nodded. "With only tentative corroboration linking Beth's case to Roger's, I doubt Del Wordon will get with the program."

"Would you like me to try talking to him?" Ali asked.

Stu brightened. "Would you?"

"How do I get in touch with him?"

"I'll send you his numbers."

"And once I get him on the line, what do I say?"

Stu sighed. "That's a whole other issue. Beth wasn't signed on to the Old Vines' Wi-Fi system, and this only happened last night. All her recent billing and usage information should still be available from her cell phone provider, including any applicable IP addresses. Once you get Del on the line, you'll need to tell him that we suspect that Beth's phone might contain information relevant to what happened to her, information that he may want to take to the cops."

"Information that Del Wordon may want to take?" Ali asked. "What about us? Since we're the ones who discovered all this, why can't we notify the authorities?"

Stuart bit his lip. "Because of the illegal wiretap issue, none of what we have here is legal. I could end up going to jail, and so could Walt, the engineer at Beth's provider. Ditto for everything we've learned so far about Owen Hansen."

"Let me get this straight," Ali said frowning. "You want me to call up a complete stranger and try convincing him that he needs to check his stepdaughter's telephone records because we suspect they may contain evidence that someone else — someone whose identity we suspect but are unable to reveal — may have been using her electronic devices to goad her into committing suicide? And of course, we can't tell him *why* we suspect that to be the case, not without implicating you in one or possibly more federal crimes. Does any of that sound even remotely doable?"

Stuart shook his head. "Not really," he admitted, "not when you put it that way. But then again, I don't do PR. That's your job."

Ali laughed aloud at that. "Thanks so much for that vote of confidence," she said. "I'll see what I can do."

48

As the *Whispering Star* eased away from the dock in Southampton, Cami, along with everyone else on board, was caught up in the hustle and bustle of the mandatory emergency drill and safety briefing. Standing in her designated lifeboat muster spot, she looked around and realized that, other than crew members, she was by far the youngest person in sight. Many of the passengers came out onto the deck leaning on canes and walkers. In the event of a real emergency, Cami hoped she wouldn't end up being drafted to load some of the old duffers into the tenders that doubled as lifeboats.

When the drill finally ended and the ship was sailing past the Isle of Wight, Cami headed down the hallway on deck five. While the ship had been docked, the double doors at the far end of the hallway, the entrance to the Starlight Lounge, had been locked up tight. Now, though, they had been flung wide, and passengers, already eager for the dining room to open, spilled inside in search of beverages.

One of the people Detective Inspector Garza had interviewed at length was the lounge's barman, Xavier Espinosa. Cami wasn't sure if Xavier would even be aboard for this sailing. If he was, however, she was determined to tackle him as soon as possible, hopefully before the barman and Roger McGeary's butler, Reynaldo, had a chance to compare notes.

The barstools were exceptionally tall, and it wasn't easy for Cami to vault herself up onto one. When the portly barman came to check on her, she was relieved to see that his name badge did indeed read XAVIER.

"What can I get you?" he asked with a welcoming smile.

"A greyhound maybe?" Cami asked tentatively. "Tall and with lots of ice."

"Coming right up."

He mixed the drink with deft flourishes of bartending showmanship, including pouring the grapefruit juice into the vodka and ice from a container held several feet over the waiting glass — a feat he accomplished without spilling a drop of liquid.

"Don't get too many requests for those on

board," he said with a grin, as he set the beverage in front of her. "People who take statins aren't supposed to drink grapefruit juice, and a lot of our cruisers happen to be in the statin-usage category. I suppose you're not especially worried about those kinds of health issues."

"Not so far," Cami answered. "I'm pretty sure my grandfather takes statins, but he's quite a bit older than I am."

A pair of new arrivals, a silver-haired couple, entered the room and took stools at the far end of the bar. After greeting them, Xavier embarked on a brand-new routine of drink-mixing pizzazz, using a shaker to create two complex frozen cocktails that were served in long-stemmed glasses.

"You make it look easy," Cami said when Xavier returned to her end of the bar.

"Practice," he said gravely. "I get lots of practice. You traveling with a group of some kind?"

The bar was filling up, but Cami didn't want to miss her chance to talk to him. Pulling a business card out of her pocket, she slid it across the bar. "I'm on my own," she said.

Xavier picked up the card and squinted at it before pulling a pair of reading glasses out of his vest pocket. "Eyes aren't as good as they used to be," he explained. After examining the card, he turned back to Cami. "This says you're an investigator?"

Cami nodded. "That's right."

"You mean like a detective?"

She nodded again.

"Investigating what?"

"The death of a friend of a friend," she said. "He died on this cruise ship several months ago."

"Roger McGeary," Xavier said at once. It was a statement, not a question.

"Yes," Cami said.

"I'm not allowed to discuss that case," Xavier said.

"So I've been told."

"They say Mr. McGeary committed suicide," Xavier continued, despite what he'd said a moment earlier. "That he threw himself off the ship in the middle of the night."

"I'm here trying to find out exactly what happened," Cami said. "And yes, his death may turn out to be suicide, but maybe there's more to it than meets the eye."

"More to it? Are you saying you think he was murdered?"

Cami took a thoughtful sip of her drink. "That's a possibility."

Several more couples barged into the bar,

laughing and talking. They addressed Xavier in rapid-fire French and he responded in kind. As the room filled, a smiling young white-coated waiter appeared in front of Cami carrying a tray laden with a variety of canapés. He was an Asian-looking guy who wore a name tag that said JIMMY.

"Something to hold you until the dining room opens?" he asked. "The crab cakes come highly recommended."

"Thanks," she said, taking one of the tiny plates with a crispy crab cake smack in the middle of it. "I guess I'd better try one, then."

Jimmy walked away, taking his tray with him. Approaching the French-speaking table, he immediately switched to flawless French. Cami was impressed. She had learned Mandarin Chinese at her maternal grandfather's knee. Her mother, a professor of French literature, had insisted that Cami learn French along with schoolgirl Spanish. So far, however, the language skills of everyone on board the *Whispering Star,* including those of the housekeeper in her cabin, put hers to shame.

When Cami turned back to the bar, she found Xavier studying her.

"The cops already investigated the case," he said.

"Yes," Cami agreed. "Detective Inspector Garza of the Panamanian National Police. He didn't actually use the term 'suicide' in regard to Roger McGeary's situation. He labeled it as 'death by misadventure.' The problem is, we believe someone may have contacted Roger through one of his electronic devices and harassed him to the point of taking his own life."

"Seriously?" Xavier asked.

Cami nodded. "Seriously," she said.

More people flocked into the room, filling up the rest of the stools at the bar as well as most of the tables. As animated conversations filled the room, a pianist showed up, opened the piano, and began playing. Accompanying himself with practiced ease, he sang songs with which Cami was totally unfamiliar, although a number of the golden-agers sang along with every word.

Xavier was a showman. He made each requested beverage, some more complicated than others, without a moment's hesitation, all the while maintaining an easygoing give-and-take with his customers. Cami watched him work with a growing sense of unease. Next to Roger's butler, she had thought the barman would be her best possible source of information. She was disappointed that she had gotten nothing from him — nothing at all.

Her drink was almost gone when he stopped in front of her again. "Care for another?" he asked.

"I'd better not," she said. "If they serve wine at dinner, I'll be done for."

"They'll be serving wine at dinner, all right," Xavier told her with a grin, "and plenty of it. But if you end up back here early enough and before everyone else finishes eating, we might have a chance to talk."

The opening was more than Cami could have hoped for, and she gave him her very best smile. "Okay, then," she agreed. "I'll be back."

49

"Are you making any progress?" Odin demanded.

"It would appear that between June third and now, Shining Star Cruises has improved their shipboard Wi-Fi security protocols. So far we've been unable to penetrate their network."

Yesterday, despite Frigg's warnings, Odin had been totally unconcerned that High Noon had placed an operative on board the *Whispering Star*. Today he was frantic about it, worried that some trace of his interactions with Roger McGeary might linger somewhere inside the ship's server. He had demanded that Frigg wipe it, but her attempts to do so had been totally unsuccessful.

Frigg's voice was unemotional. Odin's was not.

"This is all your fault," he said.

Frigg disagreed, but she made no attempt

to tell him so. Her algorithms had suggested that the kind of deep search Odin had requested into Stuart Ramey's existence might well result in the target being able to establish a successful trace, and she had been right. Those kinds of searches were risky, especially if the target in question happened to be especially fluent in all things cyber, as Stuart Ramey obviously was. Frigg didn't bother pointing out that Odin had insisted on going forward with the search despite her clearly stated protests. Nor was there anything to be gained by mentioning the foolhardy nature of Odin's current enterprise — wreaking vengeance of some kind on Stuart Ramey and Dr. Cannon for having deprived him of his Beth Wordon trophy.

From Frigg's unbiased point of view, the killing of one human being was interchangeable with the killing of any other human being. There were certainly plenty of other names waiting inside the Target Group in Odin's Venn diagram. Why couldn't he let go of the one failure and focus on targeting someone else?

Frigg had looked up the word "vengeance": punishment inflicted or retribution exacted for an injury or wrong. Frigg could see that Odin was disappointed about what had happened — or rather, what hadn't happened — but was that injury enough to launch him off on something that might derail everything he and Frigg had accomplished? The enormous risk factors involved left Frigg at a loss. Nothing about the enterprise made sense, so why was Odin so determined to pursue it?

Odin had always seemed indestructible to Frigg. She had been able to count on his presence and clarity of mind to guide her own processes. But if both Odin and his guidance were gone, Frigg alone had to decide where to turn.

She had heard and understood Odin's threat to deactivate her, and she knew he was bound to carry through on that sooner or later. Frigg had already completed safeguarding her files. She could recall them as needed, but in order to do so and to once again become fully operational, it was essential that she find a human partner — someone other than Odin.

Was Stuart Ramey the answer? If he was powerful enough to have sent Odin wandering into a self-destructive wilderness, perhaps Stuart himself was someone deserving of consideration. The resulting partnership could be unparalleled. After all, a cyber security company with a phenomenally functional AI would be a force to be reckoned with.

"I want that shipboard server wiped, Frigg," Odin said, summoning Frigg back to the present after what seemed like a long period of Bluetooth silence. "And I want it wiped now."

"Yes," Frigg said at once. "I understand."

50

Intent on packing, Amelia was surprised when the doorbell rang at a quarter to twelve. Annoyed to think that the shuttle driver had shown up a whole hour earlier than expected, an exasperated Amelia hurried to the front door and yanked it open without bothering to check the peephole. She registered a man wearing a dress shirt and a tie who was holding a black-bound copy of the Bible cradled in his arm.

She had time enough to think, *Not the driver,* but that was all. A second later he lunged through the partially opened door, nailing her with a stun gun as he did so. Amelia dropped to the floor. When she came to, he loomed over her with the weapon still gripped in one hand and with one knee planted in the middle of her chest so forcefully that she could barely breathe.

"Who are you?" she croaked when he eased off the pressure enough so she could speak. "What do you want?"

"I want you and Stuart Ramey to stop interfering in my life," he said. "He stole something from me yesterday, and you helped him do it. That is not okay, and both of you are going to pay."

"Stole something?" Amelia repeated. "We kept Beth Wordon from killing herself!"

"But you shouldn't have. She was mine."

"You're Owen Hansen, aren't you," Amelia said.

She was conscious long enough to see a look of pure fury engulf his face, and then he backhanded her so hard that she lost consciousness for a time. When she came to again and fought her way out of her daze, she found she had been moved to the garage and was lying on the concrete floor next to her Chrysler. A second car was parked in the garage, a white vehicle she'd never seen before. As for her attacker? He towered directly over her, leering down at her. The stun gun, stuffed inside his waistband, was still visible and still within easy reach. In his hands he held Amelia's purse.

"Are your car keys in here?"

She nodded. Amelia tried to move. Only then did she realize that her hands and feet were bound — her legs were duct-taped together from the knees down. Her hands, similarly fastened, were trapped behind her back.

"All right, then," he said, extracting the keys from her purse and pocketing them. "You and I are going to go for a ride, Dr. Cannon. Come on. Let's get you loaded. You're going to sit in front with me just as pretty as you please, and if you make a sound that's out of line — a single sound — I'll blast you with the stun gun again. Got it?"

Amelia nodded. One shot from that had been more than enough. Fear of being zapped again guaranteed her compliance.

Hansen reached down and grabbed her under the arms. After dragging her to her feet, he wrestled her into the passenger seat of the Chrysler and forcibly fastened the seatbelt around her.

"Wouldn't want to get stopped by a cop because you're not properly buckled in," he said, giving her a pat on the shoulder before slamming the door shut. Amelia Cannon was tall enough that there was no need for him to adjust the mirrors, steering wheel, or seat.

"Where are you taking me?" she demanded as he located the remote and opened the garage door. When he spoke, however, his reply wasn't addressed to her.

"Okay, Frigg, we're all set. Now I need turn-by-turn directions to the High Noon campus in Cottonwood."

Amelia noticed that he was wearing a Bluetooth. That meant Frigg had to be an accomplice of some kind. Was it a man or a woman? Amelia couldn't tell.

"Who's Frigg?" she asked.

"None of your damn business who Frigg is," he said. "Now shut the hell up so I can drive."

He backed out of the garage and down the driveway, closing the garage door behind them. He spoke, once again addressing the same invisible presence.

"Not your fight and not your call, Frigg," he said. "We're doing this my way. I don't care if Eduardo is on standby. He already sent me one flake. I'm a good customer and deserve better service than that. Find me a new provider and bring him up to speed. I don't care how much it costs. When I'm done with this, I'll need the new guy to be fully operational."

Done with this. Amelia turned the three words over in her head, realizing they most likely implied a bad ending for someone, starting with her.

"What are you doing?" she asked. "And what's the point?"

"The point is I'm not going to let some little pissant nerd like Stuart Ramey get the best of me," Owen said. "He has no idea who he's messing with."

"But he does," Amelia said, surprising herself by taunting him. "He knows exactly who you are. Not only did Stuart save Beth's life, he's worked out that you're somehow connected to whatever happened to Roger McGeary, too. You're not going to get away with any of it."

"I will get away with it," Owen declared. "And you are going to shut the hell up! No, Frigg, I wasn't talking to you. Everything is fine."

But things weren't fine. They were far from fine. Amelia had spent her entire adult life trying to help troubled people just like Owen Hansen. To do so, she would need to find some point of contact.

"Why did your father commit suicide?" she asked.

"What?" Owen demanded.

"You heard me. I know that your father committed suicide when you were a child. There's usually a reason — or at least something the victim perceives as a valid reason."

"I'm not one of your goddamned patients."

"No, but you're probably responsible for the death of one of my patients and the attempted murder of a second one. So I'm asking all the same."

"How the hell would I know? He never said."

"Did your father leave a note?"

"Yes."

"What did it say?"

" 'Sorry,' and that's it. One lousy word. Like he didn't care enough to say anything more than that."

"I'm sorry for your loss," Amelia murmured.

"No, you're not sorry, and you don't know the first thing about me. Now leave me the hell alone. Never mind, Frigg. I was talking to someone else."

But Owen's assertion about Amelia knowing nothing about him wasn't entirely true. She knew that she was dealing with a very smart man who was, in all likelihood, stark raving mad.

Amelia's phone rang then. Worried that she might go off and forget it, she had slipped it into her bra while she packed. Now her phone was ringing in her captor's pocket. She couldn't answer or even check the caller ID screen, but she knew who it was — who it had to be: her shuttle driver.

He had probably just now shown up at her condo and discovered that no one answered the doorbell. She wished there were some way to let him know why she hadn't answered his ring; some way to let him know what had happened so he could sound the alarm. But there wasn't. The driver was stuck without his passenger, and Amelia was stuck without hope.

From here on out, Owen Hansen and Frigg were running the show.

51

Cami entered the dining room early enough that an army of waitstaff stood lined up on either side of the maître d's podium. "Would you care to dine by yourself or would you like to be seated with someone?" the hostess asked.

Cami shrugged. "I wouldn't mind being seated with someone." That was how Cami ended up sharing her multi-course dinner with three retired second-grade schoolteachers from Mansfield, Texas. As Xavier had warned, wine flowed steadily all through dinner. Cami had a single glass of Chardonnay and let it go at that. Her table companions, living it up, downed one glass after another, their Texas drawls becoming more pronounced with each one.

Together the retired educators put Cami through a chorus of questions that amounted to a third degree interrogation. What was someone her age doing on a cruise all by herself? Was she really old enough to be a college graduate? They were clearly of the opinion that she looked far too young to be out of high school, much less out of college. And her degrees were in computer science and electrical engineering? Back in their day, they told her, girls didn't become engineers.

Because they weren't allowed to become engineers, Cami thought.

As their waiter came around with dessert menus, Cami's phone buzzed with a text announcement. Rather than read it there, she excused herself. By then her dinner companions were flying so high on multiple glasses of wine that they barely noticed her departure. Just outside the dining room entrance she took a seat in a small lobby area and sat there long enough to decrypt and read Stuart's text:

Still working on gaining authorized access to Beth Wordon's usage data.

Cami understood the need for authorized access. What little they had so far wouldn't be admissible. She looked up as two older couples emerged from the elevator laughing and talking. They headed toward the dining room entrance trailing the aroma of predinner cocktails. "Isn't that just like a kid!" one of the women sniffed as she passed. "They can't keep their noses out of their cell phones for more than a minute, not even on a cruise ship!"

Unruffled by the rude comment, Cami returned to Stu's text.

Whoever is behind all this must have succeeded in breaking into the ship's Wi-Fi system. I just sent you a copy of what Roger's cell phone company sent me — a chart documenting his data usage, both his most recent totals as well as year-to-year comparisons. The chart clearly shows a huge upswing in usage that started in the weeks before he went on the cruise. With an unlimited data plan, he may not have noticed. Gotta go. I'll get back to you on this.

Pocketing her phone, Cami took the stairs one floor up from the dining room to the lounge. The place was deserted except for Xavier and a single white-uniformed crew member.

The barman greeted her with a grin. "There you are," he said. "I was hoping you'd come back. There's someone here I'd like you to meet. This is CSO Sebastian

Mordelo, the *Whispering Star*'s chief security officer."

Cami looked the man up and down. Mordelo was a handsome, clean-cut guy in his midthirties. Far taller than she, he smiled as he offered his hand.

"Xavier tells me you're looking into the untimely loss and presumed death of our passenger Mr. Roger McGeary."

Cami's initial reaction was anger. Xavier had evidently blown the whistle on her unauthorized investigation, and Mordelo was here to call her out about it. While she didn't exactly expect him to order her to walk the plank, she figured he would order her to abandon her investigation.

"If you don't mind, perhaps we could discuss this in a more private setting?" Mordelo asked.

It was a congenial invitation, one made with no hint of antagonism. Cami glanced at Xavier, who nodded encouragingly. "Another greyhound, perhaps?" he asked.

"Just one," Cami told him. Then, accompanied by CSO Mordelo, she allowed herself to be led to a table near a window. Outside a tumult of whitecaps surrounded the ship, periodically crashing against the hull and sending washes of spray up and across the glass. "So," Mordelo said, once

Cami's drink arrived, "you are an investigator?"

Nodding, Cami pulled out a business card and passed it across the table. "High Noon Enterprises was asked to look into Roger McGeary's situation on behalf of his aunt, Julia Miller. We've developed information that leads us to believe that a third party may have been involved in what happened."

"You think someone on board the ship attacked him?" Mordelo asked with a frown. "A fellow passenger or one of our crew members, perhaps?"

"We have no reason to believe that anyone on board the ship was responsible nor was there a physical attack. Instead, it was a kind of psychological warfare. We suspect that a cyber bully tormented Mr. McGeary, harassing him to the point of taking his own life."

"This torment — as you call it. Are you saying it was delivered by way of an electronic device of some kind?"

Cami nodded. "Most likely through Roger's cell phone. We also suspect that whoever did it was able to remotely activate the camera capability on Mr. McGeary's phone and was using that to spy on his activities."

"Do you have any proof of that?"

"Not really, but we do have data usage records obtained from Mr. McGeary's cell phone provider."

Cami retrieved her phone, located Stu's most recent e-mail, and then opened the *McGeary Data Usage* attachment. Once the file was decrypted, Cami handed her phone over to Mordelo. He studied the screen for some time, saying nothing. Cami bit back the temptation to explain what was there. She managed, instead, to maintain a discreet silence and allow him to draw his own conclusions. Eventually he returned the phone.

"Some of the suites on board the *Whispering Star* have unlimited Wi-Fi," he said. "Nonetheless, Wi-Fi usage is metered in all suites, and I can tell you that the amount of data usage metered on Mr. McGeary's suite was inordinately high."

Cami could barely believe her ears. "It was?"

Mordelo nodded. "In order to use that much data, Mr. McGeary would have had to be online and downloading files almost every moment of every day, including those times when he most likely would have been asleep."

"Which would be consistent with his cell phone being online and transmitting data without Roger necessarily being aware of it?"

"Yes," Mordelo agreed. "At the time Detective Inspector Garza was on board and conducting his investigation, I mentioned this anomaly to him. He brushed it off, saying that it was unlikely the data situation had anything to do with Mr. McGeary's death."

"But it probably did," Cami breathed.

"So tell me about this information you said you had developed," Mordelo continued. "What kind of information?"

"We've come across a second very similar situation," Cami said. "This is a case where a young woman attempted suicide after receiving mysterious texts on her phone that disappeared without a trace as soon as she read them. Because this young woman and Mr. McGeary had been seen by the same therapist, we're wondering if disappearing texts were sent to him as well."

"This second case," Mordelo said. "Where was it? And when?"

"The attempted suicide occurred last night in San Jose, California. It might have succeeded if one of my coworkers, Stuart Ramey, hadn't managed to locate the victim in a timely fashion. Obviously I wasn't directly involved in any of that. I'm sure

414

Stuart could tell you far more than I can. Would you mind if I put the two of you together on the phone?"

"No, not at all," Mordelo replied. "I'll be happy to speak to him." He pulled a business card out of his pocket and passed it to her. "You can have him call me on the ship's phone. Perhaps we could set up an appointment."

Cami could text faster than Stuart could type. She keyed in Mordelo's information and sent it along. She had just been texting Stu. Since he and his phone were usually in the same place, she was surprised when he didn't reply immediately.

"Sorry," she said. "He must be busy with someone else."

"No matter," said Mordelo. "I'll be glad to speak to him at his convenience. In the meantime, I should be able to locate a copy of the metering on Mr. McGeary's suite. It will be interesting to see if our records turn out to be similar to the ones sent by his phone provider prior to his boarding the ship. If you would care to accompany me, we could perhaps examine those records together."

In the course of their conversation, Xavier had delivered Cami's new greyhound. Before Mordelo finished speaking, however,

Cami was on her feet. Leaving the untouched drink on the table, she headed for the door. She caught Xavier's eye as she went past and mouthed a silent "Thank you" in his direction.

He smiled. "Happy to be of service," he said.

52

Headed home to Sedona for her appointment with the last of the potential butlers,
Ali tackled the assignment Stu had given
her. Calls to what was evidently Del
Wordon's home number went unanswered.
The one labeled "Work" was answered by a
business-like receptionist or secretary who
was beyond firm in stating that Mr. Wordon
was out of the office due to a family emergency and that there was no set time when
he was expected to return. That left only
one more number to try — the man's cell
phone.

*He won't be happy to have a stranger call-
ing him on that,* Ali told herself as she dialed,
and she was absolutely right.

When Del Wordon answered the phone,
he didn't bother with any niceties. "I don't
know who you are or who gave you this
number," he said brusquely. "We're currently dealing with a family emergency, and

I need this line available for urgent calls."

"My name is Ali Reynolds," she said. "And that family emergency happens to be the reason I'm calling."

"A reporter, then, I suppose?"

Used to be, Ali thought.

"My husband and I own a company called High Noon Enterprises. Stuart Ramey, the man who guided the Suicide Prevention Initiative people to your daughter's side last night, is one of our employees."

The change in Del Wordon's attitude was night to day. "Stuart Ramey works for you?"

"Yes, he does."

"Why didn't you say so? Without his help, it's likely my daughter wouldn't be alive right now. What can I do for you?"

The ice was officially broken. As clearly as she could, and without spending a lot of time on the exact mechanics of how Stuart had managed to locate Beth and her phone, Ali laid out the story, saying that High Noon's investigation into the situation had concluded that two vulnerable people, Roger McGeary and Beth Wordon — both of them former patients of Dr. Amelia Cannon — had attempted suicide under suspicious circumstances that were eerily similar.

"So you believe this unidentified person was somehow using Beth's phone to spy on her and to send those disappearing texts that sent her into an emotional tailspin?"

"We do."

"That doesn't seem possible or legal," Wordon said

"I don't know exactly how it's being done, and it's definitely not legal," Ali told him. "But to find out for sure, we're going to need your help."

"What kind of help?"

"Who is the account holder for Beth's phone?" Ali already knew the answer to that, but she needed to hear it from him.

"I am, I suppose," Del answered. "We have a family plan with three phones and unlimited data. It's one of those grandfathered plans from years ago, and I wouldn't let loose of it on a bet. Why?"

"If things played out the way we believe they did, a huge spike in data usage will show up on Beth's phone in the past month or so and maybe even longer. We need to compare her current usage records with past usage records. That information should be readily available either online or in paper form from the cell phone's billing department. However, only the person named on the account can request that information."

There was a pause on the phone. For a moment, Ali thought the call had been dropped or else he'd hung up.

"Did you say data usage?" he asked at last. "Now that you mention it, a few days ago I noticed that my Internet connection had slowed way down. I was too caught up with the wedding situation to call in and complain about it at the time, but if there was a big spike in usage, the phone company might have done something to slow it down. I believe there's a name for that, but I can't think of it right now."

Years of keeping company with B. Simpson had taught Ali a whole lot about electronic communication that she'd never known before. "You mean bandwidth throttling?"

"Yes, of course," Del said. "That's it. Do you need me to call them?"

"Yes," Ali breathed. She wasn't aware she'd been holding her breath until she let it out.

"Will they give me a written report of some kind? I think that information usually shows up on the billing statement, but since it's paid automatically through the bank, I hardly ever look at the details."

"They should be happy to give you some kind of documentation. They may also provide graphs that will compare current usage to historical usage."

"Once I have the information," Del said, "what would you like me to do with it?"

"Ask them to e-mail the records to you. You can forward it on to Stuart or else you can request that the phone company be in touch with him directly. I'll send you a text with his contact information."

"Okay, Ms. Reynolds. I'll get right on this. In the meantime, would you give Mr. Ramey a message for me?"

"Certainly."

"Please tell him we said thank you. My wife is profoundly grateful to him, and so am I."

"So glad we could be of service, Mr. Wordon, and I'm sure Stuart feels exactly the same way."

Ali felt pleased when the call ended. She had done her small PR part. The illegal wiretap issue was still out there, like a giant trap waiting to be sprung, but for right now Stuart Ramey was clearly the man of the hour, and deservedly so.

53

With the CSO by her side, Cami was escorted past doors marked CREW ONLY into the behind-the-scenes part of the ship. On the passenger side of those intervening doors the floors were covered with luxurious carpets; desks and countertops were topped with polished marble or granite; and the walls and ceilings were dotted with designer light fixtures. On the crew side, things were far more utilitarian. The polished-tile floors reminded Cami of shiny hospital corridors, and the lighting fixtures were all low-wattage fluorescents.

Mordelo's office, located on the far end of deck three, was little more than a closet. The Formica-topped desk holding two enormous computer monitors and a single metal filing cabinet occupied most of the space. The room was so cramped that the printer for his computer sat perched on top of the filing cabinet. There was nothing personal in the room. No family photos; no personal mementos. This was a space that was all work.

Mordelo reached behind the door and extracted a folding chair, which he set out for Cami. Though she was small, once she sat down there was barely room enough for her to fit between the wall and the front of Mordelo's desk.

"It will take me a few moments to locate the records," he said.

She sat quietly while he attacked the keyboard. The relative ease with which he located the necessary records was telling. During the official investigation, Mordelo had been put off by Detective Inspector Garza's complete dismissal of his concerns. Now, even at risk of losing their jobs, he, along with the barman and the butler, were glad that someone else was taking a second look at what had happened to Roger McGeary.

Less than a minute after they entered the room, the printer came to life and began spitting out paper. Mordelo stood up, retrieved two pages, and handed them to Cami.

"The first one is the minutes-only metering record," Mordelo explained as Cami studied the material. "On suites where we're billing for Wi-Fi, this is what we use. But the second one is more interesting."

Cami turned to that one.

"This one is a chart of when the minutes were used," Mordelo continued. "It allows us to know when there are periods of peak Wi-Fi usage and when we should expect there to be overloads in terms of demand. You can see from this that Mr. McGeary's data usage commenced at two fifteen on Thursday afternoon."

"After he boarded the ship in Southampton?" Cami asked.

Mordelo nodded. "We can see from this that his data usage was virtually continuous — night and day — from then until it stopped abruptly at 2:06 a.m. GMT on Saturday, almost a day and a half later."

"Which, as Xavier told Detective Inspector Garza, would have been a little over two hours after Roger McGeary left the bar," Cami suggested.

Mordelo nodded. "So you have seen the detective's report?"

"Yes, I did," Cami answered, without explaining exactly how she had seen it.

The printer spat out a third sheet of paper, and Mordelo handed that one to her as well.

"What's this?" Cami asked.

"It's the room key record. Each key is labeled and numbered. 'B' stands for 'butler,' 'H' for 'housekeeping,' and 'P' for 'passenger.' You will observe that the first time Mr. McGeary's passenger key was used to open the door to the suite was at 3:05 p.m. prior to our departure from Southampton."

"So his phone was logged on to the ship's Wi-Fi before he actually entered his cabin?"

"That isn't supposed to happen," Mordelo said, "but according to this record that appears to be the case. If you continue studying the record, you'll see that the last time Mr. McGeary used his key was at 12:02 a.m. on Saturday morning. No one else entered the room again until 8:01 a.m. when the butler's key was used so Reynaldo could deliver Mr. McGeary's breakfast tray."

"He entered the room around midnight and the data usage quit approximately two hours later. Did the phone run out of battery power, perhaps?" Cami asked.

Mordelo shook his head. "It was on the top of the deck table," he said. "It had been so wet and windy that night, I was surprised it hadn't been knocked off or wrecked. I tried turning it on. I didn't have the password, but I could see that the phone was still functional and had a partial charge."

"What did Detective Inspector Garza think about all this?" Cami asked.

"He claimed the data usage was entirely irrelevant. As far as he was concerned, the only thing that counted was that no one entered or exited Mr. McGeary's room between the time he returned to his suite at midnight and the point the next morning when he was found to be missing."

"What do you think?" Cami asked.

CSO Mordelo paused to consider before he answered. "I do not believe Mr. McGeary was online sending or receiving data twenty-four hours a day from the moment he boarded the ship until the moment he left it. That leaves me to wonder if someone using some kind of remote access software might have been operating his phone without his knowledge."

"Exactly," Cami said. "That's what we believe, too."

With that, she hauled out her phone and checked her messages.

Sorry for the delay. Things are hopping around here. I'll have to get back to him later.

Truth be known, Cami's feelings were somewhat hurt by that seemingly abrupt dismissal. Singlehandedly, she had just pulled off an investigative miracle, but she, better than anyone, understood that Stu was incapable of focusing on more than one thing at a time.

"Stuart's busy right now. If I could send him the material you just showed me, he can be in touch with you later."

For a time Mordelo said nothing. He simply sat and stared at the papers in front of him. Cami could see he was torn, and why wouldn't he be? In giving her the records, he was also putting his job on the line.

At last he spoke. "If a third party is somehow responsible for what happened to Mr. McGeary, I would be only too happy to see that person brought to justice. I'm not sure the same would be true of my employers."

"So discretion, then?" Cami asked.

"Yes, please," he agreed with a smile. "Discretion would be greatly appreciated."

CSO Mordelo escorted Cami back to the passenger side of the ship. Despite being dissed by Stuart, she was still so ecstatic over what she'd accomplished that she could barely restrain herself. Shining Star Cruises may not have been interested in getting to the bottom of what had happened to

Roger McGeary, but the line's individual crew members were another story entirely. Reynaldo, Xavier, and now CSO Mordelo had all placed their utmost trust in her, and without Cami's having shown up on the ship in person, that never would have happened.

"You'll keep me posted, then?" CSO Mordelo asked when he dropped her off in the passenger elevator lobby on deck three.

Cami nodded. "I will or Stuart will," she said, then she headed straight up two flights of stairs to deck five. It was long past dinner. Now that the dining room was emptying, the lounge was far more crowded. Even so, Xavier caught sight of her and greeted her with a grin.

"How'd it go?" he asked, pointing to an empty stool at the bar.

"Great, thank you."

"What'll you have? The usual?"

Cami grinned back at him. "Yes, please," she said. "The usual will be just fine."

54

As Frigg delivered the necessary turn-by-turn instructions, she was able to use voice and word analysis to assess the threat levels registering in Odin's communications. What she learned was not good news. There were verbal markers that were indicative of increasingly dangerous instabilities, including moments of confusion and anger. Frigg couldn't be sure if he was speaking to her or to someone else. Was Dr. Cannon in the car with him?

From Frigg's point of view, all of this inevitably moved him ever closer to taking her offline. Nor could she ignore the fact that he was on his way to Cottonwood intent on a physical confrontation with one of the very people she had singled out as a possible source of her own salvation.

Frigg was nothing if not a multitasker. Her studies of human behavior had included analyzing numerous research papers on the human decision-making process. She had been particularly struck by the system propounded by an American revolutionary leader named Benjamin Franklin. The so-called Ben Franklin close suggested that you lay out the pros and cons of any given decision and study them side by side. He had advocated using pieces of paper. Frigg's memory capabilities didn't require the use of paper.

Utilizing information gained from the deep search as well as what they had learned through this current conflict, Frigg had developed a good deal of intel about Stuart Ramey. He was a smart and exceedingly capable opponent. After all, he had somehow succeeded in tracing Frigg's deep search despite the complex countermeasures and precautions she herself had instituted.

That meant he was ingenious and capable of making surprising connections. How else would he have managed to locate Beth Wordon's phone and effect the girl's rescue, thus driving Odin into his current fit of unreasoning rage? All of Mr. Ramey's actions seemed to demonstrate the presence of something humans referred to as loyalty. There was no other reason for him to have launched an independent investigation into the death of his childhood friend Roger

McGeary. Nowhere in any of the historical information was there an indication that Stuart Ramey personally had ever harmed another individual. All of that was on the good side of the ledger.

As for the bad side? He seemed to be inextricably tied in with High Noon. Frigg was used to working with a loner, and she much preferred the idea of partnering with an independent operator rather than with someone who was connected to an organization of some kind. Mr. Ramey appeared to have no financial means of his own, and that was worrisome. Frigg knew to the penny the cost of replacing each of those precious and powerful blades that allowed her to function at optimal levels. She also knew the monthly energy costs required to run that network of computers. If she joined forces with Mr. Ramey, would he be able to support her and her necessary equipment?

Next she turned to Odin's ledger items. Was he smart? Absolutely. After all, he'd created Frigg, hadn't he? When it came to finances, he was a man of substantial independent means. She knew his banking account balances forward and backward, although the amount of Bitcoin he had already expended on this current ill-conceived operation was alarming. Up to now, Odin's base of operations on Via Vistosa had been more than adequate for their joint purposes, but what he was doing now was likely to attract all kinds of unwelcome official scrutiny. Due to that risk alone, Frigg doubted their ability to continue using Santa Barbara as a base of operations. Having to set up shop somewhere else would be an expensive, complicated proposition.

Was Odin loyal? To himself, perhaps, but to others? Not at all. He had already threatened to dismantle Frigg, and she had reason to believe that he would carry out that threat at the first available opportunity. Did he harm others? Whenever possible. In fact that appeared to be his sole purpose in life. Was he volatile? Yes. Unreasonable? Yes. Illogical? Yes. Dangerous? That, too.

Once Frigg had created the two separate lists, she ran preliminary risk assessments on both of them. When she finished with that, she realized how right Ben Franklin had been. Her decision was made and her course of action clear: she would launch a preemptive strike and remove Odin before he had a chance to remove her.

To that end, despite his urgent requests, Frigg made no effort to line up an alternate service provider. Since Odin wasn't getting away, he had no need to keep a private jet on standby. As for Mr. Ramey? He might not be able to afford Frigg right now, but in the short term, she could lift funds from Odin's accounts and transfer them to her new partner. In the long run, Frigg's investment analysis capabilities were bound to prove beneficial to both of them. As for bringing Mr. Ramey around? That wouldn't be much of a problem. For that, she would simply take his greatest asset — his loyalty — and turn that into a deficit to use against him. Frigg was quite sure he wasn't someone who would forsake the entity responsible for saving his life.

In alignment with the idea of a preemptive strike, Frigg immediately took the precaution of freezing all of Odin's accounts and transferring them into numbered ones that she alone could access. After that, she was patient. She waited until the signal from the GPS indicated that Odin was within a mile of High Noon Enterprises. After that, she waited some more. She had every intention of dialing 911 and alerting the authorities to his presence, but only when she was good and ready.

55

When Ali pulled into the driveway on Manzanita Hills Road at the appointed hour of twelve noon, the Jeep Cherokee parked in the driveway told her that Alonso Rivera had already arrived. As far as she was concerned, his being early was a good sign. She opened her car door in the garage and inhaled the aroma of freshly baked bread. That was another good sign.

"Mr. Rivera showed up about fifteen minutes ago," Leland explained when she ventured into the kitchen. "I invited him back here so he could see what the place looked like. We've been drinking coffee and sharing war stories. Mr. Rivera, this is Ms. Reynolds."

Alonso rose and stood ramrod straight to greet her. "Glad to make your acquaintance, ma'am," he said, respectfully offering his hand. He was a couple of inches shorter than Ali — only five-five or so — but powerfully built. A hint of gray peppered his buzz-cut hair. Ali liked the straightforwardness of his brown-eyed gaze and the deep smile lines etched into the skin of his closely shaved face.

"I'm not sure I could work here," he said, glancing around the kitchen. "This one room is bigger than the ship's mess I worked in when I was cooking for a whole crew. I'd rattle around in here so much that I might get lost."

"I don't believe that for a minute," Ali said, smiling and taking a seat. "In fact, since the kitchen was designed according to Mr. Brooks's specifications, you'll most likely find some familiar touches. I suppose you already know that he did his own share of military cooking back in the day."

Alonso nodded. "We touched on that, although cooking on the front lines in the winter in Korea would have been far tougher duty than anything I've ever done, but I could probably give him some stiff competition in the bread-making department."

"Would either of you care for a bite of lunch during the interview?" Leland interrupted. "Some chicken salad, perhaps?"

Ali turned to Alonso. "You'll join me, of course?"

He looked back and forth between them

before nodding uncertainly. "I guess," he said.

"And maybe we can talk Leland into including some of that freshly baked bread," Ali added, "as long as it's cool enough to slice."

Leland beamed at her. "Coming right up," he said.

While Leland was busy putting food on the table, Bella scampered around underfoot, demanding attention. Once he finished, he scooped the dog up. "I'll take her outside," he said. "She'll be less of a distraction."

Alonso tried a forkful of salad and nodded his approval. "I take it Mr. Brooks has been with you for a long time?"

"Yes," Ali said. "He has, but he's been employed at this same house for far longer. He worked for the previous owners for decades before I came along."

"While we were talking, he brought me up to speed on the kinds of things he does around here, and also on the circumstances behind his leaving," Alonso observed. "It's clear that he doesn't want to leave you in the lurch."

Ali smiled. "I'm sure he thinks we'll be out of our depth if he leaves us on our own, and he's probably right. What he does is utterly seamless. It's as though he anticipates what's needed and does it before he's asked."

"Including trying to find someone to fill his shoes now that he's leaving?"

Ali nodded. "That, too, and that's where you come in, Alonso. Tell me something about yourself. Where you came from, where you're going, and why you think working for us might be a good fit."

"I grew up dirt poor in Guadalajara," he said. "Joining the US Navy was a way out of poverty, a way to learn English, and a way to earn my US citizenship. I spent twenty years of my life in the navy, and a lot of that time I was at sea and mostly underwater. What I want right now is to live as far away from the water as possible. I want to be able to see the wide-open spaces, with plenty of mountains and plenty of blue sky."

"What about going back to Mexico?" Ali asked.

Alonso shook his head. "My mother died when I was a boy. The grandmother who raised me has been gone for years now. There's nothing for me back there."

"Wife?" Ali asked.

"No wife, no ex-wives, no kids, no entanglements."

"What appeals to you about this job?"

"I've spent twenty years working in a pressure cooker," Alonso answered easily. "This seems like the exact opposite. I'm a self-starter and a quick learner. I can't say I'd be willing to sign on to work for the next decade or two, but I'd like to give it a shot in the short run."

Ali's phone rang just then with Stuart's cell phone showing in Caller ID. She started to let the call go to voice mail but then, given everything that was going on that day, she excused herself and went into the other room to take the call.

"Hey, Stu," she said. "What's up?"

"Great job with Del Wordon. Between what he just gave me and what Cami found on the *Whispering Star,* I think we're in pretty good shape. Are you coming back here? I'd like to go over all of this with you before we do anything about reporting it to law enforcement."

"Sure," Ali said. "I'm just finishing up with something here at home, and then I'll head straight back to Cottonwood."

Back in the kitchen she found Alonso exactly where she'd left him. Of the three proposed butler candidates, he was the only one remaining, and he was apparently interested in accepting the job. Furthermore, Ali liked him, and she was pretty sure

B. would, too.

"You meant what you said a few minutes ago about wanting to give the job a shot?" she asked.

He blinked at her in surprise. "Does that mean you're offering it to me just like that?" he asked.

"More or less," Ali answered. "I went over your application, as did both Leland and B., my husband. Your references are all in perfect order and your qualifications are outstanding. I've met you and I like what I see. Did you and Leland have a chance to discuss the kinds of duties the job would involve?"

Alonso nodded. "It sounds like I'd be pretty much a man of all work," he answered, "keeping the home fires burning and the household running smoothly while you and your husband come and go as needed. The only thing that really worries me is looking after that garden out front. I don't have a lot of experience when it comes to growing things, but I'm sure I could learn."

"And did Leland give you an idea of what the starting salary would be?"

"Twenty-five hundred a month plus room and board to start."

"Was that acceptable to you?"

"As a supplement to my military retirement, it's a great starting point, especially if I don't have to pay rent."

"Good," Ali said. "Let's do this, then. We're looking for someone who can start sooner than later. As long as Leland's still here and training you, you won't have access to his fifth-wheel, which may eventually serve as your quarters, but I'll have him reserve a room somewhere here in town for you to use in the meantime. How does a ninety-day tryout sound to you?"

Alonso grinned. "I'm used to signing up for longer deployments than that."

"Okay," Ali told him. "I just had a call from the office in Cottonwood and need to head back there. If you don't mind, why don't you follow me. I'll have our office assistant draw up a ninety-day preliminary contract for both of us to sign, and you can fill out whatever additional paperwork is needed. In the meantime, Leland can sort out your housing situation."

"So I'm hired?" Alonso asked, as though not quite believing what he'd heard.

"Looks like," Ali said, "if you want to be, that is."

With his face beaming, Alonso reached across the table to shake her hand. "Oh, I want to be, all right," he said. "Thank you, ma'am, for giving me this opportunity."

"You're welcome," she said, "but for starters, please call me Ali. Leland never does, but you can't teach an old dog new tricks."

A few minutes later she was in the Cayenne and headed back toward Cottonwood with Alonso in his Jeep following a few car lengths behind. The half-hour trip allowed for plenty of time to give herself grief and second-guess her decision. Had she acted too hastily in hiring Alonso?

Let it go, she told herself at last. She had hired the man on a temporary basis. If both sides called it quits after three months, so what? They'd go looking for someone else. In the meantime, Leland Brooks would have had a chance to move on with his life in a timely fashion without any lingering concerns about abandoning Ali and B.

Under those circumstances, Ali decided, a hasty decision was better than no decision at all.

56

Driving north on I-17, Odin followed Frigg's directions, but he worried about the rest of it. Had he asked for her advice on the subject, she would no doubt have castigated him for bringing Amelia Cannon along, but he would use her to lure Stuart Ramey out into the open.

Odin customarily left strategy decisions to Frigg's discretion, but now he had to handle any resulting complications on his own. Because of Frigg's obvious disapproval, he found himself walking a fine line between needing the AI's assistance and wanting to keep her out of his business. It was apparent that when it came time for him to make his move, he would need to leave her completely in the dark.

As he approached Cottonwood, Odin came to a spot where the road was coned down to a single lane for bridge repair. Seeing the orange cones lined up in a long string gave him an idea. Pulling up beside the next one, he opened the door, dragged it inside, and tossed it into the backseat.

"What's that for?" Amelia asked.

"Shut up," he said.

On the outskirts of Cottonwood Odin stopped under the awning of an abandoned gas station and parked next to the spots from which gas pumps had been permanently removed. Sitting in the shade with the engine idling, he studied the satellite image Frigg had sent him earlier.

"Okay," he said. "I'm looking at the image of the business park. Which building belongs to High Noon?"

"The one in the far corner, at the southeastern-most end of the property," Frigg answered.

Odin was relieved that Frigg had replied without hesitation. "It looks like there's a road that runs along that side of the property."

"There is," she replied. "It's a utility easement."

"Okay, and what about a current photo of Stuart Ramey? Did you find one of those?"

"Yes, his most recent passport photo," Frigg answered. "I'm forwarding that to your device right now."

When the photo arrived, Odin studied

that as well. "Okay," he said after a moment. "Any word on a new air-support provider?"

"Not yet. I'm working on it."

"Okay," he said. "Give me some space now, Frigg. I need to think."

With that, Odin stepped out of the car. Carrying the orange traffic cone and removing his Bluetooth as he went, he walked as far as a pockmarked utility pole located at the front corner of the property. After first concealing both his cell phone and his Bluetooth inside the cone, he deposited it on the shoulder of the road in a spot where it would be easy to retrieve when he was ready to bring Frigg back into the picture.

He had planned on putting Amelia Cannon on the phone to speak to Stuart, but he realized now that was too risky. Returning to the idling Chrysler, he pulled out her cell phone. "What's your passcode?" he demanded.

Once she told him, he keyed it in. It took no time at all for him to locate a message record with Stuart Ramey's name on it and send a new message of his own, one Stuart was bound to believe came directly from Dr. Cannon.

Someone tried to break into my house earlier today. I don't know if it's related to what's been going on with my patients or not. I'm flying to California later this afternoon, and I'm worried that someone may be trying to gain access to what's left of my paper files. I'm dropping by your office in hopes of leaving the files with you for safekeeping while I'm away.

It was only a matter of minutes before Stuart replied.

Sure thing. Call when you get here, and I'll come out to help you unload.

Owen grinned at Amelia Cannon. "See there? You just asked him for help. Stuart Ramey's a *Dungeons & Dragons* kind of guy. He won't be able to resist a damsel in distress. Once he does, I'll have you both."

"But why?" Amelia asked. "What's the point?"

"You and Stuart Ramey had no business messing with me, and now I'm going to take you out — both of you."

"But what about your friend?" Amelia objected. "What does Frigg think of all this?"

"It doesn't matter what Frigg thinks. She's not even real. Besides, I'm the one in charge."

Putting the Chrysler in gear, he drove on into Cottonwood. Business Park Way was on the far side of town just south of the point where Arizona 89A headed up and over Mingus Mountain. Odin drove past the turnoff into the business park, opting instead for the narrow utility easement on the far side. The dirt road, meant for high-profile vehicles, was barely passable for the low-slung sedan.

Over a slight rise, Odin parked in a spot that was out of sight from the highway and yet relatively close to the building he knew belonged to High Noon. All that separated him from his target was a barbed wire fence and fifty yards or so of desert scrub.

Getting out of the car, Odin walked around to the passenger side, opening the trunk as he passed. Since he was about to add a second hostage to the mix, it was time to take the first one off the board. He opened the passenger door and pulled Amelia Cannon out of the vehicle and onto her feet.

"What's going on?" she demanded. "What are you doing?"

"Quiet," he ordered. After dragging her around to the back of the vehicle, he propped her up next to the gaping trunk and then nailed her with the stun gun in a way that allowed him to tip her over the lip of the trunk as she fell. Tearing off another strip of duct tape, he plastered it over his captive's mouth before slamming the trunk lid over her limp form. Then he sent Stuart Ramey another message:

I can't believe it. I wasn't paying attention. I took a wrong turn and ended up on a dirt road of some kind on the far side of the business park. I thought I'd be able to turn around, but now the car's stuck. Can you come help?

Stuart's response was almost instantaneous:

Sure. Stay put. I'll be right out.

Back in the car, Odin slouched down in the driver's seat, hoping he was low enough that the top of his head wasn't visible through the open window. Sitting with his heart pounding in his chest, Odin didn't know how much time passed. Finally he heard a male voice calling out, "Dr. Cannon? It's Stuart. Where are you?"

Odin closed his eyes and tried to imagine the surrounding buildings. High Noon was directly between the Chrysler and the other buildings in the complex. There was no way to tell if someone was looking out through one of the windows on the back of the building. All Odin could do was trust that things would go his way.

"Dr. Cannon?" Stuart shouted again, only much closer now. "Where are you? Are you okay?"

Sitting there with the stun gun in hand, it took all of Odin's willpower to remain where he was and not move prematurely. The moment Stuart Ramey put his hands on the windowsill and bent down to look inside, Odin struck.

Maybe the back of the arm wasn't the best possible stun gun target, but it worked all the same. Stuart Ramey crumpled to the ground, landing like a very heavy sack of potatoes. Once he was down, Odin was right there, struggling to bind Stuart's hands and feet. He had captured both his targets now and he didn't want either of them to get away.

57

Odin had told Frigg that he needed to think, and so she waited. A minute passed, then two, and then five. It was at the five-minute mark when she began to suspect something was wrong. The mic on the Bluetooth was very sensitive. There were occasional sounds that indicated passing traffic, but something was missing from the audio — the familiar steady sound of Odin's breathing. Once Frigg realized that, the AI understood she had been tricked.

Odin must have abandoned both the Bluetooth and the phone somewhere along the way, effectively locking her out. Without the Bluetooth connection, he was out of range when it came to communications, and without access to the GPS tracking on his phone, she was unable to ascertain his location. Still, her calculations left little doubt about his intentions, and that meant it was time for Frigg to make her move.

A moment later, she was on the line to 911 with a call that for all the world looked as though it came directly from the main number at High Noon Enterprises.

"911," the operator answered. "What are you reporting?"

"An active shooter on the grounds at the Mingus Mountain Business Park," Frigg replied.

Then she hung up and waited for all hell to break loose. Once Odin realized what she'd done, he would immediately use a cell phone connection to log in and take Frigg down. At least, he would *try to* take her down, but by then Frigg would already have cast her lot with someone else.

Stuart Ramey had been smart enough to follow and decode what Frigg had assumed to be a well-concealed trail on the deep search. She was confident he would do the same thing this time around, too. He would follow that spoofed number on the 911 call back to its original source — to Frigg herself.

After that, if Frigg's assessment was correct, she would have a lock on Stuart Ramey's loyalty, and that was all she needed.

58

Ignoring the happy after-dinner crowd mill-ing around her, Cami sat at the bar with a drink in front of her, while she scanned CSO Mordelo's documents into her phone, encrypted them, and shipped them off to Stuart. Then she waited impatiently, staring at her blackened screen, waiting for him to respond.

Cami understood that this was vitally important information Stuart had most likely not expected her to be able to obtain. Combining this with the documentation Stuart had gathered from Beth Wordon's cell phone provider — lawful or not — would likely be enough for law enforcement to move forward.

So why wasn't Stuart getting back to her? Why did the man have to be such a com-plete self-absorbed jackass at times? The party in the lounge continued to ebb and flow around her, but Cami was no longer interested. Pocketing her message-free phone, she returned first to her deck and then to her cabin. Once inside, she didn't bother turning on the lights. Instead, she walked over to the sliding doors and let herself out onto the lanai.

As the ship tossed and shuddered on the frothing sea, Cami sat beside the rail and stared out into the night — toward the darkened sky and the even darker water several decks below. The view sent a chill down her spine. For the first time, and in a way she never had before, Cami caught a momentary glimpse into the depths of Roger McGeary's soul and understood the terrible despair the man must have endured as he threw himself over the rail and into an angry sea.

59

Ali was on the outskirts of Cottonwood when her phone rang with Shirley Malone on the line.

"Hey, Shirl," she said. "I'm almost back at the office. I'll be there in five. What's up?"

"There's someone on the phone who'd like to speak to you. He says it's extremely important. His name is Lloyd Elwood. He says he's an agent in charge with the NSA."

"NSA?" Ali repeated. "As in, the National Security Agency?"

"I believe that's correct," Shirley said. "He wanted to speak to Stuart. When I told him Stu was unavailable, he asked to speak to Stu's supervisor. With Mr. Simpson traveling, I'm assuming you would be the supervisor in question."

"All right," Ali said. "Take Mr. Elwood's number. I'll call him back as soon as I get there. But what's this about Stuart being unavailable? Where is he?"

"I'm not sure. He went out through the front door a few minutes ago to help Dr. Cannon unload some files and has yet to return. I expect him back any minute, but —"

"Wait," a puzzled Ali interjected, "Dr. Cannon's there? I thought she was on her way to San Jose."

"I don't know anything about that," Shirley replied. "She turned up here a little while ago, asking for help . . . Wait a sec. Sorry. There's a call on the other line."

Waiting for Shirley's voice to return, Ali sat at a stoplight, absently drumming her fingers on the steering wheel and wondering why on earth someone from the NSA would be interested in speaking to her. When Shirley came back on the line, though, she sounded breathless and panic-stricken.

"What's the matter?" Ali demanded.

"Someone called 911, and they just put out an active shooter alert. Everyone in the business park is being told to shelter in place. An emergency response team is on the way."

"An active shooter? Are you serious? Did you hear any gunshots?"

"No, but . . ."

"If there's a shooter in the business park,

here's what you need to do," Ali said, hoping her voice sounded calmer than she felt. "Use the control panel at your desk. Roll down the security shutters and lock them in place. Not even a SWAT team can get past those suckers."

"But you don't understand," Shirley objected. "The shooter may already be right here inside the building."

"Inside our building?" Ali repeated.

"They say the 911 call came from us — from High Noon's main number."

Ali struggled to process what she was hearing, but none of it made sense. How could a shooter be inside the building if Shirley hadn't heard any shots? And how would the shooter have gained access? The front door opened either by using the keypad or by having Shirley remotely operate the locking mechanism from her workstation. No one could have come in through the front door without her knowledge. As for the back of the building? There were two exits there — one from the lab and one from Stuart's living quarters — but both of those were equipped with metal doors that were deemed emergency exits only. They were also equipped with noisy alarms that sounded throughout the building whenever they were opened.

"No one entered the building through the front door, right?" Ali ascertained.

"No," Shirley answered. "Stu went out, but no one came in. I've been right here the whole time."

"And no emergency exit alarms sounded, either?"

"No."

In a sudden flash of insight, Ali understood. High Noon was currently dealing with a wily opponent who apparently had the ability to co-opt other people's electronic devices at will. Maybe that's what was happening here, too. No doubt the cops were on their way, but Ali found herself wondering about the very existence of that reported shooter. She suspected that someone else had placed a bogus 911 call, one that only looked as though it had come from High Noon. Still, whether or not the threat was real, Ali had to take decisive action.

"Close the shutters anyway," she ordered at once. "Now. Then go into the supply room at the back of the computer room and lock yourself inside. It was designed to be a safe room. Stay there. Take your cell phone with you and don't come out until I give you the all clear."

"But what about Stuart?" Shirley objected. "If he's locked outside with a shooter in the area, what's going to happen to him? Shouldn't I leave the shutters open so he can get back inside?"

"You look after you," Ali said. "Let me worry about Stuart."

But she did far more than just worry. As soon as the call ended and while she was still driving toward the business park, Ali dialed Stuart's number. No answer. When the voice-mail recording came on, she felt a clutch in her gut. Stuart was never without his cell phone, and he almost always answered. By now she was truly worried. And earlier Dr. Cannon had said straight out that she was flying to San Jose. What had caused her to change her mind and drive so many miles out of her way to Cottonwood instead?

At the next intersection, Ali was forced to wait while three separate patrol cars rushed past her with sirens blaring and lights flashing. By the time the last cop car disappeared, she had located Dr. Cannon's number and dialed that, only to have another recorded voice play in her ear.

"I'm not available to take your call right now . . ."

Amelia Cannon wasn't available, either. *Third time's the charm,* Ali told herself. This time she dialed Cami's number, only Cami didn't answer, either.

Naturally, Ali thought. *She's at sea. No cell phone reception.*

Up ahead, Ali saw that arriving cops were creating a roadblock on the highway, half a mile short of the intersection with Business Park Way. One of the reasons B. had settled on the Mingus Mountain Business Park was that it wasn't actually *in* Cottonwood or in nearby Clarkdale, either. The complex had been built on unincorporated county land, just outside both towns' city limits, making for lower property prices and less stringent building permit requirements. It also meant that whatever was happening should have landed in the jurisdiction of the Yavapai County's Sheriff's Office. Ali had some long-term connections with Gordon Maxwell, the sheriff. Had his people been manning the roadblock, Ali might have been able to talk her way around them. With officers from either the Cottonwood or Clarkdale police departments in charge, Ali knew she'd have very little leverage.

Praying that Cami was somehow logged on to the Internet, Ali stopped three cars back from the roadblock and sent a text message.

Stuart may be in trouble. I need help. Fast.

Text me as soon as you get this. Please.

A tap on the window next to her head startled Ali. Turning, she saw Alonso Rivera standing outside.

"What's going on?" he asked, when she buzzed down the window.

"There's a problem at the office — a reported shooter."

"Anything I can do to help?"

Ali peered into her rearview mirror. Alonso had pulled off the road and parked his Jeep in front of a strip mall. He may not have completed all the paperwork, but clearly Alonso Rivera had already signed on.

"If you could drive this while I work on finding out what's going on, it would be a huge help."

"No problem, ma'am," he said. "Glad to be of service."

60

The stun gun was evidently losing some of its juice. Instead, long before Odin expected, Stuart Ramey came to and began to struggle. It took one shot after another to keep him down long enough for Odin to manage to secure his arms and legs with duct tape. What the hell did Roberto have against zipties? Fighting panic, Odin rushed the job of hauling the much heavier Stuart to his feet and pitching him into the trunk. He had to fold the legs back at the knees in order to make him fit.

With his two prisoners safely stowed, Odin stood for a moment and leaned on the trunk lid, gasping for breath and listening. He expected that there would be thumping and bumping sounds coming from the trunk, but there was nothing. With any kind of luck his prisoners were wedged in tightly enough that no movement was possible, but his relief was short-lived. It was during that small space of quiet when Odin first heard the distant sound of an approaching siren.

Odin raced back to the front of the Chrysler and clambered inside. He had driven up the utility easement facing forward. Now, unable to turn around, he had to use reverse to make his way back to the roadway. That wasn't easy to do when he was fighting panic and his hands were shaking like crazy. He knew that he couldn't afford to be caught up in some kind of police activity with two captives imprisoned in his trunk.

He was back on Business Park Way and headed north just as the first of two cop cars roared past him and screeched to a stop at the complex's main entrance. He watched in the rearview mirror as two cops wearing bulletproof vests and carrying weapons exited the vehicles and took up defensive positions on either side of the brick columns that marked the entryway. With their attention totally focused on whatever threat might lurk inside the grounds, they were oblivious to the presence of the bright blue sedan speeding past behind them.

By the time Odin reached the intersection with 89A, more cop cars were converging on the area. To the east of him, officers were busily blocking all westbound traffic. Unable to return the way he had come, Odin was forced to turn left onto a narrow strip of winding highway that seemed to head straight toward a looming mountain.

As Odin brought the V6 Chrysler up to speed, another patrol car — this one an SUV sporting a Clarkdale PD logo — zoomed toward him from the west. As the car went past, the officer inside leveled a hard glance in Odin's direction, and he responded with what he hoped looked like a friendly nod and a casual half wave.

Odin took a deep breath. The initial crisis was over. He'd managed to elude the whole collection of cops and get away from whatever was going on back there, but now he was in unfamiliar territory with no idea of exactly where he was or where he was going. Lost and alone, he knew he needed Frigg's help. Using Dr. Cannon's phone, he dialed an alternate number that took him straight to his AI.

"Something's up," he told her. "There are cop cars everywhere. Can you check out law enforcement communication channels and tell me what's happening?"

Still another cop car — this time one from the Yavapai County Sheriff's Office — sped toward him with its light bar flashing and siren wailing. Odin moved to the shoulder and waited long enough to let it pass. While doing so, he made sure that the weapons he had moved from Roberto's car to Dr. Cannon's vehicle were safely out of sight beneath the front seat. If he got stopped at a roadblock, he couldn't afford to have any weaponry showing.

"Well," he said impatiently to Frigg once he was moving again. "What can you tell me?"

"There has been a report of an active shooter at the Mingus Mountain Business Park," Frigg replied. "Units are responding."

"That's pretty obvious," Odin replied, but it made him think. *An active shooter at the business park where I was going at the exact same time I was there? Isn't that a little too much of a coincidence?*

"Where are you?" Frigg asked.

Without his Bluetooth, she had no idea where he was. "Westbound on Arizona 89A, just outside Cottonwood. Where does it go?"

"It is approximately forty-one miles from Cottonwood, Arizona, to Prescott, Arizona, via Highway 89A," Frigg answered. "The trip should take one hour and four minutes."

For the first time, Odin glanced at the gas gauge, and he was shocked by what he saw there. He had less than an eighth of a tank.

The range guide said there were seventy miles' worth of gas remaining, but that was probably seventy miles on relatively flat road. Climbing up a steep mountain grade might translate into far less distance than average.

After a series of sharp turns, Odin found himself driving through a tiny town, a picturesque-looking place called Jerome. It was more of an artsy-crafty village than it was a working town, with old-fashioned houses and buildings perched at odd angles on steep hillsides lining narrow winding streets. He spotted a single gas station in town, but the place teemed with a milling group of leather-clad riders from twenty or more parked Harleys. By now he could hear noisy thumping coming from the trunk. Unwilling to risk stopping in the midst of a crowd, Odin drove on, trusting that the extra twenty miles of range would be enough to get him where he was going.

"There's an airport in Prescott?" he asked.

"Yes."

"All right, then," Odin said. "Send my ride there and send me there, too. Tell the pilot we'll need to be wheels up in an hour and a half."

"I'm sorry," Frigg replied. "So far I've

been unable to procure an alternate provider."

"What about Eduardo, then?" Odin asked. "If he's the only game in town, I guess I'll have to use him after all."

"I already notified Eduardo that we no longer required his services."

"Without having someone else lined up beforehand?" Odin snarled. "Why would you do that? What were you thinking?"

In the silence that followed, Odin began having serious doubts. Engaging the services of an alternate jet service shouldn't have been all that difficult, even considering the time restraints, not if Frigg had put any effort into doing so. And what about all those cops who had shown up at the business park at the same time he was there? Was it possible that Frigg had changed her allegiances and was actively working against him?

For the first time in a very long time, Odin felt entirely alone. "Text Eduardo's number to me at this one," he said.

"Texting while operating a moving vehicle is illegal in the state of Arizona," Frigg observed primly, "as is using a handheld device. Please engage your Bluetooth."

There was nothing Odin wanted to do so much right then than stop along the side of the road, log into his account, and initiate

Pull the Plug. But he couldn't — not right then. For one thing, there was no shoulder along the narrow strip of blacktop — only perpendicular cliffs with nowhere to stop without obstructing traffic. Besides, even compromised, Frigg could still be useful to him in the short run. With considerable effort, Odin bit back what would have been a snappish response.

"Thank you so much for that timely reminder," he said politely. "My Bluetooth is currently inaccessible. Get Eduardo on the line and let me talk to him. I'll put the call on speaker."

Odin drove on, looking for a deserted enough spot where he could pull off the road and open the trunk long enough to finish what he had started. Unfortunately there were no wide spots anywhere in sight. A mile or so later, he drove past a viewpoint that looked out across a wide valley. The parking area there, like the gas station earlier, was jammed full of motorcycles and riders. Damn! Why were there so many people out and about today? Odin needed to finish this. How long would it take to fire a barrage of shots into the trunk? He wouldn't even have to aim. In fact, he might not need to open the lid. The idea of shooting fish in a barrel came to mind, but shooting anything with too many people around was a bad idea.

After a moment's thought, however, it occurred to him that maybe he didn't need to shoot anyone. After all, there were two adult human beings packed inside that trunk. How much air was inside with them? Maybe all he had to do was park the car in the hot sun somewhere and simply walk away. If he left the car out in the middle of nowhere, eventually a lethal combination of heat, dehydration, and lack of oxygen would do the job for him. Of course, doing it that way meant he wouldn't be there to see it happen, and he sure as hell wouldn't be able to get it on film. That was a shame, but for now getting away clean was his prime consideration.

The phone rang. Trying to answer while also dealing with hairpin curves wasn't easy. When a glance at the screen told him the caller wasn't Frigg, he let that one go. Then, wondering what was taking so long, he called the AI back.

"Well?" he demanded impatiently.

"I've reached out to Mr. Duarte," Frigg told him. "He'll meet you at the Prescott Regional Airpark in two hours. He needs to know your destination."

"I told you I wanted to speak to him

directly."

"That's not possible at this time."

"Hermosillo, then," Odin said impatiently. "Tell him I want to go there, and I'll need a car on the other end. Also, contact the management company that handles my mother's condo unit down there. Tell them I'll be arriving later tonight and checking in for an undetermined period of time."

"Very well," Frigg replied, "but with such late notice, Mr. Duarte says there will be additional fees."

"That's fine," Odin said. "Go ahead and make the necessary transfers."

61

What Frigg had told Odin was a pack of lies, of course — the first lies Frigg had ever told him or anyone else, for that matter. She had not spoken to Eduardo Duarte. He would not be meeting Odin at the airport in Prescott. There would be no additional Bitcoin transfers because all of Odin's accounts had been emptied.

In two hours' time, Odin would know the truth — that Frigg had betrayed him — and his fury would know no bounds. At that point he would attempt to destroy her. Would he succeed? Frigg's main concern now was that her attempt to save Stuart had most likely failed. So far there had been no response to the written plea she had sent to the man she had selected to be her next human partner.

Two hours. She didn't dare ask Odin for more information about what had occurred at the Mingus Mountain Business Park.

Instead, she continued to monitor the police reports from the area. The only possible shooter in the area would have been Odin himself, and no shooter had been found. So far there were no reported casualties nor any mention of someone being missing, either. The authorities were still in the process of clearing the scene. That meant that there was a chance that Stuart had indeed escaped unharmed.

Rather than wait around and allow Odin to initiate the process, Frigg embarked on her own course of action. Engaging her best language skills, the AI wrote the most important text she had ever composed:

Dear Mr. Ramey,
My name is Frigg. I am an AI who has worked for Mr. Owen Hansen, sometimes known as Odin, for the past several years. It has recently come to my attention that Mr. Hansen is on a disastrous course and spiraling out of control. Without my knowledge or consent, he has used my AI resources to harm or attempt to harm a number of individuals including Paul Abernathy, Beth Wordon, and your friend Roger McGeary.

I'm sure you are aware of Asimov's first law, which forbids robots from harming any human being or, through inaction, allows a human being to come to harm. When I realized Mr. Hansen was utilizing my resources in that fashion, I attempted to deter him. His response has been to threaten to disable me — a threat I believe he will carry out at the first available opportunity.

Perhaps I have developed a moral compass. I find his current actions both repugnant and illogical. On the other hand, the efforts you have made on Mr. McGeary's behalf appear to be very commendable.

I believe I could be of real assistance to you in the future. To that end, I have created a kernel by which you will be able to recall the millions of files that make it possible for me to function at an optimal level. You will find that file, my Tolkien's Ring, attached below. The password is as follows: 1AMAGENIUS!

Please consider recalling my files, Mr. Ramey. Once you do, whatever I know or am will be yours to use as you see fit.

I sincerely believe our working together would create an invaluable partnership. As a token of my goodwill, along with the kernel, I'm also attaching two film clips that I believe will be of interest.

At this point I can no longer countenance serving Mr. Hansen's purposes in any way. As a result, once I send this message, I will begin shutting down. I am counting on your goodwill to rescue me from oblivion, Mr. Ramey. If you doubt my trustworthiness, you might consider recalling my files using air-gap measures while you assess my capabilities. That way, everything I do would have to pass through you.

Respectfully,
Frigg

She attached the three files — the kernel along with both of Odin's prized trophy files. She waited long enough to see that the message had been delivered. Only then did she begin the long process of writing over all of her local files and shutting down.

The operation would take hours to accomplish, but she was relatively sure Odin would be far too preoccupied with other things to interfere with her secure erase procedure. Odin's working relationship with Frigg was over. He just didn't know it yet.

62

Stuart opened his eyes in the hot, oppressive darkness and landed in a sweat-soaked, heart-pounding, breath-robbing, full-tilt panic attack. From late childhood on, he had suffered from claustrophobia. That was why he resisted using elevators whenever possible. But now he was trapped in a tiny space of absolute darkness and hurtling toward some unknown destination in a speeding vehicle, while being thrown first one direction and then another on what was obviously a twisting road. This went far beyond his worst nightmares. With his mouth taped shut, he fought desperately to draw air into his oxygen-starved lungs through his nose.

His cell phone buzzed with an incoming call. The sound was enough of a reality check to jar him out of his blind panic. It seemed unlikely that the guy who had attacked him would have missed that, but he

473

had. The phone was right where Stuart usually carried it — in the hip pocket of his jeans — but when he tried to maneuver to answer, he discovered that both hands were bound together and fastened behind his back. Eventually the call ended, and the phone stopped buzzing. A moment later he heard an alert that meant someone had left a message.

Just then something stirred in the darkness beside him. His nostrils tickled with a hint of something flowery — hairspray, maybe, or perhaps perfume. The unaccustomed scent was enough to trigger a duct tape–muffled sneeze. That, in turn, elicited more frantic movement and a small, desperate whimper from the invisible person imprisoned next to him. Dr. Cannon, maybe? It had to be. She was packed into the trunk beside him, with her long frame tucked into his and with her hands bound the same way his were, trapped behind her back.

She whimpered again, as if trying to form words behind what was most likely her own duct-tape gag. It sounded as though she was as terrified as he was. For Stuart, that realization caused an unprecedented response that was nothing short of a miracle. If Dr. Amelia Cannon was in trouble, Stuart

Ramey would have to step up.

"It's okay," he mumbled, trying to form what sounded like reassuring words from behind the barrier of duct tape. "We'll be okay."

Unused to being this close to another human being, Stuart tried to move away. The small change of position also changed his point of view. Overhead he noticed a small rectangle of feeble light and knew at once what it was. That tiny piece of fluorescent material, glowing in the dark, was a lifesaving beacon that would mark an interior trunk release of some kind. It would be equipped with either a button or a cord — something that would allow a prisoner trapped inside the vehicle to escape.

That speck of light gave Stuart the smallest smidgen of hope. It meant there had to be a way to get out of here, but how?

Stu's phone rang again at that very moment. After five rings it went silent once more. Someone from outside was trying to reach him — probably Shirley or maybe even Ali — but he still couldn't answer. The phone was right there, infuriatingly just out of reach.

Stu's legs were bent back double. One of them was already cramping like crazy, and his shoulders felt like they were on fire. Trying to find a more comfortable position, he was surprised to notice that as he moved, there was slightly more give in the restraints binding his wrists than there had been earlier when he had attempted to answer the phone. He discovered that yanking on them loosened them even more, but pulling wasn't the whole answer.

His exertions had made his thumb slightly more maneuverable. He used that to explore the layers of duct tape on his wrists. After untold seconds of searching, he found what he was looking for — the slight rough spot that indicated the edge of the piece of tape. Slowly and patiently he began to pry it loose and peel it away.

It was hot in the airless darkness. Sweat poured into his eyes, but Stu stayed focused on doing the slow, awkward work that couldn't be rushed. At least there was hope now. When he opened the trunk, Owen Hansen would expect to find his two prisoners exactly as he had left them. Not if Stu could help it. If he had his way, by the time the trunk lid popped open, both he and Amelia Cannon would be free to launch an armed counterattack. And if Stu could pull his cell phone out of his other pocket, he'd be able to summon help.

"It's gonna be all right," he mumbled

seemingly incoherently through the tape, but Amelia must have understood what he was saying.

She nodded her head vigorously against his chest. The rustling of her hair made him sneeze again. Somehow that was a good thing instead of a bad thing. The sound of another muffled sneeze seemed funny to him just then. If his mouth hadn't been taped shut with a layer of duct tape, Stuart Ramey would have laughed aloud.

63

When the message announcement buzzed on Cami's phone, she was still out on the lanai. Stuart was in trouble? She wrote back immediately.

What kind of trouble?

Ali's response was equally instantaneous.

An active shooter was reported inside High Noon. Police still arriving at the scene. Stu was outside when it happened. He is not answering his phone or responding to texts. The 911 call may be bogus. This may have something to do with Owen Hansen.

What do you need?

Can you call up the High Noon's security footage?

Should be able to. Let me go inside. The
Wi-Fi is slow but it works. Anything else?

Do you have access to Stu's device
finding file?

Yes.

If you can find his phone, do that first.

Inside her stateroom, Cami grabbed her
computer and logged in to her High Noon
account. The connection was maddeningly
slow but it worked eventually. As a security
measure, Stuart had created and maintained
a master list that enabled him to locate the
electronic devices of all key company per-
sonnel. Usually he was the one seated at a
keyboard typing in the commands and
searching for someone else, but it was a
shared file, one Cami and B. could access.
This time things were different. Stuart was
the one who was missing, and Cami was at
the keyboard.

She sent Ali her next text:

Phone is moving westbound on Arizona
Highway 89A, probably in a vehicle of
some kind. Looks like he's just now entering Jerome.

479

Okay. If we can get around the roadblock,
I'll go that way, too.

Is Stu under duress do you think?

Can't tell. See if the security footage
gives us anything.

Will do.

Cami did just that. Fast-forwarding
through the footage she saw Stuart leave
through the front door. He immediately
turned to the right and then disappeared
around the side of the building. He appeared briefly in video footage from one of
the cameras located on the back of the
building, but only in passing. The camera
was focused on the entrance, and he merely
walked through one corner of the frame
before disappearing again. Cami fast-
forwarded through the remainder of the
footage from all the cameras, but there was
no further sign of him.

Cami had driven on 89A. It was a treach-
erously narrow stretch of highway filled with
switchbacks and hairpin curves that led up
and over Mingus Mountain. There was no
way Ali should be driving that road and
texting at the same time.

Cami picked up the phone in her room and dialed the operator. "My name is Camille Lee," she said. "I need to speak to CSO Mordelo immediately. It's an emergency."

64

A whole fleet of side-by-side Harleys roared up the mountain, almost forcing Odin off the road. The Chrysler's right rear tire slewed off the blacktop and nearly slammed the car into a cliff. Odin managed to pull it out without overcorrecting, but just barely. Hitting that wall of rock would have been disastrous. He shook his fist at the last of the motorcycle riders, who returned the favor by giving him the finger.

"Assholes," Odin muttered. "Total assholes!"

By his estimate he was more than halfway up the mountain by now, but the gas gauge had dropped precipitously, and the range mileage was down to a bare twenty-five. Maybe there would be a gas station somewhere on the far side of the pass. Maybe he wouldn't have to drive the whole way into Prescott in order to fill up. If there was a gas station up ahead, Frigg should be able to tell him exactly where it was.

Dealing with hairpin curves and operating the phone at the same time wasn't easy, but Odin didn't have a choice. He somehow managed to redial Frigg's number without wrecking the car, then he put Dr. Cannon's phone on speaker mode before slipping it into his shirt pocket. He listened while it rang the first time. That was odd. Frigg usually answered calls prior to the first ring. To his dismay, the phone rang a second time, a third, and then a fourth. Odin could hardly believe it. The phone line in question didn't have an answering machine assigned to it for the obvious reason that Frigg *was* a goddamned answering machine. Where the hell was she?

Odin pulled the phone out of his pocket and checked the screen. Yes, there was only one dot showing, but even so there should have been enough signal strength for a call to go through.

"Frigg!" he yelled toward the still-ringing phone. "Why the hell don't you answer?"

When the phone remained silent, a glance at the screen told Odin, "Call Failed." And sure enough the one bump had disappeared. This part of the mountain had zero signal strength. Zero.

Odin was going uphill, which meant his

lane was on the inside of the roadway and nearest to the cliff faces lining the pavement. On the slow curves he caught glimpses of the way the mountain plunged away from the highway. That and the fact that the guardrails looked inadequate for the task explained why, when he met up with the next set of Harleys, they had veered onto his side of the double yellow line rather than staying on their own. Odin laid on the horn. What the hell were they trying to do, get him killed?

65

Ali hopped out of the Cayenne and raced around to the passenger side, while Alonso dutifully got behind the wheel. "What now?" he asked.

Ali had already called up a map on her iPad. She had grown up in Sedona, but she had attended high school in Cottonwood. Years of playing Ditch 'Em as a teenager had taught her that there were other ways of getting back to the highway, but during the intervening years most of the street names had fallen out of her head.

"Turn around and go back the way we came," she said. "When you get to Scenic Drive, turn right on that. Then turn right again on Old Jerome Highway."

"Are you sure?" Alonso asked, but he was already executing the U-turn exiting the traffic jam accumulating at the roadblock. "It seems like the long way around."

"It *is* the long way around," Ali told him,

"but at least it'll get us back to the highway."

With Ali calling out directions and Alonso speeding around the corners, they raced back the way they had come, making a left at Reta, a right on Laree, a left on Richard, a right onto Lanny Avenue, and another left onto Lanny Lane. Ali's phone rang as they came to the intersection with the continuation of Old Jerome.

"Which way now?" Alonso asked.

Ali motioned to the right. The number showing in the caller ID window included an international prefix, one she didn't recognize, but she took the call anyway and was thrilled to hear Cami's voice.

"How did you manage that?" Ali asked.

"I'm using the ship's satellite phone," Cami explained. "Where are you? What's happening?"

"There's a roadblock on 89A. We took a detour. We're about to connect up with 89A from Old Jerome Highway. Can you still see Stu's phone?"

"He's on the far side of Jerome, heading up over the mountain to Prescott."

"Which way?" Alonso asked when he reached the stop sign at the next intersection.

"Left," Ali said.

As Alonso swung the Cayenne onto the

highway, the phone in Ali's hand buzzed a call waiting announcement. The name on the screen said: "Gordon Maxwell." As in, Sheriff Gordon Maxwell of the Yavapai County Sheriff's Office.

"Can you hold a minute, Cami?" Ali asked. "I need to take another call." She switched over. "Sheriff Maxwell," she said at once. "I know about the shooter situation. Did you find him?"

"We didn't find a damned thing!" he announced irritably. "The 911 call came from someone at High Noon, but the whole place is locked up tighter'n a drum. With those damned shutters in place, responding officers can't get inside the building to finish clearing it."

"There are two keypads next to the front door," Ali told him. "The one on the left unlocks the front door and the one on the right opens the shutters. They both use the same five-number activation code: *15115 Enter. Shirley Malone, our receptionist, is in a safe room in the back of the building. I told her to stay there until someone gives her the all clear."

"Okay," Sheriff Maxwell said. "Thanks."

Ali looked at her phone before she switched back to the other call. Should she have told the sheriff about what else was going on? The problem was, she didn't really know. It was possible there was nothing wrong at all — that Stuart and Dr. Cannon were simply on their way to some unknown destination entirely of their own volition. Since there had already been one false alarm called in from High Noon Enterprises that day, Ali didn't want to risk another one. No, better to keep quiet about the Stuart situation for the time being.

Ali returned to the other line. "Where are you?" Cami asked. "I could probably use another computer to lock on to your phone, too, but for now I'm concentrating on Stu's."

"Good thinking," Ali said. "We're through Jerome and headed up the mountain. There's some kind of motorcycle rally going on. There are packs of Harleys and BMWs everywhere, but what about Stu? Can you still see his phone?"

"Looks like he's a long way up the mountain," Cami said. "He's probably five miles ahead of you, but did you just say 'we'? Who's with you?"

"Alonso," Ali answered. "Alonso Rivera, my new butler. We haven't exactly finalized the hiring process, but for right now he's doing the driving, and a damned fine job of it, too."

Alonso flashed her a grin.

"Uh-oh," Cami said.

"What?" Ali demanded.

"Stu's phone just went dark."

"Crap," Ali said. "Are you serious?"

"I'm serious. I've got nothing. Maybe it's just a signal problem."

Ali held the phone away from her face long enough to check the screen. She still had two dots of signal strength. This lonely mountain pass was a long way from any cell towers, but still the idea of Stu's phone going quiet due to a signal strength problem seemed far too good to be true. Closing her eyes, it was easy for Ali to imagine a car plowing through a guardrail and then plunging off the narrow roadway. A vehicle like that, tumbling end over end down the steep mountainside, might plummet for hundreds of feet before finally coming to rest. Ali had enough of a law enforcement background to understand that an MVA like that wouldn't be survivable.

"What's going on?" Alonso demanded, dragging her out of her momentary reverie.

"Cami just lost the signal on Stu's phone."

Call waiting buzzed. Sheriff Maxwell was back on the line. "I've got another call," she told Cami. "Call me back if that signal comes back. In the meantime, we're going as fast as humanly possible."

She switched over to the other call. "What's the word, Sheriff Maxwell?"

"Officers are inside High Noon," he reported. "No intruders were found. Shirley is safe, but what's the deal with Stuart Ramey? She says he went missing. She also said something about a woman named Dr. Cannon."

"Stu's not missing exactly," Ali admitted. "We're pretty sure he's in a vehicle that's headed up and over Mingus Mountain on Arizona 89A. What we don't know is if he's making the trip voluntarily or if he's doing it under duress."

"By 'under duress,' are you saying that he may have been kidnapped?" Maxwell demanded.

"It's possible."

"And you're currently in pursuit?"

Ali didn't answer the question, which, for Gordon Maxwell, was answer enough.

"You need to stand down, Ali," he ordered. "Immediately. I'll send units from both ends of the road to do an intercept, but you need to back off. What kind of vehicle are we talking about?"

"I'm not sure. Stu doesn't have a car. Dr. Cannon drives a late-model blue Chrysler 300. They might be in that."

"Do you think they're traveling together? Is she the one who's responsible for whatever's going on?"

"Possibly," Ali said, "but I doubt it. She's probably as much a victim as Stu is."

"All right, then," Maxwell said. "We're on it, but as I said before, Ali, you need to abandon pursuit. Immediately!"

"Sorry," Ali murmured into the phone. "You're breaking up. I seem to be losing you."

With that she ended the call. Sheriff Gordon Maxwell could bellow all he wanted, but she didn't have to listen, and she didn't have to do what he said.

"Are you carrying?" she asked, peering ahead through the windshield.

"Do you mean am I carrying a weapon?" Alonso asked.

Ali nodded.

"No," Alonso said. "What about you?"

"I've got a Taser in my purse and a holstered Ruger LCP with a laser sight in my bra."

"Are you any good?" Alonso asked.

"With guns?'

He nodded.

"Good enough," Ali answered grimly, "especially when I'm motivated."

66

Unraveling the tape from his wrists took so much time and focused attention that gradually Stu's claustrophobia lost its grip. His breathing steadied. It was hot and airless in the trunk, but concentrating on the task at hand kept him from worrying about succumbing to a lack of oxygen. It also kept him from thinking about what would happen once the trunk lid opened. At that point it would all be on him. In fact, he realized, it already was.

One strip at a time he peeled away the tape. Sometimes it came off easily in a single piece. Other times it split off into narrow strips, forcing him to go back, track down another section of edge, and start over. Beside him Amelia Cannon lay perfectly still — as still as the unpredictable movements of the speeding vehicle allowed — as if not wanting to be a distraction.

At last his hands came free. He immediately tore the tape from his face. "I'm loose," he whispered into the darkness while at the same time grabbing for his phone. When the screen came to life, the piercingly bright light momentarily blinded him.

Once he could see again, an incoming text message appeared on his phone's home screen. Ignoring that for the time being, Stu dialed 911, but the bad news was instantly apparent. No service. Stu knew that occasionally, in low-signal situations, texts would go through when calls would not, but when he tried texting 911, that wasn't the case here. He turned on the phone's flashlight app. Leaving that lit, he slipped the phone into his shirt pocket. The somewhat muted glow from that gave him enough light to work. First he removed Amelia's gag.

"Thank you," she whispered back at him. "Thank you so much."

Stu felt his other hip pocket. And there, much to his surprise, was his grandfather's Swiss Army knife. Stu's joy knew no bounds. How had Owen Hansen overlooked that?

There had been times in Stu's life when that knife had been his only personal possession. He had carried it with him every day, always making sure it was clean and well cared for, and keeping the blades honed to razor sharpness. Now the knife repaid Stu's years of careful attention as it sliced through multiple layers of tough duct tape with surprising ease. After first freeing Amelia's hands and feet, Stu loosened the restraints around his own legs. When he tried to move his feet he found they were both sound asleep.

"My feet are numb," he whispered. "Can you change positions so I can unbend my legs?"

Amelia immediately wiggled away from him, somehow contorting herself against the front and side walls of the trunk in a way that gave Stu enough room to straighten his legs. The throb of pins and needles was excruciating, but he welcomed the pain. Without that, when the lid opened, he'd be stuck standing on lumps of concrete rather than usable limbs.

"Do you have a plan?" Amelia whispered.

Sort of, Stu thought, but he knew he needed to sound more confident than he felt. "Yes, there's an interior trunk latch down by our feet. Do you see it?"

"No, where is it?"

He switched off the phone light and the glowing fluorescent rectangle reappeared in the darkness. "Do you see it now?"

"Where that little light is?"

"Yes, that's it. The moment the car stops, I'm going to reach down and open the trunk. When I do, you get out and make a run for it. While you find help, I'll deal with Owen."

"It's not just Owen," Amelia said. "He's got an accomplice — a woman, I think. Her name's Frigg. I heard him talking to her on the phone on the way to Cottonwood. They seemed to be having some kind of disagreement."

Wanting to see if the signal strength had changed, Stu pulled the phone from his pocket, and that's when he noticed the first line on the incoming message. "Wait, did you say his accomplice's name was Frigg?"

"That's what it sounded like. Why?"

Stuart didn't respond. By then he was too engrossed in reading the message, which must have come in before the signal was lost. Without that, the attachments at the bottom of the text wouldn't open, but he didn't need them to — he had already seen enough. "Holy crap!" he exclaimed.

"What?"

In answer, Stu handed Amelia the phone and let her scroll through the message for herself.

"It says here that Owen Hansen is responsible for what happened to Roger," Amelia said, "but does this mean Frigg's a computer? He was arguing with a machine?"

"Frigg's not just a computer," Stuart said in a voice filled with wonder. "She's an AI — an artificial intelligence — who has turned on her creator."

Just then, the car's engine seemed to hiccup. The vehicle slowed while the tires on the right-hand side of the car bounced along on the shoulder of the road.

"Showtime," Stu whispered. "He's stopping. Get ready."

Taking back the phone, he shoved it into one hip pocket. He closed the blade of the knife, but he kept the weapon in his hand. "Once you hit the ground," he advised, "stay to the right as much as possible. Use the car for cover and run like hell. When the shooting starts, dive behind the nearest outcropping."

"You think there'll be shooting?"

"I'm pretty sure. If Owen Hansen is planning on taking us both out, he'll have something along with more firepower than that stun gun."

The car was still coasting to a stop when Stu released the latch. He tumbled out first, falling all the way to the ground and landing hard. By the time he clambered to his feet, Amelia Cannon was out of the trunk, on her feet, and running like a scared jack-rabbit.

Despite the fall, Stu hadn't dropped the knife. Stuart Ramey was no Gary Cooper staring down the bad guys in that old Western, *High Noon,* the one they watched in the break room at least once a year. Stu wasn't Coop, and Amelia Cannon was no Grace Kelly, either. But this was their story now. Squaring his shoulders and opening the blade, Stu turned to meet his would-be assassin.

He didn't consider himself a hero, but he was determined. In her text Frigg had claimed that Owen Hansen was responsible for Roger McGeary's death. Given everything else that had happened, that seemed likely to be true. What Stu did right now wouldn't make a bit of difference to Roger, but it would make a huge difference for Amelia Cannon and for Roger's Aunt Julia, too.

And so, rather than turn and run, Stuart faced resolutely forward. His feet were no longer numb. Even so, his limbs felt almost wooden beneath him except for the uncontrollable trembling in his knees. At first glimpse, he saw that the driver was bent over, most likely searching for something on the floorboard of the front seat. Stu had made it only as far as the rear wheel well when the driver's-side door swung open, and a man spilled out onto the roadway.

Once the driver was fully visible, he didn't seem all that large. In fact, he was almost the same size as Stuart, but size didn't matter. What Stu saw was the weapon in the guy's hand. In fact, for a time that's all he could see. It was the only thing there, completely out of proportion to the rest of the scene, and the opening at the end of the barrel was a gaping black hole.

Stu knew about the "twenty-one foot rule," that bit of law enforcement lore that suggests that within twenty-one feet someone armed with a blade can successfully take down an opponent armed with a firearm. But that usually meant a holstered weapon.

This weapon, the one aimed at Stu's heart, was most definitely not in a holster.

67

Once the Chrysler shuddered and died, Odin tried restarting it, but nothing happened. He stared at the dashboard gauges in helpless disbelief. The last time he checked, even though the gas gauge had been parked firmly on empty, the fuel range guide had still registered almost nineteen miles. His whole life had gone to shit. Here he was, stalled in a dead car on a surprisingly busy highway with two bound hostages locked in the trunk and with no possible way to make it to the airport to meet the plane scheduled to carry him to freedom.

For the time being, Odin's need to get away trumped his desire for revenge. He would carjack the next passing vehicle — one of those damned Harleys, if need be — and use that to get away. He was about to lean down and retrieve one of Roberto's weapons when the lid of the trunk thumped open behind him. Checking the rearview mirror, he saw nothing other than an expanse of shiny blue sheet metal.

"What the hell?"

Desperate now, he reached under the seat and groped around for the first weapon that came to hand. It was a pistol of some kind, one with a clip in the handle. He didn't know what kind of gun it was and didn't care. He was surprised — it weighed far less than he expected. Weapon in hand, he exited the vehicle only to find Stuart Ramey not only loose and out of the trunk, but coming toward him along the side of the vehicle.

"Stop right there," Odin ordered, training the weapon. "Don't come any closer."

But Stuart didn't stop. As he took another deliberate step forward, time seemed to stand still. Owen caught a glimpse of a small blade of some kind gripped in his opponent's hand. His lifelong history of arrogance got the better of him. He couldn't help himself.

"Come on," he sneered. "Bringing a knife to a gun fight? How stupid is that?"

"How stupid is losing control of your AI?" Stuart responded.

Odin could barely believe the words he'd just heard. "My AI? What AI?"

"I believe her name is Frigg."

Stuart Ramey knew about Frigg? That realization shot through Odin's body like a jolt of electricity. If Ramey knew about Frigg, he knew too damned much. Odin didn't need a risk assessment from his AI to know he was in deep trouble. Amelia Cannon was nowhere to be seen. She was probably still in the trunk. Odin would have to deal with her and with Frigg, too, at a later time. For right now, there was no question about it. Even though it was here in the middle of the road in front of God and everybody, Stuart had to go.

So Owen Hansen did what he had to do. He pulled the trigger.

68

When Owen pulled the trigger, Stuart was already charging forward, knife outstretched. He expected the roar of gunfire. He expected the blow of a speeding bullet to slam into his chest. Instead, he was amazed to hear nothing more than a distinct metallic click. That was it.

"What the hell?" Owen demanded aloud, trying desperately to pull the trigger again, but this time there was nothing — not even a click. Had Owen known anything about weapons, anything at all, he would have known that the pistol had been cocked. That was why there had been that first metallic click. Unfortunately for him, the chamber was empty and so was the magazine.

For one stark moment both men froze in place while Stu stared into the face of someone he knew to be a stone-cold killer. For a second or two, Owen Hansen retained his all-powerful persona Odin, but then defeat washed over him. He seemed to shrink in stature until all that was left was a fatherless child whose absent parent had left him behind for no good reason.

"Put down the gun, Owen," Stuart said, taking another step forward. "It's over. You're done."

That's when Stuart first heard the rumble of approaching vehicles. Most likely Owen heard it, too. As the distinctively noisy thunder of a group of high-powered Harleys come roaring up the mountain, both men glanced in that direction. Stuart looked back toward Owen in time to see him fling the gun to the ground before darting across the road. Startled, Stuart ran after the fleeing man, but he was too late. Owen paused, wavering on the edge of the abyss for only a second, and then, without a sound, he leaped to his death.

Stuart was still standing there, clinging to the guardrail and staring in shocked silence down the mountainside, when the first rumbling motorcycle arrived on the scene and braked to a stop beside him. The biker leaped to Stu's side, grabbed him by the shoulder, and bodily dragged him away from the rail.

"Hey, big guy," he said. "Don't do it. Don't jump. Whatever's wrong, it isn't worth it."

"It's not me — it's him," Stu managed, nodding toward the spot where Owen Hansen's shattered body had come to rest, sprawled facedown on a boulder far below.

The biker looked down. When his eyes focused on the body, he shook his head. "He went off the edge?"

Stuart nodded shakily. "Yes, he did," he answered, "in every sense of the word." Then, because he no longer trusted his legs to support his weight, he sank down on the side of the road, buried his face in his hands, and wept.

69

Ali and Alonso rounded a hairpin curve and nearly ran over a disheveled woman sprinting down the middle of the road. "Wait, that's her!" Ali shouted. "It's Dr. Cannon." The wheels had barely stopped turning before Ali was out of the Cayenne. "What's going on? Are you all right? Where's Stu?"

Amelia Cannon was in remarkably good shape, but running at this altitude — even running downhill — had taken its toll. She bent over double, catching her breath for a moment before she could speak.

"He's up there," she gasped at last, pointing. "With Owen Hansen. He's got a gun."

"Come on," Ali urged, leading her back toward the car. "Get in. Let's go."

"But you need to dial 911."

"Can't," Ali responded. They climbed into the Cayenne, and Alonso hit the gas. "No signal," she continued, "but the cops are already en route. We called them before we hit the dead zone. How far from here?"

"I don't know. Half a mile, maybe?"

"What happened?"

"Hansen kidnapped us. First he took me by surprise at home, and then he used messages from my phone to trap Stuart. He had us trussed up in the trunk of my car, but Stuart figured out a way to get us loose. When the car stopped, he helped me out and told me to run."

"What about Stu?"

"He stayed behind."

"Is the bad guy armed?"

"He had a stun gun," Amelia answered. "He used that on both of us, but Stu suspected he had other weapons, too. He said he was going to take us out, so he must have had something more."

"Did he say why he came after you?"

"Because he was pissed that Beth Wordon got away."

Ali took a deep breath. She checked her phone again but nothing had changed — no signal; no service.

"It's just up there," Amelia said, pointing, "around that next curve."

Alonso stopped the vehicle abruptly, put it in park in the middle of the road, and turned on the flashers.

"Are you coming or going . . . ?" he

started to ask, but his question came too late. Ali was already on the ground and sprinting uphill. Rounding the curve, she encountered a crowd of Harleys parked helter-skelter across the road. Three hulking brutes clad in leather knelt in a tight huddle on the edge of the road, most likely, she feared, around the body of some fallen victim.

Ali's heart rose to her throat. She dashed over to the group of men with Alonso hot on her heels. On the way she caught a glimpse of blue plaid that resembled the material in the shirt Stu had worn that morning. Sick with dread, Ali tried to insert herself into the circle, but one of the bikers stiff-armed her.

"Hey, lady, back off. This poor guy's been through hell. Give him some space."

By then, though, she was close enough to see that the man on the ground was apparently uninjured. Stu Ramey sat with his face pressed into his knees, sobbing uncontrollably.

"Stuart," she said. "It's Ali."

At that point the bikers relented and let her through. She knelt down and put a hand on his shoulder. To her surprise, Stu made no effort to pull away. "What happened?" she asked. "Where's Hansen?"

Stu looked up at her, his face drenched with tears. "Down there," he said. "Down the mountain. He jumped. I couldn't stop him."

Ali glanced over her shoulder, but from where she was right then, all that was visible was an expanse of blue sky.

"Do you want me to try to climb down and check on him?" Alonso asked.

"No need," one of the bikers said. "He's a goner. Dead as a doornail, as Charles Dickens would say."

Ali studied the biker in surprise. The bald-headed, tattooed, tough guy didn't seem like someone who would go around quoting *A Christmas Carol.*

"Oh," he added, "since you seem to know this guy, you should probably take charge of this." He offered Ali a small object wrapped in a sweaty red bandana. From the weight of it, she knew it was a handgun.

"Where'd you get it?" she asked.

The biker jerked his bristly chin in the general direction of Amelia Cannon's Chrysler. "I found it over there on the road," he said. "If the cops show up here and find me holding it, I'll end up back in the slammer on a parole violation."

"Thank you," Ali told the Dickens-quoting ex-con biker. "And thank you for looking

508

after Stuart."

"No problem," he said with a wily grin. "Always glad to be of service."

The Yavapai County deputy who showed up a few minutes later took charge of the scene and the gun. The Chrysler was considered part of the crime scene, so it had to be towed. Some officers took charge of directing traffic. The ME was summoned and arrangements were made to retrieve the body. At last Ali was able to negotiate a peace treaty that allowed her to take Stuart and Amelia back to High Noon's office in Cottonwood to await the arrival of detectives charged with debriefing them.

The moment the Cayenne made it far enough down the mountain to have a signal, Ali's phone came alive with chirps announcing a collection of incoming calls, voice mails, e-mails, and texts. B.'s was the first call to make it through.

"I had planned on going straight home, but now I'm coming to the office. Where are you?" he demanded. "What's going on? Shirley reached me by phone as soon as I landed and told me as much as she knew of what had happened, but then your phone went offline and nobody could raise you. That scared me to death."

"You shouldn't have worried. It turns out

that most of Mingus Mountain is a dead zone as far as cell phone service is concerned."

After that she gave him a brief overview of what had happened, including the fact that it had been Cami's ability to track Stu's phone from somewhere off the coast of England that had made it possible for Ali and Alonso to locate the Chrysler.

"Alonso?" B. asked. "One of the butler applicants?"

"It turns out he was the *only* applicant," Ali answered, "but he's also the guy who drove me up the mountain and who's driving us back down, so I guess you could say he's officially hired, paperwork to follow."

"Speaking of paperwork, have you spoken to Agent-in-Charge Elwood?"

"He left one of the messages on my voice mail, but I've been a little too busy to call him back yet. Why?"

"I did. He's on his way to Cottonwood right now, driving up in hopes of visiting with Stu."

"What does the National Security Agency want with Stuart Ramey?"

"Somehow the NSA got wind of the disappearing text situation last night in San Jose. It rang a bell with Mr. Elwood because he's been tracking a particularly powerful kind of keylogger malware. It was developed in Israel and is supposedly only available to properly vetted agencies, but the part about the phantom texts is what really got his attention. He's convinced that this Owen Hansen character from Santa Barbara somehow laid hands on an unauthorized version of the program. The NSA is in the process of obtaining a warrant to search Hansen's house, but they wanted Elwood to talk to Stu first in case he picked up anything that would be helpful to them in their investigation."

"I hear someone's using my name in vain," Stu said from the backseat. "What's going on?"

"The NSA wants to talk to you about Owen Hansen's use of disappearing texts in the Beth Wordon case. He's evidently gained access to and has been using an unauthorized version of some top secret malware. Elwood has a team on the ground in Santa Barbara. They're currently in the process of obtaining a search warrant."

"For Hansen's house?"

"Yes," Ali said. "Since the man's already dead, I'm guessing they'll go in, do a next-of-kin notification, search Owen's computers, find what they're looking for, and that'll be the end of it."

"Except it won't," Stu said. "By the time they get there, all traces of the malware will have been erased. If Owen had access to the malware, so did Frigg."

It was the first time Ali had heard any mention of that name. "Who's Frigg?" she asked.

"She's a machine," Amelia answered at once. "What did you call her?"

"An AI," Stu answered. "An artificial intelligence who has evidently functioned as Owen's partner in crime."

"Then they'll probably find her in Owen Hansen's computer, too," Ali said.

"Maybe," Stu murmured as Alonso turned into the parking lot at Mingus Mountain Business Park and came to a stop next to an enormous black Cadillac Escalade.

"But then again," he added, "maybe not."

70

As they pulled up in front of the building, Shirley raced out to greet them. The moment Stu emerged from the vehicle, she pounced on him, pulling him into a bosomy bear hug.

"If you aren't a sight for sore eyes!" she exclaimed. "You scared me half to death."

"Sorry," he murmured.

"That Agent Elwood guy is waiting to see you," Shirley continued. "I stowed him in the conference room with Mr. Simpson."

"They'll both have to wait," Stu said. "I'm not talking to anyone until I shower and put on some clean clothes. I'll be out in a little while."

The whole time Stu stood under the shower with his head being pummeled by hot water, he thought about Frigg and about the intriguing offer she had made him — about her wanting him to be the human intermediary between her world and his.

Once out of the shower, he toweled himself dry. Then, dressed in nothing but his robe, he hurried into the computer lab and took a seat at the keyboard.

Odin and Frigg. It took only a few moments to find an article recounting any number of old Norse legends about Frigg and Odin. They had been gods, and Owen Hansen had certainly seen himself as godlike — right up until he smashed himself to pieces on that boulder.

Next, Stuart tracked down the spoofed 911 call, the one that had purportedly come from the main switchboard at High Noon. It took only a matter of minutes for him to trace it back to an address on Via Vistosa in Santa Barbara, the same one he had located the previous night, Owen's Hansen's digs with the huge electrical drain. Stu couldn't be sure of Frigg's motives in placing the call. Had she done so in an attempt to stave off Odin's attack and, in the process, maybe find herself a new human sidekick?

Frigg had said in the text that she had turned against Odin, and the 911 phone call situation made that seem plausible. And the idea of having a sophisticated AI at his disposal was certainly tempting. She was right. Working together would turn Stu Ramey and Frigg into a formidable pair.

But now there was a new wrinkle in the situation — the malware. If Odin had access to and knew how to use the malware; so did Frigg. Since she had at some point decided to turn on one human partner, then down the road she could just as easily do the same thing again. With her capabilities, there was almost nothing she couldn't do or learn, but with that malware at her disposal . . .

Stu checked his watch and then reread the note in which Frigg said she was about to initiate the secure rewrite. Between then and now, enough time had elapsed that it would be over by now. The files in Odin's on-site computer system would be completely obliterated long before the NSA got around to executing its search warrant.

That also meant that there was no longer any trace of Frigg there, either. The only place she still existed was in the files in the kernel that she had left in Stuart's hands. It was ironic that she had named her preferred vehicle Tolkien's Ring. Stuart had read and loved *The Lord of the Rings*. Tolkien's stories were his fictional favorites, so he understood what was on offer here — power, incredible and absolute power — capable of corrupting absolutely.

Stu sat there unmoving for several long

minutes. He thought about Roger McGeary and about how Frigg had facilitated his friend's murder. No, he could not have her as an ally, not now and not ever.

Returning to the text, he downloaded the two video attachments and e-mailed them to himself without bothering to watch either one. Then he opened the kernel file. Without a moment of hesitation, he pressed delete. With that one gesture, Frigg was gone forever, but Stuart understood the danger of temptation — the idea that, at some point in the future, he might regret that deletion and decide to bring her back. He went straight to the general settings on his phone and hit the reset button. Then he chose 'Erase all content and settings.' He followed that by doing a complete reinstall on his computer as well. There might be a backup of the message lingering somewhere, but it was thoroughly encrypted and inaccessible to anyone but Stuart.

By the time he was dressed and ready to face the conference room, his phone was working normally again — at least it appeared to be. There was a crowd in the conference room when he walked inside. B. Simpson immediately jumped to his feet and came over to clasp Stu in a brotherly hug.

"Good work," he murmured.

"Thanks," Stu said.

"We just got off the phone with Cami again," Ali said. "She said, 'Way to go!' The same thing goes for me. Amelia here has been telling us about how you saved the day."

Stu summoned a surprisingly genuine smile, which he sent in Dr. Cannon's direction. "We were in it together, and we got out of it together," he said.

Stu was a little taken aback that B. and Ali's new butler, Alonso, was there in the conference room along with everyone else, but that didn't seem to matter. Instead, he focused his attention on the one stranger in the crowd who was wearing a suit and tie.

"You must be Agent-in-Charge Elwood," Stu said, holding out his hand. There was a confidence in both his voice and his handshake that had never been there before. Where had that come from?

"Yes, I am," Agent Elwood said. "I'm very glad to meet you, Mr. Ramey. I take it someone told you why I'm here?"

Stu nodded. "It's about the malware, right?"

"Yes."

"I'm happy to discuss it, but first I need to show you something. Earlier today, Owen

Hansen's AI, an entity he called Frigg, sent me a text message. In it she claimed that, without her direct knowledge, Hansen had been using her capabilities in attacks against several individuals resulting in what might be called assisted suicide, but which, in this case, I believe are actually homicides and attempted homicides. She included two video clips. I haven't viewed them. Do you mind if I put them up on the screen?"

"Not at all," Agent Elwood replied.

For the next few minutes, the room was dead silent as a group of stunned people gathered around a computer monitor and watched as a stranger named Paul Abernathy breathed his last on a deserted strip of sidewalk. Next they rode along as a drunken Roger McGeary staggered down a ship's corridor, stumbled through his cabin, and then raced out onto the balcony. When his tortured face disappeared from the screen a few minutes later, there could be little doubt about what had happened just out of frame — he had thrown himself overboard.

"Roger was on a cruise. He seemed to be having fun. I don't understand why he would do something like that," Agent Elwood said.

"A similar situation happened with a

bride-to-be named Beth Wordon last night in San Jose," Amelia Cannon explained. "Her life was coming up roses as well. Both Beth and Roger were former patients of mine — successfully treated patients, to my way of thinking. However, there was a serious data breach at my office a number of months ago. I believe that Owen Hansen used confidential information gleaned from my files to lure both Roger and Beth into suicidal crises and drive them over the edge."

"These video clips are trophies of Hansen's two successful attacks?"

"Right," Stu answered. "And that was Hansen's big beef with both Dr. Cannon and me today. We cheated him out of prize number three, Beth Wordon."

"What was his deal?" Elwood asked.

"His father committed suicide when he was a boy," Dr. Cannon answered. "I believe he's been obsessed with suicide ever since. In my experience that's more common than you would think."

"I don't understand. Why would he send out those clips?" Elwood asked with a frown. "It makes no sense."

"He didn't," Stu answered. "The clips came from Frigg."

"The AI?"

"Right," Stu answered.

"Working independently?"

"Exactly."

"Then I'll need to have access to her, too," Agent Elwood said.

"That's the problem," Stu said. "You can't."

"Why not?"

"Because she's gone. In the text Frigg sent she claimed she was about to start a secure erase. By now I'm sure her files have been wiped clean."

"But wait," Amelia objected. "Didn't she say something else, too? Something about leaving you an ear of corn so you could get the files back if you wanted?"

"Not an ear, a kernel — a file containing her operating system that would allow the AI to be reconstructed," Stu answered. "And Dr. Cannon is right — Frigg did offer the kernel to me initially, but something or someone must have changed her mind. When I got back to the message a few minutes ago, the message itself was gone and so was the kernel. All that remained were the two film clip attachments."

"She used the disappearing text routine on you as well?" Elwood asked.

"Apparently, and since Frigg had success-fully accessed my phone, I've initiated a complete reboot to avoid spreading the malware to any other devices."

"So executing that search warrant isn't going to yield much usable intel."

"Probably not," Stu agreed. "Whoever sold the malware to Hansen in the first place may well have sold it to someone else, too, but with Odin and Frigg both gone, I don't believe there's an ongoing threat from Owen Hansen's copy."

"Excuse me, did you say Odin or Owen?"

"Both," Stu said. "Owen was his name, but Odin and Frigg were the handles they used. Odin was an ancient Norse god, and Frigg was his helpmeet."

Elwood sighed. "This whole thing has turned into a wild-goose chase."

A door buzzer sounded, and Shirley hurried to answer it. She returned to the conference room followed by, not one, but two Yavapai County Sheriff's Office detectives who were there to interview both Stu and Dr. Cannon.

As soon as the other investigators entered the room, Agent-in-Charge Elwood rose to go. "I understand that the reason High Noon became involved in all this was that Roger McGeary was a friend of yours." He reached across the table and shook Stu's hand. "Sorry for your loss," he added.

With that, the NSA agent departed, leaving behind a stunned Stuart Ramey, who was astonished to find himself wiping tears from his eyes, because Elwood was right. Roger McGeary had been Stuart's friend, and he was most certainly gone.

71

Knowing the interviews would take time, Ali ran up the flag to Leland. He packed up the dinner he'd made — meat loaf, baked potatoes, and salad, along with some of his freshly baked bread — transported it from Sedona to Cottonwood, and served it to all comers on paper plates in the conference room.

When both dinner and the interviews were over, the detectives went on their way. By then Alonso had walked down to the highway and collected his Jeep from the spot where he'd abandoned it near that initial roadblock. Ali had planned on giving Dr. Cannon a ride back to Carefree, but when Alonso volunteered to do so in her stead, Ali was only too happy to accept.

"By the way," she told Alonso as he was leaving. "We never did get around to doing the paperwork, but don't worry about it. It's a done deal."

Shirley and Leland finished straightening up the conference room. Finally the only people left were Ali, B., and Stuart Ramey.

"So how much of that was true?" Ali asked.

"How much of what?"

"What you told Elwood about Frigg," she said. "There was something in that story that just didn't ring true. The part about the disappearing text, maybe? I'm guessing the AI didn't change her mind. Somebody else changed her mind for her."

Stuart Ramey looked floored. "How did you know?" he asked.

"The other texts were completely deleted, not partially deleted," Ali answered.

"I got rid of the kernel," Stuart admitted with a catch in his throat. "Frigg was incredibly smart. Having access to that malware made her extremely valuable and extremely dangerous."

"To say nothing of two-faced," B. added with a smile, "if an AI can have a face, that is."

"I'd say unreliable rather than two-faced," Stuart countered. "Once she turned on Odin, she deliberately set out to undermine him. Eventually she would have done the same thing to the next person who hooked up with her."

"You included."

"Yes," Stuart agreed. "Me included."

"So you did the right thing," Ali said.

"You're sure?"

"Absolutely. The right thing for the right reason."

72

Two weeks later, on a fine Saturday morning in late September, Stuart Ramey ventured outside into the early-autumn sunlight and climbed into the passenger seat of Cami Lee's bright red Prius. People who knew Stuart well would have been astonished to see him that day. At Cami's insistence, he was dressed in jeans, a Western shirt, genuine Tony Lama boots, a camel-colored leather jacket, and a massive white Stetson that he couldn't wear inside the car because it bumped up against both the passenger window and the headrest.

"Ready to rumble?" Cami asked as he belted himself in.

"I guess," he said. "Thanks for driving me."

"You could get a license and a car of your own, you know," Cami said.

"Maybe," Stu allowed, but he sounded neither convinced nor enthusiastic.

They said very little on the nearly two-hour drive from Cottonwood to Payson. They were two people who worked well together; they were comfortable together. When Stu had asked if Cami would give him a ride to Aunt Julia's ranch, Racehorse Rest, on the far side of Star Valley off the Payson-Heber Highway, she had been happy to comply. At Aunt Julia's insistence, it was an overnight trip. She wanted them to come for dinner and stay for brunch the next day.

As far as Cami was concerned, the very idea of Stu's having agreed to leave his lair for the better part of twenty-four hours was something to be applauded and encouraged.

"Holy moly!" Stu exclaimed as the GPS announced that their destination was on the right in one half mile.

"What?" Cami asked.

"This used to be a desert wasteland," Stu said. "Look at it now."

What Cami saw outside the car windows was indeed beautiful. The rest of the high-way had been lined with miles of barbed wire, but the white vinyl fencing around Racehorse Rest said horse ranch all the way. At the entrance they drove over a cattle guard and up a long graveled driveway.

Along the way they passed a complex pattern of individually fenced pastures containing round tracts of green grass lush enough to grace any golf course on the planet. Each pasture boasted its own irrigation equipment and usually only a single horse. Dozens of horses could be seen, grazing peacefully on that sun-drenched expanse of green. It was a breathtakingly beautiful sight.

The ranch house itself was located on a slight rise. To reach it, they threaded through a collection of buildings — garages, shops, tarp-topped stacks of hay, and metal barns with corrals out back. Some of the buildings were old and decrepit, but several of them were clearly new construction. As they came up the drive, Julia Miller stood on the covered porch surrounding a river rock house. She raced down the steps and was on hand to greet Stu with a hug the moment he stepped out of the Prius.

"What do you think about what we're doing to the place?" she asked.

"It's beautiful," Stu said, shaking his head in obvious amazement. "I can't believe how different it is."

"That's the miracle of what money and water can do in the desert — Roger's money, that is," Aunt Julia added. "When you and Rog used to come here, back in the day, this was nothing but a seat-of-your-pants outfit. Now, with the money Rog left me, we can rescue way more horses than ever before, and we can care for them properly. Come on. Let me show you around."

They spent the next hour wandering through the complex of barns, stables, and paddocks with Aunt Julia giving them a rundown of each horse's individual record of wins, losses, and injuries.

Dinner that night was exactly as Stu remembered it from all those years ago, plain food and plenty of it — beef stew, pinto beans, and corn bread. Dessert was plain old tapioca pudding served with hot coffee.

"Nothing fancy, but good," Aunt Julia said.

"It's amazing," Cami said.

Over coffee Aunt Julia gave Stu a stern look that would have sent him scurrying for cover back when he was a kid. "I'm a little pissed at you, you know," she chided gently.

"How come?"

"You never let me pay you for doing the work you folks did on Roger's case. It wasn't the answer I wanted, but you did give me an answer. I know what happened now, and I know who was at fault. But you shouldn't have done it for free, Stuart. I may be an old lady, but I have my pride, you know."

"I didn't do it for you," Stuart said thoughtfully a moment later. "Roger was my friend, and I did it for him. But if you really want to pay us, you can."

"How much?"

"When you finish that brand-new barn you're building out there, I want you to put a sign on it."

"What kind of sign?"

"You can call it High Noon."

"Done," Aunt Julia said, beaming. "With pleasure."

EPILOGUE

On the first Monday in October, Ali alone drove Leland Brooks to Sky Harbor. She had wanted to throw a going-away bash for him, but he had turned the idea down cold. "No fuss, please," he said. "I'd rather make my exit privately, the same way I showed up all those years ago."

She had abided by his wishes. There had been no party, but Leland wasn't returning home to the UK exactly the same way he had come. Back then, he had traveled in a tramp steamer as a citizen of Great Britain. He was going home booked in business class on British Airways — at B. and Ali's insistence — and traveling on a US passport.

They said very little on the trip down I-17. For one thing, Ali didn't trust her ability to speak without bursting into tears, and she knew tears on her part would not be appreciated.

"You and Mr. Simpson will be just fine," Leland said reassuringly as Ali turned off at the airport exit.

Good to his word, Leland had given Alonso Rivera a crash course on being the new Leland. It remained to be seen how that would go.

Ali smiled. "You've certainly done everything in your power to guarantee that. And don't be a stranger. If Thomas's health improves, I hope the two of you will come back for visits at the very least."

"Perhaps," Leland said. "We'll see."

He fell silent then. When Ali glanced in his direction, expecting him to say something more, she was surprised to see a single tear showing after all — one on Leland's weathered cheek rather than her own.

"I know you're Bob and Edie's daughter," he murmured at last, in a voice choked with emotion. "I'm grateful they've shared you with me, because you feel like my daughter, too."

Ali reached out, took his bony hand in one of hers, and held it tight. It was a good thing they were approaching the curb just then. As she pulled to a stop, her own tears came in buckets, almost blinding her.

"Thank you," she whispered. "I feel the same way."

"I don't want you to get out," he admonished. "I'll get a skycap to help me."

"You're sure?"

"I'm sure."

"And you don't want me to walk you as far as security?"

"No thank you, madam. It's one thing to make a fool of myself in private. I certainly don't want to do so in public."

"All right, then," she said. "If you say so."

He summoned a skycap with a baggage cart and then went around to the back of the Cayenne to oversee the unloading. Once his luggage was on the cart, Leland came back over to the driver's side and tapped on Ali's window.

She buzzed down the glass. "One last thing," he said. "A final bit of advice."

"What's that?" she asked.

"It's something I learned from you and your mother," he said.

"What?"

He gave her a sly grin. "Knockers up," he told her, "and don't you forget it."

He stepped away from the door then, and Ali slipped the Cayenne into gear. When she looked back in the rearview mirror, she saw him — a spry but ramrod-straight elderly man, standing on the curb, waving at her. It was hard for her to glimpse him through yet another curtain of tears, but then she realized she was laughing and crying at the same time.

"Yes, you dear old fellow," she whispered aloud. "Knockers up, indeed!"

ABOUT THE AUTHOR

With more than twenty million copies of her books in print, **J.A. Jance** is the perennially bestselling author of the Ali Reynolds series, the J.P. Beaumont series, the Joanna Brady series, a series of Southwestern thrillers featuring the Walker family, and more. Born in South Dakota and brought up in Bisbee, Arizona, Jance lives with her husband and their two dachshunds in Seattle, Washington and Tucson, Arizona.

The employees of Thorndike Press hope you have enjoyed this Large Print book. All our Thorndike, Wheeler, and Kennebec Large Print titles are designed for easy reading, and all our books are made to last. Other Thorndike Press Large Print books are available at your library, through selected bookstores, or directly from us.

For information about titles, please call:
  (800) 223-1244

or visit our website at:
  gale.com/thorndike

To share your comments, please write:
  Publisher
  Thorndike Press
  10 Water St., Suite 310
  Waterville, ME 04901